8/23 $2

THE
fallout

Rebecca Thornton is an alumna of the Faber Academy 'Writing A Novel' course, where she was tutored by Esther Freud and Tim Lott. Her writing has been published in *The Guardian*, *You* Magazine, *Daily Mail*, *Prospect* Magazine and *The Sunday People* amongst others. As a journalist she has reported from the Middle East, Kosovo and the UK. She now lives in West London with her husband and two children.

The Fallout is her third novel.

@rebecca_thornton_writer
@ RThorntonwriter

THE
fallout

REBECCA THORNTON

HarperCollins*Publishers*

HarperCollins*Publishers* Ltd
1 London Bridge Street,
London SE1 9GF

www.harpercollins.co.uk

This paperback edition 2020
4

First published in ebook by HarperCollins*Publishers* 2019

A catalogue record for this book is
available from the British Library

ISBN: 978-0-00-837312-2 (b-format)
ISBN: 978-0-00-837313-9 (tpb edition)

Set in Sabon LT Std by Palimpsest Book Production Limited,
Falkirk, Stirlingshire

Printed and bound in the UK by CPI Group (UK) Ltd,
Croydon CR0 4YY

MIX
Paper from
responsible sources
FSC
www.fsc.org
FSC™ C007454

For Walter and Dom

'Silent lies are more venomous than cruel truths'

— Ben Oliveira

2 September 2014
WhatsApp group: NCT West London Ladies
Members: Victoria, Liza, Sarah, Miranda, Ella, Camilla

Victoria: Hi guys. We are absolutely delighted to announce that Otto Arthur Stuart-Brown was born yesterday to a very proud Mummy and Daddy. Hit the September baby mark. Phew! Weighed 6 pounds and 5 oz. We are totally in love. Oxytocin, ladies! It's the stuff of dreams.

Camilla: Lovely news, Victoria. Elodie was born too, yesterday. Whopper at 9.9 oz.

Miranda: Ah congrats everyone. I'm still waiting for my little bundle to arrive.

Sarah: Me too

Liza: Me three

Victoria: Oh you ladies will be absolutely fine. Just remember. Breathe, let nature work its magic. Nothing to be worried about. And remember – they're sensations. NOT contractions.

Liza: How was it? We're all dying to hear.

Victoria: Good thanks! Bit tricky trying to type with one hand whilst I feed. Just enrolling him into schools!

Miranda: Oh god. Schools? Really? Do you think I've missed my chance already? Where did you put him down?

Victoria: @Miranda – I'll ping you separately. Yes. I'd get on it. Got to do it now ladies, or you'll miss the boat!

Ella: Typing . . .

WhatsApp group: Renegades
Members: Liza, Sarah

Liza: @Miranda, I'll ping you separately – in our newly-named WhatsApp group. SMUG MUMS.

Sarah: Hahaha I know!

Liza: Shit I thought I sent that to the wrong group.

Sarah: I'm so tired I think I might die.

Liza: You're tired now? Wait till you get this fucker out. THEN YOU'LL KNOW THE MEANING OF TIREDNESS. Joking.

Sarah: Oh god. Wtf is with that school thing btw? Is she for real?

Liza: Yup. She's been banging on about it since the first step she took into our NCT class. Thank god you were there. And normal.

Sarah: I'd have to sell a kidney first. Not that they'd be worth much at the mo.

Liza: Me too.

Sarah: £6k a term or something for the one she's been talking about. PS Ella keeps typing then dropping off.

Liza: Sure she's fine. We would have heard by now if not. Think she's just . . . not into socialising too much.

Sarah: *with us*

Liza: Yup.

Sarah: haha.

Liza: Coffee later?

Sarah: Mella's? Half an hour?

Liza: See you there. I'm bringing plastic bags to sit on.

Sarah: Ping me if you hear anything from Ella before then? So weird she hasn't been in touch. I've WhatsApped her separately but nothing – she's read it though.

Liza: Yeah will let you know. Although she'd have pinged you before me anyway. She's a bit of a mystery that one.

Sarah: She is indeed. Do you think we did anything to offend her? She's posting on Facebook. Just seen pics of her and Christian from this morning!

Liza: Weird. Must be us then. Something someone said, or did. Like I said, Ella Bradby is a total mystery.

Sarah: Hmmm. She sure is. Ok see you in thirty, yeah? X

Liza: Yeah X

FIVE YEARS LATER

West London Gazette Online, 21 July 2019
Author: J Roper

A nine-million-pound refurbished health club, The Vale Club, has just opened to the well-heeled residents of West London. Based on the Acton/Chiswick fringes, the club boasts an Olympic-sized pool, a crèche, soft-play, six tennis courts and an outdoor playground.

Kirsty Macdonald, Director of Sales, says two thousand members have already joined, with staggered waiting lists already full.

'Our clients are mainly families and working professionals and we hope to provide a fantastic service to everyone in the area to keep them healthy and fit, whilst also being a great place for socialising.'

The residents are also thrilled to have this new West London club on their doorsteps.

Cordelia Banks, a lawyer and 39-year-old mother of three, says that the club will be a 'much needed central hub – a place for both children and adults to keep fit and entertained in a safe environment'. And Finlay Brown, a 27-year-old marketing executive, says that The Vale Club will 'keep the residents of West London *active', and he is looking forward to meeting 'like-minded healthy people there'.*

For further information, or to book a private tour, please visit The Vale Club website.

SARAH

'Sarah,' Liza hisses. 'Quick. Oh my God. Look who it is. My three o'clock.' She throws her head towards the soft-play, kids hurling themselves off the plastic inflatables like they're on some kind of kamikaze mission.

'Georgina Bard?' replies Sarah. 'Yes, she's here all the time. With that perfect, peachy bottom of hers.'

'No. Not her. No, look again. Behind the blondes. Hurry, she's going. Bloody hell.'

It's rare, but Sarah's not in the mood for a gossip. It's just one of those days where everything feels wrong, like a too-tight pair of trousers, except she doesn't have the relief of opening the top button.

She'd googled her symptoms this morning in bed. Mood swings, tiredness, heavy periods. Her diagnosis had said: *perimenopause*. She shivers remembering what she had read next. *Perimenopause can last for ten years during which time fertility declines.* Ten years! It seems so unfair. She's only thirty-nine after all.

She can't really see who Liza could possibly be talking about anyway. Everyone looks the same here. Block-printed

9

athleisure-wear leggings with Olivia Cunningham's brand-new *Motherhood Mania* clothing-line tops. Brightly coloured slogan tees – *Mother's Little Helper!* – complete with lozenge-shaped pills underneath. She jolts when she realises she cannot see Casper, his blond, bowl-haircut flying up and down as he leaps from level to level, before she remembers he's safely ensconced in his Champions Forever tennis lesson.

'See her now?' says Liza. 'It's a good 'un.'

'Nope.' Sarah wonders why Liza is staring at her so intently, waiting for her reaction. A Z-list celebrity, she wonders. Unbearable if it is. But, all she can really think is: why is everyone still smiling? Three days into the autumn half-term and she's done in. Yet here they are, all the other women (and where are all the bloody men today?) bouncing around. Long, lean legs, feet in pristine trainers, chatting so animatedly. Why aren't they exhausted? She knows she's probably just jealous – but what's wrong with them? She'd never stopped to think that maybe they're all normal and it's actually her with the problem. She rubs a mark off her own leggings. Weetabix, she's guessing, from Casper's breakfast.

She inspects all the other women as she tries to find the target of Liza's attention. She's distracted by Thomasina Hulme, who'd been extremely frosty with her in Zumba the day before last.

'Come on Allegra.' Thomasina sounds increasingly shrill. 'Come on. You can jump by yourself, without Mummy's help. Go on.'

Sarah wishes Thomasina would shut up and stop thinking that she is instilling *confidence* into her little one. Allegra jumps onto a red, squishy mat. Thomasina lets out a triumphant 'Oh!' and looks around, hoping for some semblance of shared joy at her daughter's leap into the unknown. To Sarah's utter satisfaction, no one else seems to be watching.

'I can't see anyone new, Liza. Just tell me who it is.' She tries to disguise the impatience in her voice. Both she and Liza had had a field day when the club had recently opened. After all, The Vale Club is the spanking new place to be for the parents of West London and their little monkeys; so far, she and Liza have pretty much spotted and done a recce on all of the members already (their best one yet being some of the cast of *Strictly Come Dancing* on rehearsal) and apparently they've since shut the waiting list.

She can see why the place is in such high demand. There's a soft-play, a gym. There's even a crèche and kids' classes, boxing, tai-chi and all, so the children can pump their little fists on punch bags instead of Mummy and Daddy.

Just as she's about to swivel her gaze back to Liza and tell her she can't see anyone, she spots her. She's in the corner, behind the soft-play, picking up a large bag with two tennis rackets sticking out. In her right hand is a bottle of half-finished water and, in the other, an iPhone. Sarah can see it has been personalised with a photograph on the back. She gasps. Liza's right. Bloody hell indeed.

Ella Bradby.

Of all people. Here. Sarah doesn't know why she hadn't expected it. She must have just joined.

It's just like Ella to waft in after everyone else. To check things at the club are tickety-boo. Ella isn't a leader of the pack in that sense. More that she would always wait. Keep everyone on their toes. Wanting to see if it *is* actually good enough for her. Sarah's mind is pulled back to their antenatal class, five years earlier. The way Ella had waited for a text message from *someone*, before she deigned to *follow on* to the restaurant that had been chosen for their final NCT lunch. *Just let me know what the food looks like, will you? Before I come all that way.* And of course that part of the discussion had taken up most of lunch, as everyone had been too scared to put their heads above the parapet – just in case it *wasn't* good enough for Ella Bradby.

'Oh my God, it's *her!*' says Sarah. 'I thought there was a massive waiting list.'

'See? I told you it was a good spot. The mysterious Ella. Back again in our lives.'

Sarah doesn't want to give Liza the satisfaction of reacting in exactly the awe-struck way she is anticipating.

'Well, she hasn't changed much, in all these years, has she? We still don't know where she went.'

'Nope. You'll catch flies in a minute,' Liza laughs. 'She's one of us now. No helping it. Ha. You going to ditch me now?'

'No, course not,' she replies, distractedly. 'Shall we talk to her?'

'You can. Happy to observe. But I don't want to go back in time. It's all history now.'

Sarah doesn't really know what 'history' Liza is referring to but she glosses over it, in favour of thinking about Ella Bradby. She had been fascinated by her for the few weeks they'd been in NCT class together, and afterwards too. She thinks about the second she'd first laid eyes on Ella. How every single man and woman in the room – including her own husband – had been looking at those never-ending legs, that self-contained smile of hers. Sarah had felt that curious pull of wanting to both look and be like her, yet feeling simultaneously threatened. The fact that Ella, too, had forgotten Sarah's name – not once, but twice – only served to make her allure even stronger.

And after that, she'd googled her obsessively and discovered with absolute glee that, back in the day, Ella had spent two dazzling years with West London-based actor, and St Paul's alumni, Rufus North. Sarah had told Liza she had known with an absolute certainty she'd recognised Ella from somewhere. And there it was! Her relentless poring over the Mail Online's Sidebar of Shame had paid off. All along, she'd been right on the money.

Afterwards, Sarah had remained intrigued for the eight weeks that Ella had been on the NCT West London Ladies WhatsApp group, before she'd quietly and deftly removed herself.

None of the other members of the NCT had said a word to each other about it. Too proud. Nursing their indignation by swiftly moving on to other matters. Nappy-rash. Tongue-ties, the colour of their newborns' faeces. (Often accompanied by a photograph. *Sorry in advance. TMI, but I'm having a massive freak out! Why is it the colour of mustard?*)

But now Ella's child, Felix, is in the same year at school as Sarah's son, though of course in a different class. And despite having looked high and low, Sarah's never once spotted Ella at the school gates.

She remembers eagerly skimming through the Reception enrolment list for The West London Primary Academy School before the start of autumn term. The way her heart had skipped when she had seen the name: *Bradby, Felix*. And she'd *known*, right away. She'd texted Liza

Rebecca Thornton

straight off and had felt a swell of validation that they'd also managed to get Casper into the local primary – even though they are precisely three quarters of a kilometre away from the school. It had still been touch and go for a minute. She had been so thankful that she and Tom hadn't had to delve into their life savings, just to be able to afford one term's fees of the private school The Little Falcons. Tom had been relieved when she'd imparted the news and, because Ella Bradby's child had also been sent to the local primary, Sarah had never again felt that she had to justify her choice to her mother – who constantly asked if Tom's job was 'going well'. A lecture would then follow, on how she and Sarah's father had *worked themselves into the ground* to send Sarah to her private school. She had clutched at this newly acquired information about Ella and Felix like it was a toasty hot-water bottle.

And now Ella is here too, at the club. Only a few metres away. She feels the lift of her earlier malaise.

It isn't that Sarah necessarily still wants to *be* Ella Bradby like she had when she'd first laid eyes on her at NCT. Not in the same way that, aged sixteen, Little Miss Average Sarah Biddlecombe, at her West London private school, had wanted to step into the glittery, platform trainers of Little Miss Popular Cassie Fox.

No. Not in that way. Or at least so she tells herself. She's had enough experience now to know women like Ella had enough trouble in life, what with the judgement that comes with their ice-cool looks and trendy jobs. The pressure of it all. No, it is something else entirely. She just wants to be *near* her, and breathe in the cool, calm essence of her. Her energy that says: *I don't really give a damn if you like me or not*, which of course, makes Sarah want Ella to like her even more.

14

Fuck, she thinks, smoothing her T-shirt over her belly. Fuckety, fuck fuck. Is this how utterly sad her life has become that she's getting off at the prospect of talking to one of the other school mothers?

'Oh, well, she's already gone,' says Liza. 'Ghosted us. Again. Remind me why we sat here?' She throws her head towards the soft-play.

'So we have prime seats so that when the kids are back with us, they can watch even more telly and we can be inside and warm.' Sarah turns to the blaring TV screen and watches Mr Tiny Tots in his weird, spotted bowtie, grinning and gurning like he's just necked a load of class A drugs. 'Hey. Want a coffee?'

'If you go, can you check on Jack? Outside? In the playground.'

'I sure will,' Sarah tells her. 'Don't worry.'

'Thanks.' Liza lifts Thea out of her pram. 'He's just there.' She points at the window, towards the sandpit. 'This little monster just needs a quick feed.'

'No probs. Cake?' Sarah nearly trips over the aggressively large bundle of bags, toys and coats that they'd used to lay claim to the seats.

'Nope. Thanks. Need to start learning some willpower. Shift this baby weight.' Liza lifts her T-shirt and unclips her nursing bra. 'But sorry – you asked me about coffee. Yes please. I *shouldn't* of course. Don't want to over-caffeinate this little one.' She gives a small smile at the ubiquitous joke they shared right back from NCT. 'But – well. You know. I'm tired.'

'Listen, Liza, Gav will come back to you. I promise. He's just . . .'

'An idiot?'

'You said it, not me.'

'Do you see him at all? I mean, I know you're still under the same roof but . . .'

'Yeah. He's always breathing down my neck about something or other. It's weird. He wanted the separation. Wanted to move into another part of the house. But still, he thinks he can get involved in parts of my life that I don't want him to.'

'Well, you know my thoughts on the matter. Thea's barely two months old. I mean when I think back to when Casper was that age, how hard it was – and now you've got two.'

Something about Liza's expression looks a little bit guilty. Sarah wants to shake her friend. *It's not your fault he wanted a break*, she wants to shout. But instead she controls her voice. 'Black, one sugar, yes?' She doesn't wait for Liza to reply. 'Let me go and get us drinks and I'll check on Jack too,' she says.

In truth, she wants to get away from the bright lights and the screaming. It's all making her head buzz. She'd drunk too much Shiraz last night and she feels sick. Not so sick she can justify fully indulging her hangover and eating her body weight in carbs, but sick enough.

She watches Liza's green eyes narrow, scanning the neighbouring cricket pitch outside – a large green peaceful space in this area of West London. Her friend looks even more tired today than she did last week, the wing of her brown eyeliner smudged underneath her right eye. The bright halogen lights are unfairly harsh on her skin. Sarah can see some new wrinkles. Or perhaps they've always been there and she's just grown so accustomed to Liza's face, she hasn't noticed.

She thinks of her own appearance. Mousy hair. Freckles. She still looks quite young, she supposes. Except

16

for the lines under her eyes. *Smile maps*, Tom had said to her once. *Don't be a dick*, she had replied. Perhaps she'd have that Botox after all. The other mums she speaks to are all at it. Botox parties. She is both miffed and elated she hadn't been invited to one. Liza still looks pretty though, Sarah thinks, despite her dog-tiredness. She watches her friend's expression as she tuts at Thea's head. 'Just stay on, will you,' she mutters down at her two-month-old daughter.

Pretty, but unmemorable, Tom had once said. *And that's why you like her*, he had laughed. *No threat. You're so predictable, Sarah Biddlecombe.*

No! She had been cross. *That's not true. I like her because she never judges me.* And she'd quickly added that Liza was also *funny and kind*.

'Bloody hope Jack is still there.' Liza cranes her neck to get a better look outside. 'Can't see him anywhere else. He's probably digging in the sand under the pirate ship. He's a good boy, at least I have that much. Thanks for checking on him, Sa.'

'He'll be fine. Be back in a sec.' Sarah walks away from the harsh sounds and noises of the soft-play area to the quieter café. What a relief. Only three more days of half-term. She can do this. But then she thinks about afterwards. She's moaning now, but what about when it's over? How empty the days will seem. How boring with the new account Liza has got her. She is incredibly grateful. But she isn't really interested in marketing old people's homes. Or post-retirement flats, as they've decided to call them.

She walks through to the café serving area and consoles herself with the thought of forty minutes of blissful peace and quiet before she has to pick up Casper from tennis.

Just before a load of other customers join the line she arrives at the food counter, where her gaze settles on a passionfruit and walnut cake. She falters for a second. Should she check on Jack first? No, she thinks. Get everything sorted and then she'll go. She'll be waiting for ages if she leaves now. He's nearly six. He's a well-behaved boy. And after all, he can't get out of the health club. At least she has made a definitive decision about one thing today. She looks back down at her phone and sends Liza a quick message while stepping one foot closer to the front of the queue.

LIZA

My phone beeps. I'm sure it's Sarah. She does this when she's forgotten our table number when ordering coffee. Normally I would pre-empt it. Not today, though, what with both kids awake all night. And of course Gav had been there, at every single turn. I'd hear his footsteps first as he ran up the stairs from the spare room, breath ragged from broken sleep.

'Everything all right?' he queried, watching me open my pyjama top.

'Everything's fine. Why?'

'Just checking. That you're doing your job.' He'd emphasised the word 'job' in such a way that made me think I'd been doing anything but. Last night, he'd stood over me, making sure I was feeding her right, until I'd asked him to leave. 'I'll go when you've finished.' He'd sat down on the very end of the bed, the furthest distance he could manage before he would fall off. As though being any nearer would poison him. He'd made exaggerating stretching sounds all through the feed, yawning and sighing.

I try to forget about Gav. I rest my handset on Thea's side whilst she's feeding. Sarah would have told me to take it off immediately. *Radiation, cancer.* She's right, of course, but I leave it there whilst I shuffle Thea into a more comfortable position. I'm having to learn independence now, after all. I look down at my screen.

Just in bit of a queue. Haven't checked on J yet.

I type back one-handed.

No worries. I've just seen his head poke out from the sandpit but please check on him after. Just to make sure I got the right kid.

I think about Sarah – how strangely she's been behaving lately. Not with it. Distant. It's as though her eyes are totally blank. That look she gets when she and I have been on the wine – the dead-eyed tipping point when I know she's totally gone. I should find out if she's OK, especially given what she went through last year. I know it can't be easy, her seeing me with a newborn, but, for the moment, I'm just too tired.

She's been a bit snippy with me today too. I want to talk to her about an email I'd got from the work contact I'd put her in touch with, but I decide to wait. I know these moods of hers. Nothing can snap her out of it, really. Except today, the reappearance of Ella Bradby had. I wonder how long *this* one will last. I think about Aria Delamere whose daughter, Emmeline, had been at nursery with Casper. Sarah had constantly meerkatted for Aria at the school gates, whilst I had been her 'steady' friend in the background. The feeling towards Aria had been quick to dissipate, though, when Casper hadn't been invited to Emmeline's fourth birthday party.

I look back out of the window, thinking about when *I'd* last seen Ella, just before she'd done a runner on us, all those years ago. The way she'd stood right by me, her fingers squeezing my arms in the pitch-black freezing winter night. Of course Sarah knows nothing about that – no one does. I pull my thoughts away from it all. Time to move on.

I look outside at the sky to distract myself. It's a greying day. It feels all at odds with the bright colours and noise inside – the swell of parents dropping their kids into the crèche, so they can race to their fitness classes. Thea starts to squirm. I move her onto the other side of me, rather optimistically latching her high up to my breast. It's only when I look down that I realise that she's nowhere near my nipple. 'Christ,' I mutter. If Gav wants out of the marriage, I dread to think how I'm going to find anyone else who I won't mind seeing my boobs. I look around. Everyone just looks so on it. So – perky. And then I give myself a good talking to. *Come on, Liza,* I tell myself. *You're better than this. Stop feeling sorry for yourself. Get on with it. The kids need you.* But despite my pep talk, there's still something about today that has turned sour. Just a feeling, if you will. Restlessness. An edginess in the pit of my stomach. And it's not just the way Gav's been behaving towards me either.

I look out the window again but my vision is pulled towards the other side of the room. And then I see a flash of her amongst the multi-colours. She stands out, in her monochrome outfit. So sleek and perfect. She pushes a tennis racket back into her bag and swings herself up, effortlessly. As though her limbs are weightless. Bet she has no issues with her boobs. I pull up my bra and try and hoik up my own at the same time.

When I look back on this moment, I will realise that this is when it hits me. This is when my mindset spirals even further. When I start to really question myself. Not that Gav didn't help me do a good job of that anyway.

It was in this moment, little more than ten minutes ago, when things changed and cracked.

This moment Ella Bradby walked back into our lives.

West London Gazette editorial notes, September 2019
J Roper interview transcript: Aaron Daniels, crèche
manager, The Vale Club

I know, I know. This is meant to be a puff piece for the
club, isn't it? You want me to tell you how fantastic the
new crèche is. My boss gave me the heads-up. How happy
the mums and dads of West London are that there's a
new place for them to drop off their children so they
can get to their Pilates and what not. How much it's
changed the area. Blah blah blah. But it's – OK – off
the record, I'm not staying for much longer. Sick of it,
I am. Especially since I moved here.

For some it's been good, of course. Not just the crèche.
This whole 'health club' thing. We've already had people
claim that property prices nearby have rocketed. Like
we need that. It was bad enough when they built that
school – West London Primary Academy, driving up the
house prices like crazy for the rest of us. A school for
the under-privileged, my arse. You should see the families
that go there now, braying at the gates with their 4x4
cars running outside. So for those people, you see, of
course this has all been a bonus.

Anyway, I'm not ungrateful for the job. I've learnt

how to handle myself much better. Especially when there's a complaint from the mums or dads that we haven't been doing our jobs properly. (I didn't know our role was to be private tutor, chef and the rest all in one.) The behaviour then is crazy. They're all rigid and polite until something is not to their liking. Then they come up, their faces all in mine. 'You mean you don't have drinks and snacks for the children? This is disgusting. I don't pay all this money for nothing, you know.' You get the picture.

Anyway, they're not all bad, obviously. Some are. Your ears would bleed if I told you some of the stuff I've seen. Put it like this, I'm not quite sure how some of them have hearts that don't explode on the running machines after a weekend of 'excess'. And by excess, I'm sure you know what I'm talking about. (At this point, interviewee mimics sniffing something off the table – ed.)

I hear them all the time in the queue. 'How did you feel on Sunday, Minnie?' And the casual tap on their noses, their smiles, all conspiratorial-like. 'Oh God,' they'll reply. 'The children were up at six in the morning. I was still absolutely awake from the night before.' Then they'll do this comedy wide-eyed expression, chewing their tongues. In front of their kids! Anyway, I'm not going into that now, when I've still got to hand in my notice.

Besides, as I was saying, some of them are nice. Polite but distant. But they're all very, I'd say . . . 'eager' to drop their kids. I understand, they want a break. We all do and I've got two of my own, so I know. But the way they go about it is quite mad, really. Jostling and pushing to get to the front of the queue. It's like they're teenagers all over again, waiting to see their favourite band live in concert. We've had to install a proper system with barriers and stuff, just so we can keep them in line.

And when I say the parents run – they've barely finished scribbling their names on the signing-in sheet before they've disappeared to get to their fitness classes. Then, when they come back it's all like, 'Oh little Freya' or 'Little Isabella, how I've missed you, have you missed Mummy and Daddy?'

Look, as I said, I've got my own kids so I know what it's like. And better they run to their fitness class than, well, to the pub. Although it appears to me they do that too.

But I think what upsets me the most is not that the members here have a place to enjoy. It's brilliant that they've built somewhere that focuses on fitness and health for both adults and children. I know most of those parents work hard. And if I'd grown up somewhere like this I would have loved to have been a part of it all.

But I suppose what I'm saying, really, is that some of the parents who drop their kids at the crèche, they see it as their right to be here, rather than a privilege.

And you know how I know this?

Well, it's been a few weeks now since the club opened its doors, and some of the first members started coming here right from the beginning. Every day they've dropped their little ones here. Same time, same place. And it occurred to me yesterday that only about half of them have even bothered to learn my name. I don't expect them to know all the staff members here. Of course not. But the ones looking after their kids? Yes. I do expect that.

I do get a vague smile, though, from most of them. I mean, we can't be totally invisible. Can we?

After all, we're looking after their little angels. It's us that keeps them safe from harm. For that window of time they are with us, we have to make sure that nothing bad comes their way. Because, of course, where their children are concerned, there's danger everywhere – isn't there?

SARAH

'Table number?' the barista asks when Sarah finally reaches the front of the queue. As well as WhatsApping Camilla, her mind's been off elsewhere. She can't seem to focus on one thing, thinking about whether it's true that sugar has an effect on fertility, and her perimenopause and whether that might just be the root of all her problems in trying to conceive. Then she drifts onto remembering to get a dodgy-looking mole checked (she'd have to remember to bring the iPad with her to the GP to entertain Casper) before starting to think about whether she's actually remembered to sign Casper into his tennis class. Whether she should put a second wash on before she watches *Killing Eve* tonight, or if she'll be too tired to stay up until it finishes.

'Oh, crap. Sorry. I was . . .' She waves a hand over her head. 'Sorry. I've forgotten. We're just by the soft-play. You know, the table by the window. The one that everyone wants.' She laughs but the waiter gives her a pitying look. 'It's like ze Germans with the sun-loungers.'

She stutters on her own bad joke. 'Oh, don't worry. Forget about it.'

'Overlooking the cricket pitch?' he asks, speaking slowly, as though she's hard of hearing. 'That's table eighty-seven.' He jabs his finger on the buttons until the till pings. *Shit.* Her mind starts reeling again.

What if her bank card doesn't work? Had she been paid for her last project? She can't remember and she hasn't checked her account for weeks. She feels hot and clammy and now look – a queue forming behind her. After all, membership here is expensive enough. *But it's a life saver*, she'd pleaded with Tom when it had first opened. *A health and fitness club. Think of the benefits.* She'd even pushed her stomach out extra hard so that he'd see it and think it was unquestionable that they join.

'Here's your receipt, Madam.' *Phew*.

'Thanks.' She snatches the bit of paper from the waiter's hand and slinks off towards the sliding window. She remembers it's her birthday soon. Tom had suggested a weekend away in a cottage in Scotland. Something to look forward to. But she can't quite bring herself to do that either.

'We have to celebrate, just for your nearest and dearest,' he'd said as he spooned overpriced, sugar-free muesli into his mouth, before he'd left for work this morning. She knows it's ridiculous, but truthfully the idea of it fills her with utter dread. The rigmarole of packing up, organising childcare, catering. False jollity when everyone just wants to slob around in bed all day. And then the invites, to boot. She can't cut her list down to *just her nearest and dearest*! What if Saskia gets wind of it? Or Matilda or Miranda? They'd be so hurt and she doesn't particularly want to keep it all a big secret. That would be far too much effort, what with the way WhatsApps spread like wildfire around the school gates. And then her mother too, on at her about celebrating this big milestone of turning forty.

A tonne of guilt washes over her. Look at what Liza is going through with Gav. Let alone the other awful things that are happening across the globe. Those Syrian children she'd seen on the news earlier. It didn't bear thinking about. And she had Tom and Casper. A nice three-bed house in a desired location to boot, and it even has a self-contained one-bed lower-ground-floor flat too, which she and Tom have plans to develop.

'Something to get your teeth into,' Tom had said.

'Don't be so patronising,' she'd replied. It still makes her cross to think about. And inevitably then she'll ruminate on all the other misguided comments that Tom has made since they'd had Casper. About work, money and all the rest. As if she doesn't have enough on her plate. They're close to Chiswick. Close to Westfield shopping centre. So privileged in so many ways. And yet it's tough, she thinks. These years are tough. Her mother is getting older. Too old to be in that ramshackle house of hers in Gloucestershire, all alone since her dad had died. Casper needs her and here she is, slap bang in the middle of the sandwich years. But should life really be such a chore? Aren't these years meant to be breezy, loving your kids, a laugh a minute? She should feel lucky she has a child at all after everything that had happened last year. Her eyes fill with tears despite vowing never to think of it again in public. By the time she reaches the balcony, she feels like she's been through ten rounds in the boxing ring.

She resolves to stop thinking like this. She needs to hurry up and check on Jack. Her thoughts have reached fever pitch. Five minutes alone and she's already lost it. She doesn't know what's wrong with her. She peers over. At first she can't see Jack but then she spots his curly hair, bandy legs wrapped around a wooden post at the back of the playground, next to the sandpit. He's halfway up, but looks like he's edging back down to safety.

She softens for a second. He's so sweet. Gifted the best of Liza's personality. Always hugging her, telling her he loves her. Then she thinks of Gav. Wonders what characteristics he's inherited from him. How he's changed lately from being fun, *up for it* Gav to someone she wants to shout and tear her hair out over. Of course, Tom hasn't noticed a thing.

'He's one of my best mates, Sarah,' he'd said when she'd brought it up. 'Don't you think I'd *notice* if he was controlling Liza?' Part of her had thought this was true. She'd watched carefully, for any signs. But it is difficult when Gav lives in one part of the house and Liza another. How weird, she thinks. Can't he just move out? Wouldn't that make things so much easier for them? It's not like they can't afford it. Something is keeping him at the house, she just doesn't know what.

She really should shout over at Jack. Motion for him to get down from the post. But before the thought segues into action, she feels a presence behind her. She turns.

It's her. She's standing on the balcony right behind her, like some sort of apparition.

Ella Bradby.

'Ella, hello.' She grabs her opportunity whilst she's alone, without Liza's sly gaze making her feel self-conscious. 'It's Sarah. Biddlecombe. Remember? We were in . . .' she trails off, waiting to see if Ella does indeed remember. Silence. 'We were in NCT class together?' she prompts. 'Years ago. You . . .' deserted us all, she thinks. 'I think you must have been busy.'

'Sarah. Yes.' Ella smiles, a flat sort of smile, showing a perfect set of bone-white teeth.

'How are you then? You . . .' Sarah is about to ask about Felix. But she shuts her mouth. How on earth would she know about Felix unless she's been keeping tabs on her? And she can't very well admit that now, can she?

'Did everything go well in the end? After your NCT? Boy? Girl?'

'Boy, Felix. He's in karate now.'

Sarah waits, ready to fill Ella in on her own news, the information on the tip of her tongue, but before she can drop in that her own little boy is at The West London Primary Academy School (surely she can't be dismissive of her after that nugget of information?), Ella's icy-grey gaze is transported downwards.

Sarah follows her eyeline to see a small, cherubic blond figure on the floor beneath them. The little boy (she assumes it's a boy but she's made that mistake before) is about six months old. She thinks about her earlier cyber-chondria. Her self-diagnosed perimenopause. This month's PMT – she had felt the familiar darkness settling on her all of last week, the downward tug of her uterus. She tries to be generous about other people's good fortune but, alas, the hand of sadness squeezes her tight around the neck.

'Oh, lovely,' she says. 'What's . . . the baby's name?'

'This one? He's Wolf.'

'Wolf?' Sarah wants to laugh, desperately – she feels

it bubbling up in her stomach. Just wait until she gets back to Liza, she thinks – but then she realises, with some frustration, that Ella pulls it off majestically. A snip of delight swiftly follows that Ella has had two boys – instead of the 'one of each sex' that she remembers Ella pining for at NCT. She hates herself for thinking it. Really, really hates herself. But she just can't help it. Not everything is perfect for the enigmatic Ella Bradby.

She watches as Ella bends down and scoops up Wolf, breathing into his soft hair, her phone in her other hand: a rose-gold-encased iPhone, with an image on the back of her and her husband. Sarah remembers Christian well from their NCT days. Who wouldn't? His beachy-blond hair, and huge, shiny white teeth. And as for his spectacular body – well, she remembers everyone at their NCT class sliding glances towards him, not daring to stare too long. The way he'd rubbed Ella's back as they'd all acted out different labour positions. She and Liza had been laughing convulsively but, somehow, Ella and Christian hadn't made it so funny. She had watched them out of the corner of her eye. The way they'd glided around making it all seem so easy and beautiful – Ella's eyes closed so serenely, as she transported herself to the birth of their baby. Sarah wonders how it would feel if anyone stared at her and Tom like that.

'We're just hanging out, Wolf and I.' Ella interrupts Sarah's thoughts, her voice low and controlled. 'Whilst Felix has got karate. Aren't we, Wolfie-Bear?'

God, thinks Sarah, the poor bugger is going to develop an identity crisis.

'God, he's just so . . . *delicious*. Aren't you, Wolfie?' Ella continues.

'He's absolutely divine,' Sarah says. *Divine*? What the

32

hell? She's never used that word before in her life. But she carries on and on, the words spewing out of her mouth. 'Just look at that beautiful blond hair.' *Just like yours*, she nearly adds, but manages to stop herself just in time.

She stands there, rooting around for more things to say but suddenly her workout top feels too tight, squeezing out all her breath. She notices the squidge of flesh spilling out of the top of her leggings, which begin to feel scratchy and hot. She's also got a nagging feeling – her stomach feels hollowed out. It's the sense that she's forgotten to *do* something. But then she hears Ella clearing her throat and her mind is transported right back to the present moment. She thinks about making a joke about it all. Telling Ella how annoying she finds this whole 'soft-play' thing. She lets out a brief laugh and then wonders how she's managed, in the space of three minutes flat, to come across as a complete twat.

'So Felix is enjoying karate? I was thinking about putting my son Casper in for a trial.' If Ella knows that Casper and Felix are in the same year, she's not letting on. The feeling her son is being dismissed, as well as her, only makes Sarah more determined to get Ella's attention.

'Yes. He enjoys it.' Ella's still rubbing her thumb on the screen of her phone, glancing down at it as though she's expecting it to ring at any given moment.

Keep going with this, Sarah thinks. Her heart's going crazy. Don't fuck this up. But Ella's attention is elsewhere. She's cooing in Wolf's ear, totally unaware of Sarah and the emotional energy she's putting into the conversation.

'We're inside,' Sarah carries on. 'Me and Liza. Do you remember Liza? She was in NCT too. We're still mates. Really good mates.' She sees something flicker in Ella's expression. A vague recognition but it quickly disappears.

She feels slightly irritated. Is Liza really more memorable than her? 'We're in the soft-play area. If you want to, you know, join us?' Liza would scold her later on for that, Sarah was sure of it. *What do you want to ask her for?*

'Thanks.' Ella doesn't say anything else to indicate she's even acknowledged what Sarah's said. She feels stung at Ella's lack of interest in her, a seed of rage pushing its way up from her stomach. Is she not good enough for her? She tells herself just to stop being so bitter. That none of this is to do with her. Ella is the way she is and that's all there is to it. Maybe something bad had happened to her when she was young. Her mind fills with images of Ella as a child. A sad and lonely orphan. Maybe, Sarah thinks, just maybe, she should try being a little bit kinder in her thoughts. Except she can't. She's furious at the distance that Ella has put between them.

Just as she's thinking all of this, Wolf's right leg kicks out and something clatters to the ground.

'Oh,' Ella gasps, bending down. But before she can get there, with Wolf now wriggling and whining, Sarah reaches it first. The phone. Ella's hand stretches out at the same time. Sarah watches as their fingers nearly touch.

'No!' Ella lets out a protest. But Sarah's already grabbed it.

'Nice,' Sarah says, turning the phone around in her hands. She feels a giddy sense of power.

'Can I have it back now, please?' Ella says, her vowels stretched high over the piercing sound of Wolf's cries. It's the first time Sarah has seen Ella experience something close to discomfort – she watches her bounce Wolf up and down on her hip. She smooths her thumb over the plastic case and, before she returns it, she turns it over, screen-side up. She doesn't know why she does it. It's an instinctive action, but she can't stop herself. She's almost unaware that she's doing it. She makes a big show of looking at it, her chin pulling right into her neck. There it is. The green background of a new WhatsApp notification.

'Look,' she says. 'You've got a message.'

Ella snatches the phone but it's too late. Sarah has managed to read and digest the entire contents, well before Ella swiped it back. Her stomach flips over. Oh my God! Her first thought is that she can't wait to get back to Liza to tell her what she's just found out. But then she realises that perhaps it's not such a good idea after all – what with everything going on with her and Gav at the moment. Her second thought is that it actually can't be true. She wouldn't. She just *wouldn't*. Oooh, but she has.

Ella, with her perfect, handsome husband. Her two blond, angelic children.

'Oh my God,' Sarah mutters, a half smile curling up her lips. *This is more like it.* The earlier power she'd felt over handling Ella's phone has morphed into something else entirely.

'Wolf. Shhhh. Shhhh.' Ella is going red now. Sarah watches as she squeezes her little boy's arm, leaving small imprints in his pudgy flesh. 'Sarah, I . . .' And then she stops, breathes in deeply and stands up straight. 'Actually, Sarah, you know what? I *have* got twenty minutes before I pick up Felix. I will have that coffee with you.'

Bingo! Now, perfect Ella is going to want to be *her friend*. At this point, Sarah doesn't give Liza a second thought. She can feel Ella's fingertips through her grey top. She allows herself to be led back into the soft-play. When they arrive, Liza's slumped on the chair, gazing into the distance. Sarah knows that she's too tired to have been thinking of anything much. That the last thing she'll want to do is socialise.

'Thea's asleep,' Liza mouths, giving a thumbs up. But then she clocks Ella and a slight frown crosses her face.

'Liza,' says Ella. 'Look who I just bumped into.' Aha, Sarah thinks. So you *do* remember. 'How *are* you?' Ella sounds almost sympathetic. Now why would that be, Sarah wonders. Ella and Liza were never close, were they?

'Oh hi, both of you.' Liza looks at Sarah – something accusatory in her expression and then, the strangest thing, she spills a bit of her coffee, and drops her phone.

'Oh God, silly me,' Liza flusters. 'So cack-handed today.' Most unlike Liza, Sarah thinks. It's almost as if she's been thrown off balance. Usually, in circumstances like these, Sarah would cast Liza a glance. One that says a multitude of things: *I know. I'm sorry, but come on, we can get the gossip. We can find out what the hell she's been doing all these years. I'll steer the convo so you don't have to make any effort. I'll make it up to you.*

'So how are you?' asks Ella.

'I'm well. Thank you. Very well. Nice to see you,' says Liza. 'And another little . . . boy?'

'Wolf,' Sarah interjects. 'Isn't he gorgeous?' Liza raises her eyebrows but manages to nod.

Sarah inwardly begs for Liza not to be in one of her narky, don't-carish moods. She doesn't have the energy to overcompensate when she's already trying to be as welcoming as she possibly can.

But then Liza jumps. 'Shit,' she says. 'Sarah, did you see Jack by the way? Is he OK?'

Fuck. Jack. *Fuck, shit. Shit*. Sarah glances outside, but he's not to be seen. The wooden post he was climbing earlier is set back behind a tree, out of view from here. If she angled herself correctly she might be able to glimpse him, but it's too late for that.

She absolutely cannot admit to Liza that she *had* seen him. That he was higher than he should have been on that bloody post, and that she'd been distracted before she could call out to him. Distracted by Ella Bradby, of all people. She can't admit that in that moment, in that very moment that she'd seen *her*, both Liza and her beautiful, well-behaved little son had become totally dispensable.

'Yes.' Ella sounds almost bored. She sticks a leg out. 'Yes, she saw him.' She pulls out a menu from the wooden holder, her grey eyes scanning the protein shakes section. 'He's fine, isn't he?' she says, without looking up. Liza looks at Sarah, pointedly. Sarah knows that look. *Why the fuck are you letting her answer?* But before Sarah can say anything else, she finds her head moving up and down, mouth open, like she's one of those freaky Mama dolls.

She tries to work out why Ella would have said that. But it's too late now to do anything else and it saves her the bother of having to admit that she had *sort* of done her job. But not quite.

Sarah looks at Ella and thinks she catches a tiny wink. Almost imperceptible. A warm glow spreads across her chest. Something to tie them together. She forgets about her shitty work. She forgets about the tug of her womb. She forgets about the way she's been feeling lately. Restless and edgy. Who gives a damn about marketing an old people's home after all? She sits up straight, buoyed by these thoughts and the connection with the woman sitting next to her. But then she thinks about those moments outside on the balcony.

The moment when she'd seen Ella Bradby. The moment that she forgot about the promise to her best friend.

She looks over to the window again, desperately trying to quash the memories of everything that Liza had done for her last year when Tom had been away on business in Sydney.

She'd been twenty-eight weeks pregnant when she'd rung Liza and told her she had a 'bad feeling' and some pains. Tom had scoffed down the phone when she'd insisted on paying for someone to take Casper whilst she went into the hospital.

'Fine,' he'd said. 'But we can't keep doing this every time you have a "bad feeling".' But then, the silence as the ultrasound technician glided the Doppler over and over the same area on her stomach. 'Just one more second,' she'd said, pressing harder. Moving it around a bit more. Nothing. Liza had been her go-to then. Liza had been the one who had gripped her hand during the long, drawn-out labour, as she had given birth to the little girl they'd named Rosie. No. She will not think of that now.

She shifts her focus onto the other parents outside watching their kids. She notices a lady craning her neck over the fence at the back of the playground – undoubtedly looking at the new tennis courts. If Jack is in any danger, she thinks, someone will have spotted it. And he'd probably have clambered down from that post now anyway. He would be under the pirate ship and they'd have twenty clear minutes with Ella Bradby. To make up for all that lost time. She clears her throat and turns to Liza.

'Yes,' she says. '*Yes*. He was at the back of the sandpit.' That much is true at least, she thinks. 'I waved at him. He's absolutely fine.'

WhatsApp group: Stuff
Members: Sarah, Camilla

Sarah: Guess who I've just spotted at The Vale Club?!

Camilla: Holy shit! Don't tell me the hottie from SCD? I read that he was there in the Mail yesterday! Couldn't come up today. Taking Elodie to dentist.

Sarah: Ella Bradby!

Camilla: Oh – yes! Gosh. How was she? Never heard from her again, did we? Did we ever find out why?

Sarah: Didn't speak to her yet. Still looks the same. Just trying to resist cake. Will try and speak to her later and get the goss.

Camilla: You ok? You looked upset this morning at school drop off. Tried to catch you but didn't want to get stuck talking to Carmen.

Sarah: Yes. 2WW. I think I'm about to get it though. PMT off the charts.

Camilla: You peed on a stick yet?

Sarah: No. Can't bring myself to see a neg.

40

Camilla: Oh I'm sorry, love. I know I've offered before but if you want my IVF doc name, just LMK. She's in Chiswick. Easy.

Sarah: Will you come with me? Just for the registration then I'll tell Tom. Don't want to put too much pressure on him just yet. We can go for lunch after? That new restaurant on Turnham Green Terrace?

Camilla: Course. I'll book the appt. Next Thurs morning ok? When the kids are back at school? I know there won't be anything wrong by the way but she'll do all the investigations anyway.

Sarah: Sounds great. Thank you. Thank you so much. X

Camilla: No worries. I'm there for you anytime. X

LIZA

Just as Ella and Sarah start up a new conversation, there's a piercing scream. It's not Jack. But somehow, call it maternal instinct, I have a feeling it might be to do with him. I half get up, then sit down. *Silly.* Don't pander to anxiety. Of course it's fine. But by then, people have begun to rush through the café, and my heart is slamming around my chest, the blood rushing to my head. The waiter is coming with our coffee. He's stopped too and is looking over towards the noise.

Everything has me on edge at the moment. The slightest sound. Someone banging into me. When Cecilia Williams had given me a 'look' earlier when I'd bribed Jack to shut up with some crisps, I'd even used the 'F' word. I know, I know – I'm not proud of it. It was a shitty thing to do. But not *that* shitty. And the only reason she doesn't do such a thing is because she has ten hundred nannies. And, well, Jack just wouldn't freaking stop. And then I'd given him another whole fistful of crisps in front of her, out of spite.

And anyway, Jack was fine only a few minutes ago. Sarah had said so. And Ella had too.

I start to feel calmer, waiting for things to revert back to normal. But then the entire place goes silent. Sarah keeps flicking her eyes over to the window and Ella – well, Ella keeps clearing her throat and looking down at the menu and I'm thinking, really? What's the point? You know you aren't really going to order anything other than that sodding green juice, so why bother? Or is she just calculating how many calories she's managing to restrain herself from? But then the silence continues and that's when I can't hold out any more.

'Jack,' I cry. And I swear to God, I *swear* it, I catch a look between Sarah and Ella. I can't read it. I would dissect it later but, right now, it's a look that says: *Oh my God. Look at her. Look at the crazy bitch overreacting.*

And I think – maybe I am? Maybe I am crazy? All this shit going on in my life, maybe it's sent me over the edge. I think about how much Sarah knows. If she knew the whole truth, she'd be doing more than just giving Ella a look. Honestly – what had she been thinking bringing her over here? I'd outright told her that I wasn't interested in being in touch with her again. When I'd seen her earlier in the soft-play, that bad feeling came over me. Why had I pointed her out and put Ella back onto Sarah's radar again? I wonder what part my subconscious had to play in it all. I'd told myself not to be so silly. That maybe I was projecting. I'm full of bad feelings at the moment, but now she's here, giving Sarah those *looks*; maybe I wasn't so wrong after all. Not only has she brought back associations of everything that happened, but it seems the minute she walked back into our lives, mine and Sarah's friendship has been immediately thrown slightly off balance – I'd been trying hard enough to keep it steady for a while now, what with

Sarah's moods and the way she takes everything to heart, but now everything feels uncertain.

'I'm going to see what's going on.' I stand up. 'Sounds like something bad.' I'm trying to be casual. Acting like I'm just a lame old nosey parker but my voice gives me away. I gesture for Sarah to watch Thea but just as I'm about to walk off, I hear the Tannoy.

'Mr Blue arriving soon, please keep access clear.' Now it's Sarah's turn to exchange looks with me. She brings a hand up to her mouth.

We know that the club has code announcements for different emergencies. Silly ones like, 'Can Mr Harry Potter please come to the front desk' (*a child has gone missing*) or 'Can Mr Snape call into reception' (*I've got a really difficult customer, please send back-up*). But I hadn't heard this one yet and the speaker doesn't draw breath before she announces it again. I hear something whisper as it falls to the floor, and I realise I've dropped my parka. Before I know it I'm running towards the café but there's no one there. And then I see a commotion by the playground.

I look around, my head twisting across the space. Then I see him. On the grass. The cricket pitch. How on earth did he get there? The only way to reach the pitch from the playground is if he had climbed over the high fence that was obscured by a tree. But – he wouldn't have done that. *Surely.* He wouldn't be capable? Or maybe he had walked back into the building and out again, via a different exit. But . . . *but* . . . I start to hyperventilate.

'Get out of the way,' I scream. 'What's wrong? What's wrong with him? I'm his mother.'

Someone's opened the gate to the cricket pitch. I run through. No one budges at first. Of course, people always look twice, given how dissimilar we are. But then I push someone, hard.

'Move,' I hiss. 'That's my *son*.' And that seems to do the trick. Everyone moves to one side and there I see his little body, his black hair flattened across his head.

I lean down over him, but I'm breathing and shaking so hard I'm worried I'll hurt him even more. At first, I can't discern what's wrong. His large brown eyes look at me and then to the fence.

'I saw him. Falling,' screams a lady. Her hands are by her mouth and she's trying to swallow but she keeps making this weird, gasping noise.

'Where's the ambulance?' I'm hysterical now. 'Are there any doctors here? Put a message out.' I'm trying so hard to be calm but it's like the breath is being squeezed right out of me.

There are no obvious injuries on him, but something tells me it's serious. His small chest flutters up and down. He's still breathing OK. But his eyes look desperate. A small whimper escapes from his mouth.

'Oh God. My darling. My boy. It's OK.' I stroke his head, careful not to press too hard. 'I love you. I love you so much. You're going to be OK.' Another whimper.

I think about picking him up. I shift myself back but then I feel force on my shoulder.

'Ma'am. Don't move him.' I turn my face to see that the paramedics have arrived. I hear the sound of their stiff uniform as they bend down. The quickness of their breath. There's two of them. A man and a woman. I hold Jack's small hand for a bit but then the man asks me to step aside.

And then I remember. *Thea*. But when I turn around, she's already there. Oh God. Sarah's at the side of the crowd, holding her in one arm, clutching Ella's elbow with the other. Both of them white.

'I've got her,' Sarah mouths, nodding down at Thea, who looks so tiny in her arms. I shut my eyes briefly. I think I'm about to be sick. Everything's falling apart. And then a voice inside my head. *No, that happened already long ago.*

One of the paramedics is talking to the woman who said she saw Jack fall. I can't hear exactly what she's saying. Part of me doesn't want to know. Part of me just wants him in safety. But then I hear something about three-point protection. I think about where I've heard that phrase before. In an old episode of *Grey's Anatomy*. Bile swills around in my stomach.

'Darling,' I say. 'You're going to be OK. I promise you. OK?' I think about Sarah and how she'd checked on him only moments before.

Yes, she had told me. *Yes. He's absolutely fine.* Sarah. Poor Sarah. I know how bad she'll be feeling. Thinking that she should have brought him in with her. That she should have stayed with him.

I'll tell her. After this whole horrendous nightmare is over, I'll tell her. *No one could have done anything different. It was just one of those things*, I'll say. He'll be fine. He *has* to be fine.

And then it crosses my mind that I should have been watching him more closely and that I shouldn't have left it to Sarah. But she'd seen him. It was OK. And then the thought swiftly disappears. I have more urgent things to worry about.

'Please, God,' I mutter. 'I know I've failed you many times. But if you are there, please, *please* help my little boy.'

SARAH

Thea won't stop screaming. Sarah flings out a load of rubbish from the bottom of the pram that Liza had left – biscuit wrappers, apple cores, old juice cartons, about three crumpled-up boxes of medicine – but she can't see any pumped milk there, or in the nappy bag. Sarah tries shushing Thea, but her arms keep giving way, what with all the adrenaline. She begins to feel maternally useless, further adding to her anxiety.

'Please. Shhh. Shhhh. Please. I'm begging you. Be quiet.' But Thea's tiny mouth keeps getting wider, lips quivering as her screams reach their peak.

Sarah can no longer hear the ambulance. The blare of the siren had gone on for what felt like hours. She imagines how Liza felt in the back and she can't stop thinking about Jack. His small face as he'd been stretchered out. *Shhhh. Thea. It's OK.* And then she remembers her earlier promise.

I'll check on Jack. Don't worry.

She thinks of Liza again with her at the hospital, after her daughter had been stillborn. How her friend had

47

silently been there for her and now she's repaid her with *this*.

'What the hell,' Sarah turns to Ella. 'What the hell do we do? You told Liza I'd checked on him. Why did you do that?'

'You didn't object. You didn't speak up. You could have gone back.' Ella's speaking so slowly and calmly. As though nothing has just happened. Like she could be talking about her summer holiday plans. Sarah wants nothing more than to slap her. All of the earlier allure has gone. Vanished into blackness.

And then her feelings turn in on themselves. It's her. This whole situation is all her fault.

Don't try and defend yourself. Just admit it, says an inner voice. *You've caused this by dumping your friend – and her son – in the shit. You've repaid your friend's kindness and loyalty, with this.* She wonders if it would make it worse, or better, that she had only made a flimsy attempt at checking on him. That she knew full well that Jack had been halfway up that post. She swiftly decides it makes things ten times worse. Or does it? Besides, it's too late now. She should have said something at the time. It would look too bad if she admitted it now. But before she knows it, she's opened her mouth.

'Listen, Ella. Actually, I did check on Jack. Or rather, I saw him. Outside.'

'You did? Fine,' says Ella. 'See? It's all OK.' She looks relieved. As though she, too, is off the hook, her grey eyes almost glittering. Didn't she for one minute think about Jack? She's not going to get away with this, Sarah decides. If she tells her the whole story, Ella becomes complicit.

'I did. But.' Ella's stopped listening now. She's pulling

a thread from the bottom of her T-shirt with much concentration, like she knows there's more coming; a petulant child with its hand over their ears. 'Listen. Are you listening?'

'Hmmm hmmm.'

'I saw him up that post.' Sarah takes a step towards Ella. 'Did you hear me? I saw him. He was halfway up. It looked like he was coming down. Or at least I thought he might have been. I don't know . . . I meant to shout out to him. To get down. But then you . . .'

'*Me*?' Ella's chin sets forward. 'You what? You aren't actually trying to blame me here, are you?'

Sarah feels the energy around her change into something dangerous. 'No,' she takes a step back. 'No. I just, that's what happened. Should I tell Liza?'

She thinks she should perhaps relinquish some of the power back to Ella and diffuse the situation before matters get much worse. After all, that's what Ella wants. Girls like her are all the same, she thinks. Or women. They're women now. Grown-ups. Oh God. Look at everyone here, playing grown-ups, not knowing what the hell they're doing most of the time. And now this has happened.

'No. Don't say anything. There's no need. Why did you tell me that?'

'Because . . .'

'Because you wanted me to carry half the burden of guilt? Am I right?' Sarah gives a half nod. This is the most she's heard Ella speak in one go.

'Look, Sarah. If there's one thing I've learnt, it's that you can't change things. It won't help if Liza knows. Will it? It won't change things. It still happened. It still *would* have happened. And Liza's strong.'

Sarah listens intently. Ella's right. In a way. But she

should do the morally correct thing. And how dare Ella presume she knows what's best for Liza.

'You don't know anything about Liza.' There's the funny look again. Sarah ignores it. 'Listen. Ella, I don't even know why we are having this conversation. We just need to focus here on Jack. On Liza. Making sure they're both OK. All right? I don't really care about anything else.'

'Fine,' Ella says. 'But do what I say. Just keep quiet, OK? Things will be much worse if you don't. You're just being selfish,' she carries on. 'Wanting to take away your own guilt. It doesn't serve anyone. Least of all Liza. So just stick to your story and all will be fine.'

At the mention of Liza's name, Sarah pulls out her phone. No new messages. And then she wonders if she should ring Gav.

'Anyway,' says Ella. 'It's time. We need to get the others.' Oh God. *Casper.* Sarah hasn't even thought about her little boy.

'You go.' Sarah turns Thea around so she's facing outwards. 'Get Felix. Then get Casper. He's in the tennis lessons on court three.' She feels too shaken up to move anywhere. She doesn't think her legs will carry her just yet. And besides, she needs a few moments alone. 'If they ask where I am, tell them that it was my friend,' she motions towards the playground, 'back there. Password for pick-up is Leo.' She thinks of Casper's lion comforter and wants to cry. 'And after that, the kids can get a snack.'

'OK.' Ella walks off, sashaying from side to side. She has that unselfconscious walk of someone totally confident with their own body. Then Sarah wonders why she is even thinking of such a thing at a time like this, and what that says about her. Has she been so conditioned to be so damn . . . *judgemental*? Or is her mind just distracting itself from the god-awful thing she's just done? She rubs her stomach, trying to make the bottomless sensation disappear, but the thought of Jack and Liza's faces keeps looming in her mind's eye.

She sits and waits, checking her phone every five seconds. She thinks back to what she'd seen on Ella's screen, moments before. How she wishes that right about now everything had been different. If only she could relive the last twenty minutes. If things had gone according to plan, she'd be WhatsApping Liza under the table right about now, as they sat drinking coffee.

> Just wait until you find out what I've got to tell you when she's gone!

She tells herself that Jack is going to be OK. That he's alive. But what if things never go back to normal? What if *Jack* never goes back to normal? What if he never walks again? What would she do then? She clenches her hands together, trying to rid them of the onset of pins and needles. How would Liza and Gav cope? Not just emotionally, but financially too? It would be a daily reminder of what she'd done. All her fault.

Just as she thinks she can't take the not knowing much longer, Ella arrives back in sight, with Wolf in her arms and Felix and Casper on either side of her. Felix looks like something from a Boden catalogue, all neat and clean blond hair swept to one side. He's wearing brown leather hi-tops, cream chinos and a sleeveless V-neck jumper over a striped blue shirt. Ridiculous. Casper, by comparison, looks like some sort of urchin child, with ragged tracksuit bottoms on and a black smudge on his chin. She's lucky enough to have her little boy. She thinks of Rosie. She must make more of an effort. She holds Thea up over her shoulder and opens her arms up to her son, breathing in his smell.

'Oh God. Casper.' She doesn't deserve him. Not after what she's just done.

'They're closing the club early. My tennis teacher said so,' he says in his matter-of-fact voice, eyebrows disappearing under his blunt-cut fringe. Sarah had hacked at it two days earlier, trying to save money on a professional cut. She'd made him look half-deranged. 'Where's Liza, Mummy? Where's Jack? Liza promised we could have half an hour play.'

'Jack has had a small . . .' Sarah places a fist on her breastbone. 'He's going to be . . .' she swallows back tears.

'He fell,' Ella says. 'Jack fell. He's just gone to be checked out. He'll be OK though. Felix, go with Casper and get some biscuits. Quick. Before they shut the place.' She presses a ten-pound note into Felix's hand. Casper runs after him. Sarah watches his legs winding up faster and faster at the thought of a sugar-fix.

'Jack – he'll tell her he didn't see me.' Sarah turns to Ella. 'That is if he . . .'

'If he what? I think you're being a bit hysterical about all of this. He's going to be just fine.'

Sarah fights an uncontrollable urge to hurt her again.

'How do you know? I was just thinking that if he does – God help us – make it out alive, he could be paralysed. Or something. So tell me, how do you know it's all going to be OK? You don't. Too busy looking at your *special* messages?'

She grabs at Ella's phone but she snatches it away.

'Look.' Sarah starts to cry again. 'We need to sort this out. I think something really bad has happened to him. If I'd just told him to get down.' She watches as Ella glances over to where he fell. For a fraction of a second, she bites her lip, before her expression turns to one of impatience, and she throws her hands up in the air.

'Look, you did check on him. OK? We saw him. From the balcony. You waved at him. He was at the bottom of the post. That's your story. He's not going to remember if he waved back at you or not. You can say he can't have seen you. But that you saw him. Or that you thought he waved back but maybe you were mistaken. Maybe he was just moving his hand around.'

'What if they've got CCTV or something?' Sarah can't believe she's even entertaining this discussion. She tries to motion to Casper, who has come back with a muffin stuffed into his pocket. Oh well. She'll have to be done for theft too. She's too emotionally wired to tell him to put it back. And then she sees a waitress right behind her, coffee cups stacked on a tray. She steps aside, heart thumping. Is her son about to get told off? She couldn't cope with it if he was. More lies – having to pretend she hasn't seen Casper pocketing their food because she certainly isn't going to own up to that now. But the waitress mercifully carries on walking, the sound of china rattling around the otherwise silent room.

'It's not going to get that far. Is it? She's your friend.' Ella pulls up her posture until she looks like she's about to launch into a backflip. 'She's going to believe you. Why would she think you'd lie?'

'I don't know.' Sarah pauses to think about why she had lied. *Ella.* Ella had happened. 'But what if he *is* paralysed or something?'

'Just wait and see what happens.'

Sarah wants to shake Ella, predominantly for not giving her the reassurance she needs, but also for seemingly not giving a damn about Jack's welfare.

'Look, I'm telling you, he'll be fine,' Ella says. 'Whatever happens, he'll be fine.'

'Whatever happens? What do you mean, *whatever happens*? So you *do* think he'll be paralysed? I can't cope with this.'

'Look, just stay calm, Sarah. Just bloody well stay calm. This is certainly not helping.'

Casper suddenly runs up to Sarah, a cereal bar in his hand.

'Can I have this, Mummy?'

Sarah bends down, careful not to jog Thea now she's finally quiet.

'Of course you can, darling,' she says, her mind being pulled in a hundred different directions. In any other situation she'd have said something, she'd have told the truth, straight away. At least, she likes to think she would. She can barely swallow for fear.

But the thought of losing Liza's friendship is too much for her to bear. *Tell the truth, lose a friend. Lie, and keep her close.* A hot flush rips through her as her brain settles on her decision. She'll do what Ella told her to. At least then they'd both be in it together. And, on second thoughts, Ella's right. Telling the truth now won't solve anything. In fact, it might make matters worse – stress Liza out even more. For the moment, they all need to do what's best for everyone and, most of all, Jack. She'll wait and see what the news is at the hospital. The Tannoy goes off again.

'In light of an earlier incident, we'll be closing the club in ten minutes. I repeat . . .'

'Fine,' Sarah says, turning to Ella. 'Let's just see what happens. Casper. Come on, darling. We're going to take Thea back to ours.' She is about to say goodbye to Ella, but she pulls up. 'Wait,' she says. 'I need your number.'

She watches a frown cross Ella's face.

'In case I need to speak to you.' Ella shrugs. Sarah lifts her chin in defiance. 'Don't you want to know what happens? With Jack?'

'Fine,' Ella breathes, and then she reels off her phone number, a bored expression on her face.

'Thanks. Fine. I'll ping you later. Felix, bye to you too.' She grabs Casper's hand and takes him and Thea back to the soft-play. She takes the pram, hoisting all the bags and coats into the bottom of the buggy before ordering an Uber. She's in no mood to take the bus home. Whilst she's waiting, she rings Tom.

'Oh God,' he says, once she's run through the whole incident. 'Is he OK? What can we do? I'm coming home now. Anything at all I can do, just let me know. Anything.'

'I don't know, Tom. I'm . . .' She tries to tell him she's scared but the words hang heavy on her tongue. 'OK, look.' She decides now is not the time to be thinking of anything else other than Liza and Jack. 'Right. Formula. Can you get some formula milk for Thea? I've got her with me. Take out the Moses basket from the loft. Oh, and some nappies and shit . . . I don't know. The steriliser. Do we still have that? What else do we need for babies? It's been a while.' She gives a small laugh which turns into a hiccup.

Images of last year surface in her mind – they seem to come back full-force in times of stress: how Liza had gone quietly to her house from the hospital before Tom had arrived back in London; keeping her mother up to speed because she couldn't face her grief as well. Liza had then spent that day putting away any reminders of Rosie's homecoming – everything shrink-wrapped and stored back in the loft so Sarah wouldn't have to see it again.

She squeezes Casper's hand. 'OK?' she mouths. He nods, looking up at his mother, a worried expression on his face. It's only when she hangs up that she realises her hands are shaking and she's got tears running down her face. For the first time in about five years, she actually *wants* to ring her mother but she's too scared that the sound of her voice will prompt her to lose it entirely.

By the time she's got Casper out of the building and manoeuvred the pram and everything else, the sky is getting darker and heavier, and it's nearing tea time. Any minute now, Casper's going to start whining and Thea's going to want her milk. She passes a small group of women by the car park.

'Awful,' one of them whispers. Priti, she's called. Sarah recognises her from Body Pump – she always wonders how she manages to be so compact but springy at the same time. 'Investigation . . . I mean, my little one plays out there all the time. Lord knows what could have happened. Someone could have been killed.'

She wants to tell them all to stop gossiping. To go back home and have a little respect. She watches all the 4x4s, streaming out of the barriers. People are waving at her left, right and centre. Why can't one of you just offer me a lift, she thinks. She stands scanning the roads for her Uber, when she realises she doesn't even know what she's looking for. She puts the brake on Thea's pram, checking it's on with her foot, three or four times. Something about the conversation she's just overheard has made her even more nervous.

'Casper. Away from the road.'

'I'm not near the road,' he says, but she yanks him back so he's standing right close to the hedge. He looks shocked.

She pulls out her phone and brings up the Uber app. Tom's words play back in her mind. *Anything at all I can do, just let me know.* And that's when she knows. That she'll do *anything* to make it up to Liza. To Jack. Liza won't know why, but that's fine. Somehow, even if it means putting her own life on the line, she's going to sort out this awful, sorry mess. Maybe she should do some googling – *falls from a great height*, or *paralysis* – but then she knows her fear will take over.

She puts her phone firmly in her pocket, and then she sees Priti, leaping into her car. She plays back the conversation she's just overheard; the self-righteous tremble of Priti's voice. *Investigation. Someone could have been killed.* And that's when she jolts. Investigation? Surely not. It was an accident. That's all. Surely they wouldn't go that far? And anyway, she couldn't come clean now. She thinks of Liza's face. The relief when Sarah had told her that her son was OK. *I saw him. He's fine. This is the way I paid you back for your friendship and love, Liza.*

Her stomach tilts. She watches Priti's car swing out of the space and into the road, the flash of her diamond ring winking in the weak sunlight. It's far too late. She's sure the investigation won't happen. And if it does? Well, she has a story. She is going to stick to it and that, she tells herself with a lurch, is that.

LIZA

I'm taken into a waiting room, whilst Jack is rushed into the operating theatre. Gav arrives soon after, motorbike helmet clamped under his arm. I stand up, and we hug. Something we haven't done for months now. It doesn't last long. I extricate myself from him, terrified about what's coming next.

'What happened?' he demands as he crosses his arms and takes a step forward, encroaching into my space.

'He fell.' I take a step back from him.

'How?'

I'd worked out the explanation already, yet now that Gav is here I'm finding it hard to speak.

'He was climbing.'

'Climbing what? A tree?'

'No.' I lower my head. 'He was outside The Vale Club. In the playground.' My vision tunnels.

'And?'

'Look, please,' I tell him. 'I was with Thea. She was screaming.'

'That's not what I'm asking you.' I look into his eyes.

58

Ever since we'd separated and he'd moved into a different area of the house, he's been distant, unreadable.

'He was outside. In the sandpit.'

'And you were doing what, exactly?' His voice takes on a menacing tone. 'Can you please explain? That's my son in there.' He narrows his eyes. '*Again.*' Cold rises up in my blood and I take another step back. I know we're both thinking the same thing.

'I was . . . I told you. I was with Thea. He was fine.' I think back to just before it had happened. How Thea had just fallen asleep. How finally, that day, I thought I'd have three minutes to myself. Until Sarah had turned up with Ella Bradby.

'He was fine. Sarah checked on him seconds before. He obviously . . .' I trail off, unable to think of his small body impacting the ground. I swallow. 'The doctors are, well, they've been good.'

'What have they said?'

'Nothing much. Just rushed him into theatre. They think he might have damaged his neck.'

'Damaged? What the fuck do you mean, damaged? Broken?'

'Gav. Please.' I cover my mouth with my hand. 'Please. Keep your voice down.' I'm used to Gav's emotions going from zero to a hundred miles per hour within the space of a few seconds.

'You weren't watching him, were you? Busy in that café with Sarah? Please, just tell me you were doing your job as a mother.'

'I was,' I try, but the words sound hollow. 'I was. He was fine.'

'And you trusted Sarah? What did she say? That he was OK?'

'She said,' I look up, trying to recall what she had said. 'She said that she had waved and that he was fine.'

'Well, you shouldn't have left it up to Sarah. She's so dopey sometimes she wouldn't notice if her arse was on fire.'

'That's not fair. And nor is it relevant.'

'What about the club then? How could they have something so dangerous? In the kids' playground. I'm going to fucking have them. I'm going to . . .'

'Listen.' Now he's turned his attention to The Vale Club, at least it's off me and Sarah. 'We have to focus on Jack.'

'Well, it's all relevant. He was under your watch, after all.' He stares me down. I know what he's thinking.

'Look.' My voice comes out in barely a whisper. 'He was in the sandpit. I had seen him minutes before. Sarah checked on him. There's nothing else that we should have done. I know that . . . I know you're thinking of . . .' I can't bring myself to talk any further, but I don't have to because he takes a big breath. The room feels dry.

'If anything happens,' he points a finger at me but then tempers himself, rubbing his face with both hands. *If anything happens, then what*, I want to say but I sit down, defeated.

'And I'm going to make sure they damn well do an investigation into all this. The club. Someone's going to have some answers. I want answers. I'm going to sue.'

This is the thing about Gav – he always needs answers. Even when there aren't any. I'm torn between pushing the spotlight off me – and the fact that I hadn't been outside with Jack – and getting Gav onto the fact that it might have been The Vale Club who was at fault. Eventually, however, he runs out of steam and we sit in silence, Gav fidgeting in his seat. He picks up his motor-bike helmet, clicks and unclicks the clasp over and over. I give him a warning look but he carries on.

I'm scared. So scared. I've been through every single outcome of the fall. From the best to the worst options. Jack is alive, but what about his quality of life? What if he never walks again? One of my greatest fears come true. And then all these other fears start careering through my mind. If he *is* paralysed will we be able to afford it? How will I cope? I don't want to be thinking of money at a time like this, but we'd have to make arrangements. Change the house. Maybe Gav's right? Maybe we should sue? Maybe that's the only way we'd get enough to pay for his care. I try and be sensible and give myself the advice I'd give Sarah. *Wait and see what the doctors say. Stop making things up before they've happened.* But I feel sick at the thought of my son going through all of this.

'Please can you stop making that noise with your helmet,' I finally snap. 'I'm finding it distracting.' He stands up. 'I mean, not you,' I add quickly, in case it makes him flare up again. I've just got more important things on my mind right now than stepping on eggshells around Gav. 'Just the noise.'

'I'm going,' he says. I feel the familiar stone drop in my stomach. *Where to*, I want to ask, but I keep my mouth shut. 'I need to know what's going on.'

He walks out of the room and I start to sob. I pick up my phone, mainly as a distraction from the sensation of dread hanging over me. There's a text from Sarah. About Thea. My God. *Thea.* All this time I haven't even thought of Thea. I feel the tingle, the swelling of my milk ducts. Oh God. She needs feeding. I *am* a shit mum.

All ok with Thea. We've given her formula. She's fast asleep. We're thinking of you. We're here for you if you need anything at all.

Thanks, I text back. Still waiting. Jack in surgery. Can Thea stay the night in case we aren't back? Not sure what's happening.

Of course, comes the swift reply. Don't think about anything other than Jack. Let us know any updates if you can Sx.

I start typing a reply. Telling Sarah that she needn't berate herself about what happened, but I put down my phone. I've got to concentrate on the matter in hand.

The doctor comes in with Gav. She's still in scrubs, her dark hair pushed up under her cap. She's very pretty, with kind features and a reassuring expression, which makes me want to start crying all over again. I stand up and go to Gav's side. Without realising it, we are gripping each other's hands.

'I'm your surgeon, Mahim Qureshi,' she says. 'Nice to meet you. Sorry I didn't catch you both earlier.'

Please, tell me he's going to be all right, I plead in my mind. *I'll die if he's not. I'll die.*

'Jack is going to be OK,' she says. 'He's going to survive.'

Gav snaps his head up, ripping his hand out of mine. 'Survive? What do you *mean*, survive? I had no idea . . .' I will the doctor to start talking, to put us out of our misery.

'He had a very lucky escape,' says Dr Qureshi, looking at me. 'He's broken a wrist. And he's had a greenstick fracture on the seventh cervical vertebra. That's to say that in adults, it would have resulted in a clean break. But children's bones are a lot more supple. We've operated on his wrist but you'll have to keep him lying down for the next few months whilst his vertebra repairs and he'll have to be in a neck brace. He'll be able to move a tiny bit. But it'll be painful for him and we can't be a hundred percent certain that it won't have a future impact on things.'

For a second, I think about asking *what things* but I'm unable to process everything she's saying to us. The only words that are flashing through my mind right now are *survive* and *lucky escape*.

'So he'll be OK? He'll be able to walk again properly and everything?' I ask, desperate to hear one more time that he's going to be all right.

'With the right care and support. But at the moment, I cannot stress to you how important it is that you keep him still. No knocks. The bone needs to heal right.'

I think of how the hell I'm going to do this but then I don't care. I don't care. He's alive. He's going to be OK. I feel like collapsing with relief. My boy. My beautiful boy. It's all going to be OK. I start to cry.

'You might want to arrange things at home so that . . .' her gaze flicks from me to Gav, 'it's comfortable and easy for you to reach him.'

'We're . . .' I can't bring myself to use the words, even though it has been weeks now.

'We're not together any more,' Gav finishes for me. I look over at him. His presence fills the entire room. 'But I still live there and am watching Liza and the kids all the time.'

He glances over at me. I imagine him ending the

separation. How we might be able to make things work if I can show him that we're meant to be together. That we are a family unit of four. That I'm a good person. A good mother, who has just made some mistakes in her life.

'It's OK,' says Dr Qureshi. 'I'm sure you'll work it out and we'll send support for you, of course.'

I think about our house. My room in the loft. Jack's on the floor below and the living area two more floors beneath that with a spare room attached to the end, where Gav sleeps.

I'll move downstairs, or move Jack to the bottom room, and then we can be together. Thea can be in the . . . *fuck*. My mind feels like it's spinning with all the options. Gav would never, ever agree to moving back upstairs to the room we used to share. And I can't move downstairs to be nearer Jack – I wouldn't be able to cope with being on the same floor as Gav, breathing down my neck all the time. And besides, Jack would pick up on the bad atmosphere if we're forced to spend long periods of time together.

I'd begged Gav, after all, to move out. To end things in a better, cleaner way than him still living in the house. But of course, he'd refused over and over.

'I'm staying. To watch you,' he'd warned me.

What am I going to do?

And then, a flash of an idea. And I think about Sarah's earlier text.

If you need anything at all.

Sarah and Tom. Their lower-ground-floor flat. It would be perfect. They aren't getting it developed for another year. Maybe, just maybe, I could ask if we might stay for a bit. We'd all be on one floor. Me, Jack and Thea. I'd have to get Gav onside, and no doubt he'd be over every five minutes. But I'd know that Sarah and Tom would be right upstairs if I needed them. It would work perfectly. If I could get them to agree. Do I dare ask?

'I'd best get back but I'll come and see you later to answer any questions you have,' says Dr Qureshi, leaving the room.

We both sit and my phone pings. Sarah.

What's going on? I can't stop thinking of you all.

He's ok. Fractured his neck.

Oh my god. Oh my god. I'm so sorry. Liza, I'm so sorry.

Why are you sorry? I'm just grateful you were there to take Thea.

What does that mean? He'll be able to walk again, won't he? Will he be ok?

Doc says he'll be ok. But very difficult. We won't be able to move him at all for a bit otherwise it'll disrupt his healing, so he has to lie flat on his back. It's going to be tough. For him mostly. And I think she said there might be knock-on effects. But was too overwhelmed to ask what they were. I feel so upset for him. He should be running around in the park with his friends. Not lying like this in a bed for the foreseeable future.

I think about asking her there and then. Just come out with it. She wouldn't say no now. But then I tell myself to slow down. Wait, at least, to find out if Jack is going to be OK. Focus on his recovery. And then, only then, will I think about how to move on from this.

To: J.Roper@westlondongazette.com
From: 54321@freeserve.com

Hi

I saw you've been covering quite a lot of The Vale Club's new opening of late. I'm not sure if you've got some form of tie-in with them but I thought you might like to know that there was an accident there earlier today. A small boy fell off from high up a post in the playground. I believe he is ok but I thought you should have a look at what went on – us residents and members would be keen to know the truth behind it all.

Yours,
Derry

SARAH

That night, Sarah lies in bed, terrified of Thea waking up. She listens to the snort and shuffle of tiny arms and legs. She hovers over the Moses basket, holding her hand under Thea's perfect upturned nose. She's breathing. This time five years ago, she'd done the same thing every night, with Casper.

She thinks back to when they had first brought Casper home from Queen Charlotte's and Hammersmith Hospital. She had snapped at Tom for being too rough with the car seat as he tried to click it into the back of their BMW. She'd held her breath at absolutely every jolt on the road, both for the baby's sake and her own – she had been torn from back to front. She winces remembering the pain as the metal had tugged Casper right out of her. And then the rest. The ensuing images at every turn of things that could go wrong: Casper choking on her milk, suffocating in his Moses basket, inhaling smoke particles from family members who held him. The list had been endless. She rubs her stomach wistfully. She'd do it all over again in a heartbeat. And just like that, she has a vision of Rosie being handed to her in the hospital. She remembers wanting to breathe life into her daughter, so desperately. To impart some of her own living soul into the tiny creature that lay in her arms. Liza's presence strong and calm right beside her. The doctors. *We're so sorry. Nothing anyone could do.* She shivers.

She hears Tom downstairs, the soft monotones of the cricket commentary on the TV, which she normally finds so comforting. Tonight though, she wants to shout down to tell him to come and help her. But, she reasons, he has probably fallen asleep. She doesn't want to leave the room in case the creak of the door wakes Thea.

Her mind traces the events of the day. Jack fracturing his neck. His small body lying in the operating theatre, the anaesthetic needle puncturing his tiny veins. She curls herself up into a ball as she replays the events preceding the accident. And then Liza's WhatsApp. She flicks back onto it, reading and rereading the conversation she'd had with her earlier: *there might be knock-on effects.* She puts her phone down. He's alive. That's all she should be focusing on. She thinks about whether Ella was right. *He still would have fallen. Whether you'd checked on him or not.* She'd never know.

And anyway, where the hell *is* Ella? Does she really not give enough of a damn to at least contact her and ask about Jack? Especially given the thing that Sarah had found out earlier. And then Priti mentioning the investigation. She knows, rationally, that the club will be duty-bound to look into what happened. She also knows they won't want any bad publicity from this. They'll shut it down as soon as possible. They might want to speak to her. That's OK. She'll tell them what she told Liza.

She takes a breath and recites the words in her head. *I waved at him. He was absolutely fine.* And then she goes through the various responses to any given questions they might ask her. *Are you sure you saw him properly? Yes. He was playing. Are you sure he was OK? Yes.*

Oh God. She wipes her hands on her top and shuts down her thoughts. She needs to focus on Thea. Do the best for her friend and try and make things up to her. And then she remembers Liza's earlier text. How Jack would be flat on his back. How this is all her fault so she needs to be doing more to fix it – especially if he never quite recovers properly. The taste of bile floods her mouth. She can't quite believe that she's been responsible for something so hideously awful. She's done some bad things in her life – she'll never forget lying to her parents time and time again so she could go to the Palladium nightclub – but this, this is something she could never have even imagined experiencing.

She thinks about their lower-ground-floor flat. It's free at the moment. Perhaps she'll ask Liza and Jack to stay with them for a bit so she can help out. Try and make things all right. It would give Liza a break from Gav, too. The way he calls her out on everything. *Look at you*, he'd say. *Look at the way you're doing that.* And he'd get up and take over. Tutting and asking Jack if he was OK, gliding his eyes over his little boy's body in exaggerated movements. *Anything your daddy can help you with?*

She didn't know how Liza stood it, really. He never used to be like that – controlling and anxious. And it's even weirder now, given that they're actually separated. In any case, it would be good for Liza to get away from him. Give her some breathing space. Sarah's absolutely sure that Gav is not going to be happy about the fact they'd both been inside The Vale Club, and not out in the sandpit with Jack. He'll probably try and sue and then she'll have to speak up in court. Oh God. But before the thought maps out into anything further she hears a small cry.

Shit. The milk. It'll be freezing cold. She should have boiled the kettle earlier instead of being held hostage by her thoughts. Perhaps she should go downstairs and get her bottle first? Or take Thea down with her so she doesn't start shrieking at full pelt? Shit.

Before she knows it, she's running downstairs.

'Tom,' she hisses. 'Tom, she's awake.'

'Hmmm?' She watches as Tom stretches out and moves a pale, freckled hand towards the remote.

'Tom?' She's exasperated now. Has he no sense of urgency? She swallows back her 'nagging' voice, as he calls it. 'Tom,' she continues. 'I'd really love it if you could go upstairs to Thea while I get her milk. It would be really helpful,' she monotones. 'Because you're so soothing with babies.'

It's a trick she'd learnt during their stint at Relate last year – after they'd buried Rosie. She still feels resentful that Tom hadn't been with her, even though she knows that wasn't his fault. Would it work tonight? Would it fuck.

'*Tom*!' She picks up the remote and hurls it across the sofa.

'Jesus.' He leaps up. 'Sarah. What the hell has got into you?!'

'Oh God.' She can hear Thea's cries getting more intense. 'I'm sorry. Can you just go up?'

'Going.' He stands, his expression bordering on sheer

71

terror at witnessing his wife in such a state. She has no idea why she's freaking out so much. She's looked after a baby before. Surely this should be a doddle? She goes to the kitchen and counts out the formula scoops, checking and rechecking the amounts on the back of the blue box.

When she's satisfied she's got the right number of scoops, she shakes the mixture in boiling water and places it in a bowl of ice. The crying slows down.

At least Casper will stay asleep, she knows that much. Her one saving grace. She stares at the milk, willing for it to cool. 'Hurry up,' she mutters. By the time she goes upstairs Thea's screams are at full pelt.

'You calm now?' Tom gives her a look, as though she's one of those potty pigeon ladies who cover themselves in breadcrumbs in the park.

'I'm calm. Look. Today. I . . .'

'I know. I'm sorry,' he says. 'I should have realised how traumatic it would be for you and I'm sorry. Oh love, why don't you go to bed with Casper? I'll sort Thea out. Just go and get into your nightie and I'll do the rest.'

She wants to resist. She feels she owes it to Liza to be the one looking after Thea, but the lure of lying down and ignoring the world is too strong. She pulls out her old grey nightie from the wardrobe – the one that she used to comfort her stonking hangovers – and sits on the bed. She watches Tom angling the bottle into Thea's mouth, her small, fuzzy head resting in the nook of his elbow.

'Shhh, there we go,' he says. 'All OK now. It's OK now.'

'I forgot how good you are at this.' She nods at Thea.

She sniffs at the hem of her T-shirt. *Don't let me think about it. Last year. Please. Not now.* But it's too late and she starts to cry.

'We'll be OK, love,' he says. She knows what he's thinking. *This should be our child.* 'Don't you worry. You've had a long day. No wonder you're feeling tearful. Now go on. Get into Casper's bed and try and get some sleep.'

She can't think of anything she'd rather do less than move from where she is right now. The tiredness has hit her like a truck.

Tom looks down at Thea and smiles. 'Well done, little girl.'

Sarah pulls down the soft, pink eiderdown and climbs into their comfy king-sized bed from Loaf that they'd saved up for last year.

'I want to sleep with you.' Sarah's sobs subside. She needs to feed off Tom's calm presence. If she's near Casper, she'll start to feel more anxious. What if karma is real? Tit for tat. That kind of thing. What if he fell too? *Please, Casper, no. Stay safe.*

After Tom has got Thea back down, he goes straight back to sleep. She listens to his slow, rhythmic breathing. Not a care in the world. No lasting adrenaline from the baby crying. How lovely to be him – able to switch on and off at the drop of a hat. She can feel her heart still thrumming from earlier. She tries to still her whirring mind and fall asleep, but it's no use. She listens to the tick-tock of the bedside clock, her limbs restless. She watches three rectangles of light strobe across the ceiling as a car drives past.

Maybe she'll feel better when her PMT subsides. Then she'll be able to rationalise everything. No. *It's guilt, warping into something even worse,* says a voice.

'Tom,' she hisses. 'Tom, wake up.'

'Go back to sleep,' he murmurs.

'I never went to sleep in the first place.'

'Shhh. You'll wake the baby.'

She goes quiet for a few seconds.

'Tom?'

A short jab in his ribs has the desired effect and he drags himself up onto his elbows.

'What is it?' He squints over to the small Ikea side table. 'Three in the morning. Oh God, Thea's due a feed soon anyway. What's the matter?'

'Liza. Jack. And,' she nods over to the Moses basket. 'I was just thinking.' She stares at the shutters on their bay window, wondering when they'd last been cleaned.

'Thinking what? He's going to be OK. You know that. I spoke to Gav.'

'No. I know but . . .' She takes a breath. If Tom agrees just to this one thing, she knows, in her heart of hearts, that everything can be OK. Not in an OCD, everything-has to-be-in-threes kind of way. Just in a make-her-peace-with-what-she's-done kind of way. She'll *show* Liza just how sorry she is. She won't say anything at all about what happened, but she is absolutely convinced that if she gives her life over to Liza, just for a little bit, then everything will be OK. She'll have paid her dues for her wrongdoing. She wonders whether to wake Thea while they're talking but decides not to. She wants Tom's full attention and he's always moaning that she can't multitask.

'OK. Well, I was thinking. Our downstairs flat. Well – we're not using it. I know we were going to Airbnb it before we renovate, but how do you feel about Liza and Jack moving in? With Thea, of course. That way they'll all be on one floor. Easy access. That kind of thing.'

She holds her breath. Tom's kind. He'll always do anything to help out. But before she's allowed herself to exhale, he shakes his head.

'No. No way. Not now.' He throws back the covers with more force than is perhaps necessary and walks over to Thea. 'I'm going to feed her now. Before she starts screaming. Then hopefully she'll sleep till seven.'

Tom always has been a stickler for routine and she has to admit that, for Casper, it had worked a treat.

'Look, I know you want to help. But this is not the way to do it. Besides.' He lifts up Thea's small body and places her gently over his shoulder. Sarah watches the paleness of his skin, reflecting against the moonlight.

'Besides what?'

'Besides. What about us? *Our* baby? I need you to focus fully on our situation, Sarah. We can't put our lives on hold. No matter how awful Liza is feeling. There are other ways we can help. Jack is going to be OK. You know that, don't you? You,' he takes a breath, '*we*, we aren't over what happened to us last year. Please don't give your entire self over to Liza.'

She wants to tell him she owes it to Liza, in more ways than one. She wants to shout at him that he wasn't even there when Rosie died, so how dare he try and tell her what Liza does or doesn't need. But she is too exhausted.

'How do you know? That Jack will be OK?'

'Because I know. This bit will be tough for them. But you know what Liza's like. She's got it in hand.'

An image of Liza's pram from earlier floods her mind's eye. The piles of rubbish. The medicine boxes and the rotting apple cores. She isn't so sure.

'OK,' says Tom with a sigh. 'How about you move in

with Liza for a couple of days? Stay with her just while Jack settles back in. I can take some time off work. Look after Casper. That way you can help out but we can still focus on *us*. On our baby, Sarah.' He squeezes Thea tight. 'You know how much this means to us.'

She opens her mouth. She's about to tell him about the IVF clinic appointment next week, but something stops her.

'OK, Sa? Is that OK? Good enough?'

'Yes.' She wraps her arms around herself and shivers into her T-shirt. 'Yes, it's fine.'

But in her head, of course, she's thinking something totally different. No. It's *not* good enough. It's absolutely not good enough at all. She doesn't want to move into Liza's; with Gav giving them both the evil eye every time they open their mouths. She wants to be right here with Tom and Casper. And she wants to, she *has* to, do the best by her friend. There'll be a way to get Tom to agree. And she's damned if she isn't going to find out what it is.

Liza: Hi all. I hope everyone is surviving half-term! I'm sorry to be the bearer of bad news. I just wanted to let you all know that Jack has had a terrible accident and fractured his neck and broken his wrist. I'm doing the best I can but I'm trying to put everything into place now, before we leave the hospital, so that I can focus on him and him alone as he's going to be flat on his back for a while. He's doing ok (champion that he is) but it's going to be a long recovery. And thankfully, I think he's going to come out of this relatively unscathed (physically, at least.) So – I wanted to let you all know that I'll be stepping down from my role as head of the Christmas fair this year. I know it's not far away so I wanted to let you all know sooner rather than later so you can get things in place. I've started off with a bit of the sponsorship money – some leads but there's a lot of work to be done. Need to raise 10k for all the stuff on the school enrichment fund. This is the most important thing so any leads at all please, please chase them up. This is a full-on task, so anyone that is interested needs to be aware of that. Thanks all.

Millie: Oh my god, Liza. That's so dreadful. I'm so sorry. We're all here to help.

Charlotte G: Oh, Liza. We are all so desperately sorry. Jack is such a spirited little boy that I know he will cope with this brilliantly. Do let us know how we can all help.

Liza: Thanks so much all. But please – use this thread just to sort out the Xmas fair, so I don't have to worry about it! If you want to send any private messages to me or Jack please do.

Ems: Typing . . .

Charlotte G: I'll do it!!! I'd love to

Mimi: ME!

Shereen: Yes. Liza, we are here for you if you need anything.

Charlotte T: I'd LOVE to do it.

Charlotte M: I can't. Sorry! I've just got so much on with the little ones at the moment and work – I think it'd be silly to take it all on at once. Don't you? I'll help out of course in any way that I can though.

Bella: As you know, I'm not a SAHM so I just don't think I can offer any more of my time. But like Charlotte M says – I'm happy to help.

Fizz: Just FYI I'm a *SAHM* and my time is limited too! I don't think we should be talking in terms of time. It's not helpful when we are all exceedingly busy with our children and everything else.

Sarah: Guys – let's just focus on Liza here please and getting the fair sorted so she can concentrate on Jack. Anyone who offered to help out, we'll have a meeting the first Thursday back after half-term, in the green café at ten am. I'll send out a reminder before then. 10k is a heck of a lot. We need to get focused. Ok?

WhatsApp group: School mums VIP business
Members: Charlotte G, Bella

Charlotte G: Was that the 'incident' I heard about at The Vale Club? Do you know? Apparently someone wasn't watching their kid and they had a fall? There'd better be an investigation of some sorts.

Bella: I don't know. Maybe. Awful.

Charlotte G: Must be. I'll try and find out. They shut the club apparently. I wasn't there, of course. Had all three kids at home crafting. But by the sounds of it, someone's head's going to roll.

Bella: *rolling heads emoji*

LIZA

The next morning, I meet Gav in the hospital café. I'd slept on a guest bed next to Jack, whilst he'd gone home to get some rest. I'd barely shut my eyes, listening out all night for any change in the rhythm of Jack's breath.

'Ready?' I hand Gav a black coffee. Two espresso shots, just as he likes it. He nods and takes the cup without a thank you. We get the lift up to floor three, Paediatrics. I shield my eyes from the other patients in wheelchairs and trolleys. I can't stand any more heartache right now. Selfish, I know.

We stand close to each other as we walk towards Jack's hospital bed. My little boy is there, his head on the pillow, stilled by a foam neck brace. I'd only been away from him for about ten minutes whilst I went to meet Gav but I'm already overcome with the feelings I'd been battling all night – fear, guilt, sorrow, relief that he's alive. There's a flickering halogen bulb to the side of him, the blue concertinaed curtains drawn so that I can only see half his sleepy face. It all feels a bit eerie now the lights have been switched on, especially when

I see the cannula tape, puckered over his small arm. There's a plastic jug of squash next to him, still full with a bunch of limp-looking straws next to it.

'You OK?' Gav takes my arm and pulls me forward. For some reason this small act of kindness makes me want to cry all over again, until he seems to physically push me forward with the palm of his hand on my back. He wasn't being kind after all – he was just steering me into the right direction, I think. My feelings can't keep up with his actions and my throat constricts. It seems that neither of us knows how to behave in light of this trauma. 'Just . . .' I manage.

'Come on. Let's not let him see us upset when he's fully awake.' Gav grabs two plastic chairs and places them next to Jack. There's an awkward moment, when neither of us knows who should sit first, but I go ahead and lean over to my son.

'Jack? My little one? It's OK. Mummy and Daddy are here.' His eyes look all droopy and a small tear rolls its way down his cheek. I feel the heat of his breath on my hand. A lone, thick eyelash has made its way onto his cheek. 'We love you so much. We're so proud of you.' I lick my finger and press it over the eyelash. 'I'm doing it for you. The wish. OK?' I shut my eyes and blow as hard as I can. *Please, please make him better.*

'I'm sorry,' he whispers. 'I didn't mean to be a bad boy.'

'Oh darling, you could never, ever be a bad boy. It was an accident. A dreadful accident.'

I would never, ever admit this to Gav, but I think about the fact that I had been inside The Vale Club. That I should have been with Jack, watching him. How easy it had been for me to be sitting in the warmth, as he

81

had climbed higher and higher up that post. How poor Sarah would probably feel guilty for the rest of her life that had she checked on him just minutes later, she might – just might have seen him. Too high. Not that she should feel bad. Of course, she couldn't have changed a thing. But – I know Sarah. I know how she is, she'll obsess over this. My stomach feels like it's about to fall out of my body.

'Never let me hear you say that again, darling.' I smooth back his hair. His eyes look glassy. 'You're OK. You're going to be all OK. I promise.'

I hear the creak of Gav's leather jacket as he leans forward and wraps both of his arms around Jack's small legs.

'I love you, big guy,' he says, his voice muffled by the sheets. 'I love you so much. You are my hero. Always remember that.'

A small smile hovers on one side of Jack's mouth. I look at Gav, who is chewing the inside of his lip, eyes closed.

'It's OK,' I tell him too. 'He's OK. He is.'

By the time we both look back at Jack, he's fast asleep again. It's only then that I feel drops of liquid pouring out from my boobs.

'Shit.' I look down at two, large damp bullseyes on my Breton tee. 'Shit. Thea.'

'Is she OK?' Gav snaps his head up. 'She's with Sarah – are you sure that's the right person to—'

'Yes, yes of course. It's just that,' I point to my chest. The movement seems grotesquely intimate, embarrassing even, given Gav hasn't been anywhere near that area since Thea was conceived.

'Do you reckon you could just go to the maternity

ward?' I think back to when we'd last set foot in there only eight weeks ago. My bladder feeling like it was going to explode as I bounced up and down on that purple, rubber ball. 'Just explain the situation and ask one of the midwives if I can borrow a pump? That nice girl, Lucie. See if she's on shift? She'll remember us.'

Gav lets out a deep sigh. 'I'll go and see. Anything else?'

I look up at his brown eyes. I want to ask him why he had felt the need to separate from me in the first place. How if he could explain it to me fully, perhaps I could help, *do* something. Anything, to make it better. But he'll shut down. As he usually does. Say that things have changed since Jack had been born, and that's that. *Then why did you have another child with me*, I want to shout. *Why?*

'No thanks. Nothing.' My whole face hurts with the effort of trying not to cry. My chin feels numb.

Why didn't you love me enough to stay with me? To try and work things out, I want to ask, even though, deep down, I know the answer.

He's gone for a long time. I watch the other kids in the ward. Listen to the shuffle of feet and swish of mops. A tall male nurse with a sharp face comes over to take Jack's blood pressure and temperature.

'Lovely boy.' He breaks into a grin. I nod but can't say anything. By the time Gav gets back, Jack is still asleep. He wheels in a large yellow hospital-grade pumping machine. We both smile, thankful that the distraction – and size of it – has broken the tension. 'Jesus,' I say, as he pushes it around the bed and moves his chair out of the way. 'Looks like it could milk an elephant.' I try and be light-hearted for Gav. Make jokes so that he might recognise the old me. The one he fell in love with and perhaps, then, things would be all right.

'Someone's coming,' he says. 'With all the other . . . you know,' he waves his hands around his own chest, 'stuff.'

We sit and wait. Eventually someone arrives and hooks me up with all the bottles and tubes. Both boobs are stuffed unceremoniously into two rubbery cones.

'Let me,' says the midwife, ramping up the dial. Almost instantly, the *drrrr drrrr* sound starts up.

'That noise,' Gav says, mimicking the sound of the machine and placing his palms over his eyes. 'Gives me nightmares.'

We both laugh again. I remember how we'd both spent hours working out how to use the damn thing when we'd first brought Jack home. I see Gav shaking his head, as though ridding himself of the darker memories that followed. I wonder when it got so bad between us. We'd managed, in spite of everything. But then he'd snapped after Thea was born, around the time she reached the three-week mark. All those memories of what happened with Jack had surfaced again. I tell myself to focus on the now. I go through the things I'd been taught when Jack was tiny. Focus on things you can see, touch, smell and hear. I watch the rise and fall of my son's small chest, thankful that Gav's earlier rage has dissipated. This morning, I had been braced for his harsh remarks and his sharp temper but, so far, he's managed to contain it and I've managed to keep the mood buoyant. *Somehow.* It's exhausting, but my focus now is on keeping things calm for Jack. My son is here. *He's alive.*

When both bottles are half-full of milk, I hear my phone vibrate.

'Shit.' I shuffle my hip towards Gav. 'Sorry about this. Can you just . . .'

He reaches over and slides out the phone from my pocket. I notice how careful he is not to touch me – whether he can't bear to, or he doesn't want to give me the wrong impression, I don't know.

'God, this old thing. Never could work your bloody keypad.' He presses in my code – Jack and Thea's birthdays – and I watch his eyes flicker over the screen.

'Well, there are about a million messages from school parents from about two hours ago. And there's one here from . . .' he squints and brings the handset close up to his eyes. 'Unknown number?'

'Weird. What's it say?' This feels so like how we used to be. Comfortable and free. My heart aches again. 'Go on, read it then.' I almost drop the bottles of milk as I lean over, willing him to hurry.

'Wow. This is something else.'

'What?' I wonder what on earth he's talking about.

'But there's no name. It's just a random number.'

'Read it out then. Come on.'

'It says: *Dear Liza. I'm so sorry about Jack. I've paid for a maternity nurse to come and watch Thea for the next two days and nights, whilst you get adjusted. She's called Mary. We had her after both Felix and Wolf were born and she's a saint. I had some problems after Wolf and she still managed beautifully. Here's her number. She'll start today. Please text her your address.*'

For a minute, I have absolutely no idea who has texted. Who would be so generous and do something so extraordinarily kind? But then the names Felix and Wolf ring a bell. Felix. Wolf. I had heard that only yesterday. Who could forget the name Wolf? And *bam*, out of nowhere, I know. It's her.

No explanation of how she'd found out what happened, nothing to indicate how she'd got my number. It's so like her, I think, from what I know of her. How she was at NCT: so confident in her choices. I think of those grey eyes. The way they'd scanned the drinks menu in the café. Her long limbs, supple and loose. The strong line of her nose and pale skin. And then I think about when I'd seen her after Jack had been born, in the street – she'd been kind to me then, offered a hand of friendship as I'd stood in the street, shivering, unaware of who I was – but I'd just pushed it to the back of my mind. I think about Sarah – how her body had gone rigid the minute she saw Ella Bradby in the corner of the room yesterday. The slackness of her mouth. And then afterwards, when they had both walked over together into the soft-play, after checking on Jack. The way Sarah's eyes had darted around the room. *Look at me. Look at who I'm with.* And then, the conspiratorial apologetic look she had given me, which I had studiously chosen to ignore.

I'd felt suspicious then, but maybe I had just been jealous? Maybe I had thought badly of Ella all this time and actually the problem was with *me* and the association of when I had last seen her – when everything started to fall apart.

'Ella,' I say to Gav. 'Oh my God. It's Ella. Remember her? NCT?'

In fact, I know he does. No one could forget her.

'I do,' he replies. 'I totally do. She went AWOL, yeah?'

'Yes. No one knew why. But well, I bumped into her yesterday. Just before . . . Anyway. Her kid is at school with Jack but not in the same class. And neither me nor

Sarah have ever laid eyes on her at the school gates. Guess she's back and nicer than we thought.'

'Oh. I'm surprised you didn't mention it. I know Sarah was obsessed with her. Anyway – it appears that yes, she is back,' says Gav. He looks over at Jack and nods his head. 'And two days' maternity nurse? Wow. I think she might just be our fairy godmother. It will be good to have an extra set of eyes on everything.'

I guess, despite everything that's happened in the last two days, despite the fact my son is lying in a hospital bed next to me, despite me wanting to shake Gav to come to his senses, we've agreed on one thing, at last.

Are you sure this is anonymous? I mean, my job could be on the line. I've been with my family for three years now: two little girls. I'm a live-out. But I still know them back to front because I babysit twice a week and I've been on holiday with them. They employed me fresh out of Norland College for Nannies. They expect full loyalty – so, they must never, ever find out I've been speaking to you. It's this code of conduct thing. They know we all gossip about them behind their backs. For us it's work, you see?

'Oh, you must hate us,' they say. 'And talk about how awful we are to all your other nanny friends. I hope you don't think our children are too bratty.' But they don't mean it. Really, they're just looking for reassurance that we haven't been discussing their children – or their parenting habits. But of course, we have.

So I was there. When it happened. I didn't see the actual fall. For me it was just a normal day. Pretty intense because it's half-term but a group of us had met that morning. It was the same as it normally is, just on hyper-mode; all the parents competing all the time. Perfect little children, perfectly dressed up. And if one of their children starts to have a meltdown, they speak extra loudly – just so everyone knows they're disciplining their child. 'Maximilian, do we do that at home? No we don't.' (And let me tell you, Maximilian definitely does do that at home.) Or they just give in to save face – 'Here, Maximilian of course you can have ten chocolate bars,' whilst hissing at him on the sly that he's going to have his favourite toy taken away later on.

But anyway – it was all a bit busy. We were going about our business, when we heard this terrible scream. Everyone froze for a minute. Then I saw this one woman – she had brown hair and was in leggings – rush outside. I thought she looked like she was going to faint. It must have been her son because when we looked outside she was sobbing over him. She was at the table where you can see outside into the playground, so I suppose she must have been watching but, you know – if it had been one of us nannies in charge, it would have been a totally different ballgame. For a start, we would never have been sitting there, we would have been outside. It's an unspoken rule at the club, that that table is reserved only for mums and dads.

Because, you know – there's a list of rules us nannies have to stick to. No phone during working hours. Engaging with the kids at all times. Always be next to them. Healthy food. Consistency with discipline. All the things we'd do anyway. But – it's like, we're held to a totally different set of standards to the parents.

I spend all day with my two charges – seven a.m. to seven p.m., doing exactly what their mum and dad ask me to do – and I work hard to do it. But then the parents get back from work and undo everything I've achieved that day. They sit there on their phones as soon as they get back from their jobs. Slumped on the sofa and then they wonder why their kids are jumping all over them, demanding their attention. And then – the cheek of it, I've spent hours preparing freshly pressed juices, fresh salmon and the likes – the parents let them eat what they like. 'Yes of course you can have a bowl of Coco Pops.'

I tell Mum and Dad, 'They've already had a very healthy dinner,' and you were the ones that implemented that bloody rule anyway, I want to shout, but they look at me and then they look directly at their child, and say, 'It's OK. Mummy said you could.' It drives all of us nannies wild.

I'm not saying anything shady went on, just that – well – if it had been us nannies on patrol, then I doubt this would ever have happened. And if it did? You'd find us on the front page of the paper, wouldn't you? I said as much to my boss and she didn't seem very happy with me. Mumbled something about mums being exhausted all the time and 'mental load' – whatever that is. Does she not think I'm exhausted, taking care of her kids?

As I said – it's one set of rules for them, and one set of rules for us.

But please, I'll lose my job if anyone finds out I've been talking. I'm sorry. I hope you don't think I'm too awful. It's just that this is exactly the way it is. And our rule would have been very clear. We would have been outside, all that time. Rain or shine. We would have been watching that poor little boy, and so really – he never would have fallen in the first place.

SARAH

She wants, desperately, to go to the soft-play at The Vale Club. She's trying to plan the day as best she can so that she's busy but stress-free. After Tom had left for work, she'd managed to get Thea asleep, whilst Casper had been absorbed in endless rounds of that ghastly *PAW Patrol*. (She'd tried over and over to get the theme song out of her head but it's there, like a sore tooth.)

She'd signed Casper up for a mini football class, giving herself at least an hour to concentrate on Thea, without Casper mooning all over her pram. And Sarah needs time with her own thoughts. Predominantly, in a moment of self-flagellation, to replay in her mind the events of yesterday.

She has enough sense to know that it isn't going to help matters. She had thought, at six o'clock this morning, that it might go some way in soothing her twitching limbs, her thumping heart; but every time she revisited the look on Liza's face as she realised her small boy was on the floor, Sarah started to feel as though she might pop. Ha! Perhaps *that* wouldn't be such a bad thing.

Perhaps then all her innards would slide out and she'd shrink to her ever-elusive target size ten – since Rosie, she's managed to totally change shape. As she drinks her lukewarm tap water, she imagines herself back at the club. She should go now. Strike whilst the iron is hot. Get her fear over and done with, but she cannot. When she thinks about stepping foot into the place, her hands start to shake.

The idea of the investigation lingers on the periphery of her thoughts. She hasn't been able to bring herself to look on The Vale Club Facebook group, to see what everyone is saying. People must be going mad. The group is active enough at the best of times – constant grumblings about the food taking too long, the towels being too scratchy, the lockers not being big enough. She can't imagine what people would be saying about this.

She also can't bring herself to tell Casper he's not allowed outside. That she never, ever wants to see that wooden post again. Even if they removed it, the empty space would be a stark reminder of what had happened.

'Casper?' She walks into the living room to find him slumped on the sofa like a teenager. 'Five minutes. OK?'

As the words fall out of her mouth, she knows full well she doesn't mean them. Five minutes, in television time, would actually translate into an hour or more. Especially on days like today.

'Where we going?' he asks, eyes locked onto the screen.

'I don't know. Where would you like to go?' She tries to leave the decision up to him, but he doesn't answer, just plucks the material on his jeans. She doesn't bother pushing it and leaves the room to check on Thea. She's in her buggy, fast asleep. She remembers this time five years ago when Casper used to have his morning nap, manically using the precious moments to swipe crumbs off the counters, do a quick floor-sweep and hastily shove a piece of half-burnt toast in her mouth. She takes a picture of Thea's heart-shaped face with her spiky black hair and sends it to Liza. She looks so peaceful. So like Jack had when he was that age. She wonders with a shrinking heart if Rosie would have looked like her brother.

All happy here, don't hurry. Thinking of you. Her friend is offline. She scrolls down to Ella's WhatsApp. Online. Her heart thuds. Should she? It's a better option than going to The Vale Club. Yes. Why not? After all, they are tied now. Bound together in complicity.

Ella. Just wanted to check in. Wondered what you were doing today? Whether you wanted to meet up. Her hand hovers over the keyboard. Should she add something extra? Something about yesterday? No. Don't be foolish, she thinks. She stands and stares at her phone, waiting for the message to be read. Two blue ticks appear on the screen.

'Mummy,' shouts Casper. 'Mummy change the channel.'

'Wait, darling,' she shouts, shaking her handset in the hope it might elicit some sort of response from *Ms Bradby*. Her teeth clamp together. Nothing. But then she has an idea.

Or – just thinking. Don't suppose you'd like to come with me to do a shop for Liza? It isn't that she wants to deliberately trap Ella into replying. But she *had* planned to buy stuff for when Liza and Jack got home.

Can't today, comes the reply. Got plans, but I've sorted something for Liza. Perhaps we could meet up tomorrow. Sorted something for Liza? What on earth does she mean by that? And there she is, dangling herself so self-importantly in front of her. Tomorrow indeed. Sarah's had enough, the weight of disappointment nearly crushing her bones. She resolves to put this all to the back of her mind. And with that, she claps her hands together and gets to work.

Firstly, she changes into her best jeans. The ones that she has to squeeze closed but that look good with the right jumper. She's going to get Ella out of her mind. Go shopping for Liza. Get Tom to agree to let them stay and, in the meantime, she'll think about the Christmas fair. She'll boss it with both Casper and Thea. There'll be no screaming tantrums in the supermarket. She'll be a fully present and loving mum towards her son. No raised voices. *Empathy. Compassion. Kindness.*

She feels her blood pressure rising.

'Right, Casper darling. Telly off.' She looks at her watch.

'Five more minutes,' comes the wail.

'No,' she says. 'Listen, darling, I thought since we've got Thea, we'll go to Sainsbury's. Have a really fun trip there. You can steer the trolley? Be like Captain . . . America, is it?'

'Nooooooo Mummy. Noooo. I want telly.'

She inhales. *Kindness and calm.*

'No. We're going to Sainsbury's. Like I just said. And please. You'll wake Thea.'

His voice starts to rise, his legs thumping into the sofa.

'Fine,' she snaps. 'Just turn off the telly. I'll buy you a toy if you come with me now.' She regrets the words as soon as they're out of her mouth; she's already gone way over budget this month and she had to teach Casper to do what he was told without a bribe. But with a tiny zing of relief, she watches as he leaps up off the sofa.

After she's been to Sainsbury's (thankfully, Thea had remained asleep) and thrown anything and everything sugary that Casper wanted into the bottom of the pram, just to shut him up, she decides to go straight to Liza's.

She always has her spare key which Liza had handed to her when she and Gav had separated. She'll open up, organise everything in the fridge, put the fish pie she's bought into a Le Creuset and trim and arrange the bunch of purple lilies she's bought in preparation for their homecoming.

Casper can hang out in the playroom and she'll feed Thea and pray she lies there quietly whilst she gets everything done. This will be the start of everything, she tells herself. The start of making it up to Liza. She'll need a morning or two to sort out the flat if she and the kids are to move in. But that's OK. She'll make up the beds, check everything is in order. She'd started doing it last week, after all, when they'd planned for Airbnb renters. And then she'll get Tom to come round. He would soon enough. They've had such a difficult time this last year. It would be a chance to start afresh.

'Casper? Go to Jack's playroom when we get in. And don't start pulling everything out.' She pulls out her key and struggles inside with the pram. 'Thea, I'm coming. Time for food.'

She's always been envious of Liza's house. The sleek, marble open-plan kitchen. The black barstool and the big island with the copper drop lighting. It even has three holes in it in which you can drop different types of rubbish. There is also the abundance of unlit Jo Malone and other smart looking candles (Liza thinks it a dreadful waste to ever use them), soft, fluffy cushions and sharp lines that draw the eye to the end of the house. But today, without Liza, it feels cold. Today Sarah sees it for what it is – which is a place totally at odds with her friend's laid-back, slightly chaotic, down-to-earth character. It's all Gav, she thinks, totally up his street. Liza must be more beholden to him than Sarah ever realised. She thinks about her strong, feisty friend. How recently she'd agree with Gav in front of his face – whatever he said – and then afterwards, she'd say something totally different. It's almost as if she'd do anything to get back with him. It hadn't been like that when they'd first met. In fact, it had been Gav doing all the running. His tall frame, following Liza around the room, eyes sparkling at the sight of her. What the hell had happened?

'There, there Thea.' Sarah makes a token effort at spinning some coloured beads on the bar of Thea's bouncy chair. She empties the dishwasher (that's more like Liza, she thinks – everything thrown in higgledy-piggledy piles), cleans out the fridge (also more like Liza – wilting coriander stalks, broccoli stems and soggy aubergines: evidence of her failed weekly good intentions) and puts two loads of sheets in the wash.

She transfers the fish pie into a dish, cling-filming the top. She writes a message on a small, pink notepad. Thirty five mins @180, and she tears off another piece and writes a list of what she's done and what food she's bought. She's starting to feel a little better. Thea starts to whine. Sarah makes up her milk and goes into the playroom, where Casper is building Duplo.

'You OK, darling? Mummy's just going to feed Thea now. OK?'

'Can you help me Mummy? I want to build a space station.'

'Of course. Just tell me what you want.' She rests Thea's bottle in her mouth and uses her elbow to keep it upright. 'Here.'

She passes her son a plastic cube, in an effort to look as though she is engaging with him. *Be present*, as all the Mama blogs say. *This time goes much too fast. Before you know it, they'll be teens and they'll never let you kiss their sleepy heads again.* (She'd always silently told the authors of these blogs to go fuck themselves at three in the morning when the prospect of sleep was impossible, and then felt teary-eyed and guilty about that too.)

He takes it without looking. Thea sounds content. Phew. She's done it. She can do this. *Breathe.* Just as she's starting to feel on top of things, she hears a key in the lock. It must be Gav, or Liza. They have no parents between them, and she knows Liza's cleaner is not due today.

'Hello? Liza? It's me, Sarah,' she shouts. 'I let myself in.' No answer. Weird. Despite the surge of adrenaline, she doesn't move. Thea's too settled – better Sarah gets hurt than wake the baby – and she's quite frozen.

'Liza?' she shouts.

'Oh!' says a voice. 'Someone's here,' and then another, quieter voice in the background. 'Hello? It's Mary O'Sullivan here. I've come to help out.'

There's a rustle of plastic bags and more footsteps and then the living-room door opens. The bottle of milk falls out of Thea's mouth and she starts to cry.

'Oh hello.'

Sarah looks up at a short-haired lady dressed in full Norland Nanny uniform.

'Like I said, I'm Mary,' she smiles. 'Oh, and look at that delicious, gorgeous little bundle. Here, let me.'

And before Sarah can say another word, Mary has whipped Thea out of her arms, bottle and all, and is cooing in her ear. 'There, there. Is this Thea then? I've seen a picture. Isn't she gorgeous. Aren't you gorgeous?'

Thea stops crying.

'Yes,' Sarah says, before she has a chance to do or say much more. 'Thea and my son Casper.'

'Yes that's right. Liza said you had Thea. You must be Sarah. And you must be tired,' she says, shushing Thea. 'I've been asked to go and collect Thea from you. To give you a break. I was going to go round to yours after I got settled in here but – it looks like you got here first, didn't she ducky?' Mary's now got a wrinkled finger in Thea's mouth. 'Your mummy's friend got there first.'

If she hadn't known better, Sarah might have thought there was something accusatory in Mary's tone.

'Oh,' says Sarah, struck dumb. It was so unlike Liza to have any help. 'Well, I suppose, well, you don't need to now.'

'And I've brought Liza all her food for the next couple of days. I'll tidy the house, get ready for them to come back from the hospital. That poor, poor boy. Falling like that when there were so many people around. You would have thought someone might have seen him. Don't you?'

Sarah inwardly pleads for Mary to be quiet – every word like an arrow piercing her heart.

'Oh gosh, you do look white. It must have been a dreadful shock for you all. You go on, love. Get home with your boy and have a nice, relaxing time. I'll work out where everything goes. That nice young man Gav told me all the important stuff.'

Sarah opens her mouth. She's about to tell this lady not to bother. That she's got the fish pie and done all the other stuff, but before she can say a word she finds herself alone, standing with her son and the blaring television.

'Right,' says Sarah weakly, slightly dizzy with confusion. 'I'd better get on with going home then.'

Gav is always reluctant to have anyone in their house – probably so he can control Liza in private, she thinks, but then she hears the front door creak open.

'Mary?' says a throaty voice. 'I'm just bringing all the ingredients for Jack's smoothies. I'm going out to get some calcium powder. To help with bone healing.'

Sarah's about to start packing up but she can't bring herself to move. She thinks of the clean fridge, the fish pie. She knows who it is but she cannot for one moment believe that it would be *her*.

In her best friend's house.

In her heart of hearts she knows it's a good thing. That Liza deserves all the help she can get, no matter who it's from, but she can't help but feel a little stung. Or something else. She searches for the word, just as Casper decides to throw a piece of Duplo across the room.

'Now, now,' says Mary, who's appeared back into the room out of nowhere. 'Casper, who taught you to do such a thing? Now pick it up, then, there's a good boy. Your mummy's had her hands full.'

'No one taught him that,' says Sarah, feeling both defensive and teary. 'He's just . . .'

'Just probably seeing you with the little one,' says Mary, stroking Thea's head. 'Now come on, Casper, there's a good boy, pick it up,' she continues, before Sarah herself has had a chance to open her mouth and berate her own child. Casper still doesn't move. By this point, Sarah's blood pressure is stratospheric. She silently begs her son to do *something*.

'Oh,' the door opens. 'It's you. What a surprise.' Except there's so little surprise in Ella's voice, Sarah thinks she could be asleep. 'I didn't know you were going to be here.'

She opens her mouth. What she wants to say is: *Why the hell wouldn't I be here? At my best mate's house. Helping her out.*

'Well, I've had a key for a long time,' she says. 'I'm Liza's only other trusted key holder.'

But Ella doesn't even seem to be listening. She's too busy humming and scanning through the label of some special powder – no doubt mixed with frogs' legs and lotus plants – to notice.

Ella glides off into the kitchen. 'I went, just now to the hospital. I saw them.'

She saw them?

'I was going to get Gav to drop the key with Mary, but – you know, an added thing for them to think about,' she says, as though Sarah hasn't made any effort at all to think about the wants and needs of her friend. She's so confused. She's dumbfounded. Ella had seen them? At the hospital? And now she's here? She doesn't understand a thing.

She follows Ella into the kitchen. She can hear Mary getting sterner and sterner with Casper, but she can't be bothered. If she wants to tell him off, let her. She'll pick it up later. She watches Ella unload a box of tinctures, laying them out neatly in rows. Then she pulls out some beautiful, boxed candles. Oh God. Sarah had coveted those candles for years. And a soft, grey cashmere throw. What in hell's name is this all about? Throwing money at her guilt? Sarah thinks of her own overdraft and smarts.

'I know I haven't seen you and Liza for so long. I don't want to be too over the top, given I hardly know Liza now, but, well, I can't very well witness what I did yesterday and not do anything. Can I?' Great. Ella's now reading her mind. 'I mean, there's no such thing as "too much" when someone's going through something like this. Is there?'

Sarah shakes her head. Maybe she's got Ella wrong. No. No, she hasn't. The phone. The message. The way Ella had dumped her in it yesterday, telling Liza that Jack was fine. *No.* There is something else at play. *Don't be duped*, Sarah tells herself. Ella has an answer for everything. Anything Sarah says will leave her looking mean and nasty, so she shuts her mouth tight.

Sarah leans over and picks up one of the candles. She recognises the label. *Aurore.* It's a shop in Chiswick that she goes into every now and again, just to see the kind of lifestyle that's just out of her reach. She'd once bought a small ornament from there and left it on her mantel-piece, in the hope that it would transform her home. But it had just left her feeling worse.

'Hmmm.' She sniffs. 'Spiced ginger and citrus.'

'Delicious, isn't it?' says Ella, passing her another flavour. 'I thought it would be soothing for the autumn.'

Sarah looks at the fish pie in its dish. It already looks soggy, pink tips of salmon peeking through the top. The ink on the instructions she wrote has started to bleed into the paper so that it's almost illegible.

It's Liza she should be focusing on now. Liza and Jack

and how best to make them feel comfortable. Not the way she feels about this surreal situation. But at this very moment she feels something else. Angry? No. That's not it. Envious? That's not it either. And then, as Ella pulls out a jar of raw manuka honey and sets it on the counter, she sees it. Damn.

Redundant. There it is. She hates to admit it, but that's exactly what it is. She feels totally and utterly redundant.

LIZA

When I see her, I burst into tears. She's there, at the doorway to my home, with Thea nestled in her arms, her coat dress all starched, the classic beige with a white collar. I had no idea these nannies still existed.

'There, there love.' Mary leads me in through the hallway and pushes me gently onto the sofa, cushions all plumped up and in a neat line. 'You poor thing. I'm going to make you a nice cup of tea. Some food. And then you're to go and have a shower and have a rest.'

I nod, mutely. I can't do anything else. She passes Thea to me. I press my nose into her little belly and inhale.

'I'm here,' I tell her. 'I'm here. But it looks like you have been in good hands.' I put my feet up, aware that if I get myself too comfortable, I'm going to fall asleep there and then. But I know that when I shut my eyes, I'll probably lie awake, body on fire with everything that has happened in the past day – just like it has been since, well, just after Jack had been born really. I have four hours before Gav and I change shifts. In that time, I need to get fresh clothes for me and Jack, sort myself out and shower. Just as I feel my eyes close, Mary's back.

'Let me take Thea. Come on, have a quick supper and then you're to go to sleep for a few hours. I've made your bed. Put a fresh nightie out.'

'Oh, Mary. You are an absolute star. Thank you. I couldn't have done this without you. I don't have family here. So this feels amazing.'

I think about if my mum and dad were still alive, and how much they'd want to help me. How much they would have loved Jack and Thea. My heart squeezes. I don't want to start getting upset about them now. I walk into the kitchen. Everything just looks – sparkling. So clean and fresh and there are three beautiful candles lighting up the island. It almost feels homely, this place. I think of all my candles, which I've never lit. How much of a difference a little thought and care makes to the atmosphere. Gav had insisted on designing our house and, although I like it, it has never really felt very 'me'. But now, today, with the fresh smell of . . . spiced ginger, is it? And a beautiful tray of brownies and other things laid out, there's an atmosphere that has always been lacking. There's even a new plant in the corner of the island, in a pink and white vase. To think, this is all it had ever needed – a homely touch.

I pull up a barstool. Mary takes Thea and pops her down in her bouncer. Lined up in front of me is a mix of concoctions and brown bottles, each with little labels on them. Hand-drawn, with little pictures on each bottle.

'Oh wow, look at the calligraphy on this.' I pick up one of the potions. *'Jack's get-well magic liquid. Three drops under the tongue twice daily.'* I can't believe all this. And look at that beautiful drawing in the corner of the label. The little shaded flowers. So much attention to detail. 'Was this Ella?'

'It certainly was, my dear. Thoughtful like that, she is. When I stayed with them she was always leaving me little things lying around the house. Small gifts under my pillow. Lavender scent for when I was doing the night shifts. Isn't she amazing?'

'But I don't understand.' I inhale one of the scents. Orange blossom and honey. 'I barely know her.'

'I know, she's just like that. It's in her nature. She can't see something bad happening to someone and not step in. When we arrived she came straight in here whilst I was with Thea. She must have unloaded the dishwasher, tidied the place. She looked busy. She can't help herself.' Mary's eyes scope the landscape, preening at her old boss's good deeds, almost as if she is responsible for them herself.

'How exhausting for her.' I laugh but Mary looks serious.

'Well, the thing is,' she takes out a plate from under the island. 'Ella is one of those people. She's just never tired. She's had her fair share, after all.'

I want to ask Mary what she means by 'fair share' but, before I can, I'm beset by the thought that Ella is exactly the kind of person that Gav should have married. Always on it. Always looking good with everything under control. As I think about this, I smooth a hand over the island surface trying to get rid of any crumbs. Just as Gav likes it – he's an absolute neat-freak.

'Now look here, what would you like to eat?' Mary guides her hand around the food offerings. 'She dropped off these lovely home-made salads. Immune boosting, she said. So you feel strong.'

'Mmm, that looks lovely.' My mouth waters at the sight of the juicy, fresh strawberries on a bed of green leaves. Crisped noodles and shallots and the smell of tangy dressing. 'What a treat. I never eat like this any more.'

Since Gav and I started to lead totally separate lives, using the kitchen at different allocated times, I can't remember when I'd last actually prepared anything more for myself than cheese on toast. I watch as Mary uses two wooden salad servers – I can't work out if they're even mine or not – to lay my plate with food. She passes it over, along with an ice-cold drink of water.

'There we go, love. Eat that down and then get straight to bed.'

I nod. No one has looked after me like this since before Jack was born. I remember the way Gav used to care for me, rubbing my neck at the end of every day of the pregnancy. How it had all stopped soon after.

'It's OK, love, he's in the best hands,' Mary says. And then I realise guiltily that I hadn't even been thinking of Jack.

'I know,' I tell her, crunching on a roasted cashew. 'It's just that – I don't know. It's all so quiet here.'

'Don't you worry. It'll soon be loud enough.'

'I don't want to get too used to you, Mary,' I laugh. 'It's going to be a shock when you are gone. Mary Poppins. My Mary godmother.' I give a tiny laugh and think about what will happen when she *is* gone. And the thought of being alone. How appealing the idea of being in Sarah's flat is. Away from the horrid, oppressive atmosphere of the house. The knowledge that Sarah and Tom would always be around. Especially at night.

'You OK?' says Mary.

'I'm fine. I've just got a headache. I know it'll stop me from sleeping.'

'Oh love. I've got these with me.' She goes over to her bag and unclips the clasp. 'I take them when I stop doing night shifts. To get my timing back to normal. In fact, Ella introduced me to this. It's all herbal. Natural. She had them made up for me when I couldn't sleep one morning after I'd looked after Felix during the night. She did a course in all that herbal healing remedy stuff when . . .' She looks like she's said something she shouldn't and then quickly changes the subject. 'Anyway, I'm sure it's fine with breastfeeding. In fact, I know it is because Ella fed whilst taking them.'

'How does she know all this?' I ask, wanting to find out what she'd been talking about just now.

'Well, she just does.' Her eyes darken. 'Don't ask me why. Or how.' She hands over a couple of small, greyish-coloured pills and starts to pour me a glass of water. 'Go on, you'll be fine. Don't stand there too long, you need to get to bed or you'll be no good to anyone. Take them.'

I don't have the strength to argue. I think about the alternative. The insomnia and what that will do to me. I get a flash of Jack, just after he was born. And then of me and everything that followed. The grip of blackness that I couldn't shake off and how that had made me behave. I shut my eyes to make the thoughts disappear.

'Thank you.' I take the pills, feeling them in my hand, like small sweeties.

'What you waiting for? Don't you worry. Drink some more water too. And look at this little one.' She picks up Thea from her bouncer and pats her head. 'She's just beautiful. You've done a great job. You're a fabulous mother. Very lucky, those kids.' I feel a stone of guilt drop right through me.

'You think?' My voice sounds tight.

'I do. Right. Sleep. Now. Oh by the way, I met your friend. Sarah was it?'

'Oh?' I can't think how she would have met Sarah. If she'd been told about her by Ella, or had met her somewhere else, but my mind is too foggy to continue the conversation. 'Ah lovely.' I turn away from Mary to signal I don't want to continue chatting. Thank God she seems to get the message, I'm just about finished. I watch as she starts to clear the island, Thea in one arm. She stacks all the bowls, wipes the surfaces and keeps whispering into Thea's ear.

'And what's this too?' I follow her eyeline, to the small Le Creuset dish that we use every day – the one that I bung anything and everything into, any old leftovers I can find that look vaguely palatable. 'Looks like some potato thing. Ella didn't bring it, so it must have been here before . . .' She swallows. 'Before you left.'

'God knows, Mary,' I shrug. 'It's probably been there for *days*. I'd chuck it if I were you. Dread to think what the hell it is. It looks gross from here. Probably poison us all. Some old fish pie. How embarrassing. We're not normally such slobs.' I don't look too closely. But then she picks up a couple of small, yellow Post-its.

'These too?' She positions her glasses at the end of her nose. 'I can't quite read the writing. Must have got wet.'

She passes the notes over to me but again I'm too exhausted to look. I think of the bottom of my pram. How messy it is. The piles of rubbish, unpaid bills, empty boxes that I threw there. A bottomless pit of admin and stuff, all confined to one area. I almost tell her to go and put the Post-its in the pram. But then I shake my head. No more crap, I think. Streamline things. I'm going to have to now, if I want to be on top of things for Jack.

'Chuck it.' I wave my hand at the pieces of paper. 'If you can't read them, just chuck them. And that too.' I point to the Le Creuset. 'If that's OK.' Normally I'd do it, but my bones feel like they're turning to lead. 'I'll just go up now for a sleep. I'm so grateful,' I start to say but Mary puts a finger to her lips.

'Shhhhhh.' She waves her hand at me. 'Go. Just go. I'll deal with the rubbish here and the leftovers.' I watch gratefully as white slop pours into the bin, the Post-its crumpled up in her hand. 'There we go,' she says. 'All gone.'

WhatsApp group: Renegades
Members: Liza, Sarah

Sarah: Thea ok? Thinking of you so much.

Liza: She's great. Thanks so much for watching her. Back home now for a quick kip. Got back to a load of candles, incredible salads all laid out on the island. And I've just come upstairs to find my nightie laid out on this incredible cashmere throw. All from that shop we love down in Chiswick. WTF? Can you believe it? Ella is an angel! In disguise! Sending a maternity nurse and everything. Feel bad how I dissed her earlier.

Sarah: Was there anything else?

Liza: What do you mean?

Sarah: Anything else you noticed? Any other food or anything?

Liza: Anything else? Surely she'd done enough! A maternity nurse, all those gifts. No, nothing else. Steady on Sa! I know she's amazing but there's a limit!

Sarah: Ah – I didn't mean that. I just . . . never mind. Just thinking of you and Jack and hoping that you are ok. Quick, go to sleep now and make the most of it. I'll check in later. Ok? Loads of love to you.

Liza: You too. By the way, will you come over when Jack gets out of hospital, whenever that is? I need you there with me. I'm already feeling shaky about it.

Sarah: Of course. I'd have been there anyway.

Liza: I know. Thank you. X

SARAH

She's exhausted. Her mind's in a spin. Casper is watching telly again, which is making her feel horrendous. They haven't even done his half-term homework. '*Find different types of autumn leaf, stick them in a scrapbook.*' Nothing to it and she hasn't even managed that. Liza can't have noticed the fish pie. Or everything else she had done. The cleaning and sorting, emptying the dishwasher. She must have thought Mary had picked up Thea from her house. Not that Sarah cared. She didn't want praise. She didn't want gratitude. She just didn't want Liza to think that she'd done *nothing*. At least Liza had asked her to be there when Jack gets discharged from the hospital. She is still needed. She flops down on the sofa next to Casper and squeezes his small, sockless foot.

'Mummy loves you darling,' she pulls at his little toe. 'I love you very much.' She feels her eyes close. Just half an hour. One more episode of *PAW Patrol*. That would allow her twenty-five minutes of rest. Time in which she can let go of her absolute fury with Ella Bradby. *I've sorted something for Liza* indeed. Then she'd get up and go to the park with Casper before Tom got home. Just as she's sliding into a deep, black sleep, she hears a key in the lock. She jumps. It can't be Tom already? But then she hears a soft, Irish lilt.

'Only me.' *Fuck*, she thinks. It's Friday. Helen is here to clean. And she can't very well be lying on the sofa now, can she? ('Don't be ridiculous,' Liza had told her time and time again. 'You're paying her, you can do what you want.') But before she knows it, she's stood up too quickly, feeling like she's about to pass out.

'I'm just in here, Helen,' she shouts too loudly, in a bid to disguise the sleepiness in her voice. 'Just sorting out Casper's toys.' Her eyes dart around the room to a small box in the corner, which she leaps towards. She empties out all the plastic crap into the middle of the room and scatters it about her person. 'Just doing a big tidy-out. Very busy,' she says but Helen has already walked to the kitchen and is pulling out the Hoover from under the stairs.

'It's OK, love. I'll just start upstairs and then I'll come and say hello to my favourite little boy when you're done.'

Sarah slumps back down onto the ground, shoving the toys back into the middle of the room with a sharp kick. For fuck's sake. She rests her head on the wooden floor. What a mess. She needs to *do* something. But instead, she just lies there, feeling the guilt weighing her down, like it's going to push her right through the floorboards into the dust-filled cellar below. But then what would happen? Would anyone find her body? Would anyone care enough? Would the police turn up with Casper sobbing for his mummy? Get a grip for crying out loud.

*

By the time Tom gets home, she's still catatonic. Casper is fast asleep – thank God. She'd managed to time everything perfectly so that he didn't get too hyper before bed. She can congratulate herself on that much, at least.

'Takeaway,' she mumbles from the sofa. 'I'm sorry. I went shopping for Liza. Didn't even remember our supper.'

'Want me to nip out and get something now?' Tom asks.

'No. I need to talk to you. We'll get a delivery.' She holds her breath, waiting for him to say something about money and how he's trying to get fit. She watches as he grabs his stomach and starts to say something before giving up.

'Fine,' he says. Thank God for that, she didn't even have to guilt-trip him into it. 'Thai?'

'Yeah.' She's relieved he hasn't gone off-piste. She can't face a row and some revolting food that doesn't satisfy her voracious need for comfort.

'Great, your usual?' She thinks carefully about her order. Pad Thai. No chilli. Pork dumplings. She really should go for something a little different. Try something new. She's always promising herself she'll push her own boundaries, after all. And her takeaway order is as good a place to start as any. She runs through all the other options in her mind, none of which are to her taste tonight.

'Fuck it,' she sighs. 'The usual.'

'Fine.' He swipes his mobile and taps the screen in three deft moves. 'All done.'

'Red or white?' She gets up. 'Or something else?' A glass of something is exactly what she feels like but she can't even decide what she wants to drink.

'Should you be?' Tom slides his phone into his pocket and looks over at her. 'I mean, didn't we decide the night before last that would be our last? We need to get your . . .' She stops in the doorway, feeling a swell of anger radiating around her.

'Tom,' she clenches her teeth. 'I've had a fucker of a day. And yesterday. A glass of red wine isn't going to kill me off. Nor is it going to affect my—'

'How do you know?'

'I don't. But what I do know is that if I'm as stressed out as you're making me now, it's never going to happen. I've been off my head before when I've got pregnant.' She watches him bite his lip, the familiar bolt of pain settling itself at a midpoint in her chest.

'Fine. Red.'

'Fine.' Just as she walks into the kitchen, she tells herself to calm down and start thinking about things rationally. Except, she tells herself, there's nothing rational about this situation at all. She's fucked up. Badly. She's trying to sort it out. But Ella sodding Bradby keeps scuppering her at every turn. She grabs the first bottle of red from the wine rack. A Malbec that she'd won in the summer school fair raffle, donated by the local wine deli. She pours them both a glass, and takes a large slug from her own. And then from Tom's for good measure.

'Here.' She walks through to the living room, hands him his glass. She puts down her own carefully on the coffee table (they had initially agreed no drinking on their brand-new sofa from Made.com, and she'd been paranoid ever since that it would be her to ruin the soft bottle-green velvet) and slumps down on the cushions. 'Well, this is nice. Isn't it?' But she knows her voice sounds all sharp and forced.

'It is.' Tom frowns. 'Are you OK?'

'I'm fine,' she takes another slurp. 'It's just that, I feel bad for Liza. That's all.' As the wine hits her stomach, she feels the softening of her limbs, her mind fuzzing. She hesitates and takes a deep breath before continuing. 'You know, I wonder if there was something I could have done. Yesterday, I mean. To stop things.'

'What do you mean?' Tom puts one foot up on the coffee table. 'There's nothing anyone could have done.'

'But what if there was?' she says. 'What if I could have stopped it?' She feels the spread of warmth from her stomach. 'If I, I don't know. If there was something I should have thought to do?' She's testing the water, she knows. She needs to be careful she doesn't go too far. Tom would be horrified. He'd probably divorce her if he knew the truth. She starts to sob.

'Sarah, love, don't cry. He's fine. He's going to make a full recovery. You're just probably thinking these strange thoughts because – well,' he starts to mumble, 'because of Rosie. You're always questioning yourself. Like the counsellor said. But there's nothing you could have done.'

'But what if there was?' She takes a big breath to stop herself from sobbing out loud. 'And please. I've told you before. Don't talk about Rosie like that.'

She feels the press of his hand on her back. 'Look, The Vale Club will be on it. Hopefully they'll do an investigation, so whoever is to blame will get the flak. And that most certainly isn't you.'

'They *are* doing an investigation. See? You don't understand, Tom!' She's shouting now, she can't control it, his words have panicked her beyond belief. 'You know nothing.'

'Look. It's fine. Like I said, I'm here. Casper's here. It's OK. If you need to talk, just talk to me.'

'Fine,' she sniffs. She can't get any more words out.

'Look,' he reaches over for her glass. 'You're exhausted, shall we just go to bed?'

'Are you fucking joking me?'

'No, I didn't mean . . .'

'You didn't?'

'No. I thought you might need some sleep.'

'Oh, so am I not attractive to you now?'

'You are. You are, it's just that . . .'

'I know. I'm not attractive. I'm a snivelling mess.'

'You're not. You're beautiful. And this will all be over soon.' She desperately wants to believe him. 'And then we can focus on, you know.'

'What?' she snaps.

'Well, giving Casper a little brother or sister.'

She tells herself not to be silly. That Tom is being very calm and not putting any pressure on her. She should be following his lead and looking to the future, instead of getting all worked up. But, she reminds herself, he has no reason to be stressed. He can be as relaxed as he wants. He hadn't, after all, been at the hospital when it all happened. When she really needed him. No. That had been Liza. So of course he can be calm, which is just making her feel even more enraged. And now, to top it all off, she feels like she's about to lose it with the thought of the investigation hanging over her.

'I thought we could go away for the weekend.' His eyes glance towards the fireplace and settle on a blow-up photo canvas that she'd had made for his birthday last year. A montage of all their holidays together, pre-Casper. 'Just you and me. Imagine. We can leave Casper with my brother? He'd like to hang out with his cousins. What do you think? Nowhere expensive. I thought I'd take Greg up on his offer of a stay in his lodge in Oban. What do you think?'

It *does* sound nice, she thinks. Roaring log fires, freshly caught fish. But before she's replied, she hears an intake of breath and only when she starts coughing does she realise it's her own.

'I can't very well leave Liza now,' she says. 'What kind of a friend do you think I am?'

'A very good one.' He takes her hand. 'OK. For the moment, let's focus on Liza. Let's see where we are in a few days when she's back home and settled. And then revisit things.'

Her mind races forward and traces over her calendar for the coming week. The IVF clinic appointment. Casper would be back at school, thank the Lord. She wants to share all this with her husband but, in the end, keeps her mouth shut. After all, she doesn't want to give him any cause to disrupt the equilibrium.

'And also, the flat. Downstairs,' Tom says. Wow. This is it, she's thinking. He's changed his mind. 'I've just been thinking,' he carries on squeezing the palm of her hand like it's putty. 'I think we should rent it out. Now. For a year. We need to save up. If there's any sort of treatment.'

She hadn't let her mind linger on the cost of IVF and how they'd fund it. In fact, she hadn't even really calculated that side of things at all. Typical of her, she thinks. Head in the sand. She thinks guiltily of the amount she's been spending from their joint account recently. And then she thinks of her own lack of work. The minimal effort she's put into finding a job. She feels bleak.

'Well, about that.' She takes her hand back. 'I still think we should let Liza, Thea and Jack stay for a bit.'

'A bit? How long is a bit?'

'Well, until they get back on their feet. You know. They're going to struggle in that huge house.'

'Well, Liza's not short of a bob or two. Nor is Gav.'

'You know Gav doesn't like people in the house. And it's so difficult for Liza at the moment. What with Gav's strange behaviour. Wanting to separate but not letting Liza go.'

'Well – Gav always said it wasn't quite so simple as that, Sa. So you know, you can't presume to know what's going on in other people's marriages. Can you?'

'But he's controlling her. He's there, every move she makes. It's manipulative, it's like he's checking up on her. And she's different around him now. So acquiescent. Not like Liza at all.'

'Well, as I said, he's probably just trying to be around for his kids, isn't he?'

'Why doesn't he move out? What the hell is wrong with him? It's like he's keeping her captive by staying there.'

'Lord knows. I told you. It's nothing to do with us.'

'It's everything to do with us!' she shrieks.

'Look. Why are we arguing about them? This is their problem to sort, Sa. We can't do that for them. It's between Gav and Liza to sort out the terms of their separation. It's not your job.' Tom rubs at his cheek, leaving a red mark on his skin. 'If we let Liza and the kids stay for a week it might just be months before they go. Who knows. Look, I know you feel indebted to her. That she was at the hospital with you when everything happened, but you have to stop thinking that friendship is like that. She was there because she loves you and because she's a good person.'

Sarah starts to cry again.

'And now, we have to save money, Sa. IVF is expensive. And I just want you to focus on yourself after last year. You haven't been doing enough of that. Remember what the counsellor said about distraction?'

'Well I thought that Liza could do some babysitting.' Sarah tries to keep herself from exploding or she's not going to get her own way at all. 'I mean – if we're going to go ahead with this IVF route, then we'll be out a lot. Won't we? She'll be there to watch Casper. He can entertain Jack.'

'You're now telling me that you're going to dump our son on Liza? In the same breath that you are telling me you are desperate to help her?' He makes an annoying whistling sound through his teeth. 'You consider then,' he continues. 'You consider what's more important to you.'

'Fine,' she snaps. She watches as he pulls himself off the sofa, his salmon-pink jumper fraying at the elbows. 'I will.'

She finishes her glass of wine and defiantly pours herself another, then drains it and slides it across the coffee table. A drop of red streaks across the wood. If Tom isn't going to play ball, she'll just have to go ahead and take matters into her own hands. Sod it, she thinks. She picks up her phone and composes a text. She feels a pull at her gut. One that says that what she's about to do isn't quite right. But – she thinks – it's the right thing to do *on paper*. She thinks of Tom again. Selfish. How dare he pull the IVF card on her. True, they aren't rolling in it but, for God's sake, they can help a friend out. She's going to get Liza, Jack and Thea to move into the flat. She'll tell them they can only stay for a few weeks. Just until Jack gets stronger. *Whoosh*. It's sent. She expects to feel vindicated. But out of nowhere, a deep surge of fear ploughs through her.

Shit, she thinks. What has she done? She can take it back, surely? She wonders how she's going to tell Tom. Perhaps she'll have to tell him that she had no choice. That Liza really, really needs her. She hears him coming back downstairs. He's changed into his tartan dressing gown and pale-blue pyjamas.

'Just come down for some water. Going to bed now. Can you save my takeaway for tomorrow? I'm not that hungry after all. Too tired.'

'Oh, yeah sure.'

'All OK?' he asks. 'You look worried? What's going on?'

'Nothing.' Her phone pings. She knows it's Liza. She can sense it. She just can't bring herself to look at the screen. Another ping. Hopefully she will have turned down Sarah's offer. Then all will be OK and she'll be able to move on. Liza will know she was trying to help. Then she'll start giving Ella Bradby a run for her money. After all, Ella is only a very recent friend of Liza's. Except, she thinks, sometimes those friends are the most dangerous; Liza no longer needs to make much of an effort with Sarah, after all.

'Who's that?' Tom tightens his dressing gown cord. 'Pinging you. Why are you looking so . . . shifty?'

'Oh.' She slides the phone under her. 'It's no one.'

'Well, it must be someone.' He takes a step closer. She presses her bum down into the cushion, hoping to mute any further sound. Just as she's about to leap up off the sofa and make a run for it, she feels his lips on her forehead.

'OK. Well, get some rest. I'm here for you. You know that, don't you? I'm here to help. I'm not the enemy. We're a team, Sa.'

'OK,' she says, her body rigid. 'Thank you,' she squeaks. 'And goodnight.'

'Night.'

She watches him leave the room. She wants to look at her messages, but the fear of what Tom will say is paralysing her. Not to mention the guilt about everything. One more minute, she thinks. One more minute of not having to be responsible for her actions – not knowing the outcome of what she's done.

One more minute and then she'll find out her fate.

West London Gazette editorial notes, October 2019
J Roper interview transcript: The dads, witnesses, The
Vale Club

Will: *Well, we don't spend time with them alone – not when they're in their big mum groups. (Interviewee does a mock shudder.) Certainly not if we can help it. It's not like we can get a word in edgeways, is it? I can't tell you what goes through their heads. Because we just watch them in astonishment thinking: what are you on about? Why are you making such a big deal out of nothing? And you know if we dare ask them – is it that time of the month? (Interviewee pretends to strangle himself.) Anyway – we were all there the morning it happened.*

Theo: *We were training. Before work. We're doing the half marathon together in Paris early next year. Lads' trip. Get away from the wife and kids for a while. (Interviewee guffaws.) We go together to The Vale Club because to be honest it's a bit tricky to go when all the ladies are there. It's better that we leave them to get on with it and . . .*

Freddie: *. . . talk amongst themselves. We can't keep up with anything they're saying really. They leap from one convo to the next, like rope-jumping monkeys. And* one will be talking about one thing and three others about something totally different. But somehow, they'll get what each other is saying . . .

J-J: But really it's like they're talking in tongues.

Will: And then someone will say something and they'll all go a bit silent – and then the chatter will start up again. Except when they're talking about something really sensitive. Like, y'know, vaccinations or something. And then everyone's shouting, trying to be heard. They're just waiting for the other person to shut up so they can get their point across quickly.

Theo: So yeah – we missed the actual fall. But when we all left that morning, it was already getting crowded. Half-term craziness. So that might have been an issue – people losing sight of their kid. My wife goes crazy sometimes, that I'm not watching our little boy. But then two minutes later there she is doing the same thing – yakking to her friends or on her phone.

Freddie: It's crazy, isn't it? They hover, but often aren't paying attention anyway.

Will: And they have this weird capacity to make a small deal into the biggest deal possible. Like – if they feel someone's slighted one of the kids or something . . .

Theo: Haha and that's it – they're off on one. It's like something primal gets switched on. My wife threatened to set up a smear campaign once – against a lady who made a comment about our eldest. Wanted to buy a domain name and everything and start spreading anonymous rumours online. It's honestly batshit.

Freddie: They say we don't understand it. That we don't have the same reactions that they do because we're not mums and don't have that maternal thing. But I must admit to being shaken up by that fall. We all know

them – the family. They're always here. Everyone recog-
nises everyone so we did get quite a shock. And everyone's
been on the case, trying to work out what happened,
just to make sure it doesn't happen again. Because you
can say what you like about us men around here but
we're definitely proactive about that kind of thing, and
we care. We get stuff done.

* **Will:** Yeah – we do. But they'll still find a reason to*
have a go at us, won't they? (Interviewee makes clucking
noises.)

Interview ends to lots of laughter and slapping of thighs.

LIZA

I tell Sarah I need to think about it. Just give me a few hours to speak to Gav, I'd written. I want her to know I've taken her offer seriously. For her to realise how much I appreciate it and that I haven't taken her friendship for granted. But deep in my heart, as soon as I got her message, my blood had gone hot with relief. *A few weeks*, I'll tell her. *At most.* Just until Jack's physio has started to work. Just until he's at least more mobile. Because the idea of doing this with Gav in the house, with the horrific and tense atmosphere, is too much to bear.

I look around my room and mentally prepare myself for the packing I'm going to have to do and all the things that Jack will need. We'll all be on one floor. Safe. Sarah and Tom upstairs. With their help, I think, maybe I can manage this. And Casper could even come and entertain Jack. It's a win-win for us all.

I hear Mary downstairs, the hiss of the boiling-water tap; her shushing Thea. I think of Jack. He'll be asleep now, I hope, but the lure of seeing my little boy is too much. I get up and ignore the drag of tiredness in my limbs. By the time I get to the hospital, it's nearly midnight. Gav is asleep, with his arms crossed, on a plastic chair next to the bed. I can hear the soft whistle of Jack's breath.

'Gav.' I shake his arm. 'Gav, wake up. Is he OK?'

'Huh?' He opens his eyes and, for a minute, I think he's about to smile at me in that old lazy way of his; the moment before he leans in for a kiss. But then he recognises me and the glimmer disappears.

'Fine. He's just been asleep for hours. He complained a bit about the pain. But the nurses have been great. Oh, and Doc says he can come home tomorrow.'

'Really?' I ask, thinking about how we're going to manage, but before I can say much more, he pushes himself up from the chair. 'Right, I'm going.'

'Wait,' I say. 'Wait.'

'What? I'm tired. I'll be back tomorrow. First thing.'

'Just that, Sarah and Tom . . .' I take a deep breath, wanting to get this done and dusted as soon as possible, so it's not weighing on my mind. Gav can be cranky when he's tired – I've learnt that the hard way – but at the same time I know he'll want to wrap up the conversation and get home. 'Well, they've asked if we want to move into the downstairs flat. Me, Jack and Thea. I mean.'

'Really?' his eyebrows shoot up. He's wide awake now. 'You and the kids move out from ours?'

'Yes,' I say cautiously.

'Firstly, Tom was telling me only yesterday he wanted to rent the flat out.'

'Oh.' Any feeling of hope or power drains from me. 'He must have changed his mind. Sarah was pretty adamant. Here, look at her text.'

He scans the screen of my phone.

'Hmmmm,' he nods. 'That changes nothing. You know full well you aren't moving out.' He gives me a warning look – a brief flash in his eyes. 'You aren't going anywhere. You need to be where I can watch you.'

'But . . .'

'No buts. How do you expect me to see the children? Are you deliberately trying to keep them from their father? Is that what it is? Because if you even think, Liza—'

'No, no of course not.' A needy tone creeps into my voice, mixed with irritation that he constantly has this effect on me. That with Gav, I'm this deferential being – totally different to how I perceive myself in the outside world. 'As if I'd do that. You can see them whenever you like. It's just that I think it'll be easier for you. For me. For us both. Given the tension. It won't help Jack's recovery. You know that. Don't you?'

'Liza. That's not happening.' He moves closer towards me. I can see the muscles straining from his neck; the tic of a vein down the side of his forehead. 'What did I just say?'

'It's OK.' I've made up my mind now. For Jack's sake. This rowing will be no good for him. 'Sarah's said we can move in. That's what we will be doing.' I swallow back my fear. I know I'm going against orders, that this all might blow up in my face, but I force myself to stick to my guns.

'What about night times? You'll need help. With the kids. I need to help. To make sure everything's OK.' He sounds panicked now but I widen my feet in an effort to try and stand my ground.

'We'll be fine.' I want to add the words, *without you,*

but I know what will happen if I do. 'I mean, you just come and *watch* me feed Thea.'

'I do more than that, Liza, and you know it.' I feel winded. I look around. His voice is getting louder and Jack is starting to rouse.

'Yes, yes I know. We're so grateful for everything you do.' I see Gav's shoulders drop just a touch. 'And you are the most amazing dad. I really couldn't do it without you. You know that.'

'It's nothing to do with that, Liza, and you know that full well. Have you really forgotten everything that happened?'

'Well, how about as a compromise I ask Sarah if you can have a key too?' I feel sick at the thought of him letting himself in unannounced, anytime he wants. But I know this is the only way he'll let me agree. 'And we can set Jack up with a temporary mobile, so he can call you direct whenever he wants. And you can call him. That way you know everything's OK.'

He takes a deep breath. I notice his hands sliding over his knees. I'm suddenly aware of my own quickened heartbeat.

'OK, Gav?' I try and steady my voice. 'It'll be good for us. I think you need it.'

'Trial run,' he says after a pause. 'A few days. If things go like before, then you have to move straight back in. Understood? And I'm allowed to let myself in at any time. You promise?'

'Fine,' I whisper. 'That's the deal.'

He gives a great sigh like something heavy has been moved off him.

'OK.' And then we both stare at Jack.

'Well, we don't need much. Just the physio, who is

coming over every day. Except now you're not going to be in the house, things might need a little more organisation.'

'OK.' I'm not reacting to his pointed comments. 'Also, we need to think about a tutor too. Perhaps I'll ask Ella for a recommendation. I'm sure she must know someone. And we need to sort out one of those mobile potty things. Can you order one? To go straight to the house.'

'Fine. I've got to go. I'll be back later.' I watch him disappear and as soon as he does I let out the breath I've been holding, pull out my phone and text Sarah.

Yes, I reply. I start to type, It's all agreed, then I delete it. Sarah's always having a go at me that Gav seems to make all the decisions in the house. One million times yes. Thank you. So much. I don't know whether a part of me is doing this to spite Gav but, as soon as I hear the message go, I start to cry. I can feel the delayed shock kicking in; all the fear and worry; my mind racing with everything that needs sorting out. But most of all, gratitude. I am filled with a deep gratitude that, despite everything – Jack's accident, a marital separation – Sarah is there, and I know she'd do anything for me.

SARAH

Sarah has a spring in her step for the first time in ages. Or rather, a sense of *purpose*. Jack is going to be OK. It will be a hard road. But there is no lasting damage, thank God. Liza had also texted to say he is being discharged from hospital. The relief! She'll pop over as soon as they're back, just as Liza asked her to do. She hasn't heard anything about any investigation just yet and she's just dropped Casper at Camilla's to see Elodie – if anyone knew anything about a looming investigation, Camilla would, and she hadn't said a thing.

Sarah had to admit, though, the guilt about what had happened at The Vale Club is still rumbling away, embedded deep into her subconscious, manifesting in some strange and twisted dreams in which she wakes thinking Casper had fallen from a great height. She startles constantly in the night, throwing off the bedclothes and gasping for breath. And on top of this is the fear of having to tell Tom she's offered Liza the flat. But at least she's *doing* something, she's trying to salve her conscience. And Liza would be away from Gav, able to make her

131

own choices. From the outsiders' point of view, Gav is a hands-on dad. *Oh isn't he wonderful*, the other mothers would coo. *I wish my Dave was like that instead of sitting there with his hand down his pants*. He's always attentive, Gav. Always up with the children, watching over Liza. Making sure she has water whilst she's feeding Thea. But Sarah knows better. She senses something else is at play – it's obvious in how much Liza changes when she's around him. Trying to please him all the time; always compensating for his abruptness.

The rest she can cope with. And Ella – well – their secret will bind them together and, in part, she feels relieved someone else is to blame too. If only she plays ball. It's unsettling, being complicit in something so huge, with someone she barely knows. Never being sure whether Ella can be trusted to keep her mouth shut. It makes Sarah feel like the ground is about to be pulled from beneath her at any given moment. Yet today, she is going to force herself not to let that get in the way.

On the bus on the way back from Camilla's she runs through the list of things she needs to get done in the next few hours. If she's lucky she might even have time to grab a coffee and bran-wheat banana muffin from Hollister and Tailors, on Turnham Green Terrace. They taste sugary enough, but she's checked time and time again on the small, hand-written card stuck in a dish of pink Himalayan salt crystals. *Home-made. Agave syrup*. Her mouth waters. She'll buy something for Tom too. Perhaps one of those Portuguese custard tarts he loves. And for Casper. She reminds herself to ask all the shops she goes into if they'd consider donating something for the school Christmas fair. She'll have to start channelling Liza – who normally raises thousands for the school. It's time to up her game. They don't have long to get the sponsorship, after all.

When she gets off the bus, it's cold but the sky is a ferocious blue. The roads are empty. Everyone must have gone away for half-term. She spots a few West London Primary parents in the playground next to the High Road. She'll say yes to Tom and her going to Oban – perhaps not now with all the furore, but maybe early next year, when things have hopefully settled. She inhales the wind. Something to look forward to. A long weekend. It'll be so good for them. She'll miss Casper, of course. But a long lie-in! She feels her body unwind at the very thought.

Her phone rings; it's her mother. Sarah contemplates answering – but she still doesn't feel strong enough to pretend that everything is all right, so she sends her a text instead. Just busy at the moment. Is everything alright? Her mother replies that yes, everything is fine, and the slight feeling of panic that always arises when her mother gets in touch disappears.

What would *really* make her day now, Sarah thinks, is if she bumped into Ella Bradby. She imagines how the situation might unfold. *Ella! How are you? Yes I'm just doing some shopping and organising, because of course, Liza and the kids are moving in. Oh! She didn't tell you? I guess she's been so busy with Jack. She just needs to be around her closest friends right now.* She wonders when the perfect moment might arise, in which to discuss Ella's little secret with Liza. Or indeed, Ella herself. It gives her a delicious little thrill to know that she has some information on Ella Bradby. She'll have to use it wisely, though. Keep it safe, in case Ella decides to pull any of her ridiculous one-upmanship tricks again.

First, she skips into Nature and Beauty, a health food store in Chiswick. Camilla had texted her earlier and told her to get magnesium and zinc, and something called Agnus Castus – for fertility – which she thinks sounds like some sort of witch's brew. She knows she definitely isn't pregnant this month, but at least her horrendous PMT symptoms have abated. She'll buy that and then she'll whizz round and collect all the cleaning products she needs to make the downstairs flat sparkle.

She picks up all her potions. Thirty-five pounds for the pleasure. Shit. Again. She tries not to gasp when the cashier pings the till. In fact, she lets out a small laugh. *Pah. Thirty-five quid? Nothing!* But really, she should have known. This is Chiswick, after all. She should have foreseen this and stopped off in Acton instead. She hands over the cash (she had taken out one hundred pounds – she couldn't bear the dread of thinking her card might be declined every time it was put to use) and hums a song to distract herself from all the feelings that threaten to overwhelm her.

'Thank you.' She feels she should be well-disposed towards the moody shop assistant today, despite wanting to punch her lights out for charging her such a bomb. But she gets no response. So she huffs pointedly, picks up her bags and makes her way down the high street to Robert Dyas. She's going to buy a hand-held vacuum to pick up all the corner dirt, some mould cleaner and whatever else she can find. By the time she gets there she's feeling a little less energetic – the thought of cleaning the flat is a bit exhausting – but she still has her bran muffin to look forward to and one whole hour to go before she has to pick up Casper. She grabs all the stuff she needs and is pleasantly surprised to find she has more than enough cash left over to satisfy her sweet craving.

When she leaves the shop, her gaze catches on the IVF clinic opposite with its peppermint-green clapboard.

Her earlier mood dips. She takes a step forward. She doesn't want to get too close – she'll leave that until Thursday when she's got Camilla holding her hand – but she wants to read what they have to say about their treatment.

Calm. Safe. Fantastic results. That's good, she thinks. She needs all of those things. She's been warned that it's a long, hard road. But nothing could feel harder than what she and Tom had been through last year. Just as she's squinting into the reception window, she sees a small, blonde lady with skinny jeans tucked into black ankle boots, coming out of the clinic. She's struck by how poised she looks. Happy, almost. She's turning her head, chatting to someone. Sarah hopes that she will be like that on Thursday, instead of the shaky wreck that she's envisaging. But then she sees who is behind her. He's holding a bunch of leaflets, sliding his wallet into his back pocket. She recognises his stance. The way he fills up the entire space. His leather jacket that's such a part of him she can't ever imagine him without it. She takes a step backwards. What the fuck, she thinks. Gav? *Gav?* She can't quite believe her eyes.

'Oh God, sorry,' she mutters. She's bumped into someone now, but she barely notices. She's too busy watching Gav and the blonde lady as they hurry off down the road towards Gunnersbury. He bumps his shoulder into the woman's body, the way he does when he's making a joke and he wants to highlight just how amusing it is.

'Sarah?'

She doesn't, or rather can't, respond for a moment. She stands there, suspended in time.

'Charlotte. Oh. God sorry. I'm not with it today. Just, you know.' She holds up all her shopping with an apologetic smile. She knows she looks vacant but inwardly she's panicking. Should she tell Liza what she's seen? She should probably speak to Gav first. Come straight out with it. She's good at detecting a lie. She's known him for long enough. But recently he's been so weird with her that she doesn't know if she can face it. Or maybe, just maybe, she should pretend she never saw it. But if Liza finds out she'd known and hadn't told her . . . Oh God. It's starting all over again. She knocks her temple with her knuckles. Just shut up, brain, she thinks.

'Hello Charlotte,' she sighs. Charlotte G. The one person on the planet she can't cope with seeing right now. Perky Charlotte, who's been gunning for Head of the PTA position for months. Sarah braces herself – she doesn't have the energy to escape.

There's nothing else for it. She may as well give in to whatever else today has to bring. But she has a feeling, from the smug look on Charlotte G's face – the upwards curl of her pursed lips – that it's not going to be good.

West London Gazette editorial notes, October 2019
J Roper interview transcript: Waitress Zara Hollis,
witness, The Vale Club

I'd been on the long shift. I'd left home at five that morning. The club opens at six, you see. For all the people who want to do their workouts before going to the office. I was a bit jittery. Had mainlined coffee in fact. So when I heard that scream, my heart was right up in my mouth. I knew something terrible had happened.

Anyway – we had word that the club would close pretty quickly after the boy fell. Most of the mums and dads who were with their kids scarpered. I suppose they'd had a shock and didn't want their children exposed to it all. I'm not surprised really. No one wants to see a badly injured child being carted off in an ambulance, do they?

So anyway, there was this really strange atmosphere and I was closing up the tills and doing the last bits of clearing away. I had just scooped up all the last cups and saucers that were left on the tables. There were only about two people in the café at that point. Two women and their kids. One of them was like this supermodel. I remembered her because – well – she was just one of *those types that look like they work out all the time. The other one seemed very upset. She must have known the boy or something because, come to think of it, she looked like she was in dreadful shock. I nearly asked her if she wanted a cup of tea. I stopped right behind her but they were talking so intently that I thought I would just let her get on with it.*

Strange conversation they were having. Something about the security cameras here and whether she could have done anything to stop the fall. I mean, how could she have done? She's not God or anything, is she. The only way that that fall could have been stopped was if the post had never been there in the first place. I wanted to tell her that. But my arms were aching and I thought all the china was about to slide off the tray. She shouldn't have worried though. It's not as if she was responsible, is it?

LIZA

Gav's right. Jack *is* being discharged. I hadn't really believed him yesterday – had assumed he'd misheard, got it wrong, even though he's prone to checking things three or four times when it comes to the children. I want to be happy about it. I *am* happy about it. Of course. But the idea that Jack is here, in the hospital where he can be looked after, where there are people around if anything goes wrong, is more comforting than I'd possibly realised. I feel better after texting Sarah and letting her know we are coming home. I know that seeing her face will make it all easier for us. It's ten thirty in the morning by the time Dr Qureshi comes to see us for her ward round. Jack has fallen back asleep.

'You managed to get some rest?' She looks over at the table, cluttered with the hospital-grade pump and two freezer bags of milk. 'Looks like you've been busy.'

'I slept OK actually.' My headache has finally subsided. I squeeze the back of my neck, grateful to Ella for her herbal sleeping tablets. 'My husband,' I stutter, realising he's anything but at the moment, 'he got the good shift.

But I went home for a few hours last night and had a good rest then, before I came back here. Thank you. Is everything all right then? Any updates?'

She looks over at Jack's sleeping form. 'He's a strong boy. Luckily. And the fracture will heal well. If you stick to what we told you. Keeping him still and well hydrated. We need you to see the physio this afternoon. You can liaise with her about appointments at yours but, for now, we need you to keep him lying down. Until then, you can get ready. To go home.'

I nod, only just grasping the gravity of this – how on earth I'm going to keep a five-year-old still.

'Books,' she reads my mind. 'Audio books. Telly. Lots of it. There are some forums online that will be able to help you. And soft foods. He'll be able to sit up a bit. But we'll go through all this with you anyway before you leave.'

'Right. Thank you.' I feel so unprepared. How will I know if there's something wrong? If anything happens, who will I call?

'Can I put together a list of questions?' I say. 'Before we go home? I just feel – I don't know.'

'Of course you can. I'll leave you for a bit until he wakes up then I'll come and see both of you. A nurse will be over soon to do his observations but everything is in order at the moment.' She looks at me, and then at Jack. 'He's a very, very lucky boy. Things could have been a lot worse.'

As she leaves our hospital bay, I try and focus on what's happening around me. I try not to let her words affect me. I try not to imagine the 'what ifs'. I try to keep my mind on the here and now. What help will catastrophising do? That's Sarah's bag, not mine. I let out a small chuckle and mentally remind myself to call her and make plans for us moving in. And then I text Gav. He'd told me he'd be in earlier. It's late now, almost ten forty-five. I jolt as I realise he's now nearly four hours late. What *is* he doing? What on earth can he be doing that's more important than our son? He's never been late before. Always hovering, waiting when I'm meant to bring the kids back for him. Pacing the hallway, the kitchen. Again, I steel myself against the rage, and try and focus on my little boy, whose eyes have started to open. He blinks three times in quick succession before looking at me.

'You OK, love?' I lean over and stroke the underside of Jack's good arm. 'Good news by the way. Home time soon. We'll be back before you know it. And I want to talk to you about something.'

'What?' he stares up at the ceiling. 'I know Father Christmas is not real.'

'Oh,' I laugh. I'm always surprised by how quickly he wakes up. 'Erm, no. It's not that. Something else.'

'Am I in trouble?' He looks scared, his gaze focused on the same spot above him. I shield his eyes so he doesn't stare directly into the bright glare of halogen.

'No, of course not.' I squeeze his hand. I don't want his mind going back to the fall. I know I'll have to talk to him about it at some point. Just not now. 'Don't be daft. I wanted to tell you that we're going to move in with Casper for a little bit. And Sarah and Tom. How nice will that be. Your best mate. Just until you get better.'

I wait for his reaction. Thank God. Something to lift his spirits. But he doesn't say a word.

'Jack? Love? Did you hear me?'

'Yes.' But his little face stays focused on the lights. I start to panic. Perhaps his cognitive function *has* been affected by the fall? Perhaps I should ask for a brain scan? My body starts to tremble.

'Jack? Are you OK?' I move to shake him a bit then realise this is the worst thing I could do. 'Jack. Listen,' my voice gets louder and louder. And then I sit down. *Stop it*, I tell myself. *Trust the doctors.* 'Sorry. Sorry love. Are you OK?' I don't want him to see me worried. I don't want him to absorb all my panic. 'Just want to make sure you're OK.'

'Yes Mummy.' I think I see his eyes fill with tears.

'Oh love. Are you not pleased?'

'I am. But what about Daddy?' he says.

'Daddy is going to be with us too.' I don't go into the business of the spare key. Jack has never asked why Gav had moved out of the main bedroom. Just jumped up and down that he was going to have his daddy closer to him. 'He's going to basically be living there too. But this will just be a chance to have some extra hands with Sarah and Tom, whilst we make sure you get better. And company with Casper. Sound good to you?'

'Can we play superheroes?'

My heart squeezes.

'Phew.' I kiss his hand. 'That's good. Because I was thinking, we could set up the telly so that you can watch it from your bed. And you and Casper can have superhero bedtime feasts together. OK? How does that sound?'

'Good,' he says, but his voice goes all quiet. He's just feeling weak, I tell myself. Poor little thing. Of course he's not going to be jumping up and down for joy. How could I ever think he would be? Not even six years old. A fractured neck and a broken wrist? Give him a break. 'It's all going to be OK, little one. It's all going to be OK.' But I don't know who I'm trying to convince. Him, or me.

Liza: Gav?

Gav: What is it?

Liza: Just wondered where you are? It's past ten thirty. I thought you said you were going to be back at seven this morning.

Gav: Seven?

Liza: You said you'd be here first thing and we're meant to be getting out today.

Gav: First thing? Well, it's still first thing. I'll be there in twenty. Just leaving home.

Liza: You call this first thing? Where have you been? I've just tried your landline. No answer. You're normally so *exacting* about time – especially mine – I just thought you might deign to be here at a normal hour. How do you know we haven't been discharged already and are waiting for you?

Gav: Don't start, Liza. Don't even go there. I wouldn't, if I were you.

Liza: I'm not starting. You said you'd be here for when he woke up. And you aren't. You are every other time. Except when we really need you.

Gav: It was just a figure of speech Liza. You have to take everything I say so literally. I'll be there soon.

Liza: But where have you been? What could have been more important than being here for your son?

Gav: I had a doctor's appointment this morning.

Liza: Doctor? You had a doctor's appt? You couldn't cancel?

Gav: No. See you soon.

WhatsApp group: Renegades
Members: Liza, Sarah

Liza: RANT ALERT. Fucking Gav. The fucking, fucking fuck-wittery arse-wipe. Said he'd be here at the hospital first thing this morning. For Jack. It's now ten-fifty and he's still at home. Said he had a fucking doctor's appointment. And we're meant to be getting ready to leave.

Sarah: Typing . . .

Liza: Sa? Where are you? I'm fucking furious. Twat. Absolute, fucking arsehole.

Sarah: Shit, Liza, so sorry. Hang on. Just trying to get rid of Charlotte G. Just bumped into her. Ring you in two, I promise.

SARAH

It's coming up to eleven o'clock. Time is ticking quickly and Sarah just wants to be polite and extricate herself from any long conversation with Charlotte G. Bran muffin. Coffee. Home. Instead, she knows she's going to have to listen to Charlotte go on and on about absolute rubbish. Her mind grapples for an excuse. And then her phone goes. She glances down at the screen, not caring that Charlotte will undoubtedly complain to another parent about this later.

Liza. Shit shit shit. She scans her message. Gav has told her he's been at the doctor's. What the hell is she going to say? She wishes Liza would just tell Gav where to go. Sarah has no idea how her friend can let him get away with his behaviour.

'Sarah?' Charlotte peers closely into her face. 'You OK? I mean, I know things must be pretty stressful with Jack. You heard any more by the way? About what happened at The Vale Club? Apparently they're in awful trouble. For letting that happen. There's going to be an internal investigation into it, I hear.'

145

'I'm fine.' Sarah tries to keep the anger out of her voice but then she registers what Charlotte G has said. 'Just full on,' she says. 'Kids and stuff. And yes. Obviously, Jack. And The Vale Club thing? That's just people being nosey and disrespectful.' She gives Charlotte a warning stare. 'People trying to create gossip. No one knows what's going on at the moment. Everyone's main concern – which of course as it should be – is the welfare of Jack, and Liza.'

'Well, of course. I know that. But, well, it'll be interesting to hear what they have to say.' Charlotte G sniffs censoriously. 'And management's reaction to it. I mean, you'd think for the price we're all paying . . .'

'Where did you hear that stuff, by the way?'

'Hear what?' Charlotte G stands up to full height.

'That there is going to be an investigation?' Sarah is trying to act casual but out of nowhere she can hear the rush of her heartbeat in the depths of her eardrums.

'Oh, well.' Charlotte G's clearly delighted to oblige. 'On The Vale Club Facebook page, of course. Everyone's going mad, saying they're not taking their kids back there until there's been a proper, full-on investigation into the health and safety of the club.'

'Right.' Sarah gulps. She wonders if she can bring herself to look later. She hopes it's not gaining too much traction with The Vale Club members – given that half of them are parents at Casper's school. Not only might she be caught out, but every single person on the planet could find out what she's done. 'Oh yes. I do remember hearing something about that.'

Her skin is prickling. Sarah desperately needs this conversation to end. She thinks of Gav again too, and wonders what the hell she's going to say to Liza. She quickly types a message that will buy her some time and gives a short, sharp smile in Charlotte's direction. One that says, *Listen up, bitch. Say another word and I'll have you for breakfast.* Unfortunately, it doesn't quite translate as she hopes.

'Oh, Sarah. You *do* look exhausted. I know how stressful it is. Yes. Of course I do.' Charlotte gives her a patronising smile. 'What with part-time work at the shop. Three children under three and no real help at home. It's just exhausting. But of course I'm so lucky to have Mike. He's such a present and loving father. One must count one's blessings.'

Oh do fuck off, thinks Sarah.

'Getting ready for the Christmas fair then?' Charlotte G continues. Shoot, thinks Sarah. *Shoot, damn and fuck.* She hasn't even asked the shops for the raffle prizes yet. Her one task for the fair today and she can't even remember that.

'Yes, it's going super well,' Sarah says. 'Got some fantastic prizes. And I'm starting to make real headway with the sponsorship money. I hope you'll be at the meeting after half-term?'

'Ah, the *meeting*.' Charlotte G has a strange look on her face. If Sarah didn't know better she'd think it was almost one of pleasure. They both go silent, until Charlotte can't help but break out into a full-on smile. 'You do . . . you do *know*, don't you?'

'Know what?' Sarah feels her lips freeze. She can't take much more of this. Her head is still reeling with Gav and the talk of the investigation.

'The meeting?' Charlotte's voice grates, like a toddler playing the recorder. 'Oh, have you not been on your WhatsApp?'

Sarah pulls out her phone again. She has studiously ignored the reams of messages that she muted earlier that morning. She can't concentrate. She can't even seem to punch in her security code.

'*Ella*,' Charlotte goes on. 'She's pulled in the sponsorship money.' She takes in a big gulp of air. 'Would you imagine? The entire lot. I added her onto the WhatsApp chat just a few minutes ago. She wants to head up the Christmas fair this year.'

'Head it up?' Sarah feels like someone is clawing at her throat. 'I said I'd do it. Take over. To help Liza.'

Part of her is thinking: *phew*. She really, *really* can't be arsed to do it anyway, and she'll be cutting off her nose to spite her face if she kicks up too much of a fuss. But alas, the pride engulfs her before she can shut her big trap. What the hell is Ella playing at now?

'I mean, I'd organised *everything*.' Sarah immediately wishes she could take back the lie. But it's too late. 'I've been working all hours.' What the hell is she saying? Her mouth just will not stop, despite her brain telling her otherwise.

'Really?' says Charlotte, her eyes bulging with the pleasure of imparting such important information. 'Well, Ella's managed to secure ten thousand pounds in sponsorship. Ten thousand! Typical Ella. Probably just had to introduce herself and the business owners would be climbing over each other to sponsor us. So – you know – we need to think of that, really. Don't we? Maybe it could go to vote? I mean, if you've organised everything already then maybe you could . . .'

She takes a long swig from her Thermos flask, which has a sticky label with *Charlotte G* written on it, in small, black writing (of course it does, thinks Sarah, bitterly).

'Y'know. You could, like, do it together? What a fabulous idea. I mean, that saves you having wasted all your time. And it lets us keep the sponsorship money that Ella's raised without, well, offending anyone.'

Sarah wonders if she should offer her the Nobel Peace Prize.

'I'll ping everyone now, shall I?' Charlotte pulls out her iPhone. Sarah watches helplessly.

'There,' she says, waving the handset in the air. 'All done.'

'All done,' Sarah echoes. Just to think, this time last week, she would have jumped up and down at the thought of spending time with Ella. How her heart had swelled when she'd first seen her again after all those years, gliding around The Vale Club. Her thoughts had swiftly tumbled through the imagined scenarios of their burgeoning and sisterly friendship, before Jack's fall had ripped everything apart.

All of it seems so plain sailing for Ella. Even in the direct aftermath of the accident. Not an eyebrow out of place – her clothes effortlessly crease-free. She is just so *clean* and crisply turned out. How *easy* and how much better Sarah's own life would be if she'd just been born into Ella Bradby's shoes. *But*, she tells herself again – *no one can be that perfect.*

And how in hell has Ella brought in all the money anyway? And why? Is this all part of her perfection? Or could it be something more sinister? Sarah's mind is now racing like a trapped hamster on a wheel. Liza had already spent weeks working to pull in funds. The more Sarah thinks about it, the stranger it seems.

She looks at her watch. And now she's late. No relaxed coffee and muffin. She could try and ring Liza on the bus. Or at least WhatsApp her. She reminds herself about being there for Jack's homecoming but the thought swiftly disappears, to be replaced by images of Gav and that lady, and the echo of Charlotte's yapping in her ears. She needs to think about what she's going to do. She's filled with a deep, rotten hatred towards Charlotte G.

'Isn't that brilliant?' says Charlotte, bouncing up and down on tiptoes. 'You and Ella steering the ship together?'

'Absolutely brilliant,' replies Sarah. 'Brilliant.' She picks up her shopping. Screw the bran muffin, she thinks. She says goodbye to Charlotte, and marches off in search of the most sugary, buttery, icing-covered pastry she can find.

LIZA

It's all quiet when we get home. The ambulance drivers stretcher Jack in and take him straight into the living room. Never in my life have I imagined having to see my own child in this situation. The relief he's home is momentarily overshadowed by 'what if' scenarios and I'm flooded with feelings of anger, mainly at myself, that this has happened. *He's here. He's OK, we can all move on from this*, I tell myself again and again.

'Here?' the stocky, blonde-haired lady interrupts my thoughts. 'On this one?' Gav has managed to assemble a bed from upstairs which has been in boxes for months.

'Thank you,' I tell her. 'That will be fine. My . . . Jack's father is on his way so he can help if you need anything. He's just gone to pick up some provisions.'

'We've got it.' The paramedics heave his small body up. 'We're used to this. You should see some of the people we have to lift.' The woman pretends to mop her brow.

I watch as they place my little boy onto the mattress. He stares up at the ceiling. I should have put something up there. Some pictures of superheroes. Or something.

151

Why didn't I think of all of this before? And then Mary comes downstairs.

'Little one's asleep.' She puts her finger up to her mouth. 'Oh, hello young man. Fancy seeing you here.'

Jack smiles. A true Jack smile, for the first time since the accident. I look at the art-deco clock above the sofa – another one of Gav's finds. I've never really liked it but he'd come home with it a few months ago, pleased as Punch. 'Yes it's lovely,' I'd told him. 'You can put it in the living room. Pride of place.' Five hours until Mary leaves. Five hours until I have to do this alone – just me and an ex-husband to battle things out.

'Listen.' She walks over and puts her arm on mine. I start to cry. 'Oh love. Listen. I thought I'd stay. Just for tonight. I've got no jobs until the day after tomorrow. I thought you might like some company whilst you settle in. Your . . . Gav, he said he was sleeping somewhere else tonight. Would you like that, love?'

For one minute, I'm struck dumb by the kindness. At Ella having arranged for Mary to come in the first place. But then I wonder where else Gav can possibly be sleeping and how strange it is for him to do such a thing.

'Oh, Mary, thank you. But I'm going to pay you. I can't not.'

'You are doing no such thing. I'd never expect payment for the likes of this little lad over here. And you.' She walks over to Jack and perches on the bottom of his bed. 'I've got a surprise for you. I'm Mary by the way.' I watch as Jack's throat bobs up and down. Another smile.

'A surprise?'

'Yup. Not from me actually.'

'Ooooh, Jack, a surprise,' I say. 'And I know for a fact

152

that you've got lots of other surprises coming. From all your friends.' He smiles again.

'This one's a good one,' says Mary. 'Wait there.' She quickly turns to me as she realises that, of course, Jack can't go anywhere. We sit and wait and the female ambulance driver packs up and ruffles Jack's hair.

'You get well soon, young man,' she says. 'Now no climbing those tall posts.' I freeze. Jack's eyeline tracks me. I want to lean over and tell him it's OK, but I'm so cross with her for interfering that I go down the hall and open the front door, waiting for them to leave.

'Here we are.' I go back into the room and watch as Mary comes out of the kitchen, holding a neatly wrapped parcel and a pair of scissors in her hand. 'Jack? Are you ready?'

'Yes, I'm ready,' he says, his unbroken arm pounding excitedly into the mattress. His eyes swivel towards Mary. 'What is it?'

She unpeels the paper, pulls open a cardboard box. Then she slices through the tape and lifts out a small iPhone handset.

'Oh my God,' I say. I've banned Jack from my phone – predominantly because he is so bloody obsessed with the thing. I want to take it away from him but something stops me. I remember I'd promised Gav I'd get Jack a handset – that he'd be contactable at all times.

'Now wait.' She turns it over and peels off a little note and starts to read aloud. '*This is not for watching videos, or for playing games. That's for when you are a bit older. But I've pre-loaded a whole load of audio books that me and Felix think you will love. Maybe your little friend will come over and listen to some with you.*'

Ella. To the rescue, once again.

I'm torn between feeling annoyed I hadn't thought of doing that myself and guilt that I'd been so awful about Ella when I saw her at the crèche. Sarah has been right all this time. Ella Bradby *is* a mystery, but a good one. And then my mind turns to Sarah. It's after lunch and I haven't heard a thing from her. She'd promised she'd call me back. I check my phone quickly and scroll back to our last chats. There it is in black and white: Just trying to get rid of Charlotte G. Just bumped into her. Ring you in two, I promise. And then, when I hadn't heard from her, I'd followed it up with another WhatsApp – Are you there?

And she hasn't even bothered to bloody answer. She's read it, I can see that much. And she's online. My finger hovers over the keypad, ready to chase her again – but then I stop. Why should it be me doing all the work?

She'd also promised she'd come over when Jack got home. Surely she'll turn up later? Really, what could have cropped up that she would jeopardise our friendship, especially at a time like this?

I have more important things to think about. I know that. Honestly. Come on Liza. I can't have high expectations all the time. But then I look at Jack's face. His small hand stroking the iPhone screen like it's a soft, furry animal. The sheer look of wonderment on his face. His other hand all strapped up. And I can't help but think about just how attentive Ella has been.

But then I wonder, what if something's not right with all of this. That it's weird for Sarah not to be phoning. Not to be texting or coming to see us. And that I should perhaps see if everything is OK. Maybe she's having problems – like last year. *Rosie.* She'd made me promise never, ever to mention it again, which I'd honoured. But in return, she'd also promised she'd let me know if there was ever a problem. Just as I remind myself to ask if she's OK, I'm distracted by the shiny screen of the handset. The list of new audio books and podcasts that flash up. Jack's small fingers sticking out of the cast. The whiteness of the small crescents on his nails. And then Gav rings.

'I was going to kip out tonight. Mary said she'd stay another night. But I think I'll come back home after all. I was going to drop the shopping back anyway and get Jack settled. Don't really want to be away from the kids.' He gives a small chuckle down the phone except I don't really know what is so funny.

'You sure?' I'm itching to ask him where he had been intending on staying.

'I'm sure. See you later.'

We both hang up and I stand for a moment, silent, still clutching the phone. Aware of the tension in my muscles I feel them freeze all over again. I hadn't realised how much Gav's presence had been constricting me. How his behaviour infiltrated all areas of my life – so that every action I made, every breath I took, was not without the menace of his voice in my head. *What are you doing, Liza? Are you doing a good enough job?* And then the other thoughts start. Memories surfacing. The birth. The blood. Jack. Those sleepless nights and the inky blackness shrouding my psyche. And then everything that followed. That night Ella had found me on the street, my skin dripping with sweat despite the freezing cold night, hair hanging damply around my cheeks. I shudder at the thought of what I'd done, desperately trying to stop those memories in their tracks.

I put down my phone, take Jack's hand and squeeze it tight.

'From Ella,' I manage. 'The mobile. She's Mummy's new friend. Isn't she wonderful?'

'Yes,' says Jack settling on David Walliams, and pressing play. I think about the accident. How it could be a force for change. For bringing more positivity into my life. And if that means Ella Bradby stepping right in, I'll welcome her with open arms. 'Yes, she really is.'

SARAH

Her hair is damp from all the scrubbing and mopping. She's changed one T-shirt already. She feels absolutely filthy and can't wait to soak in a long, hot bath as soon as Casper has gone to bed. She glances over at her son. He's busy working with a toy screwdriver, his tongue lolling out to the side like a dog. She is most satisfied that she's managed to keep him off the television so far. Perhaps they'll go up to the high street for a quick supper. She can't even muster up the energy to cook an egg on toast. She doesn't know why the thought of trekking out to a café in the freezing cold is easier than shoving an egg in a saucepan. But by God, it is. Her parenting standards are sinking by the minute. And her lungs are starting to feel a little tight. She picks up the mould remover and scans the label.

It doesn't say anything about fresh air, or toxic ingredients. But then she pulls up. Casper. What if it burns his little lungs? What if it isn't suitable for children? *Oh God.*

'Casper, out,' she pulls him up by his arm. 'Sorry. You

can't be in here.' She feels like collapsing in on herself. What has she done now? She can't even be trusted to keep her own son safe, let alone . . . oh heavens. 'You can go and watch telly. Just for five minutes. Then we're going to get something to eat.'

She takes him up and settles him on the sofa and double locks the front door. Just in case. You can never be too careful, she thinks.

'Listen. I'm just going to clean off the last of this stuff downstairs. OK? I won't be long.' But her son is categorically not interested in what she has to say. 'Casper. Can you hear me? I'm going to the downstairs flat. All right? I'll be five minutes.' He manages to nod.

She grabs some water, takes some to Casper and then races down the small staircase back to where she'd been scrubbing. The place had been filthy but she thinks she's done a good job. She'll leave the back windows open. There's going to be a two-month-old in there, after all. She's even found some baby-proofing things. Not that Thea is old enough to move anywhere, but – well – it's the thought that counts. And she's had more than enough thoughts about Liza. She doesn't know what to do. She's desperate to get in touch. She knows she must ring, or text, to find out about Jack. It's probably the longest they've been without contact for over a year. And then she remembers with a sinking feeling she was meant to go over and see them. She feels sick and has a sense of loss, almost, about her friend and the purity of the relationship that they'd had only two days ago. She knows that Liza will be expecting to hear her voice.

She should stop thinking so manically and *just do*. Just pick up the damn phone. Apologise for not turning up or replying to her messages. But she is too scared.

She is too scared that she's going to fuck up Liza's life even more. That she'll let slip she saw Gav with another woman. A desperately pretty, younger woman. Coming out of an IVF clinic, laughing and looking like the Gav that she had once known before Jack had even been born. So carefree and fun. The Gav that would lean down and peck Liza on the nose or cheek every five minutes. The Gav that wouldn't be eyeing her best friend's every movement, making snide comments every time she opened her mouth, or tended to their children.

She's also terrified she's going to let slip what had really happened at The Vale Club. She sees Jack's face in her mind's eye. Then Priti and Charlotte G's faces merging into one, indefinable blob. *The investigation.* Before the images can really take root, she picks up the dust rags and cleaning paraphernalia and bolts up the stairs to Casper.

'Right, young man. We'll head down to Chiswick. Franco Manca pizza?'

'Pizza! Yes Mummy,' he shouts.

'OK. Great. If we leave now, we'll be back and ready for bed before Daddy gets home. So turn off the telly, get your shoes on.' For once, he does as he is told and she grabs the leftover money from her earlier shopping trip. Just as she goes to grab Casper's coat, her phone pings.

It's Ella. She knows it before she's even read the message. She thinks how powerful Ella Bradby must be, imparting her energy through the damn phone waves.

Want to come over for a playdate? Drop by if you're about. I've just been with Charlotte G. Seems there's a lot for us to discuss! Wld be good to do it before we go back to school and we're away tomorrow. E.

What on earth is she up to? Sarah thinks about Ella's house. How desperate she would normally be to see it and how she'd revel in telling Camilla and Liza all about it. How much they'd gossip over her interior design (she thinks she has a fair idea already of what her house would be like) and the way Ella behaved when she was in her own space. Her next thought is that she could discuss the investigation with Ella. What they would say if they were asked outright. How they'd play it. She exhales with relief. Then she thinks about what else she might find at Ella's – a chance to uncover any interesting things about Little Miss Perfect. See what life behind Ella's closed doors is *really* like. Damnit. She wishes she hadn't told Casper they're going to Franco Manca.

The curiosity stops her in her tracks, as well as the overriding desire to get some sort of reassurance that if The Vale Club is going to look into Jack's fall, everything will be all right. It's like she's going on a bad date, she thinks. She knows she should say no. She knows that she should be sensible – and she's been sensible all her life. But now is not the time to start anything reckless. She remembers the way Ella had been at The Vale Club. The casual way she'd spoken up when Liza had asked if she'd checked on Jack. *Yes. She saw him.* The gleam in her eyes just after she'd said it. *Damnit. And damn you, Ella Bradby.* Maybe, just maybe, she could do some digging. This would be a fantastic chance. Before they get caught up in the Christmas fair. She could find out more about Ella's secret. Shift the balance of power back into her court and then she'd go and see Liza.

Sarah looks up at Casper, her gaze pulled over towards the large canvas of her and Tom. Before her mind can hover over any alternative solutions and suggestions, her fingers have begun to type out their reply.

Yes! How lovely! she says, but then deletes it. She cannot appear too keen. We'll swing by, she types. That's better. And say a quick hello to discuss things. But have to rush back. Address? She's careful not to add a kiss, either. Or maybe she should? Show her that she doesn't care what she's typed? *Fuck it.* She sends the message and then she waits. And waits. Casper starts to moan. She can't leave the house just yet. She wishes she could send Ella a middle finger emoji. She's got a frigging life to lead, doesn't she know? But she sits down and pulls Casper onto her lap.

Once again, game, set and match Ella, bleeding, Bradby.

LIZA

The house is beautiful. Grey brick with huge white balus-trades. The kind you see on the front of *House & Garden* magazine. There's a big front lawn with a sculpture of a small boy right in the middle, and a vintage car parked up on the right-hand side. I'm absolutely desperate to text Sarah, she'd love the scoop on Ella's home, but she hasn't been in touch yet, so I leave it. I'll wait until she gets in contact – if she ever does – and then I'll tell her everything. She'll be agog. The cellar and a huge, bloody great gym. In her house! There's even a small, private school next door. I wondered why, then, they've chosen to send their children to the local state primary, which isn't actually all that local?

I press the buzzer, amazed at how free I feel all of a sudden. No leaking boobs on account I'd just pumped enough milk to feed an army of babies before I'd left Gav in charge.

'Liza, she's going to need more please,' he kept saying. 'You don't want her to go hungry, do you, just because you are in such a rush to go out?' He was right, though.

I *was* in a rush. I feel an inkling of the essence of *me*. I take a deep breath.

'Ah Liza.' The door opens but I can feel her presence, even before I see her face. 'I'm so glad to see you. I didn't know which one of you it was.' I'm about to ask her who else she's expecting, but before I can get much further, a suited man comes to take my coat and ask me for my order.

'Order?'

'Thank you, Barnaby,' says Ella, sashaying through the hallway. 'A pot of tea would be lovely. We'll have it in the living room. Liza, follow me. The kids are out at the park with our nanny, so we've got a few minutes alone. They'll be back soon.'

I follow her, drinking in the interiors. It's not quite what I expected. More modern. Full of those new-fangled sculptures. A mesh hare in one corner. Beautiful, plumped cushions. Cosy throws everywhere. And *wow*, the artwork. Huge art-deco pieces. Bright colours that lift the room. There are photos of Ella with a girl that looks quite like her – long beachy golden hair, the widest of smiles.

'Sister?' I ask, pointing at one, but she doesn't reply. Just focuses on trying to open a large sash window. There's a baby grand piano, just next to a huge window facing the garden, dripping with purple flowers from the outside. I notice a silver-framed picture of a dog on the wall – *Bramble: 2002–2017* it says. I jolt. Bramble. And before I can open my mouth, they start again – memories from that night. My heart constricts. Before I can say or do anything, I'm thinking about Ella and the time I'd bumped into her walking her tiny terrier. The moonlight glowing. The expression that had crossed her face when she'd seen me – a mix of fear and disbelief.

'He died,' she says, after she manages to pull up the window.

'I remember him,' I tell her, willing my pulse to slow down. I inhale some of the fresh air that's filling the house. 'Wow, it's so beautiful in here.' I walk around the rest of the room. A pony-skin rug fills up nearly the whole floor and then I take a step back to admire a huge, black and white photograph on the wall behind the piano. It's her, of course. Her unmistakeable stature. The quiet confidence and the way she holds herself upright – like she doesn't even know her own beauty. It's an image of someone so innately comfortable in her own skin that it's never crossed her mind to be self-conscious. She catches me staring at it and then gives me a smile and pats the sofa.

'Come, sit down.'

'Thank you.' I fall into the cushions, my body swallowed up by the soft material. 'I can't be too long. Thanks for asking me over. Gav's at home. And it's nice to be out of the house.' I feel a stab of guilt. Jack has only been home for a few hours, after all. 'I mean, it's going to be a long road, so it's good to have time to myself.'

'Gav. What happened, there? You guys separated, right?'

'Yup. Just after Thea was born.' I don't ask how she knows. I assume that word just gets around the school gossip channels. 'But he's still in the house. Weird set-up, I know. But, it works.'

'Wow. That's upsetting for you.' Ella's voice remains so flat it could be mistaken for sarcasm. 'What happens if, well, one of you starts seeing someone?'

I'm surprised she's asking such personal questions so early on in the conversation. But it seems like she doesn't care for what's right or wrong; she has her agenda and she sticks to it. I wish I could be more like that.

'We haven't really discussed that yet, at length.'

'Why don't you ask him to move out?' For some reason, I don't mind the questions. It feels refreshingly honest, actually. Instead of all the skirting around the subject that happens at the school gates.

'Well, I don't know. I guess it just came at a bad time, I suppose. I'd just had Thea. She was tiny. But we'd had some difficulties with Jack. When he was born.'

I look over to Ella for her reaction, but she doesn't give any.

'What kind of difficulties?' She's treading on dangerous ground here. What had felt like an innocent conversation now feels like more of an attack. Once again I think back to the last time I'd actually seen Ella, before she ghosted us all. I wonder whether she remembers it in detail. She'd given no hint that she had any recollection at The Vale Club. I wonder if what I tell her now is going to trigger her memories, or whether she'll gloss over it all? Or perhaps she's actually known all along and just wants me to admit it openly? I realise that my heart has started hammering again.

'Oh just, you know. Stuff.'

'So what happened? Got too much for him?'

'Yes. And no.' I think back to when it all did happen. And feel momentarily disloyal to Gav for letting people believe he was the bastard in all this. 'Well, it's a bit more complicated than that. Things got in the way.'

'Oh?' She leans forward and reaches for a biscuit, as though preparing herself for a night in watching television. 'Poor you. What went down?'

'Well,' the earlier feelings of defensiveness melt along

with her sympathetic voice. It's just so *hypnotic*. The cushions are so comfortable. Her entire world is so comfortable, so far removed from my own, that I start to think: what harm could it do if I just trusted her for one minute? She has it all so sorted. She could give me some good advice. Maybe some of her luck would rub off onto me. God knows I need it.

'It started right before my pregnancy. Before we'd even met at our NCT.' I grab a fuchsia cushion and fold my arms over it. 'He was already anxious about everything going OK. He was constantly questioning whether we'd be good parents. Gav had a screwed-up family life, you see. Wanted to make sure history didn't repeat itself. And then, well, this is the difficult bit. Because it makes him look bad for leaving. Or me. I'm not sure which. But please, don't judge.'

'Of course I won't.' She takes a bite from the biscuit and leans even closer to me. I can hear her breath quicken ever so slightly. 'I wouldn't. I've had enough issues of my own not to judge others.' Her face remains totally expressionless but she looks over to the far corner of the room, to a small collection of photographs. And out of nowhere she looks like she might cry.

'Anyway,' she sniffs. 'Go on. You were saying?'

'Well, I guess it all really kicked off after I had Jack. The rows. The change in our relationship, I guess. You know how it is.'

I'm sure as hell she doesn't know how it is. But she nods and I think about asking her outright then – if she remembers seeing me all those years ago. But something stops me.

'And that's when it started. For me, at least. He came home one night and . . .' I swallow, remembering the shame that had engulfed me. 'It had been a normal day. Jack had the most awful colic. Those first couple of months . . .'

I take a deep breath, trying to drown out the memory of the constant screams. The way they jarred right down into my soul so that I feared I'd snap at any given moment. I shut my eyes.

'Anyway, I was anxious. A first-time mum. Everything was a big deal. I was always second-guessing myself. So I never actually slept at all. That whole time. Jack had been making these noises in the night that I would convince myself were him taking his last breath. So I'd be up and down, leaning over his cot and holding my hand on his chest, to check it was rising and falling as it should be. So, that day I was doubly exhausted. And when Gav had left for work that morning – I hadn't been sure how I was going to make it through the day. I had pleaded with him not to go into the office. That whole period from about three a.m., I had been terrified of him leaving me. I just knew that come eight o'clock, after he'd given me a bit of time to shower and change, I would be left by myself, and it would start all over again. That feeling. And well, we're meant to feel so lucky. We *are* so lucky, I didn't really feel I could say anything. And no one else seemed to be having any problems.'

'I know that feeling.' This time she looks like she really means it. *You must be a bloody good actress*, I want to say. 'Go on.'

'Well, I hadn't slept for weeks.' I feel the usual tightening in my chest. The sense that the room is being sucked of air. She tilts her head and gives me a quizzical look. I take a deep breath.

'Gav did leave. Looking back on it, I don't think he realised just how bad it was. He thought I was just bored. Or lonely. That I'd get used to it. Perhaps I didn't explain it well enough.'

'Shhhh, shhhh, it's OK. You're safe here.'

'And then, I was all alone and Jack was screaming, screaming.' I pull at a thread of cotton. 'I don't know if I can bring myself to tell you what happened after that.' I hadn't realised it but I'm shaking.

She removes the cushion and shifts up closer to me. I can smell her. An apple-y coconut smell.

'We've all done stuff we regret.'

I feel myself starting to properly shiver. But just as I'm about to carry on, the doorbell goes. Saved by the bell, I think, except this time I really hadn't wanted to be saved. Ella gets up and looks over at the clock on the mantelpiece, a confused expression on her face. She opens the front door and I immediately recognise the voice of the person on the doorstep.

'Hello, we're so grateful to have been asked for a playdate,' she's saying. 'Casper, be polite. Use your words please. Say hello to the lovely lady. Ella. Her name is Ella. Can you say hello?'

I hear the pitch of her voice getting higher and higher. What on earth is *Sarah* doing here? She'd gone totally AWOL and now she's here?

'Oh wow, thank you,' she's saying. 'Let me just give you Casper's coat too.' I hear Barnaby shuffling around. 'Casper, just give me your arms,' Sarah says, through gritted teeth. I want to get up and stop the awkwardness in its tracks, but for some reason I have no idea what I'm going to say. I'm just so annoyed that she hasn't been in touch with *me*, or turned up to see me when we'd got back from the hospital, but has quite happily accepted an invitation to Ella Bradby's house.

When she walks back into the room, Ella appears totally unfazed. But then Sarah follows behind her, Casper looking cross. I watch as her entranced gaze travels the entire room, drinking in the beautiful contents, and then, as her eyes swing towards me, my stomach swoops. I know she's going to feel bad that she's been caught out. Too busy to have time for her best friend, but here she is. Standing in Ella's sumptuous living room.

'Oh my gosh,' Sarah trills. 'Liza, what a surprise. I'm so sorry.' She shifts her weight from one foot to another. I notice she's wearing her black boots, the ones she saves for going out, or for smart events. 'I have been meaning to ring. I just . . .' She swallows and looks down. 'How is Jack?'

'He's OK,' I tell her. I try and keep the irritation out of my voice but everything's catching up with me and my legs start to wobble. 'He's OK. He's with Gav. Ella just asked me over.' I offer her the get-out, so she can explain what she's doing here too, but she doesn't.

And then I catch a look on her face, before she manages to hide it. A look that suggests she's been caught out stealing, or worse. What the hell?

'Ella, your house is beautiful,' she says, swiftly changing the subject. 'Where are Felix and Wolf? Casper is so looking forward to seeing them. Aren't you, Casper?' She yanks his hand a little too hard and he starts to whine. Oh God.

'Oh well, they're just in the park at the moment.'

'Park? Didn't you say come over for a playdate?' I know she's trying to act casual, to come across as all light-hearted. I know Sarah back to front. And I know how difficult this must be for her. But for the moment, I can't help. I don't have the energy.

'Did I?' says Ella. 'Playdate? I must be going mad. The kids are out. Sorry. I'm just so used to, I don't know.' She waves her hand again and motions for Sarah to sit next to me. 'Hey, Casper. Want a biscuit? That OK?' she asks Sarah.

'Of course. Casper. Just one please. And make sure you say your pleases and thank yous.' Casper gingerly puts his hand out, searching for the biggest, before settling on one at the bottom of the pile. I hear Sarah gasp as the biscuits slide perilously to the edge of the plate. 'Oh goodness, Casper, do be careful.'

'It's OK,' says Ella handing him another one. 'Don't worry at all. You can't be too precious with kids around, can you.'

Sarah retreats into herself as though scolded for being uptight. 'Exactly. Totally get it. You really can't be. Not with these monkeys around, pulling everything off the shelves and everything. Not that yours probably do that,' she hastily adds. She pulls out her phone. 'Oh and by the way, the Christmas fair? Liza – I said I'd take over but, Ella, you said you wanted to discuss it? Before Thursday's meeting?' I can see panic all over Sarah's face. The way she repeatedly blows strands of hair out of her eyes.

'Oh God,' Ella ruffles Casper's hair. 'The Christmas fair. Let's not discuss that now. *Tedious*.' Sarah opens her mouth and closes it. 'Let's just have fun, shall we? Give Liza a good time whilst she can get out of the house?'

'Yes,' replies Sarah. 'Yes. A good time. Of course.'

'Oh thank you,' I mumble. We all go silent, and watch as Casper reaches for another biscuit. I stop myself from filling in the conversation. That should be Sarah's job. After all, it's because of her strange behaviour that we're in this awkward situation. But for the moment, no one says anything. My cheeks heat up at the excruciating lack of chit-chat.

'So,' Sarah says, eventually fumbling for things to say, never one to sit with a silence. But she doesn't do a good enough job, and then she just gives up and uses Casper as a distraction.

'Have you got a loo I can use?' She stands up and wipes some imaginary crumbs off her trousers. 'If you could just keep an eye on Casper here please.' Her tone is businesslike and curt. I start to feel angry and defensive. What has she got to be peeved about, I think. But then I see the inwards pull of her lips. The weird stare in her eyes. And I know that look. I know it very well. And it's at that point I realise my friend is about to burst into tears.

SARAH

Sarah tells herself she's being ridiculous. *Absurd*, even. But she has no idea what's wrong. Her hormones have levelled out after her PMT. Jack is going to be OK. She thinks she'll make her peace with everything but something feels *off*. Not depressed quite. Or 'down in the dumps' – as Tom had referred to it after they'd planted Rosie's tree. Just the pull and squirm of anxiety, in the pit of her belly; residual guilt that she has a feeling is never, ever going to go away. And now Liza's here, Sarah can't very well speak to Ella about the investigation.

She follows the directions into a cloakroom at the end of the corridor, just past the study and off the biggest kitchen she thinks she's ever seen. The design – oh God – the design. The loo has a beautiful antique-looking wooden seat and the wallpaper is to die for. Small, intricately hand-painted birds with gold leaf patterns around them. It smells like a spa. She thinks of her own hastily pulled together attempt at a bathroom when they'd renovated last year. The way her used loo rolls have piled up and up from her attempts at saving them for crafting

172

'rockets' with Casper. No such luck. They're more likely to be shredded by the mouse she had discovered in the living room last week.

After she's scanned all the black and white photographs of the Bradby family, she switches on the soft lighting just above the mirror and peers into it. No eyebags in the reflection, but she knows they're there. She presses her fingertips, pulling her skin around her forehead taut, like the celebs in the magazines. Hmmm. She could probably pass for early thirties. She knows she's lucky to have come this far in life relatively unscathed. But it doesn't stop her from feeling the way she does. She wonders why she had felt so stung back in the living room. Ella hadn't said anything particularly nasty. She didn't know whether the comments about tedium had even been directed at her. But she *feels* that they had. And that's surely enough?

And why had Ella asked them both over anyway? Sarah thinks back to Ella's earlier text. Want to come over for a playdate? And she'd said she'd wanted to discuss school stuff. So – why on earth had there been no kids when she'd arrived? And Ella had shut her down when she'd tried to discuss the Christmas fair. She can't work any of it out. She just wishes things could go back to normal, but it seems that the wheels have spun too far out of control.

It's like being back at school all over again. She gives her face a few good slaps. 'Pull yourself together,' she says out loud. She remembers to flush the loo – she hopes she doesn't actually need to go anytime soon – and makes her way back into the living room.

Casper is sitting on the floor, winding up an enormous crane that she knows he'll be asking for, on repeat, until the run-up to Christmas. And Ella and Liza are shaking.

She steps forward. Oh God. *Liza*. She's about to put her arms out to hug her, and tell her she'll be OK, when she realises she's actually *laughing*. She hasn't seen Liza laughing like this for weeks. Liza looks up, her hand covering her mouth.

'Oh, Sa . . .' She starts to explain the joke, but can't get any further before she's struck again by the most convulsive giggles. 'Stop. Oh God, Ella, I can't take it any more. Oh, thank you. Thank you so much for cheering me up like this. You are exactly the tonic I needed. As well as the actual tonics you gave me for Jack . . . oh God.'

And there they both go again. Sarah contemplates making a quip about gin but she senses it will fall flat, so she leans down to Casper and attaches a piece of Lego onto the hook of the crane.

'Get off, Mummy.' He pushes her hand away. Great, she thinks. Even her five-year-old doesn't want her around. She stands up and tries to start laughing too, just to feel less awkward, but the tears are streaming down both Ella and Liza's faces and she's too isolated to join in now.

'Come on then, darling. We'd better get going,' Sarah says as she holds out her hand to Casper, despite knowing he is going to ignore her.

'Oh no,' Ella says. 'Wait. You've only just arrived.'

That's not my fault, Sarah thinks to herself. If you'd bloody replied earlier to my text, we wouldn't be in this position.

'Please, don't go yet Sarah. Liza has to be off soon. And you really have only just arrived.'

Despite herself, Sarah feels a puff of pleasure that Ella wants her to stay.

'And besides,' she goes on. 'The kids will be so upset if they don't see . . .' she misses a beat. Can't even remember his name, Sarah thinks. 'Casper here,' Ella manages to save herself just in time. 'They always love having friends around.'

'I know but we actually have to get back for tea.' Sarah's not giving in so easily. 'I promised Casper we'd go out, didn't I darling?' He looks up and nods. Good boy, she thinks.

'Oh, do please stay for tea. Barnaby will rustle up Felix's favourite. Home-made fish and chips.' At the mention of fish and chips, Casper's head darts up.

'Fish and chips?' His eyes shine. 'Please, Mummy. Fish and chips.' He turns to Ella. 'And have you got ketchup too?'

'Ketchup? Of course we have. You can't have fish and chips without ketchup, can you?'

Sarah's surprised. She didn't quite see Ella giving her children ketchup, but Ella gets up and takes Casper by the hand. 'Come and find it with me.'

Sarah watches her little boy dutifully stand – for once – and take Ella by the hand. 'See?' she says, her long body twisting to look back. 'How can you say no to that?' Very well, thinks Sarah.

She's now left alone with Liza. It feels unbelievable that she can't think of anything to say. She refocuses on Casper and then Liza starts to talk.

'Gav's at home. I guess I'll get going. How's Tom?'

'Oh, yes OK, thank you for asking,' Sarah says, wanting to cry. Wishing she could just come out with everything, get all the guilt off her chest – after all, there's nothing they haven't shared since they'd both given birth to their first-borns. Apart from, come to think about it, that weird time Liza had gone totally AWOL on her just after Jack was born.

'He's all right,' she repeats. 'I've been thinking about you, Liza.' Silence hangs in the air. She wants, so much, to explain why she hasn't been in touch. 'How's Gav?'

'He's, you know. Gav. You spoken to him?'

'Me? Why would I have done?' Sarah snaps her head up.

'No reason.' Liza looks taken aback.

'No, no I haven't spoken to him.' They both go quiet until Liza gets up to leave.

Sarah feels hurt. Hurt that her friend pays more attention to Ella when they say their goodbyes, giving her a hearty hug, when she gets a distant kiss on the cheek. It's only when Liza and Ella go out into the corridor that she decides to give herself a mental kick where the sun don't shine. What the hell? She's nearing forty and behaving like she's at school again. She's got to take charge here. Stop playing the victim. Stop being so damn *passive*. She has to take Ella by the horns and get this situation back where she wants it. She doesn't know what's happened to her. She used to be so on top of things. Head of Marketing at Sainsbury's. And then – she had Casper, and it had all fallen to shit. Not that she's blaming parenthood, of course.

But enough of this. Most importantly right now, she needs to behave more kindly towards Liza. It doesn't matter what she knows about Gav – that's irrelevant, she's done wrong by her friend, and she won't say a word about it. She's going to forget the whole matter exists and ignore what she saw today in the IVF clinic, and she'll park the chat with Ella about the investigation and discuss it with her later.

Next, she's going to find out what the hell Ella Bradby thinks she's playing at. With both Liza and the PTA and the secret she's been harbouring all this time. And she's going to get on top of things, and become the Sarah she once was. Imposter syndrome to the max – fake it until you make it and all that. She goes into the kitchen. Barnaby is there with Casper, preparing supper for the children.

'Hi.' She sits down on one of the sleek, chrome barstools. 'I'm a friend of Ella's. Sarah. Our kids are at school together.'

Barnaby is her ticket, she thinks. Someone who probably knows all of Ella's secrets. She remembers her father's words of advice when she was a teenager, about the men she dated. *Watch how they treat staff.*

'Thank you,' she says, 'for feeding the kids.' The door slams. She can hear someone running up the stairs.

'Hey, Sarah,' Ella shouts down. 'I'm just going to send an email before the kids get back. Make yourself comfortable. I won't be long. Barnaby will look after you.'

For once, Sarah is delighted that Ella doesn't seem to want to talk to her. This way, she can have Barnaby all to herself.

'No problem,' she shouts back up. 'Take your time. I'm very happy here.'

She turns back to Barnaby. 'You must be tired,' she says and starts to sweep up some crumbs from the middle of the island. 'Here. Let me help you. It can't be easy,' she claps her hands clean over the electronic bin in the corner of the room, 'working in a house as big as this.'

'It's hard,' he says, switching on the hob. 'But Madam – she's a very good boss and her husband very kind. And her children. Perfectly behaved.'

Sarah's stomach sinks. For fuck's sake, she thinks. Of course she is. Of course her kids are perfect. She looks over at Casper, who is squeezing huge globs of ketchup onto a plate, smearing his fingers in the red sauce.

'Ah that's lovely,' she says as she walks over to the plate. She thinks back to the text message she had seen at The Vale Club. Surely, Ella would want to keep Sarah on side, not create a distance between them? She can't really understand it all. Ella is a law unto herself.

'And Sir, he's a very good dad. Very hands-on. You know some of these men. Not hands-on. But Sir, when Madam is away on the trips, well, he's always there. Up at night. Takes leave from his job to take full care of them. Very well-adjusted kids.'

'Her trips?' Sarah says, opening the fridge door and putting back the ketchup. She hardly dare turn around, the breath stuck in her chest. It must have something to do with what she'd seen on Ella's phone. She replays the message back in her mind. *That makes so much sense.*

'Of course, yes. Her big trips. I think I remember her saying,' she sings, casually. 'Where does she go?'

'Ah, just work.' Barnaby shuts down. 'Abroad. You know.'

'What kind of work?' Sarah is not going to give up easily. 'I thought Ella had stopped working?' She knows Barnaby knows something. 'Christian doesn't mind? That she's away? He's fully behind her?'

'Behind her?' says Barnaby, throwing pieces of crumbed fish into the fryer. 'Of course he's behind her. Why wouldn't he be?'

Great, she thinks. Now she sounds like a right old bitch.

'Just – that – you know.' He clearly didn't. 'If she's

not working, is she on holiday? That's amazing Christian doesn't mind. You see,' she leans forward and whispers conspiratorially. 'I wish my husband was the same. But if I even suggested so much as a spa day away, God – all hell would break loose.' She feels momentarily disloyal to Tom but shunts it aside.

'Well, Madam is obviously doing important things.' Barnaby squeezes his lips together.

Sarah thinks again of Ella's face as she had tried to snatch her phone back from her just before Jack had fallen. Important things indeed. Like trying to hide a huge lie from her husband and family, she thinks. Maybe she'll try and go upstairs, have another snoop. And when she's done, she'll present her findings to Liza.

She rubs her hands in glee and moves towards the door, feeling emboldened. Soon, life will go back to how it should be. Just her and Liza. And the debt that she owes her friend for betraying her? That would be done and dusted.

WhatsApp group: The Vale Club update
Members: Millie, Becky, Isa, Georgina

Millie: I want to take Raffy today to TPC – we haven't been since Jack fell. But I'm just worried, y'know? I don't know. This whole saga has left a sour taste in my mouth about the place.

Becky: I would hold off if I were you. *Apparently* I heard that there's something else going on. The staff at the Club are all saying that there's more to it. And that the manager keeps getting weird calls and stuff and everything's hush hush. That's what Greta told me anyway – that lady who is in charge of the memberships.

Georgina: oh my god are you serious? But what 'more to it' could there be? Jack fell. Unless . . . god, no one pushed him off or anything weird did they? Another child? Something like that?

Isa: Shit. Maybe?? I mean I can't think what other kind of thing it would be?

Millie: Jesus. I don't know. I'll try find out.

WhatsApp group: *The Fall*
Members: *Millie, Florence, Kate*

Millie: Hey ladies, Becky Granville just told me that she thinks that Jack was pushed before he fell. Or something weird happened surrounding the accident. Something that no one's talking about. Any of you guys know anything?

Florence: Pushed? Seriously? Are you sure it's not rumours getting out of hand? You know what this place is like!

Millie: Well normally I'd agree but I've just been on the Chiswick forums. Everyone is talking about it. Saying that there's something amiss. Because they're all being so coy about it at the club.

Florence: Shit. Guys. There *must* be something going on. You're right. I'm on the green with the kids and I've just seen Liza going in to Ella's . . . and then Sarah B also went in just now! They've never been friends before. Ella doesn't hang out with them. Maybe they're there to discuss it all? Sally told me they were together just before the fall.

Kate: Sarah, Liza and Ella? I've never seen them together before. Odd.

Florence: Me neither. Sarah walked straight past me without saying hello. Not sure if she clocked me or not. But she looked distant, worried. Maybe she knows something about what happened?

Kate: Maybe. Well, something weird is going on. There's an odd atmosphere around the place. And we all know the saying, don't we? No smoke without fire.

LIZA

It's Sunday morning. Gav's running late, again, to hang out with Jack after going for a haircut. Thea's having her morning nap, and Mary's gone. The doorbell goes and it's Sarah with a brown paper bag and a steaming coffee in her hand. I hadn't asked her over; it seems strange I'm now questioning why my best friend is turning up unannounced. We used to do this all the time.

'Here,' she passes the bag to me. 'From that new place that looks amazing – Fed and Watered.' She doesn't say anything about the day before at Ella's. No apologies for not turning up for Jack's homecoming. Just walks in as normal, plonking her bag down before she sits next to Jack.

'Hello little man,' she says, giving him an oat and raisin cookie. 'I brought your favourite. Casper might pop over later too. He's at home watching telly in bed with Tom. We've all been talking about you non-stop.'

She breaks it into small pieces for him. She doesn't look at me, but I know she's trying to make things right. I know she's trying to get our friendship back on an even footing. Yet, I'm still angry with her, even though I tell myself I'm being silly and childish.

'Thank you, Aunty Sarah,' says Jack. My heart swells. Still so polite, even when he's in pain.

'Did Ella tell you anything yesterday by the way, when I was out of the room?' she asks, staring at Jack's Spider Man duvet cover. She looks like she's deliberately avoiding my gaze.

'Tell me anything about what, exactly?' I push, but she crosses her arms and looks away. 'Sarah?'

'Nothing,' she says a little too brightly. 'Just wondering what you guys spoke about.' A beat of silence and then she changes the subject. 'Did she mention her trips abroad then? About going away or anything?'

'No,' I reply. 'What trips abroad? Is this what you came over to ask me?'

'Oh don't worry,' she ignores my dig. 'Just I thought I overheard her saying something about some private big thing she's doing. Just being nosey, that's all.'

'We didn't talk about anything of importance you know. Just chit-chat.' Sarah visibly slumps her shoulders, as if in relief – as if I've just told her she's got a free holiday with childcare thrown in. 'It was nice. What's up? You seem to have gone off her all of a sudden.'

'I haven't. It's just that . . .' She picks up a crumb of cookie off the wrapping and puts it on her tongue. 'It's just that, well I don't know. I was just wondering if there really is more to Ella than she lets on. You know. All this polished nonsense. This image of, like, oh look at me,' she screws up her face. 'Well, I'm sure behind closed doors, it's not all as perfect as it looks.'

'Probably not.' When Sarah's in this kind of mood I just have to ride it out, allow her to get everything she's been harbouring overnight off her chest. I want to ask her if that's why she's come over, rather than to see me, or Jack. 'But she's quite open about everything.'

'I bet she is,' she says with such vehemence that a fleck of her saliva lands by my feet.

'Well, you don't need to worry,' I tell her. 'She may look like she has it all, but you're much more fun than Ella Bradby.'

'That's not what I'm worried about. Except with the comparison you've just acknowledged the fact that I'm definitely not as perfect as her. But it's not that.'

I wonder whether I should push it. Ask her if not that, then *what*? But I sense it best not to pursue the conversation further.

'You don't need to worry about anything, Sa.' I lean over and squeeze her wrist, because, sometimes, all Sarah needs is a bit of reassurance. 'Why ever would you need to?'

'Well . . .'

'She may have a nice house and look like a celebrity. And indeed, once screwed one. But, she's not you. Is she?'

I feel sorry for Sarah when she's in this frame of mind. Something sets her off and she can't ever quite seem to shake the stream of negativity in her mind, often leaving it to me to pick up the pieces. Except at the moment, I don't have the emotional bandwidth to keep Sarah's emotional fallout at bay. And she should know this. Perhaps she'll realise, take that side of things into hand and stop making me a repository for her insecurities.

'No. But what would you do if she *was* hiding things? If she wasn't quite the person you thought she was?'

'Why are you out to get her?' I feel the earlier irritation

rising again. I've given her the reassurance she needs. Can't she just drop it? 'I don't want to hear anything bad about Ella,' I tell her. 'Not now. Not with Jack – no negativity. And after all she did for me. It feels wrong, OK? And like I said. She's not you.'

'Fine.' Her scowl stretches into a half smile and then she looks at Jack and something crosses her expression.

'I can't stop thinking about it,' she says, nodding at my little boy. 'The moment he fell.'

I'm still not ready for Jack to hear us talking about it. Not yet. And perhaps, in truth, I'm not ready myself to revisit what happened. And neither by the looks of things is Sarah – she's shaking from head to toe. Without answering her question, I motion for her to be quiet. She leans forward and strokes his hair.

'I'm here for you,' she whispers. I've never seen such a serious expression on her face. 'I'm here for you for whatever you need, whenever you need. OK?'

'Well, you're having us as guests in your home. That's enough,' I tell her. 'Gav of course doesn't want me to go.' It feels good to confide in Sarah after my earlier annoyance. To show my vulnerabilities to her after the weird dynamic that had been put in place since Jack's accident. 'He was going mad about it all if I'm honest.'

As if on cue, my phone pings. It's him. **Everything ok?** he asks, not for the first time that day.

'Was he now,' Sarah says. 'Well, I think it will be really good for you to have your own life. Without anyone constantly questioning you.' She nods her head as though agreeing with herself.

Lots of feelings pass through me at this point. Irritation that she's implying I can't stand up to Gav, probably because I know it's the truth. Then anger. Then a weird sense of loyalty to him. And then guilt again for what happened to Jack. It's exhausting and, to top it off, my sleep problems have come back in full force.

'Me too,' I say, not wanting to get into an argument about my ex-husband's behaviour. 'Hey, by the way, Gav also said something about Tom wanting to rent the flat out? He doesn't mind about me, Jack and Thea, right? You're sure it's OK?'

'I'm sure,' she says, but she doesn't look me in the eye. 'Course I'm sure. He's fine with it all.'

'Great. I'd hate to think that we would come between you two.'

'Nah. You come first in this situation,' she says. 'Especially . . .'

'Especially what?'

'Just, well, especially. He's really happy we can help.' Sarah always does the same thing when she lies. She grasps at her necklace, although today I see she's not wearing one and her fingers just graze her neck. But, I absolutely cannot believe that Tom *wouldn't* be happy to help. I must have it wrong. After all, Gav's one of his best friends too.

'Wanna hand packing?' She half stands up. 'The flat's all done, so whenever you feel ready.'

'Don't worry,' I tell her. 'I'm going to start it later. I've actually got a bit of a headache. Again. I'm not sure why. They keep creeping up on me. Lack of sleep, I suppose.'

'You have? Oh no, go and lie down right away. I'll stay here with Jack. It's probably stress, you know.'

'You mind if I just go upstairs for ten minutes? I won't have a full-on lie-down. Just a moment's quiet.'

'Of course I don't mind. Do I need to give Jack anything? Meds or anything?'

'It's OK – we've got a private physio coming today. I gave him his meds earlier. Thank you, though.' I leave the room. Thank God Sarah seems a little more normal after her tirade about Ella.

I walk up the stairs right to the top of the house. When I reach my bedroom, I do some neck exercises. Rolling my head. Stretching my muscles, except everything just seems to get worse. I had felt the pain slowly at first, moments after Sarah had arrived. It had wrapped itself around the bridge of my nose, and then tightened its noose – like a blunt trauma to my face.

This is the second bad headache I've had in the past week. I'm not normally very anxious about my health. But I sit on the bed and I think about the pain. How much it reminds me of when I'd just had Jack. The way my skin felt like it was burning from fatigue, and then it all comes flooding back to me – those newborn days with my son. The constant screaming and crying. The funny, colicky, choking noise he would make in his sleep. I never knew what was normal or not. In the end, I'd watch over the rise and fall of his fluttering chest, until I heard the sound of the bin lorries chugging their way up and down our road, the sunlight bringing around yet another day. Thank God Thea, so far, has been an easy baby. An easy sleeper.

I shut my eyes. All these thoughts jostling for attention when all I really need is to numb myself with some shut-eye. I don't know if I can pack and look after Jack and Thea feeling like this. I could ask Sarah but I sense she wants to get back to her own family. And God knows she seems on edge too. I text Gav, asking him to come back soon instead of going clothes shopping. After everything that happened after Jack had been born, I wouldn't be surprised if he came racing back, desperate to start breathing down my neck again.

I need a hand, I type.

I'll come back soon, he replies straight away.

I wonder if he really is clothes shopping. And his haircut too? He never normally gives two hoots about his appearance; generally, he can pull off any look he wants without making any effort at all. And anyway, he always goes to the vintage shop in East London to get his clothes, which isn't actually open on a Sunday. Why had he been so late to come and see Jack the other day, too? He seems so distant, and off. It's like I don't know the man I'm married to at all.

I open the wardrobe to get out a jumper and stare at the now half-empty side that used to hold all of Gav's clothes – his multitude of colourful jackets and suede shoes. His rows of old rock band T-shirts: The Rolling Stones, The Kinks, The Ramones, and then the more obscure ones that he'd wear on nights out. The reminders of his absence are everywhere, and yet still – still he won't let me go.

SARAH

Sarah has a sense that Liza doesn't want her in the house. She doesn't know why, really. It's just something she's picked up on. She tells herself maybe it's just everything on her friend's mind. The fact she'd been feeling off earlier with a headache and mentioned she hadn't been sleeping. And anyway, as Liza's best friend she needs to make sure she's there to pick up the pieces. Which is exactly what she's doing, isn't it? The school Christmas fair, them moving in. But maybe Liza just needs a bit of space. After all, the physio is arriving soon, Gav's apparently on his way back, and she doesn't want to be in the way. By the time Liza comes back downstairs, Sarah's made up her mind.

'Hey, I'm going to make us some tea and then make my way home. Shall I take Thea with me? Whilst the physio comes for Jack?'

'Home? Already?' Liza sounds so surprised that Sarah wonders if maybe she got it wrong. Maybe she does need her after all.

'Well, I just thought that you could do with some space.'

'It's OK. Could you just wait with me for Gav to get back?'

'Oh, of course. I wasn't trying to go. I was just aware you might want to be alone.' Strange, she thinks. Liza is mostly one to enjoy her own company.

'No. Go if you need to. It's important you spend time with your family too. Before we move in.'

Sarah wonders whether she's imagining the note of resentment in her friend's tone. 'But I don't mind staying at all. Of course I'll stay until Gav's here.'

Oh God, she thinks. It's coming out all wrong. She wants to tell Liza she'll be there for her. She doesn't know whether to stay or go. Why is she second-guessing everything? Why can't she just do the right thing, for once in her life?

'OK.' Sarah claps her hands on her knees and stands up. 'Right. I'm going to make us a nice cuppa.'

Liza seems slightly cheered by this.

She feels a bit bad about Tom and how little time they've spent together recently, but they have a lifetime of it after all. And she still has to tell him about Liza, Thea and Jack moving in. She swallows back a sour taste. Shit. What the hell is he going to say?

'Listen, we haven't set a date. For you moving in. Anytime from Tuesday is fine. I can help drive over everything.' If she's got a deadline, she thinks, she'll soon be forced into telling Tom.

'Great. Tuesday,' says Liza. Sarah can't quite place it but she swears there's something off about her friend. She wonders if she knows – if somehow Liza knows what she did and is waiting. For retribution. Or to find the right time to probe her about the accident. She starts to shake. Or maybe Ella had said something after

190

all and Liza has been keeping it under her hat until the right moment. Surely Liza wouldn't trap her like that?

She's playing this all wrong. She needs Ella on side. She needs to up her game. Oh God. How has it come to this?

'Perfect,' she trills. 'Lovely. Tuesday it is. Earl Grey?'

'Coffee,' Liza frowns. 'When have I ever had Earl Grey? That's Ella . . . But actually, I don't think I'll have any caffeine. I'm trying to sort my sleep. I'll have herbal. Thank you.'

'Oh gosh. Sorry.' No caffeine. A first time for everything. Liza really must be tired. Sarah runs into the kitchen and prepares the drinks. She sees the candles that Ella had brought for when Jack came home, the wax half-sunken, and picks out a wick that's embedded itself right down into the wax. Great globs of white stick into her fingernails. She presses a bit harder and thinks of Ella. A bit like a voodoo doll. She finishes making the drinks, brings one back to Liza and thinks about her next steps. She wants to discuss things, have a nice chat with her friend, but an awkward tension hangs in the air. Instead they both focus on Jack, who is looking at pictures on Liza's phone.

'What's that then, Jack?' asks Liza.

'A llama?'

'That's right darling,' claps Sarah. 'Do you remember when we saw that llama at the zoo?'

She turns to Liza, but she doesn't hear her. And just as she's about to say something else, Jack tracks his gaze towards her.

'Hey, Aunty Sarah. Were you there? Did I see you?'

Oh God, she thinks. This is it. He's remembering

now. The fall. The moments before. He must have over-heard someone talking about how she'd been there to check on him before the accident. And now he knows she's lying. She supposes the anaesthetic is wearing off. He'll be more with it as the days pass. She should have thought about all of this. She grips her hands together and manages a smile, ready to spout out her rehearsed lines.

'Oh,' laughs Jack. 'I remember now, Casper was there – he wanted to see the lions – but not you.'

'Ah yes,' Sarah says, burning with an adrenaline over-load. 'Oh the *zoo*. Yes. Oh yes,' she squeaks. 'You mean the zoo. Of course I was there. Wouldn't leave you and your mummy to go on a special day without me, would I?' She's overcompensating now, relief making her almost hysterical.

'Look, Liza,' she says, dizzy with it all. 'Let me sit here with Jack. Please. Thea's going to wake up soon. You go to sleep. Please. You look exhausted.'

She's speaking but she has no control over any part of herself. This is a terrifying glimpse into her future, where anything that anyone says or does could have a potentially lethal double meaning. Christ. *What has she done?* She swallows, the poison of her thoughts seeping through her limbs.

'I need to stay awake until Gav gets back.' Sarah recognises this strange mood in Liza. She thinks back to when Jack was tiny. The few weeks before Liza had gone totally AWOL. She had discussed it night after night with Tom.

'I think she's got postnatal depression,' she had said. 'Or something. How can I help her? She's not sleeping. She's being weird.'

'Are you mad? Are any of us sleeping? Or is Liza's sleep more important than ours?'

'No, it's not just that. She's all, like, shaky and odd and . . . I don't know. She said something happened the other day and ever since then it's just, she's been quite distant.' And then her friend had gone missing for weeks on end. Initially, Sarah thought she'd been ghosted. Until she realised no one else had seen her either.

'Talk to her?' Tom had said. And boy, had she tried. Sarah had called and called, and hadn't laid eyes on Liza once during that entire period. She had even texted Gav to ask what was going on.

She's just going through some stuff, he had replied. She'll be back soon. Her *little disappearing act*, she had called it, and neither of them had ever mentioned it again.

By the time Gav gets home, Liza's pacing the floor, looking twitchy. Sarah wants to tell her that the more worked up she gets, the less she's going to be able to sleep. But she knows it won't go down well, so she keeps her mouth shut.

'I'm back.' Gav slams the door shut, looking around the room to check everything is in place. 'Everything OK? Kids OK?'

'Yup,' Sarah says. She looks over at Liza who seems to have been struck dumb, the air pulsing with Gav's angry presence. 'I'm going to make a move now, I'll leave you alone. Liza needs to sleep.'

'Well, I'm here now, so she can. Although I've got to pop out in a bit. So if you do really have to go, do it now.'

'She's pretty desperate for some shut-eye. Aren't you, Liza?' Sarah tries to be loyal. To get Gav to understand that Liza really is exhausted. 'We all know what happens when we're deprived of sleep, don't we?'

She laughs but doesn't expect the mutinous expressions from both Liza and Gav; the dark look on his face as he snaps his head towards the children. And then the inquisitive look towards Liza – which she reads as: *What have you told Sarah, what does she know?* How peculiar. But then this whole thing is peculiar, she thinks. Suddenly she can't wait to escape this horrible atmosphere that's descended upon them.

'Anyway, Gav, you got anything nice planned?' She tries to keep her voice on the straight and narrow.

'Not really. I'm going up to The Vale Club. Make sure they're running the investigation properly. Doing the right things.'

'Really?' She pinches the fleshy bit of her left palm, still reeling from thinking Jack was about to out her.

'Yup. They've been quite on it so far but they're going to want to talk to the people involved.'

'Like me?' she manages to say. 'Will they want to talk to me?'

'I believe so. I'll see what they say later. They've brought health and safety in from outside. And now they'll want to chat to the people who were there.'

'OK.' She doesn't know how on earth she's managing to stay calm. 'Bye then everyone,' she shouts, but Liza has already disappeared upstairs and Jack and Gav barely register she's leaving. 'Bye,' she shouts again then shuts the door behind her.

When she finally gets home, she collapses on the sofa with Tom and Casper.

'Why are you so fidgety?' says Tom, patting the cushion. 'It's like you've got ants in your pants.'

'Don't talk to me like I'm Casper,' she snaps. She finds a position in which she doesn't feel quite so sick. 'I'm just so, so glad to see you both,' she rolls over and leans into them. 'So happy to see you.'

'Don't be daft.' Tom pats her head as if she's a dog. 'You've only been gone a couple of hours.'

'Feels like an absolute lifetime. You're watching *Paddington Bear*? Again? It must be the tenth time you've seen this film.' She snuggles up into Casper's warm body, feeling like she wants to sob. 'So glad you are here.'

'Me too,' Tom grabs her hand. 'It's been a tough old week. Liza OK?'

'Sure has,' she says. 'And yes. Liza's OK.' She's too exhausted to explain what happened and she can't bring herself to mention the investigation, the words strangling her. Tom closes his eyes.

Sarah pulls out her phone. Now she has a minute's peace, she's going to face up to a few things. After that, she'll cook lunch for them all and *then* she'll tell Tom that Liza's moving in. She shuffles her body to the side, so no one can see her screen, and she starts to do some searches.

She types in *The Vale Club* first. That's about the best she can do, for the moment. Slowly does it. She scans down the list of results. Nothing, other than links to the websites of all the different *Vale Club* clubs around England. She's going to have to brave it. Go right in at the deep end. *The Vale Club, boy fall, West London.* Her finger hovers over the enter button. Can she do this? Yes she can. She presses the arrow key.

When the page is fully loaded, she flicks down the screen. There are forums dedicated to *Five-year-old fractures neck in West London's Vale Club* on just about every single parenting website there is – let alone the local West London forums. There's chat on Mumsnet,

Facebook pages, there's even a piece about it in the *West London Rascals Magazine*, which she can't bring herself to read. *The Vale Club Loses Members After Five-Year-Old Boy Fractures His Neck.*

She thinks there's something lodged in her throat, until she realises she's choking on her own breath. Everyone is talking about it. How can she have missed all this? She scrolls down further to see all the other forums dedicated to the fall. She reads about how The Vale Club members are baying for blood. There's even a Twitter hashtag *#boyfallatTheValeClub*. Oh good God. She hears herself make a spluttering noise. This is all her doing. She's been burying her head in the sand for the last couple of days, keeping busy, consuming herself with Ella Bradby's motives. But seeing all *this* online brings the cold truth firmly home. What will she do? She certainly cannot come clean now. She wants to. How she wants to. Maybe if she says something this minute, it will all go away. But then her imagination goes into full pelt. Headlines scroll across her mind's eye. *Best friend of mum to blame for boy's fall.* She imagines all the journalists outside her house waiting to catch her; the parents at school looking out for her to put any foot wrong. And then Liza – after everything Liza has done for her.

'You OK?' Tom leans over. She snatches her phone away from him.

'Fine.'

'You're making these weird gasping noises. Like you've got sleep apnoea. Whilst you're awake.'

'I'm fine,' she says again.

She puts down her phone. Then picks it up again. She quickly types *Ella Bradby* into Facebook, careful to ensure she's not inputting her current status. When she reaches Ella's profile, she scrolls through her timeline and looks at her header. It's her and Christian on some beach somewhere looking impossibly glamorous.

She scrolls through all of Ella's friends, feeling grateful that she'd had the guts to befriend her all those years ago. She remembers how her finger hovered over the request button. *Should she? Shouldn't she?*

Ella had posted a fair bit right up until Felix had been born and then it had all stopped. No one had commented on her page – nothing. Until very recently. Strange. Obviously Sarah had spent a fair bit of time stalking Ella's photos after she'd first met her at NCT. Examining the people in them. Clicking on the tags, careful not to inadvertently 'like' an image, or befriend someone. But now, now she is going to do some proper detective work. She is going to delve deeper into Ella's life and find out if there are any hints about her 'big trips'. Just as she's got about forty tabs open and thinks she's getting some-where, Tom's phone pings.

'Bloody thing.' He opens one eye and shuts it again. But then he grabs the phone towards him.

'Weird,' he says. 'Message from Gav.' He re-scans the text and then looks over at Sarah. 'He says – *let's go for a drink when Liza and the kids move into yours. Catch up mate, it's been a long time. Thanks for having them by the way. I know they'll be safe with you.*' He shifts his whole body weight up. Sarah can feel the energy around him shifting. Casper pulls the remote control towards him.

'Daddy, be quiet,' he says. 'Mummy, can you turn it up?'

'What does he mean?' Tom's voice rises a few notches. Sarah puts her phone down and bites her lip. What is she meant to say? She had planned it all carefully. She was going to ask Tom first how he felt that Liza was all alone. And then build herself up to come out with it. Now that's all scuppered she has no clue what to do – and anyway, she's still reeling from finding out how many people are talking about Jack's fall. She just can't be dealing with this too.

'I . . . I was going to say something to you first,' she stands up. 'But you'd said no. You made it so difficult to even discuss it. Guilt-tripping me into agreeing with you. And, well, Liza is all alone. I was there, Tom. I saw the whole thing. But of course,' she's shouting now. She can't stop herself. Casper turns up the volume. 'Of course you got your way.'

She wishes she could admit what's really on her mind. That she has wronged her friend. She so desperately wants to rid herself of this ache around her chest. But she knows she cannot. She wants to cry. She wants to tell Tom that she knows he's right.

'Look. I'm sorry,' she takes a breath and changes tack. 'I'm sorry I didn't say anything. I was going to tell you.'

'Well, un-tell them.' He stands too, placing his palms flat against the wall. 'Bloody well do it. Now.'

'You know I can't do that.'

'You can and you will.'

'For God's sake,' she explodes. 'It's two weeks. That's what I told her. Two weeks.' *A lie.* She'll have to remember to tell Liza. 'Surely you can survive it for two weeks. I'll start preparing the Airbnb listings now then, shall I? So you know there's a cut-off point. So we all do. I'll say that we will start taking renters in two weeks. And if you must know, she needs to get away from Gav. I think he's dangerous.'

Tom snorts in her face. He actually snorts. She doesn't know where to start.

'Gav? Dangerous? Gav? You must be off your head, Sarah. I've thought you've been acting a bit odd lately. But this? You're positively deluded. And you know she'll stay longer. Liza and the kids. She'll rely on you. Of course she will. Just get a little bit cosy. Away from Gav. If you say he's so *dangerous*. And I know what you're like. You'll get so wrapped up in trying to help and then we'll never get on with trying for number . . .' Sadness crosses his expression.

'Three,' she interrupts. 'Number three.' They both go quiet. 'Of course she's not going to stay. If she knows in advance. OK? Give me two weeks. Please, Tom. Please. I'll do the listing on Airbnb today. So I'm on top of it.'

She thinks about telling him about the appointment at the IVF clinic on Thursday to change the subject totally, but she knows that's going beyond the pale.

'Fine,' he sits back down, crosses his arms and slumps back onto the pillow. 'Do it now. I want the bookings coming in for two weeks' time exactly. OK? So everyone knows where they stand.'

Sarah breathes a sigh of relief. 'Fine. I'm doing it.'

She picks up her phone and opens up her browser. Screw him, she thinks. She'll have to pluck up the courage to tell Liza she needs to move out in a fortnight. And that if that's too short a time for her, then to stay at home. But Liza's packed already and, *oh God*. How will she explain?

She types *Airbnb* into the Google search bar. But then she remembers what she was doing earlier. She was in the middle of looking up Ella Bradby on Facebook. She'll have a quick look at her profile again and then she'll go back to the Airbnb listing. She flicks onto the familiar blue page and taps on *Ella's friends*.

There's seven hundred and sixty-two of them. She starts slowly at first, skimming through each and every one. She recognises a few celebrities. TV presenters and the likes. But no one massive. There are pictures of Ella and her family. Sarah clicks on their links but they've all been totally closed off to the public. She sees a few of the school mums in the other class. How have they befriended Ella, she thinks. She carries on scrolling.

There! There he is. The actor linked to Ella, Rufus North! It's got to be. Something inside her takes flight.

'You going OK?' asks Tom. 'With the listing? Make sure you show me later, yeah?'

'Hmmm? Yes. Yes. It's good,' Sarah says, her tongue sticking to the roof of her mouth. 'Yup. I'll show you later. But shhh, I need to concentrate.'

She clicks on Rufus North's profile. It's got to be him. And of course, his profile is going to be blocked to the public. But when she opens it up, she sees that it's open. Hurrah! And look! All those albums she can nosey into. There must be some information there on Ella. Some old photos. Look – there are even pictures of him filming that Merchant Ivory piece from the noughties. He did that film right at the time he was supposedly seeing Ella. Sarah remembers googling her right after their first NCT class in wonderment – staring at old pictures and footage of them both: of Ella's forever legs on the red carpet, his arm wrapped tightly around her waist, her smiling right into the camera. How she'd told people she *sort of knew him* after that.

Maybe – just maybe – she'll find out more of Ella's secrets here. Maybe there'll be some information about why Ella is taking these big trips now, because Sarah knows it's all linked to her past. It all fits into the puzzle somehow, the mystery of Ella Bradby. Then she stumbles on some photo of a party from a couple of weeks ago. She scans the background.

'Ella's launch party,' it says. She types in the company name that's emblazoned on all the balloons with the green logo underneath it. Not one thing is returned on Google, except a link to Companies House. *Echo Limited. Directors, Ella and Christian Bradby*, it reads. How weird. And then she spots some of the school mums in the background and she forgets to carry on her search for the company, because she's wondering how she's got from Rufus North to Miriam and the other mums in one fell swoop. She cannot for the life of her work out how she's arrived at this point. She's trying to connect the dots. It's all so strange. Do they all know each other? Is there some weird conspiracy going on? And is this company something to do with Ella's big trip? She hadn't thought so – she was sure it had been to do with the WhatsApp message she'd seen just before Jack's fall. So many questions, so little time it seems, before the Christmas fair, before things really get hectic. She feels a slight swell of panic. What on earth is she going to do?

And as she thinks about the fair, her to-do list starts creeping into her thoughts, before rocketing right through her brain – *Casper's homework, Liza moving in, renting out the flat when she moves out* . . . But somehow, despite all of this, she still manages to be distracted and fixated by Ella Bradby. She doesn't know why she bothers. Why she can't just get her out of her mind. It isn't as if she can ever bridge the gap between her and Ella from a superficial point of view. But Sarah's entire being demands – no – *craves* Ella's attention. It's as though her entire identity has become embroiled in Ella's approval, or *something* that to her is still indefinable. And if she gets it? Perhaps – then – she'll feel good enough.

LIZA

'He's doing so well,' Jan, the physio, says as she packs her things into a small, black holdall and turns towards Jack. 'The movement in his arm is picking up and I think his muscles are strengthening. You're doing so brilliantly, aren't you, young man?' I notice Jack doesn't reply. 'OK then, bye.' She ruffles his head and he scowls at her. 'And that little cutie over there,' she nods her head towards Thea, 'is so well-behaved. Look at her just chilling in her bouncer.'

'Yes she is. Gosh, sorry,' I laugh. 'It's not like Jack not to say goodbye. But – he's probably just exhausted. Aren't you darling?' I think about my own heavy limbs. I'm a bit stronger, but still feel like I could sleep for a decade.

I show Jan out and then I come back into the room. The lights have been dimmed and there's a soft sound of classical music coming from the other room.

'You OK, J?' I lean over and unclip Thea from her bouncer, kissing her soft cheek. 'Not surprised you feel like this to be honest. You don't need to put on a brave face at the moment, OK? I'm not saying don't be polite.

Just – if you don't feel up to talking, don't. Save your energy.' I stand up and then Jack says something inaudible.

'Sorry?' I step towards him.

'Milk,' he says. 'Or juice.'

'No problem. Are we missing a word here, young man?' I keep a lightness to my voice. He doesn't need me haranguing him, after all. But he doesn't say anything, just stares right at the ceiling.

'Jack? Like I just said, I know you are feeling bad, but just say please.' I stand there, waiting for his usual little voice to pipe up. *Please Mummy*. But it doesn't come. I'm torn. Set the boundaries, or just let it go. I tell myself to stop. That I have to let it go and that I just need to get through this. Jack can forget his manners today.

'OK. I'm going to get you some milk. But when you're feeling up to it I want a please, or thank you. Can you manage that?'

Silence.

'Jack,' I snap. I feel bad then. I turn back to him. 'Jack. Are you OK? Sorry. I didn't mean to . . . I just – are you feeling OK?'

I rest my hand on his forehead. He feels normal.

'Just feeling down, are you? I'm not surprised, my love. I'll be back in a sec.'

I tell myself to keep calm. That Jack needs peace and quiet. I bring him a cold glass of milk, but when I try and angle the straw into his mouth, he resists.

'I'll leave it just by you. Please tell me when you want some. I'm just going to quickly feed Thea.'

By the time Gav arrives, Thea is screaming to high heaven, Jack is listening to *The Twits* on audio book and I'm clenching my jaw tight.

'Where have you been?' I ask lightly, although it feels like my insides are being boiled. 'Just that you said you were coming back.'

'I nipped into The Vale Club on my way home.' He pats Thea on the back. 'Tired, are you?'

'She's had her nap.' I try and keep the triumph out of my voice. 'Why did you stop there?'

'To meet Arlene, the manager of the whole club. She's having a meeting with the staff first thing tomorrow. I wanted to make sure she's on it and going down the right route. Everyone's up in arms about it too. So they've got to do something.'

'Up in arms?' I had heard bits and bobs – but I suppose with looking after Jack so intensely, I'd totally stayed away from all forms of social media.

'Yup,' he nods his head but doesn't say any more. I wonder if he's protecting me from something.

'Are you sure it's wise? Chasing it up with the club? I mean – as you keep telling me – I should have been . . .' I fumble for the right words. This is only going to highlight the fact I was inside the club, and not outside watching over Jack. 'I mean – you know – I was inside. When it happened.' I hadn't even felt bad about it until Gav had brought it up. I had been keeping an eye on Jack after all. And of course, Sarah had checked on him. She said so.

'But there still needs to be an investigation into what actually happened. That area is meant to be a safe zone, isn't it? I mean, who knows if the post was unstable, or anything like that. They've taken it down now. Not before health and safety did a check though.'

'I see what you mean. Oh, by the way,' I say, eager to change the subject, 'I've got some reading practice for

Jack from his teacher. A few school projects they're doing in class, that are meant to be fun. She said he can do them from his bed if we help him. So that'll be good for him to do the same things as his friends.'

'Fine,' Gav says. 'I saw his teaching assistant earlier today, she said they all miss him a lot.'

I feel like I need to get some air into my lungs. 'I'm going to head out for a quick stroll,' I say. I need a breather, the house suddenly feels claustrophobic. I hand Thea to him, grab my keys and run before he can even question it.

By the time I get back, Thea's gurgling and hungry. I don't have the energy to feed her myself right now.

'I bought formula.' I hand him the orange bag. 'Can you feed her?'

'You aren't feeding?' He takes the bag but doesn't open it. 'How come?'

'I've got mastitis.' I don't want to explain but I'm feeling tired. Guilt rips through me, but I need a break. I think about Jack and the time I'd stopped feeding him myself. The constant undercurrents of recriminations. *You do know that breast is best?* But – at that point, for me – it hadn't been. My mind starts to spiral.

'If you must-itis know,' he replies.

We both laugh and then I stop, waiting for some sort of grenade to be thrown into the conversation. It's the first time he's made one of his awful jokes for a long, long time and it's caught me totally off guard, this glimpse of the old Gav. My stomach sinks, wondering what's coming next – if this is the calm before the storm, and whether he's prepping me for something much worse. I feel wobbly. Or maybe he genuinely is feeling happier. Less stressed about something. Perhaps he's actually relieved that I'll be moving out; realising that some space between us can only be a good thing. That he can still watch the kids growing up from afar and that I am, despite his thoughts, despite the things that have happened, a good mother.

'I wish you'd stop that.'

'What?'

'Making light of everything.'

I try and act all cross but I'm so pleased that there's been some shared camaraderie that it's virtually impossible. Gav looks pleased too, at his own crappy joke and the fact it's been appreciated. I look over at Jack, he's smiling as well now, his little molars gleaming in the light. With Gav appeased, and Thea about to have some milk, it feels to me, for one tiny moment, that everything has been forgotten. Like we are a real family again.

West London Gazette editorial notes, October 2019
J Roper interview transcript: Callie Simcha, witness, The
Vale Club

I'm twenty-six years old. I've got a boyfriend but we haven't even discussed having kids. In fact it's the furthest thing from my mind. I think we'd both freak out at having that conversation. Especially when we go to The Vale Club together and we see parenting in its full glory. It's like the mums and their prams rule the world there. Or they think they do anyway. The dads are often even worse in truth. They pretend they're all, like – oh sorry we're in your way, are we? But then they don't move a muscle.

They come barging into me, without even noticing I'm there. I understand it must be difficult to be lugging a pram along with screaming children – but we exist too, you know. Us child-free people. The other day this woman bashed me in the head on the bus with her kid's scooter, which she had slung over her shoulder. I flipped. It fucking hurt! She was carrying her other kid and looked really harassed. You know, the type of mum that will never wear make-up again.

I swore at her under my breath. I'd had a bad day

too. My mum's in hospital with early onset dementia. My job is full on. Yet of course why should that matter? This mum can't get on the sodding bus properly with all her shopping and she can't even muster up the decency to say sorry. And then her kids were screaming, and she was getting more and more stressed. She was obviously one of those women that would sit at a wedding with the kids rioting through the service – not thinking that anyone else might like to hear what's going on. It's like – just leave. Just take your screaming brats outside.

Anyway, when she heard me muttering to her that she should have bloody well apologised, she had the absolute cheek to say to me: 'Just you wait until you have kids. You'll see what it's like then.'

I wanted to go mad at her there and then. I was thinking: how do you know I can even have children? I could be infertile, for all she knew. Or not want them at all. I wanted to say, you aren't reinventing the wheel you know. Millions of mothers have done this before you. Some with no money. Some under awful circumstances. Yet you think that for some reason, the world owes you a favour – you with the nice house and perfect kids, because you feel a bit stressed on the bloody bus.

Phew. Sorry. I didn't mean to let off such a rant. I'm sorry. It's just that if she had behaved like a normal human being, I might have thought a bit differently.

Anyway – all of this meant that I didn't realise at first what had happened when that little boy fell at The Vale Club. All I saw was this woman running – she was sitting in the soft-play area and then she suddenly got up and barged past me as I was leaving the club. I swore at her then too. But she was doing this weird jagged breathing thing, like she was about to freak out but trying to stay *calm. So she definitely wasn't with him at the time. Which is another thing – why are these mothers so bloody stressed out if all they're doing is drinking coffee whilst they aren't even with their kids?*

But anyway – I just thought, oh, another mother, pushing into me – not even giving anyone else a second thought. But then this weird atmosphere settled just as I was leaving – and I stuck around for a bit in reception just to see what was going on. I heard them on the phone to the ambulance, saying something about the boy falling and that it was serious. I had a horrible taste in my mouth for the rest of the day because I mean – they may be annoying – those mums and dads, but obviously, no one deserves something as awful as that.

SARAH

By the time Tuesday rolls around, Sarah is feeling more positive. In some part it's down to where she is in her monthly cycle. In other parts it's down to the fact that Tom has come round to Liza and the kids moving in – for just the two weeks, mind – and of course her own role that she has to play in making things up to her best friend. At least she can get moving on that now. At least there's no more dreadful waiting, the itching sensation that she needs to do *something* but she just doesn't know *what*.

And then there's Ella. Sarah had spent the best part of nine hours stalking her on Facebook. Oh, the things she'd managed to glean from doing her extensive search! She'd found some old photos of Ella and Rufus North, tucked away in one of about four hundred albums on Rufus' profile. They hadn't been easy to find. But she'd stuck to her guns and kept going and the rewards had been great and she thinks she has a surer idea now of what is going on. Except there is still the missing period from after Felix had been born, when

Ella had gone totally silent. She'll have to find out about that another way.

Tom leaves for work humming and singing. Thank God he's in a good mood this morning. It's OK for him, she thinks. Going off to George Jones' new restaurant for lunch with a client.

'Any more thoughts on your birthday?' he says, as she unloads the dishwasher.

'Hmmm. Yes. Anything,' she replies. 'Although nothing big actually. I still like the idea of Oban. Just you and me.'

She can't think of anything worse than having to put on a cheery face in front of a crowd at the moment. Then it crosses her mind she still hasn't told him about the IVF appointment. Maybe she'll mention it in the morning on Thursday, after she drops Casper off and before the morning meeting about the Christmas fair. That will be a busy day and so there'll be no room for discussion about the whole thing, which is exactly how she wants it; fair, then lunch then IVF appointment then pick-up.

And there are a million and one other things she has to do in between. Help buy Liza's shopping. Type up the agenda meeting from the fair. She wants to be *on it*. She had to be. After all, she'd become detective, helper, PTA organiser, mother and all the rest in the space of about two weeks. She isn't used to all this. And then she remembers Liza's contact. The one from the old people's home that she'd tried to link her up with for work. *Shit*. She needs to ring them too – she's been meaning to. They'd left a message just before the weekend that she's only just picked up. She's got to do that before Liza moves in and asks her. It's OK, she thinks. The busier she is, the more she'll forget about the incident with Jack.

And then she wonders why she hasn't told Tom about the IVF appointment. He's agreed to let Liza move in, so she no longer needs it as leverage. Is she scared about it? Or is it something else? She can't quite put her finger on the feeling.

'Oh, by the way.' She hands Tom his keys from the kitchen sideboard. 'Before you go,' she leans down and shuts a drawer that Casper is opening and closing. 'Don't do that, darling, you'll trap your fingers. I said, don't do that. For God's sake.' She sighs; she doesn't need more stress this morning. 'Before you go, have you spoken to Gav lately?'

'Gav?'

'Er. Yes. Gav. You know. One of your best mates? Lives two roads from us?'

'Right. Casper, *what did Mummy say*?' Tom leans down and presses his foot against the drawer. 'Sorry. What were you saying? Have I spoken to Gav?'

'Yes.'

'Oh – I'm seeing him tonight actually. Liza's moving in with the kids today, right?'

Casper starts to whine and moves over to another drawer that he starts slamming open and shut.

'Yes. Today. Look, can you ask Gav what he's been up to? Anything unusual? You know. Just see if there's anything that strikes you as odd.'

'You think he's seeing someone?' Tom turns back to face her. 'Seriously? Already?'

'Who knows? Liza thinks something is up.' She throws him off the scent. She doesn't want to have to explain that she saw him at the IVF clinic. And then have to go into the discussion about their own attempts at having another child. 'He's just been a bit, well, AWOL recently.

It's not like him. Being late when he's said he'll be there for Jack. That kind of thing. He's normally so on it. So onto Liza, as I've been telling you.' But Tom doesn't pick up on her pointed comment about Gav's controlling behaviour.

'Hmmm. That doesn't sound like him at all. Weird.'

They both go silent. And then there's a great slam, followed by piercing screams. For a minute, Sarah is reminded of Jack. The fall. She's right there, back at the club. Her anxiety rockets and she turns to shout at Casper.

'I told you,' she shouts. 'I told you to stop.' She knows she shouldn't be raising her voice so much. But her heart is threatening to burst out of her chest in fear and Jack's small body keeps looming in her thoughts. The strange angle that he'd been lying at. And then the memory of him halfway up the post.

'Sarah,' Tom says, dragging her back to the present. 'Stop it. He's just being a child. What's wrong with you?'

'Nothing,' she whispers, her heart going at full throttle.

'OK.' Tom leans down to peck a crying Casper on the head. 'Just chill out, will you.' She watches him walk down the hall and pick up his briefcase that she's forever telling him to put away.

'And wait,' she shouts out as she hears the door go. Her anger is rising up, like a wound she needs to scratch; she wants to get back at him somehow for telling her to chill out. 'You'd better be back,' she shrieks. 'For bedtime. You can go out with your friend *Gav* afterwards.'

'Fine.' She sees Tom's shoulders slump as he leaves the house.

Once the energy of their row has dissipated and Casper

214

is settled playing with his Lego, she gets a cup of very strong coffee and goes back to her computer to look at all the information she's found on Ella. She's still trying to work out timings – events. What the hell is Echo Limited? And just as she's scrolling down further into her rabbit hole of stalking, her email pings. She reads it once, then twice. There are only two words going through her brain at this point. Holy. Shit. She looks at the sender: J Roper. A journalist.

She types out a reply. Just leave me alone. Her eyes feel all blurry. And then she realises she shouldn't engage. That anything she says will be written down. Shit. She can feel sweat pouring down her back. She doesn't know if her body can take this much longer. Her fight-or-flight response is going to go into overdrive and she thinks she might combust. But then she thinks of Liza – how their friendship would be destroyed if she admitted the truth. She thinks of all she's going through with Gav. She needs to be there, to protect her from him. And then she thinks of how everyone would react to her, knowing what she'd done. The flurry of whispers at the school gates. Walking the plank to the classroom to drop off Casper. She shudders. And then she thinks about Charlotte G and how she'd pretend to be taking the upper hand in all of this. *Oh, Sarah, what a terribly awful thing to happen. You must feel so dreadful – what with Liza being your best friend.* She simply can't even face the idea of it.

The squirming feeling in her stomach is getting worse by the second – like there's a wild animal inside of her, clawing to get loose. The only way she can stop it all is by shutting down this communication. By doing what Ella told her to do. *Just stick to your story and all will be fine.* Sarah replays Ella's voice in her head – for all

215

her faults it calms her down, knowing she's not in this alone. Her thoughts follow into actions and she decides once and for all what to do.

Spam. That's what she'll say. She never got the email. She reads through it one last time, committing the words to memory.

Gav Barnstaple said you'd talk to me . . . She skims through the rest of it. No. She's not going to talk. Not to a soul. And with one swift stroke, she hits the delete key, and slams shut her computer.

The Vale Club Official Facebook Page

Post: We'd like to alert you to our new EARLYBIRD Christmas offer of THREE personal training sessions for the price of 2!!! Get ready for those festive parties!!!! Sign up at reception.

Lara Keystone: Hey – @Valeclubofficial – instead of pulling the wool over our eyes with crappy offers that you run all year, can you tell us what is going on after that boy's accident? Lots of us aren't bringing our kids until we get some word or reassurance that this won't happen again. I know loads of people are blaming the mother but still – this SHOULDN'T HAVE HAPPENED.

Clemmie Brigstocke-Mathers: I heard something truly awful the other day from a mother at the little boy's school. Apparently there is a chance that someone could have pushed him. I really don't want to believe this. But please clarify and tell us what you will be doing about it and the safety in the rest of the club. We're meant to trust you with our kids! And for those who don't have children – I'm sure they're pretty horrified too. Sort it out, Vale Club!

Georgina C: Pushed? And @Valeclubofficial, you haven't told us or sent your members a letter? DISGUSTING. Aren't you meant to report all of this or at least let your PAYING members know?

Tom Hoopman: haha – PC, you're really messing about with the wrong clientele here!!!

View 567 more comments.

LIZA

'I'm so sorry.' I try not to look at Sarah's face as I drag the last of the storage boxes down into the basement.

'Yeah, don't worry,' puffs Gav, 'she's not moving in permanently or anything.' I'd received Sarah's text telling me that we'd need to limit our stay for two weeks, just after I'd packed ninety percent of the boxes. 'Liza, I'll grab that and you go and check on Jack.'

'Fine.' I go down into the living space that Sarah's created for us. She's done it beautifully. I barely recognise the place. A large, divan-type daybed that has a pull-out single truckle bed underneath it, and she's even put a brand-new bedpan in the corner of the room.

'I got the pull-out,' Sarah says. 'So Casper can lie with him and watch films.' 'Wow, this is amazing.' I look around. Everything looks so easy. The kitchenette is just to the side of the living space with a small bathroom and my bedroom is at the end of the corridor. 'This is just going to be so much easier than sleeping on the blow-up bed. Thank you so much, Sa. I don't know how we are going to repay you.' A funny look crosses Sarah's face.

'No need for that,' she says. 'No need for that at all.'

'You OK?'

'Oh God. I'm fine.' She's clutching her phone and she keeps looking down at it, as though she's expecting some big news or something. 'It's just – yes, I'm fine.'

'Good. You sure this is OK?' I look around the room, at all the bits and bobs stacked up. 'Bit late now, really, though,' I joke.

'What is all this stuff anyway?' she laughs but I detect a note of panic in her voice.

'God only knows. I just overpacked. I kept thinking we'd need everything in the house.'

'OK. Maybe I'll just push it all to one side. Just before Tom gets home?'

'Fine. No problems. Jack, you OK, darling?' He scowls at me. 'Nice to see Aunty Sarah?'

'No.'

'Oh God,' I say. 'I'm so sorry. He's happy to be here. Excited to see you and Casper. He's just struggling at the moment.'

'Of course, I understand that. Jack, would you like Casper to bring down his monkey fingerling that he got for his birthday?'

'No,' he snaps. Sarah looks over at me, her mouth pulled into an O-shape.

'Ignore,' I mouth over to her. I walk over to my little boy and sit next to him. I don't say anything at all. Just make sure that my presence is known and that I don't expect anything of him. 'He's very up and down,' I say softly.

'Shit. I'm so sorry, Liza. It's going to be OK. I'll get Casper down here. He's with Helen.'

'Oh my God. It's not Friday, is it? I don't even know the days any more. Wait. It's Tuesday, right?' I feel a pang of nostalgia as I say this. That I know Sarah so well I know when her cleaner comes. I know when she skips breakfast. I even know when she and Tom have got some nookie in, but lately, after Jack's accident, everything seems so strained. I can't quite put my finger on her behaviour. It's not her usual anxiety. I know those moods as well. It's something else. Like any wrong word could shatter her brittle façade in one fell swoop. Maybe she's been traumatised by Jack's fall. Perhaps I've under-estimated the impact it's had on everyone.

Then I remember the way she had looked at Jack the other day. The way she had looked so sad when she'd asked if I thought he remembered it at all. I don't have it in me to discuss it with Sarah and to help her too. But soon, when everything is settled, I'll look after her. I'll tell her that it's all OK. She can move on.

'I just got Helen in for a few hours extra this week to give us a hand. Here,' Sarah beckons me to follow her. 'Let me show you your room. I've made the bed and I've used the double tog duvet but if you need more, there's blankets in this cupboard here.' She waves me over to the room. It overlooks a small lightwell, under the main garden. She shuts the door. 'How are you and Gav getting on?' she whispers. 'Is it affecting Jack whilst he's so vulnerable?'

'We aren't really fighting at the moment actually. And Jack's absolutely fine when me and Gav are together. It's so weird.'

'Really? What about when you are apart?'

'I don't know. It's like he senses when there's tension and he flips out. Gets all moody. So I'm trying desperately hard with Gav, I need to stay on his good side.'

'Ah Liza. You have to forget just thinking about Gav. You need to look after yourself.'

I'm not entirely sure what she means by that. If she thinks I've given myself over to Gav, she'd be right. But, then again, she doesn't know the full story of everything that has gone on in our relationship.

'It's just that I think Jack has been way more traumatised about all this than I realised.' I don't want Sarah thinking it's all about me and Gav. I can't cope with her breathing down my neck about him as well. She'd been hinting to me for ages that she thinks he's getting too involved in the way I parent. And then I'm struck with the persistent thought I might not be able to sleep again tonight, which in turn means I probably won't. And then the panic sets in. I think back to how the insomnia affected my parenting before. How I can't let that happen now – not with things as they are. I'll have to do something about it, and quickly. Just then, the door whooshes open and Gav's standing there with two more boxes.

'Interrupting something, am I? You two putting the world to rights?'

'No.' Sarah crosses her arms, turning her back towards him and looking down at her phone again.

It's like she can barely look at him. How weird. For all Gav's behaviour towards me in recent times, he and Sarah usually had some sort of banter going on. Does she know something I don't?

'Could you just put those boxes out there?'

Gav looks at me, frowning. I shrug. He leaves the room.

'Has Gav said something to you?' I ask. 'Or has he offended you somehow? You seem—'

'No,' she interrupts. 'I just want things to be absolutely perfect for when you move in. I'm just making sure everything is right for you and comfortable for Jack. OK?'

'All right. Thank you. You have no idea how much we appreciate it. How nice it is not to be alone. Especially now that Mary has gone.'

'I bet. But Gav was with you before, wasn't he? I mean, he didn't move out and you said he gets up when you deal with the kids at night?'

'Well, he gets up to . . . Oh, never mind. It's all very tedious.' I barely have the strength to deal with my own life, let alone others' judgement of it. 'I just need to focus on Jack.' But it seems that Sarah's wheels are set in motion now.

'So Gav said he wanted a break – for a bit. Just after Thea was born. Don't you think that's a bit odd? And he still hasn't explained to you why, but he thinks he can still tell you what to do? Is that right? Please,' she pulls down her T-shirt over her thighs – a move she usually makes when she's feeling deeply uncomfortable, 'correct me if I'm wrong.'

I want to tell her she's being like a headmistress. But then I think of the pact we had made, Gav and I. How I'd broken it. How I couldn't possibly tell Sarah – *anyone* – what I had done. How in parts, Gav has actually been protecting me and our family. If Sarah knew the truth, I doubt she'd ever want to be my friend again.

'Anyway,' Sarah goes on. 'The day Gav was late to the hospital. Remember? When you told me he said he had a doctor's appointment. Did you find out more about that?'

If she's somehow hinting that she's got some sort of information on Gav, I don't want to know what it is. But then I think of how he's been taking more care over his appearance recently. His new washboard stomach. The way he's been late to various things.

'What? Sa – I don't know why you're bringing this up. What the hell have you got against Gav all of a sudden? You've had weeks to get used to the fact that he left us. Well, me. He left me.'

'It's nothing.' She sighs. I think it's all over but then she takes another deep breath and cocks her head. 'So?'

'So what?'

'Did he tell you where he went? Why he was late? There must have been a good reason. You were furious, remember?'

'Sarah, come on.' I feel my whole body fire up. The way it does when I try and fall asleep at night. 'Stop. You're being weird. And super aggressive. I don't like it. And you'll wake Thea and they can probably hear you outside.'

'Oh God.' She slides her phone back into her pocket. 'I'm sorry. I'm just very protective over you. That's all. I didn't like the way he was behaving towards you before all this happened. Even before you separated. It was like he wouldn't let you have your own life.'

'I know. But you don't need to be. I'm fine, I can handle it. Jack is OK. We're good. OK? So no need. Promise?' But she doesn't reply. She just looks to the door where we can hear Gav singing a song to Jack. I can't possibly tell her a thing. And then we hear Gav's phone ring. She looks over at me but I pretend not to notice.

'Right. Sure,' he's saying to the person on the other end of the line. Who could he be speaking to?

Then the door swings open and there he is, phone in hand, looking serious, his features pinched. I stand up, fearful of what's coming. What could it be? Has something else bad happened? I can't take any more bad news. He clears his throat.

'I've just spoken to the manager at The Vale Club.' Phew, I think. It's OK. An update. I turn to Sarah and for a brief moment I think she's got the hiccups. Her hand is placed flat against her breastbone, as though she can't get enough air into her lungs. Gav looks over at her too, eyebrows raised.

'Look, it's all right,' he says. 'It's just that they want you both in.'

'Who?' Sarah asks, as though she can't grasp a single word of what Gav has been saying. 'What are you talking about?'

'The Vale Club. They've finished writing up the health and safety. They want you to go in so they can chat to you about what happened. Just before the fall. And during.' I hear Sarah gasp again. 'But, Sarah,' Gav continues. 'Apparently they've been trying to get hold of you? Said they've rung and left a few messages. I've told them I'll email your number again or that you'll go up. Maybe they took the wrong one down?'

Sarah pulls her phone out from her back pocket and makes an exaggerated show of unlocking her screen, scrolling through her numbers. I notice she's shaking.

'No.' She tries to put her phone back into her pocket but it clatters onto the floor. 'Shit. God. No. Sorry. Weird. I've had no missed calls. Must have been the wrong number.'

'OK,' says Gav. 'Well, they're speaking to people, it's good they've got the ball rolling. I've talked to someone already from the *West London Gazette*. Sarah, I said you'd be happy to talk to them too – in fact maybe they've already been in touch?'

Sarah shakes her head again. 'No,' she says. 'Weird. I'll check again.'

'And apparently some other news orgs are looking into it. A good sign. It means they're taking it seriously. I want The Vale Club to know we won't take this lying down if they are culpable in any way. And if they aren't, then we need to raise awareness of this kind of thing happening. Get to the root of what happened.'

I turn to Sarah and see she's still got a hand clamped to her chest; she looks a little pale.

'I might push the press a little bit more, too,' continues Gav. 'Make sure they don't try and sweep it all under the carpet. You know how these places can be.' He sounds lighter all of a sudden. 'I told them they had to wait to speak to you properly. Liza, I know you've already given a statement but they want more details. That OK? And you, Sarah, I think I've mentioned this a few times, but they definitely want to speak to everyone who saw or spoke to Jack before the accident, so if you don't hear from them could you drop in? Like, soon?' He takes a breath, his eyes flickering to both of us.

'Of course,' I say and look over at Sarah whose anger towards Gav seems to have taken on a new life form. I think about stepping in but Gav needs this – his control over The Vale Club investigation. It's his way of making everything OK again. 'Sa?'

'Yup.' She clasps her hands together. 'Whatever you need.'

'Brilliant,' says Gav. 'Thank you all. Right.' He's taken on an entirely new demeanour. 'Let's get this show on the road, shall we?'

He doesn't look at either of us – just walks out of the door, totally oblivious to the atmosphere he's left behind. Sarah doesn't even say goodbye, so I look over to her – the colour in her face is gone and she's pulling out individual strands of hair, wrapping them tightly around her fingertips.

'Sarah? You OK?' I walk across the room. 'Do you want a tea?'

But she doesn't respond. I'm about to yell to her again – tell her to wake up – but then I catch the look on her face. Those brown eyes of hers, frozen in one position. It's almost like she's not here, with me. As though her mind's completely gone – like she's trapped in her very own waking nightmare.

To: G.Paphides@westlondongazette.com
From: J.Roper@westlondongazette.com

Hi George

I'm so sorry to disturb you on your holiday. I know you told me not to and I've just been getting on with things. But I've been looking into the boy's fall at The Vale Club. I hope you got my original email about that. I was just looking into it for a very small online report to keep members up to speed with things. But it seems to have caught on. And the preliminary investigations I've done make me think something is amiss. Just that – no one's quite being straight with me. And a waitress overheard something pretty odd. And it doesn't match with what the boy's father is saying. Nothing concrete yet. Just a journalistic hunch so to speak! Could I look into it more? I would really love to get a cover story. I think this would be perfect.

J

The Fallout

From: G.Paphides@westlondongazette.com
To: J.Roper@westlondongazette.com

I've just caught up with your emails – I've been in the middle of a game reserve with no wifi.

May I remind you that the West London Gazette *is a family-friendly local paper – and may I also remind you that The Vale Club is one of our main sponsors for this year's lifestyle magazine?*

Happy to give you a cover story when you find something in line with our editorial. I know you've been working hard and we appreciate it. You've done a great job since you started here and you've sailed through your internship and probation period. How about doing a more meaty feature – something about the new W4 development? A positive slant on what it's doing for the community?

If you want to look at something a bit more 'investigative' then please do something on the dog poo problem on the Chiswick / Acton fringes.

Cheers,
George.

PS back in a week. Please hold the fort until then.

WhatsApp group: Christmas fair committee
***Members: Ella, Ems, Liza, Sarah, Bella, Millie, Amina, Charlotte
T, Charlotte G, Charlotte M, Amelia, Shereen, Fizz, Becky D,
Becky G, Isa, Marion, Mimi, Camilla, Hozan, Weronika***
Created by Ella Bradby

Ella: Typing . . .

WhatsApp group: Stuff
Members: Sarah, Camilla

Camilla: Hang on – I thought you were doing this? Ella Bradby?
How come she's suddenly in charge? She's been typing for
hours. What the hell can she be saying?

Sarah: Don't. She's taken over the whole thing now. Charlotte
G organised things so that we're now in charge 'together'.

Camilla: God. It's mad. Anyway we can discuss over a nice
lunch. I've managed to get a booking at the new rezzy! My
treat. By the way . . . ALL the sponsorship money? Where the
hell from?

Sarah: Oh shit – thank you. I'm so sorry. I should have done

230

it myself. Just had so much on. And who the hell knows. I can't face asking. Can't face the smugness of her reeling it all off. God help me.

Camilla: Don't worry at all. I said I'd help.

Sarah: Oh for fuck's sake. Incoming from Ella. What are they all on about now?

WhatsApp group: Christmas fair committee
Members: Ella, Ems, Liza, Sarah, Bella, Millie, Amina, Charlotte T, Charlotte G, Charlotte M, Amelia, Shereen, Fizz, Becky D, Becky G, Isa, Marion, Mimi, Camilla, Hozan, Weronika

Ella: Dear all. Hello and welcome to the Christmas fair committee WhatsApp group!

Sarah and I will be running the show. Please come to us with any questions. Let's raise the roof for our children's enrichment fund!!! Give them the best possible start in life.

Please follow the school guidelines for the group: This group is to be used for Christmas fair committee communication ONLY. Sarah's organised the coffee morning after drop-off today. Sarah, please ping the group with details and we'll see you there.

Charlotte G: Typing . . .

Sarah: 10am at the Green Café. Looking forward to it.

WhatsApp group: CFC board
Members: Sarah, Ella

Ella: For any Christmas fair committee communication between us two! Off the record, of course! And given I've got all the sponsorship money so far, you may want to take ownership of something for yourself. Just so it looks like things are fairly divided. We don't want people thinking I'm doing all the work now, do we?

Sarah: No. Of course not. I know there's a lot to be done behind the scenes – I always hear there's so much more to the school fair than just the money. Community spirit, for one. I'm sure you'll agree. Anyway, see you later!

SARAH

Sarah's phone hasn't stopped pinging since she woke up this morning. She feels like throwing it out of the window. She can't keep up. All these other mothers (again – where are the fathers in the group? Do they just silently lurk? Or do they just renege altogether? Seriously – where the fuck are they?) and how does everyone else have time to keep up with all the chats? Do they type in their sleep?

'Tom, get Casper dressed for school. NOW!' she bellows in a fit of misdirected rage. She's still sore over the email from the journalist. The words keep ringing in her eyes, all day and all night. *Gav Barnstaple said you'd talk to me.*

She hadn't slept one wink last night, going over and over how she was going to avoid speaking to this J Roper character.

'It's late,' she shouts down to Casper. 'We're going to be late on the first day back. And I've got so much to do.'

Tom appears, skin red from his seemingly five-hour-long shower. 'Sorry?' He rubs the towel in his eardrum, shaking his hair like a dog. 'What have you got on?'

'The Christmas fair. I told you, I'm in charge. And I've got a meeting today too, as it *happens*.'

'A meeting?'

'A meeting.' She still feels bad she hasn't told him about the IVF appointment yet. But she's since realised her silence is down to the fact that if it's a problem on her side, she wants to find out without having the upset of seeing that delayed, lopsided smile Tom has when hiding disappointment. And if it's her body, she's sure the problem is going to be exacerbated from all this stress. And she can't face him telling her he told her so. That having Liza and the kids move in with them was a huge mistake. That once again she's putting everyone else before them.

'Great. I'm so pleased. I wondered if you were getting a little bored. I thought that might have been why you were so keen to have Liza and the kids here. To fill your days a bit. Speaking of which – you can't hear a thing, can you? Downstairs in the flat? It's great.'

She nods. Although she had heard 'a thing'. In fact, she'd heard 'things' all night. Jack had been shouting at midnight. Thea had started to cry at two in the morning. And there was a strange clattering sound at around three thirty. And she hadn't managed to get back to sleep. She'd lain there, heart racing its usual panicked rhythm, alternately trying to work out if she should go down and help, and relentlessly checking her email for any more communication about the fall.

She rubs away the familiar sinking sensation from her stomach, the guilt that has been growing and multiplying like soap suds, and now with Gav prodding her to go and talk to management at The Vale Club, she can't stop repeating her lines, over and over: *He was fine. Bottom of the post. Playing. I waved.*

'You think I'm bored?' She manages to keep her voice steady. Lord knows how. 'Bored? I don't have much time to be bored. What with Casper, and his school stuff and running the house.'

'Let's not have this row now, shall we? Casper?' he shouts. 'Casper? Up here now.'

She hears the scramble of feet up the stairs. Why can't he do that when *she* shouts his name?

'I'm going down to do breakfast,' she says. 'Casper, you want porridge?'

'No. Chocolate.'

'You can't have chocolate for breakfast.'

'Sweets.'

'You can't have sweets for breakfast.'

'Crisps.'

'*For fuck's sake,*' she mutters. 'OK, how about porridge and honey?'

'Yes, yes.'

'Please, Mummy?'

'Please, Mummy.'

She goes downstairs, her phone still buzzing in her dressing gown pocket. Despite being awake since the very early hours, she still hasn't managed to get dressed. The act of putting her jeans on, a quick slick of make-up (*Why do you bother? You're only going on the school run*, Tom would ask daily), felt all too much for her. She daren't even think about how she looks at the moment. The worst triumvirate: drawn, tired *and* plump. She thinks about how pulled together Ella will look at the Christmas fair meeting. *Stop comparing – you have attributes that Ella doesn't have*, she tells herself, but when she tries to think of them, her mind is mysteriously empty.

She pulls out her phone. Sarah's organised the meeting,

Ella has written on the WhatsApp group. Organised? Organised! She'd told everyone where the meeting was going to *be*. That had been the extent of her organisation. What else did it require?

She scrolls up to the WhatsApp group members – scanning through the names. There are at least fifteen who've requested to be part of the Christmas fair committee. Fifteen! Shit. Shit shit shit, she realises that she should have rung the café ahead of schedule and asked them to reserve the back area. And done some sort of agenda. *Double shit and fuck*. There are only fifteen minutes before they have to leave for school. She's not dressed. It had crossed her mind last week but she'd obviously forgotten. It will be OK, she breathes. She'll beg Maureen the manager to reserve a spot for her, but she thinks of the post-drop-off rush and how busy the café gets at exactly the time the meeting would start. Shit. Why hadn't she done something about it?

She can already envisage the look that Charlotte G will give her – the slightly skewed mouth, leaning into some sort of insincere smile. The one that says: *I'll pretend I'm onside with you. But really, I'm judging the shit out of you*. Agh, she clenches her fists. She brings up the number of the Green Café on her phone. Please. *Come on. Come on*. But there's no answer. She can't risk it; being shown up in front of Ella. In front of everyone else. Charlotte G. After she'd kicked up a fuss about organising the damn thing in the first place. She imagines the moment when everyone would have to file out into the street – wondering where else to go.

She's going to sort this. She is. She remembers who she's doing this for. Liza. Perhaps they could use the school kitchen? But then she has an idea. She could host it at hers. She'll just have to put aside all her worries for two hours and be done with it.

She'll throw money at the situation. She'll stop off at Sainsbury's. Get a bag of croissants and some tea bags and that will be sorted. One hour. She'll do a quick whizz-around tidy and the house will be passable. The idea of having Ella at her house would normally send her into a dizzying snowball of stress. But today – the alternative is worse. She thinks of the lovely hot-water tap that Ella has at hers. How useful it would be right now but she can't bring herself to ask Ella to host. She'll warn Liza to stay downstairs and remember to put some music on in case Thea starts screaming. Brilliant.

After quickly making Casper his porridge she runs up and pulls on a pair of jeans and a jumper, slathers her face in bronzer and puts on three coats of mascara.

Just as they have two minutes to put on coats and shoes, Sarah is surprised to see Liza appear. (They have set a few rules for Liza's stay. Or rather, Tom has: 'I want to be able to walk around naked in my own home without worrying that Liza is going to see me,' he had snapped. 'No walking into the other person's space without prior warning.') Thea's asleep in a red papoose around her front.

'I'm so sorry to be asking you more favours when you've already done so much for us with the flat.' Liza's rubbing her head that way she does before she's about to come down with one of her migraines. 'I really am, but Gav just rang. He can't make it today. I have something really important I need to do. Could you watch Jack later on?'

The IVF appointment, thinks Sarah. Twelve p.m. She feels she can barely breathe.

'Please?' Liza has started tapping on her phone, so hasn't caught the expression on Sarah's face. 'Please, please, please.'

Sarah thinks of Gav. Rage, swelling inside her, that he would do this. Gav should be bending over backwards to help out at the moment. He should be available at every given opportunity. He's set up his own web development company for God's sake. He's his own boss. He can come and go as he pleases, yet all this time he's acting as though Liza is making ill-placed demands on him. Sarah tightens her lips. And she also knows that Gav isn't being honest. She wants to tell Liza that she'd seen Gav. That he'd lied to her. That he'd been with another woman. She wants to tell her friend so badly it's physically hurting her to keep it a secret.

'I can't today. Liza, I'm so sorry. I had . . .' She wants to tell Liza about her plans. That everything had been arranged by Camilla for her IVF appointment and it was something important, but then she thinks of Jack. She thinks of how that journalist wants to speak to her and she's absolutely paralysed on the spot. She doesn't have time to explain anyway. Her fault. Her fault. She has to say yes. From now on, her life comes a close second and that's all there is to it.

'Sure,' she relents, thinking of Camilla. Her kindness. How she'd gone out of her way to arrange the appointment and to do her a big favour. But Liza had also been kind, last year. 'Anything,' she tells her. 'I'll do anything for you at the moment.'

'Thanks,' says Liza, although she doesn't look particularly grateful. 'Sorry. I barely slept last night. Same insomnia. Killing me.'

'By the way. I'm just about to WhatsApp everyone.

They're coming here. At ten. For the Christmas fair committee. So if you don't want to see anyone just stay downstairs, OK?'

'OK,' she says. 'Thank God you warned me. I couldn't cope with that. Ella got all the sponsorship money, I hear? Crazy. You know who from?'

'No idea,' Sarah shrugs. 'Sure you don't want to come up for a bit?'

'I'm sure. Very sure. I think.' She massages the back of her neck. 'I think being part of that chat would probably tip me over the edge. You know, send me really insane.'

Sarah laughs, and so does Liza. A little too manically. A bit too close to the bone, she thinks. Perhaps this is it. Perhaps they really are going insane. She feels it, certainly.

'OK,' Sarah says, a bright grin plastered across her face. 'Ta-ra then. See you later. All good here.' She shuts the door on Liza and sinks, deep down onto the floor.

WhatsApp group: Christmas fair committee
***Members: Ella, Ems, Liza, Sarah, Bella, Millie, Amina, Charlotte
T, Charlotte G, Charlotte M, Amelia, Shereen, Fizz, Becky D,
Becky G, Isa, Marion, Mimi, Camilla, Hozan, Weronika***

Ella: Typing . . .

WhatsApp group: Stuff
Members: Sarah, Camilla

Sarah: Mils, I've got something awful to tell you. I said I'd
watch Jack and Thea for a bit. Liza's got an appointment and
Gav is God knows where. It seemed pretty urgent. After all
you've done for me – booking the appointment and lunch
and everything. I'm so sorry.

Camilla: Ah no worries. We can do it again and we need to
think of Liza at the moment. I totally understand.

Sarah: Yes, I know – I feel bad saying no, especially with all
that's happening. But I'm so sorry again about all the hassle
you went to.

Camilla: No hassle. We'll do it again soon. Promise. And don't worry, I'm not pissed off! In truth I could do with the time to get some stuff done. See you at that ruddy meeting.

Sarah: XXXX THANK YOU I LOVE YOU.

Camilla: Love you too

WhatsApp group: Christmas fair committee
Members: Ella, Ems, Liza, Sarah, Bella, Millie, Amina, Charlotte T, Charlotte G, Charlotte M, Amelia, Shereen, Fizz, Becky D, Becky G, Isa, Marion, Mimi, Camilla, Hozan, Weronika

Ella: Morning everyone. Hope everyone is ready for the Christmas fair meeting later. Please bring issues or concerns you'd like to share with us. This is a safe space for us all to be completely open. Otherwise looking forward to seeing your enthusiastic selves soon!

Sarah: Hi All. Yes, looking forward to seeing everyone later on. Venue has changed to my house – 10 am. 64 Heathville Road. W3. See you there. Top buzzer, please! I'll provide croissants and tea! (And wine, or gin, if anyone should have the urge!)

WhatsApp group: CFC board
Members: Sarah, Ella

Ella: Hi Sarah. Next time it would be really great if you could give me some warning if you're going to change the arrangements we had. Or discuss it with me first. Thank you!

Sarah: *Warning*?

Ella: Yes – if we're going to work together on this as a team, I need to be making these kinds of decisions with you. Also should you really be making jokes about alcohol on here? People not drinking for religious reasons, and there's at least one mother that has to abstain from alcohol for her own personal reasons, if you catch my drift, so I think it's highly insensitive of you to make jokes like these on a public forum.

Sarah: Typing . . .

LIZA

I'm on the end of Jack's bed and he's sitting up a bit now, my little boy, looking pleased. Jan the physio is busy packing up her things.

'You've done incredibly well,' she says, patting his good arm. 'It's almost miraculous. These little people, they heal so fast, don't they?' She doesn't look at me as she speaks. I'm not sure what to read into that.

I want to ask her about Jack's behaviour but, of course, just as I'm about to summon up the courage to even go there, I hear the click-clack of footsteps and the clearing of a throat. *Sarah.*

'Oh, gosh, sorry,' she says when I open the door. I feel bad – opening the door to her in her own home. 'I just wanted to ask you a quick question.'

Her eyes look dull and she's breathing fast. Her make-up is slightly orange, a few white streaks from trails of sweat. Normally I'd point this out to her and we would laugh. *You've been Tangoed*, I'd say. Not today.

'You OK, Sa? What's the matter?'

243

'Matter? Nothing. Oh hello,' she waves to Jan. 'Sorry, am I disturbing you?'

I want to tell her that yes. Actually – she is. But then I think of earlier – asking her to watch Jack and Thea whilst I go out. She'd been on the verge of saying no. Surely it must have been important, for her to be dilly-dallying about whether she could watch the kids for an hour. In truth, I'd caught the look on her face. Startled and bewildered, hunting for an excuse not to help me out, but I'd looked down at my phone and ignored her.

I'd felt crappy afterwards. Leading her on to believe that I had something urgent to do. I thought about what I was *actually* going to do – which was helping myself before things got much worse. Before the memory of Jack's fall and the bad things from years ago threatened to overwhelm me and I lost everything.

I look over at Jack and Thea, her little chest juddering up and down, and I feel like I'm going to cry. If only I could explain.

'Listen. I'm in a hurry,' Sarah says, opening the door a little wider. 'I just wanted to ask you about the Christmas fair meeting. Have you got an agenda? Ella – she's . . .'

'She's what?'

'Already driving me mad. Potty. Control thing. It's weird.'

'Really? I guess someone needs to just be on it in terms of organisation. She's probably just making sure everything is going to run smoothly. That's all.' As soon as the words come out of my mouth, I regret them. I watch as Sarah's two front teeth sink into her lower lip. 'I mean, I know you're on it, Sa. It's just that, well – Ella is that type, really. Isn't she?'

I watch Sarah's chest rise. She exhales, a thin stream of breath, cutting through the air. 'Look, Liza. I know you're busy. I just wondered if you had an agenda that you go through? I didn't have time to . . .'

She shuts her mouth again. I think of the last time she told me she hadn't had time – she couldn't find a minute, apparently, to ring back a work contact I'd given her. *It's not time you need*, I'd told her.

'Sure. Sure. I'll dig it out.' I wait for her to start moving but she stands there. 'Oh sorry. You want it now?'

'Please. I'm sorry. It's just that they're all coming in an hour. I know people will be early. I wanted to give everyone a chance to go home and tidy up breakfast and stuff but I guess some will be quicker than others.'

I go over to my computer and send her the file. 'There, all done,' I tell her. 'And thanks again for looking after Jack and Thea today. There's just some stuff I need to get done.'

She opens her mouth, ready to ask me what it is, but quickly shuts it again. Normally the words come out so easily between us.

'Listen,' I say. 'As far as Ella's concerned at the meeting – just stand your ground.' I watch her shoulders drop.

'I know. Also,' her eyes start to shine, 'our Ella Bradby, you'll never believe what I've found.'

'Mum!' shouts Jack. 'Mum.'

'Liza, I'm off too.' Jan picks up a large, black leather bag. 'I've got to run to my next appointment. Jack, see you next week, Mister, I'm not on your rota until then. You keep doing those exercises.'

'Listen,' I say to Sarah. 'Sorry. I'll talk to you later, shall I? Once I've got back from . . . the thing?'

'Sure.' Her voice sounds all falsely cheery. 'Bye

everyone,' she waves her hand around the room. 'I'll see you later.' But I notice she doesn't make eye contact with anyone at all. Least of all me.

SARAH

It's the third time today Sarah's wiped the kitchen counter. She's ready. She knows she is. But she just needs to *do* something. After all, it's probably only a matter of minutes until the first person arrives. She has a tiny bet with herself it will be Charlotte G – her FOMO overriding any desire for etiquette. (Because of course, Charlotte G is hot on etiquette.) Next it will be Ella. And then the others will stream in and out in groups of two or three.

At least she has everything organised. The croissants should be ready at ten fifteen – she's bought the frozen ones that she's used to, she'd daren't try anything new and exciting today – and all the prep had taken less time than she'd thought. For a minute, she'd thought the printer wasn't going to work but then the machine had started and she had a beautifully presented Excel spreadsheet in her hands, complete with a financial document and a list of things they need to do. She had felt a tad disloyal, deleting Liza's name from the top, but she wants to show Ella a thing or two. Prove to her she wasn't quite so incompetent as her majesty had made her feel.

She takes one last look at her reflection in the back of a spoon. She has reapplied her make-up and prayed no one had looked at her too closely at school drop-off. In the autumn sunlight upstairs in the bedroom she'd noticed smears of orange on the side of her left cheek. Normally Liza would have rubbed it off, as though she was a child. And where is Liza off to anyway? Why is she keeping it a secret?

Ah! The doorbell. The first guest is here. Sarah lifts her chin, clears her throat to try and rid herself of the pre-hosting flutters. She glances over at the oven timer. Four minutes to ten. She smooths down her black-and-red-piped Boden T-shirt (she's decided to wear something 'accessible' today) and walks to the door. She'd been right. Charlotte G is there and, standing right next to her, is Ella.

She takes in Ella's workout gear. She looks so well put together. All matching, even down to her fingernails, which are a deep grey colour, just to go with her leggings. She's wearing beautiful diamond earrings – which Sarah recognises as Maria Tash. She'd been coveting them for ages. Charlotte G looks – well – Charlotte G-ish. All neat and sensible. Tapered jeans, a good practical jumper and clean, leather boots.

'Oh hi, both of you.' Sarah pitches her voice down a tone or two. 'So nice to see you. *Do* come in.' She wonders why she's chosen to accentuate the word do, like she's the queen, or something.

'I expect you want shoes off?' Charlotte G points a toe in Sarah's direction.

'No, of course not. As long as you haven't stepped in anything,' she laughs, aware she sounds totally neurotic. 'Go into the front room. Sit down.'

She hasn't dared look at Ella's face yet. She doesn't want to know how she's being judged – Ella's beautiful house flits through her mind. But she does notice that her hallway mantelpiece is looking a right tip. Tom's spare change on the side, one of Casper's toy cars. A diffuser that looks old and battered. Why hadn't she thought to clear that up?

'I'll bring you a cup of tea in. Builders' OK with you?' But neither of them reply. 'I'll just be a sec. Make yourselves comfortable. If you could answer the door if it goes that would be great.'

She pours the boiling water into a pre-prepared tea pot, and reappears into the living room. 'Here. Milk, sugar. Help yourselves. I often find it's easier that way. I'm just going to check on the croissants.'

Just as she goes into the kitchen the doorbell goes. She's starting to feel a little overwhelmed now, the heat of the oven blasting in her face. She hears Camilla. Phew. She wonders how she's going to make it up to her friend for missing the IVF appointment. Camilla will never quite be Liza but, recently, she's been coming up a very close second.

'Jesus, Sarah,' she hears a harried voice behind her and jumps. 'Ella and Charlotte G.' Camilla shuts the kitchen door behind her. 'Why are they acting all . . . weird?'

'What do you mean?'

'Like. I don't know. Awkward. Or something. It's like I've done something wrong.'

'God only knows. Quick, help me with the tea, will you? Fill up the kettle again? Jesus, Mils, this is a shitshow. I can't cope with it all.'

'Liza OK? I forgot to ask how it's been with her downstairs.'

Sarah opens her mouth. She wants to tell Camilla the truth about how strained it's been between them. But she feels disloyal, especially given her behaviour, her lies, are at the root of it.

'It's been fine so far.'

'Really? Not too much pressure on you guys? I saw Tom this morning. He looked a bit – well, stressed.'

'Oh, Tom is always stressed at the moment. Work stuff. And anyway – you'll never guess who I saw. The other day. With another woman.' Sarah puts her hand over her mouth the minute the words come out. She can't believe what she's done, but there's no going back now.

'What? Who?'

'Gav.'

'Oh my God. What the hell? Does Liza know?'

'No. I haven't told her. Can you believe it? Please, please don't say anything. I just needed to tell someone.' She doesn't quite know why she needed to tell anyone at all. But she feels both better and worse that Camilla now knows. 'Oh fuck, the doorbell again.' She opens the kitchen door and Ella is standing there, looking at a large picture in the corridor. She jumps. Shit. Did Ella overhear their conversation? Impossible.

Sarah turns back to Camilla, eyes wide, motioning her hand forward for her to hurry up. And then the doorbell goes again. She doesn't have time to worry, or think about whether Ella overheard, but she feels slightly shaky. She'll do a few testers later and ask Tom if he can over-hear her talking in the kitchen so she can know for sure. And at least Ella's expression looks totally blank. But then again . . . and oh God, there goes the doorbell again.

Five minutes later, nearly everyone has arrived. The

chatter in the room is getting louder and louder, and small groups have already formed. She hears Charlotte G commanding the audience, talking loudly about little Mimi's home learning (or homework, as Sarah still calls it – she can't get used to all this new-fangled positive language).

'I'm *so* lucky with Mimi, she just gets on with it. Just loves doing all her home learning. I mean, we didn't do anything to encourage her but she's just so *disciplined*.'

Fucking disciplined, thinks Sarah. She still hasn't collected the leaves to stick into Casper's home-learning book. And any efforts at practising phonics had fallen on deaf ears.

'And oh *look*,' Charlotte carries on. 'Dear Casper. Look at that wonderful photo. Is that the Highlands? Isn't he just delightful, with his wonky fringe. So cute.'

'He's very cute,' says Sarah. 'God, we haven't done any of our home learning yet.' Her small act of rebellion. She really must try harder, though. Letting Casper down because *she* can't cope. She inwardly promises she'll make it up to him. Hire a tutor. Something.

'Oh,' exclaims Charlotte G, her head tilted to one side. 'I mean, I saw Casper playing tennis the other day. Perhaps he'll be our very own Tim Henman, forget the academics. But they all *do* go at their own pace. Don't they?'

Excuse me, thinks Sarah. Why is she presuming that Casper is as thick as two short planks?

'They do indeed,' Sarah replies, aware that everyone is listening. 'But of course, your kids must be speeding ahead with the private tutor you hired for them.' Charlotte G pinches her lips together. 'Casper is into his Roald Dahl at the moment.'

She thinks of her son, agog in front of the film version of *Matilda*, until she remembers Charlotte G runs the school library and so will, of course, know exactly how far Casper is into his reading.

Ella has remained silent all this time. Has neither nodded in agreement at Casper's 'cuteness' nor mentioned Felix's own home learning. Sarah watches her writing down notes in a beautiful velvet-covered Moleskine notebook. She lifts her leg every time she stops writing, as if deep in thought. There is not one part of Ella that is out of place. Sarah cranes her head over to try and see what she's been jotting down, her stomach lurching at the thought she could have overheard her conversation with Camilla. And then she remembers everything she had unearthed about Ella. Her blood fizzes. No matter how Ella Bradby is making her feel she must not, she repeats, must *not* forget that she has something on her.

Just as she's thinking about Ella, she realises that the conversation has turned. She catches someone saying something about Jack. And then the chat turns full-tilt, the volume dialled right up, as though there's an exciting part on the television. She's not even aware of who is talking and she's too frightened to make eye contact with Ella.

'The Vale Club.'

'It's all bloody weird to me.'

'Oh sorry,' Charlotte G interrupts, 'how insensitive of us, Sarah. I mean, you're so close to Liza that it must all be very upsetting for you. And when you were *there* too. But it is weird, that's all, that this investigation stuff is being talked about all the time but no one official has spoken up.'

Sarah wonders how long Charlotte G can continue talking without taking a breath.

'It's all hush-hush behind closed doors. And anyone who dares ask at the club – *well* – don't you think it's a little strange? I mean, Sarah, what do you think about it all? I can't remember the details – did you actually *see* what happened? I can't even imagine how frightening that must have been for you all.'

This cannot be happening. No, Sarah thinks. Don't let my body give me away. With every word that Charlotte G utters, she feels like a noose is being tightened around her neck.

'Sarah?' Charlotte G titters and then looks around the room for moral support that she's done the right thing by bringing it up.

Come on Sarah, *do or say something*, she tells herself. Before she blurts it all out. The pressure to come out with it all, right now, is overwhelming.

'Oh God.' The noose-feeling tightens – she can almost feel her eyes bulging. 'Let's not discuss that now.' She can't think of a reason as to why not. But then she sees Ella, in the corner of the room widening her eyes. She feels a sense of comradeship and relief that Ella has given her the go-ahead to be more forceful.

'Right,' Sarah claps her hands. 'As I said, enough of that. Otherwise we won't fit in the full agenda.' She gets into her stride, despite feeling like a small figurine shaken up in one of those snow-globes, about to crash head-first onto the floor. 'Let's all start. Shereen isn't here yet but let's get on, shall we? So, we're together to discuss the Christmas fair. I've got the agenda here.'

She reaches over to pick up the papers she'd printed off earlier, that she'd left on the table for show. 'There are about six things we need to share between everyone. And we need to discuss who is going to be in charge of which stalls at the fair. And everything else on the list.'

She's winging it now. She has no idea what she's talking about – she still feels like she's underwater after the earlier discussion about Jack's fall. She can barely hear her own voice, but she'll just work her way through the list and hope for the best. She vaguely remembers last year's meeting – bits of it anyway; she'd been too hungover to properly focus.

'So we have the leaflet to sort out,' she says. 'I've got a list of all the stalls here. I'm going to read them out – if you could just put hands up please to man each one.' She carries on. She's rather enjoying this now, using it as a distraction from things, her voice firmer and more in control.

'Wait,' says Ella. 'I've got a sign-up sheet here.' She pulls out a bunch of papers from the back of her notebook. 'I'll just leave them here, shall I? On the table. People can sign up after.'

But they won't, Sarah wants to say. *Why would they?* But before she's said anything, Charlotte G has grabbed the paper and is scrawling her name on the top of the sheet.

'Oh, good shout, Ella,' Sarah says, hoping she's keeping the bitter note out of her voice. 'Brilliant. Thank you. Now, for the sponsorship.'

Charlotte G turns to Ella. 'Ella, you should really be doing this bit?'

'Well, let's wait until we hear what Sarah has to say, shall we?'

Sarah is at once grateful and suspicious. But maybe she can use the opportunity to ask her where Ella got the money. *Shit.* She's lost her stride now and forgotten what she has to say. She leans forward to look at the agenda sheet and, as she does, her hand knocks something. A teacup. Blast it. She feels liquid on her feet. All over the carpet. Fuck it. The agenda sheet disintegrates into the table. She almost laughs and cries at the same time.

'Damn. One minute, guys,' she says. 'Just going to get some kitchen roll.'

'I'll take over for a bit, shall I?' Ella stands up and everyone's eyes train right on her. 'So first of all, let's all just take a moment to think about Liza and why we are here instead of her.' Bitch, Sarah thinks. 'I'm sure many of you know now that I managed to get the sponsorship money. All of it,' she says with a curtsy. *She actually curtsies.*

Sarah leaves the room. She can't take much more. When she gets into the kitchen she sees her phone on the side. She grabs it and flicks through her messages. Mercifully quiet. Of course – they're all here. Liza's offline, and Tom is too. And that's about the sum of it. She flicks through to her search toolbar. Types quickly what she's looking for. She starts laughing at what she is about to say to Camilla. She knows she shouldn't. She knows it's mean. A burst of delight flares up within her stomach. Delight, mixed with horror. But she does it anyway. Yes she does.

Just when she thinks she's finished typing, she hears Ella droning on and on. Except she's not really droning. If Sarah listens hard enough, she can hear real intent. Lovely, relaxing intent. But she'll call it droning. And so she carries on writing her message. Tap, tap, tap. The more she writes, the better she feels. Or at least, a small fix. Of something. Meanness, *Schadenfreude*, mixed with a massive dose of *fuck you, Ella Bradby*. She doesn't read through her message. Send. There. *Whoosh*. It's gone. And by the time she's about to lift her finger up off the screen, she realises what's happened. She presses her finger back down, hard onto the screen, in the hope that, somehow, the message will be magicked back. She's too late. It's sent. Whoosh! Whoosh, whoosh and triple whoosh, straight to Ella Bradby.

She daren't read back the message to herself. She can't bring herself to. A metallic taste seeps into her mouth, her heartbeat pulsing right up her neck until she can hardly swallow. *Shit*. What can she do? And then she remembers the *delete for everyone* function on WhatsApp. Ella won't have her phone on her. Of course she won't. By the time she finishes the meeting, the message will be gone. But then Sarah remembers when she'd first seen Ella out on that balcony. The way Ella had been clutching onto her handset as though her life depended on it. Well, she would too, if she had a secret like Ella's.

She flicks back through her WhatsApps to the Christmas fair chat that Ella had started. She opens the kitchen door and starts to rush towards the living room, and then she hears Charlotte G talking. Something about Ella's phone vibrating on the table.

'Oh,' she hears her exclaim. 'It's from Sarah. How funny. She's just in the kitchen next door. I wonder what can be the matter.'

Sarah feels her hands shaking and she presses the three small dots in the corner of her phone but, somehow, another chat appears on her screen. Fuckety fuck. She's pressing the wrong buttons. And then there's silence from the room next door. By the time she's found the delete function she sees the ticks in the corner of the chat turn blue.

The Fallout

It's too late. Far too late. Ella's read every word. Laughter bubbles in her stomach. And then her hands start to tingle. What has she done? What the hell has she done? And she knows that there is absolutely no turning back from this. But – well – maybe this is a good thing. Maybe Ella deserves this. She hears Liza's voice in her head. *Don't get all defensive. You need to sort it out.* She takes a deep breath and leans her forehead onto the fridge. Perhaps it will work as a cheap version of that new cryotherapy freezing wrinkle technique she'd read about. She presses harder.

What to do now? She looks at her watch. She can't be gone for much longer. But she has no idea what she will do or say. None at all. She's trapped in her own kitchen. And what is worse is that she's somehow managed to involve her own son in all of this. Jesus. Casper. This is his school, after all. She deletes the message and makes the slow and interminable journey back into her living room.

West London Gazette editorial notes, October 2019
J Roper interview transcript: Anon, teaching assistant
at West London Primary Academy

I know Jack Barnstaple. He's a really great little kid. Always polite. Always very generous to the other children. Only five but knows how to behave and is a very popular little boy. We all felt awful when we heard what had happened. I mainly know his mum because she gets involved in the school stuff and she's nice to speak to. Which is increasingly rare these days. You should see some of the way the parents behave. It's as if they're paying through the nose for their children's education.

Like they expect us to devote hours and hours to their bloody children's welfare – they don't realise we have thirty children in the class and limited resources. Or even worse, they do and they just don't give a damn. They come storming in anyway demanding to know this and that. Of course, they're usually polite but we always know the subtext: My kid's a genius, so how come he's not being treated like one? *Or,* My kid's shit at maths and it must be your fault.

Anyway – the Barnstaples – the mum does a load of fundraising for the school, which is brilliant, and genuinely helpful for the kids, and so we see her loads around the place. She actually came in to see Miss Harbell last month to explain that her and her husband were on a break – just in case Jack started playing up. She seemed a bit shaky to be honest, rather than upset. Kept looking over her shoulder – like she was worried he was going to turn up. And then she got up really quickly, clutching her bag tight and saying she had to rush off.

But ever since Jack's fall, everyone seems to be on hyper alert. You know how it is – all the parents thinking: That could totally happen to me. *Because that's one of those things – isn't it? That could happen to anyone. So we see everyone doing the helicopter-parent thing for a few days after something like this happens. And then everyone lets up a bit.*

But there has been a strange atmosphere around the school since the fall. I can't explain it. Everyone seems a bit edgy. I hear whispers of politics amongst the parents. Fallouts in the WhatsApp groups. A lot more complaints to the teachers and requests for meetings with us to talk about totally irrelevant things. It's all quite exhausting. As if we don't have enough to deal with.

Honestly – sometimes I really do wonder who the grown-ups are here.

LIZA

'You OK, Sa?' I look at my watch as I open the door to the flat. 'It's just that you're early.'

'I'm great.' But she sounds put out at the implication that she's on time, for once. I'd told her I needed an hour to get to my appointment, just because I know what she's usually like.

'You look dreadful, Sa. What happened?'

She moves forward and I think she's about to tell me but she gives this weird little laugh. 'I'm fine. I just had a long day, that's all. I think I might have upset Ella. We had the Christmas fair committee meeting.'

'Ella? Of course you wouldn't have upset her. She strikes me as pretty unflappable.'

'What, and you think I am?' she snaps. 'God, sorry. Sorry. I know, this isn't what you need right now.' Her eyes glance over to Jack. Thea starts to cry.

'No worries. Here, listen. I've got to go but let's talk properly later, yeah? Sorry about them.' I put on my coat and shoes and start walking out of the door. 'Oh, I've left their food – Thea's powder is all ready to go and three sterilised bottles. I mean, I'll only be a couple of hours. And Jack's tutor is coming in a bit.'

'Sure.' She sounds totally flat. 'Like I said, anything you need. Now Casper's back at school it'll be a lot easier.'

I think about what Sarah means by this. How she's told me over and over that she'd lay down her life to help me out after Jack's fall. And she's bent over backwards. But she seems so exhausted by it all.

'Bye,' I say. She looks like she is near to tears. Like she wants to say something of utmost importance. But before she can open her mouth, I close the door and I'm gone. When I turn the corner, I order an Uber. Guilt swells in my stomach. I ring Gav but he can't talk. He's in a place that sounds echoey and he's whispering – like he's in a library or something.

'What's that?' he says.

'What time you coming later?'

'Oh shit. Um. Six. You left Sarah in charge? Are you sure she's OK with them? She'll watch Jack?'

'I'm sure. And Jack's tutor is coming soon too.' I'm sure I can hear a female voice whispering down the phone – and the rustle of something. 'Where are you off to anyway? Anywhere nice?' I feel the familiar punch in my stomach. I don't think I'll ever be ready for the answer, whatever that may be.

'Just doing a few bits and bobs. Catching up since the hospital. Y'know.'

'OK.' I resist asking more. 'Bye Gav.' I hang up and wonder what else I can do to distract the edginess that is taking hold. And then I remember Ella's earlier WhatsApp. That's exactly who I need. I ring her once I'm in the car.

'Liza? Everything OK?'

'I just thought I'd say hello. See how everything was going?' If Ella thinks it's odd I'm ringing, she doesn't say.

'How lovely, how are you?'

'So nice to speak to you. I've just been downstairs at Sarah's. It's been quite claustrophobic, actually. With the kids and stuff. Not at Sarah's, I mean. Just with Jack. He's been difficult.'

'I'm so sorry. Poor little thing. You could always come here afterwards?' She sounds so breezy, so kind, that I'm tempted to say yes.

'I couldn't. Thank you. But I'd love to come and see you. Just to get out of the house.'

'Well, how about next week?'

'I was thinking tomorrow or something. Or we could go and get something to eat?' I feel disloyal. But I don't want to invite Sarah along. I can't deal with her weirdness at the moment, on top of everything else. I need calm.

'Well, I'm actually going away soon so I need to pack and get myself sorted. But yes. I'm sure we can fit something in.'

Away? Something that Sarah had said about mysterious trips echoes in my mind. Where could she possibly be going?

'Oh?' I don't want to pry, of course. But then again, I do. She doesn't catch the bait. 'You all right?' I try again. 'Everything OK with the family?'

'Yes, great,' she says, barely giving me anything. 'Thanks.'

And then I think about something Sarah had said earlier. About Ella hiding something. How I'd batted her down because I didn't want to be gossipy after all Ella has done.

'Hey, by the way,' Ella takes a breath. 'About Sarah.'

'Yes?'

'Do you think she's OK?'

'Yes? As far as I can make out. Why?'

'Just that she behaved very oddly at the Christmas fair meeting. I can't quite explain. Everyone commented to me about it afterwards. A bit manic, I suppose. Or like she was terrified of doing, or saying, the wrong thing. I can't quite put my finger on it. I'm sorry to involve you. It's just that you know her the best.'

She pauses, waiting for me to talk, but before I can open my mouth she carries on. 'I wondered if she was all right. Whether I should be relying on her to carry on with organising the fair. Or whether it's just all too much for her. She seemed just so odd the other day too, when she came to mine. Don't you think? And she was saying some stuff . . .'

'Hmm,' I say. 'Some stuff? What stuff? I do think she's been a bit odd, yes. I put it down to her being upset about Jack.'

'Yes. Of course. That's affected us all.'

There's a silence. I think about how glad I am that Ella walked back into our lives, and the kindness she's extended towards me. The way she's known exactly what to say and do, at exactly the right time. Something that Sarah has been struggling with.

'It's probably that,' I say. 'She was a bit odd before the fall, though, come to think of it.'

'Really?' I hear an intake of breath. 'Like how?' She sounds all casual again.

'Well, just not really with it. Vague. Not interested in

anything. I hadn't seen her laugh for ages. Not a proper Sarah laugh anyway.' I think of my friend. The way she would throw her head back and slap her knees when I made a bad joke.

'Come to think of it, she did mention something that stuck with me,' Ella says. 'About you.'

'What?' That's what Ella must have meant in her earlier WhatsApp. 'What about me?'

'Oh well, you've got enough on your plate. Nothing much. Just that, well, she sent me a bit of a weird message. And then I heard her talking to Camilla about something. I think it was to do with you and Gav but I couldn't really hear properly. Don't mention it to her though. Will you?'

'No.' I shake my head down the phone.

'I think you should just focus on Jack,' she tells me. 'It's totally irrelevant.'

It's not irrelevant, I want to say. If it's about *me*. I start to feel all shaky again. But I don't want to look too needy. Too desperate. I give a small laugh.

'Go on, Ella,' I say, knowing that if I don't get it out of her now, I'll want to know later. 'Just give me a bit of a heads-up.'

'Oh God. Don't be silly. It's not a big deal at all. Just pathetic school stuff that we don't need to be involving ourselves in. Do we now? When we have bigger things to think about.'

But you were the one who brought it up, I want to shout. Instead, I grip my handset and hold onto the door handle as the Uber swerves in and out of the wrong lane. We're on the Westway now. Shooting past the grey, high-rise buildings. The green heart on the hoarding to my right. *Grenfell in our hearts forever*. I want to let out a sob. What the hell am I doing? What am I doing caring about what Ella Bradby thinks? Projecting my own feelings on to what is probably an innocent conversation. What am I doing racing in an Uber, having left my kids in the care of someone else who's already done so much for me? But I need to do this, or God knows what could happen. It could be even worse than last time with Jack and I know I can't trust myself in this state. I shift myself around the car seat, pulling uncomfortably at the seatbelt. I watch a lorry rattling past my window.

'Hello?' Ella's voice echoes down the phone.

'Oh.' I clutch the phone again. 'Reception went. Sorry.' I swallow back my tears. I think about getting the driver to turn around. To swing back right to my house. I feel overwhelmed with everything and I want to curl up in a ball. *But it's too late*, I tell myself. *Too late for that. Nearly there.*

'Anyway, how are things going with Gav?' Ella sounds so chilled, she could be asking about the weather. I try and concentrate on giving her some sort of reply. But it's too far gone for that. Ella's planted the seeds about Sarah too, and they haven't been sprouting, but burgeoning into huge, socking great weeds, strangling my brain.

'He's OK. He seems to just want to come and see Jack and Thea and not really speak to me. He checks up on them a lot. On me.'

'Really? You can put a stop to that, you know. You have the power to do that. You are separated after all. He wanted to leave.'

'Hmmmm.' I think about the things that Ella doesn't know. The things that are still keeping me awake at night.

'Just, you know, set your boundaries with him. OK? You can do it, Liza.'

Despite the fact she's made me paranoid, Ella has also made me feel better. Just the image of her house, her lovely comforting sofa, makes me feel all warm and cosy. The way she lets me talk. It feels like I'm being truly heard for the first time in ages.

'Where you going by the way?' she says. 'Sounds like you're driving.'

'Oh, nowhere.' I look ahead of me at the lines of traffic up Marylebone High Street. I'd spent a lot of time here after Jack had been born. After I'd gone AWOL from, well, my own life and Gav had to pick up the pieces. All the old associations come flooding back: the Waitrose where I'd lurked around in the aisles before every visit – not really focusing on what I wanted but killing time until my appointment, hating myself for what I'd done.

I told Sarah I'd be a couple of hours. I feel a thrum in my chest, birds trying to escape from behind my rib cage.

'I'm going absolutely nowhere.'

SARAH

'Jack,' she cajoles. 'Chocolate biscuit?' But he remains mute, his eyes resolutely on the ceiling. 'Your mummy is coming back soon, Jack.'

Sarah can't help it but his silence is making her nervous. A five-year-old! But it's almost eerie – a painful reminder of what she'd done. Does he know something? She's still reeling after the miscommunication of the zoo conversation. Or maybe he's so traumatised he's begun to lose his voice. It just gets worse and worse.

She remembers wondering if Casper's silences last year had meant anything either. Oh, how she'd googled and googled variations, looking for answers for her child's temporary muteness.

'He's only four. He's just trying to focus on his own things,' Tom had told her. 'They do that at this age. They're in their own world.'

She'd even gone so far as to ask Tom's mother when she'd been alive. Just for peace of mind. Except she hadn't quite got the answer she'd hoped, when she'd been told that maybe it was a sign that her grandson was a genius.

'Einstein didn't talk until he was four,' she had told her. 'Not a dickie.'

Sarah loves her son and he is a bright little boy but genius he is not. But she had been in an odd state of mind and she had *wanted* to look for problems. She'd been totally convinced that her son was exhibiting behaviour of *something*. She'd spent hours on the Mumsnet forums, trawling through any sign that might be good or bad. She remembers seeing one poster – *Anna Banana* – she can still remember the avatar to this day, three unicorn emojis and five exclamation marks with a ridiculous acronym. *DDD2*. Was that dear darling daughter? Anna Banana's daughter DDD2 had exhibited signs of the same thing. Sarah had been relieved. She'd thought it might have been a boy thing. And she'd scrolled down to find out that Anna Banana's DDD2 did indeed have something wrong with her. Selective mutism. *See?* She had shaken her iPad in Tom's face. She had good reason for her anxiety! It had, of course, turned out to be nothing.

But this time, with Jack, it's different. It's not her being overly anxious. How could her friend have said such a thing? No. This is out-and-out post-traumatic stress syndrome. Or anxiety. Or depression. Sarah knows it. It's perfectly obvious, and perfectly unsurprising, given what has happened. *Given what has happened.*

'Jack. Are you sure you don't want something?' He doesn't reply. 'It's lunch time soon. You have to eat. Your mum said you could sit up a bit. She'll be back soon.'

Nothing. She's seen Jack smiling before, at his physio. It's just her then. Maybe he's picking up on her mood – after everything that had happened with Ella this morning. And the WhatsApp message. And the weirdest thing of all is that Ella hadn't mentioned one word about it either.

'All OK?' Ella had said when Sarah had walked back into the room. Sarah knows Ella had seen the message. She had still been holding her phone for God's sake, looking at the screen and then towards her. But it was as though nothing had happened at all. Ella's face remained impassive, those grey eyes of hers combing the room. Charlotte G had practically been panting at this point, craning her neck to see what the message said.

'Oh, Sarah,' Charlotte had said. 'There you are. Funny. You just texted Ella.' Sarah had looked over then just to catch Ella's expression, but there was none. This, for some reason, felt even more dangerous. Her skin had prickled and she had felt her cheeks go cold. What was she up to? All these walls of silence.

She looks down at her best friend's son, pale and staring straight up at the ceiling. And then she has an idea. She'll ask Jack directly about the fall. She knows Liza doesn't want him reminded of it yet. But she has to know. She has to be warned if Jack is going to say anything at all. All this god-damn not knowing.

She won't be obvious. She'll prod him just enough that she can get some information but not enough that she jogs his memory. When she's made herself a cup of tea and replied to a weird message from Liza (who still hasn't bloody told her where she's gone), she pulls up an old chair that she'd meant to have reupholstered.

'Jack, do you know where your mummy went?'

Silence.

'She'll be back soon, you know. Just in case you were wondering.'

His arm twitches. She tries another tack.

'You want to know where Tom is going this weekend? Which football match he's going to?' Ha! That got his attention. But just as his gaze catches hers, he closes his eyes. 'OK, little one, I'll leave you to sleep. But just before you do, I wanted to say that you've been a very brave little boy. Since the fall.'

'Go away,' he says. 'I don't want you here.'

Indignation rises in her and then she feels sick. He's broken his neck for crying out loud. She should take the role of the adult here instead of being so childish.

'OK. I'm going,' she says. 'I love you Jack. I'm always here for you. You know that, don't you?'

And for the first time since the horrific event, she feels the full force of what she's done. She's been so caught up in trying to make things up to Liza that she thought she'd taken stock of things. But she hadn't. This – this is much, much worse. A sucker punch right in the gut. She's never actually stopped to examine her own feelings towards the whole thing. And she's barely given Jack's feelings a second thought. He is going to have to carry the weight of fear from his fall for the rest of his life.

A sick and shaky feeling rushes over her. She doesn't know where to turn. Tom? No. Perhaps she should confide in Camilla. Not tell her everything. Just edited bits. No again – she needs someone who knows the whole sorry story. The only person she can get help from – the only person she can talk to – is the exact person that she's come up against since the fall. Could she make herself vulnerable to Ella Bradby? Perhaps if she did, it would change the dynamic somewhat. Swing things into balance. She'd forget all about Ella's secret (despite the thought of it still festering away in her mind) and she'd apologise for the vicious things she'd said earlier on WhatsApp.

She knows Ella is going away soon. Barnaby had said so. And she'd seen it on the fridge calendar too – this week's diary laminated and colour-co-ordinated. So she knows she probably can't schedule something in – she knows how hard it is to get close to Ella. There's only one thing for it and now she knows where Ella lives. She'll have to turn up unannounced. She has to go and speak to her anyway about what they're both going to say to The Vale Club – she's decided she's going to persuade her that they go together. She's pushing her own temptation. Then a loud ring makes her jump. The landline. How extraordinary. She'd totally forgotten they even had one installed. She goes over to the sideboard in the hallway and picks it up after the fourth ring.

'Hello?' She's fully expecting some random caller or wrong number. The crackly echo of a sales call before the person on the other end of the line dives into some irritating pitch. She's already bracing herself to tell them to go away.

'Hello, is that Liza Barnstaple?'

'It's . . .' But before she can tell the lady on the line that it's not in fact Liza, she carries on speaking. 'We were given your details by Hammersmith hospital. I tried your mobile a few times with no luck so we thought it best to try the second number you gave us.'

Sarah nods down the phone and is about to stop the speaker in her tracks before she feels a jab of curiosity.

'Yes?' She picks up a dried flower petal from next to the phone. She has no idea where it has come from but she squeezes it between her fingers until it crunches into small, sharp pieces.

'It's social services here. We'd just like to speak to you about the fall. Your son's fall.' She drops the last bit of the flower on the floor and notices that her finger is bleeding. She squeezes out the droplet of blood, letting it rest on her fingertip.

'Oh yes?'

'It's protocol. When someone has a fall like that we need to speak to them about the surrounding circumstances. Make sure everything is OK at home. Can we send a health visitor over? We've got you down on our records anyway, Mrs Barnstaple, so we should have your details but I'll need to make sure they're all up to date.'

'Health visitor?' Sarah doesn't know why she's speaking the way she is. She knows perfectly well what a health visitor is – she'd had plenty of them coming to see her after Casper was born, checking to see if she was OK. And then she wonders why on earth they have Liza's records on file. Liza, who is such a natural mother that she makes everyone around her feel bumbling. Why would they feel the need to come and check in on Liza?

'Yes. Just to meet your son. Tomorrow a good time for you? Nothing at all to be concerned about, Mrs Barnstaple. We can send someone over at, what – say, four o'clock?'

'Four o'clock. Do hold on.' She adopts a very strange voice and grabs a tissue from the hallway table, to wipe her finger. It's a voice that sounds nothing like Liza – her accent verges on mock Australian, for God's sake. 'I'm sorry, Jack has a physio appointment then. Could I call you back? With a time? I'll have to make sure my husband is here too.'

'Yes. Please do call us back. My name's Beth. It's either

me or my colleague Theresa who'll be in the office later and tomorrow morning. Have you got a pen?'

'Pen? Oh, pen. To take your number. Of course.' Sarah has no idea what she's doing, or why she hasn't just told the truth – and that she'll get someone to call them back – but she pretends to pick up a pen and write down the digits that Beth recites down the phone. Ridiculous, she thinks. This whole pantomime charade of acting out the motions when no one can even see her. But it makes her duplicity feel somehow . . . better. She shudders as she realises this whole thing has been a reflex reaction – what kind of person does that make her?

'Thank you.' Beth is talking about the nice day outside but Sarah has stopped listening. She places the receiver, very carefully, back in its cradle, and with both arms and legs shaking, she makes her way back to the front room, where Jack is silently waiting.

WhatsApp group: Renegades
Members: Liza, Sarah

Liza: Just had weird chat with Ella who said something about a strange text you had sent? Or something like that. Couldn't get to the bottom of it! But said it might have something to do with me?

Sarah: Oh yeah – that. I was just talking to her about the meeting and the Christmas fair stuff. Said it was quite boring. How is everything? Where are you now?

Liza: Will be back soon. All ok there?

Sarah: All good. Just having a chat with Jack. He's certainly not his usual self, is he?

Liza: No. I'm going to have to do something about that, for sure.

Sarah: Like what?

Liza: Not sure. But thank you for pointing it out. I needed to hear it. Asking physio. Therapy or something? To try and help him process the fall and the moments that happened before. Not sure yet. Gotta run see you soon. Thank you again.

LIZA

'Jack, I'm here. I'm back. Mummy's back. All OK, I'm here.' Despite where I'd just been – the past revisited – the shattering guilt – or maybe even because of it, I still feel that mad rush of love for my kids. 'Thea? Little one, you are so cute.' I kiss her squashy nose and plonk down on the sofa. 'Sarah, thank you for watching. I really appreciate it. Wow. I'm done in. Go, go go.'

'Sure? You look zonked. Or like you've been crying? Are you OK, Li? Where have you just been? Did you see Gav?'

'No, no.'

'What were you doing when you headed out?' Sarah is trying to sound casual, looking down at her phone. I suppose I am, too.

'I just went for an appointment. Just doctors. To see about,' I wave vaguely at my head, in the hope she'll just be quiet, 'just about sleeping and stuff.' I turn away from her, thinking about the small square room I'd just been in. The green plastic chair, the moulding of which was so familiar to me. The polystyrene cup of tea with a slightly soapy aftertaste.

'So earlier you were saying about Ella?' Sarah says. 'Something about a phone call?' I should have known – Sarah will always come full circle to Ms Bradby.

'Oh, she was saying all sorts of stuff I couldn't work out.'

'Sure she's not doing anything weird? Trying to come between us, show her power?' There's a sharpness in her voice that Sarah has when she's scared.

'No Sa, I just think she has everyone's best interests at heart and I think she's quite genuine. She's got a good nature. And just wants to help. Mary said so. And others I spoke to.'

'I dunno. I feel anxious around her. And like I said – I know she's hiding stuff.'

'I told you, I don't want to hear about all that.' I can't believe I'm having to tell her this again. But she looks up at me with a gleam in her eye.

'Then I won't tell you about how I've been doing some research and the things I've found out on Facebook. I think it's quite plausible that Ella has a love child with Rufus North. I think the child's abroad. Somewhere. And I don't think her family know what she's up to.'

For a second I want to admit that she's piqued my interest. Of course she has. But I can't let myself get further involved in this game of Sarah versus Ella at the moment.

'That's crazy, Sarah – seriously . . . nuts. I – I can't deal with that. I need to just focus on Jack right now.'

'Yes. Of course. But I'm telling you again, Liza, there's something amiss about her.' She clenches her fists. 'She's up to something weird.'

'Ah love, you're just projecting. It's because she's ghosted you once. Probably don't know where you stand with her. You know?' I watch Sarah shake her head. Ella had ghosted everyone and I feel slightly mean for pinpointing it to Sarah – but really, I'm fed up with her obsession of trying to turn me against Ella. 'But I think we've just got to accept that she's different from us. She doesn't have the same hang-ups. In fact, I don't know if she has any at all. And as for hiding stuff – we all have stuff we want to keep quiet. Don't we? But honestly, a secret love child is insane.' My tone is sharp. It seems mean, and churlish, after all Ella has done for me, to entertain this kind of gossip. I think about the effort she went to with hiring Mary, with bringing all Jack's potions and medicines, and *really* listening to me the other day at her house.

'Fine,' Sarah says. 'But you'll see. She is not who you think she is.' She looks like she wants to say more but she sees my warning face and shrugs. 'Anyway. I've got to go. Tom wants a quiet night in. Just rang me from work. He's going to cook. Want me to bring anything down?'

'No, thank you though.' And she walks out. I notice again she sends only a fleeting glance in Jack's direction. Nothing more. And when she does, she gulps back air and looks towards the front door. Strange. That's the second time she's done that.

When Sarah's gone, I set Jack up with an audio book, feed Thea and put her to sleep. I text Gav and tell him that all is OK – that everything is under control – and I take pictures of the kids so he knows what's going on.

Then I shut the door to the kitchen and go into my room – it's the first time I've really sat in here in the daylight. I look around. Sarah's added so many little touches that I hadn't noticed before. There are two little photos on each of the bedside tables – one of me and her during our first night out after we'd had Jack and Casper. There are our two faces, cheeks squished together. She's holding a sparkler and screwing up her nose, I'm holding up a champagne bottle. Crowds of people are behind us, strobes of flashing purple lights behind us. And then on the other side is a photo of Sarah and Jack together at the park. Gav had taken the photo. Jack had only been one month old. We'd gone for a stroll, with him in the buggy. I remember Gav clowning around, everyone laughing. How easy things had been back then. Before Jack had turned eight weeks old and disaster had struck. I think back to what I'd been like at the time. Fretful and worried. Sleep-starved. On the brink of a panic attack at all times.

I pick up the photo and stare closely. I feel happy looking at it. But then a sort of sadness closes around me and I find it hard to breathe. Sadness that Sarah had gone to so much effort to make me feel at home and I hadn't appreciated, or even noticed, it. Nostalgia for times past.

Sarah had been through so much last year. 'Well, everyone goes through shit like this,' she'd said, shrugging her shoulders. 'Don't they? Just have to move on and ask for help when you need it.' Except she hadn't really discussed Rosie again. But I wasn't going to make the same mistake. I pick up my mobile and dial Jan, the physio.

'Hi,' I say. 'I was going to ask you earlier. It was just all a bit of a rush.' I explain what I need. What *Jack* needs. A recommendation of someone to talk to about the trauma he has been through. Some sort of outlet so that he doesn't suffer any mental and emotional conse-quences from the fall.

'Of course,' she says. 'I'll see how I can help. Anything for that cheeky little chappie. I've grown very fond of the boy.'

I begin to feel much, much better. Something has lifted. I feel better after my trip out. I feel better after seeing that old photo of Sarah and Jack. The memories of times when Gav and I had been a unit with each other. I do something I haven't done in ages, and text him to ask if he wants to have supper.

I know the separation still stands. But – just as a family? I'll cook. I'll explain to him then about getting Jack some therapy. That he is traumatised and needs help and that I've already paved the way by asking Jan to help us find someone. We can spend the time discussing things as two adults. Something we've missed for a long time.

Sure, he replies. Sounds good. As a family. Hope starts to bloom in my chest.

'Hey, buddy.' I walk out back into the room where Jack is listening to *The Twits*. 'We're going to be OK. All of us. We're going to be OK. You understand?' His gaze moves towards me and for the first time in ages, I see him give an almost indeterminable nod. Only I, as his mother, would have known it was there.

I think about the look that Sarah gave me before her departure earlier. The look she had given Jack. How her silence towards him had prompted me to do something. At the time, something that had passed her features had made me feel uncomfortable. I'd dismissed it. *Don't be daft*, I'd told myself. I'd put it down to Jack and the fact he was so desperately miserable. But then the more I replay the expression in my mind, the more I recognise it from somewhere. And then I realise – it's the look she gave Ella, right after we'd heard Jack scream. I still can't read it. But if I didn't know better, I'd put a bet that there was horror in there. Horror, mixed with a flash of something, like guilt.

Now *why*, I think to myself. Why would that be?

To: G.Paphides@westlondongazette.com
From: J.Roper@westlondongazette.com

Hi George

   Hope you are having a great holiday. No problem
at all. I'll do what you suggested and I'm about to
interview Harry Framlingham from Savills, Chiswick
branch, about the most expensive house in W3 being
sold yesterday – just on the road up from The Vale
Club. 2.8 mill. A positive piece.

   Kind regards
   J

SARAH

Once she's dropped Casper off at the school gates, she makes a mental list of the things she needs to do today. Book Casper an appointment at the dentist (she's been feeding him far too many sweets lately), do the washing and ironing and change all the sheets. She'll Hoover too. Despite Helen coming once a week, the house still manages to look grubby after a few days. She normally loves Friday mornings. Her 'housework' day before Helen arrives when she tidies things and puts away the washing. (She had always complained when her mother had told her to tidy before the cleaner arrived. 'Why would I do that? Surely that's what a cleaner does?' But now she knows.) She feels no pressure to *do* anything on Friday mornings, other than her task at hand. And she can put the matter of finding a 'real job', as Tom calls it, to the back of her mind. And as she's thinking of a real job, she remembers she hasn't done the Airbnb listing. She and Tom are having supper tonight and he's bound to ask. She can't hold it off any longer. She races to the downstairs flat and knocks on the door.

'Ah, Sa, how are you?' Liza looks agitated. She's in an old, holey T-shirt and her hair's scraped up in a bun.

'Good, thanks so much. Just came down to take some photos for the Airbnb profile.'

'Oh yes, of course.' Liza doesn't react in quite the way Sarah had expected. In fact, she doesn't seem to react at all. 'Go for it. Go right ahead. Jack's tutor is here so I'll go have a quick shower and get ready and you can do your magic. Thea's just asleep in that room so if you could go in there last that would be great.'

After a beat, Liza continues: 'Have you been to The Vale Club yet? They actually rang me just now.'

Shit. Sarah thinks about the social services phone call she'd put off earlier and how this is all getting out of hand. She hasn't even been able to ring her mother back, who is now sending her frantic texts.

'Sure they just want to look like they're doing stuff but I know the press has been on to it – and you know how set Gav is on everyone saying their piece. So if you could chat to them soon that would be great. Then we can hopefully just move on.'

'Fine.' Sarah defies her voice not to waver. 'That's absolutely fine. Of course I'll go later on. Just as soon as Tom gets back. Then I won't have Casper pulling on me, wanting attention.' She's aware she needs to shut up. That she's sounding a bit bonkers but she just can't seem to stop. 'You know how these children are.'

'I do,' Liza frowns at her and walks away. 'OK, just going for that shower . . .'

Sarah watches her friend go into the bedroom – she looks at the way her shoulders slope, the shush of her slippers as she slides her feet unenthusiastically across the floor. It reminds her exactly of how Liza was acting after Jack had been born. And then, as she's thinking about that, a vague memory of Gav floats into her psyche. A memory that she didn't even know was there. It was something he'd said to her after Liza had gone AWOL, when Jack was only a few months old. He'd said: *Perhaps it's best for everyone if me and Liza separate. Then I can take Jack.*

She must be imagining things, surely. Getting her times muddled up. But then she remembers how she'd laughed at him – telling him not to be absolutely ridiculous. Why would he want to take Jack? And he couldn't punish Liza for feeling like crap. She had just had a baby after all. He'd gone silent then and looked close to tears. She'd put it down to things taking their toll on him but, looking back on it, perhaps this was when things had really started to change between those two.

She'd ignored the problem after that. She had a newborn herself after all. Tom had talked her down. Told her to focus on her own life. And Gav had never elaborated after all. But something now starts to ring alarm bells. Something she can't get a firm grasp on.

Other memories from long ago start to surface. Gav 'wetting the babies' heads' with Tom. Tom had come home slurring his words – he'd woken her up. Something about Gav. Liza. How something awful had happened. *Very dishstreshing.* Tom had repeated it over and over. He had stumbled on the carpet. But then the next day they'd argued about Tom not pulling his weight and they'd both forgotten about it. Had she missed something awful? About why Liza had gone AWOL, and why Gav had left? About why he'd stuck around to control her? Sarah's mind is going crazy now. She doesn't know what to think, and she's still reeling from having caught him with another woman.

She hears the shower go in the main bedroom. Jack is doing his phonics. His tutor is holding up cards just above his eyeline and is distracted. She sees Liza's phone on the table just underneath the lower-ground bay window, tantalisingly within reach. She takes her own mobile, lining it up as best she can to take a good photo of the flat. She extends her arms in exaggerated movements, just so the tutor has no doubt as to exactly what she is doing – she really will use it for the Airbnb site too – and she tells herself she's not being so deceitful after all.

She sits on the table and takes some more pictures. But when she is sure that no one is looking, still holding her own phone up, she picks up Liza's phone and presses the screen.

Never had a password, Liza would always tell her. *Got nothing interesting to hide.* Sarah has no idea what she's looking for. Something. Nothing. Everything.

She scrolls through a few WhatsApps. She sees a conversation between Liza and Ella. She shouldn't look. She knows she shouldn't. But one quick glance wouldn't hurt? Surely. Just a quick scroll. Just as her finger hovers over the screen, she sees a notification for an unread email from yesterday. Uber. Liza's Uber account. Of course – she'd gone somewhere yesterday and she'd never explained where – other than to say she'd been to the doctor about her sleep. Seventeen pounds the journey cost. Hmmm. It must have been quite far away. Liza's always moaning about how expensive Uber has got these days. But she can't just have popped round the corner. Sarah pulls up Liza's Uber app, whilst contorting her body into different positions to take pictures out of the window. 'Ah lovely,' she says out loud, desperate to keep looking at Liza's phone but knowing she has to keep the charade up. 'Sorry. I'll be out of your hair soon.'

'Not to worry at all,' Liza replies. 'It's nice to have someone around.'

Sarah hears the water being turned off. The bang of the shower door. Jesus – she doesn't have long. She holds off a few seconds, terrified Liza's about to come out. When she hears silence again, she glances back down, still feeling sick at the thought of being caught out. Yet the urge to find out the information is too strong.

Marylebone? How peculiar, she thinks. What on earth could Liza have been doing in Marylebone? She thinks of all the boutique shops there on the high street. Nothing jogs her memory until her eyes fall onto the name of the actual street that Liza had visited. She enlarges the map that's come up from Liza's previous history and, bingo – there it is. *Devonshire Street*.

The name rings a very faint bell. She takes a mental note of the exact address and puts Liza's phone back. She takes a few last pictures, and by that time Liza has reappeared from the bathroom.

'Wow, that feels better,' Liza says, brushing through her hair with her fingers. 'Much better. Guess who's coming over for supper tonight? I'm going to make a real effort. Not that anything's happening, of course. It's just the first time we've been together as a . . .' She pinches the top of her nose. 'Well, you know. Family. Family time.'

'Gav's coming to supper?' Sarah hears alarm bells ring. 'What on earth for? Are you letting him back in your life, just like that? After the way he's been treating you?'

She spits out her words. Only when she sees Liza's face does she realise she's gone too far.

'Treating me?' Liza looks furious, her mouth set in a tight line. 'Treating me? What about the way you've been . . .' She stops. Sarah wonders what Liza was about to say, but she doesn't know if she can bear to hear the answer.

She wishes she could just tell Liza why she is so anti Gav. She's held her tongue up until now, but perhaps she *should* tell her about that pretty blonde lady, laughing along with Gav outside the IVF clinic. Just as she's working out what to say next, she realises that Liza has almost reared up at her, the anger flashing in her eyes. Any tension between her and Liza has never blown up into a fight like this before – they've had unspoken hurts that, granted, have become more frequent lately, but they've always smoothed them over. Today, she's going to have to be the bigger person. She has an agenda, and she has to stick to it.

'Liza,' she says firmly, adopting a school-teacher tone. 'I'm just looking out for you. I don't want you to get hurt. That's all. You know that Gav's been a bit off lately – *more* than off.'

'You don't want to hurt me?' Liza's raising her voice now, not caring whether Jack and his tutor can hear. 'By pretending to know what's best for me and Gav? If you knew what was best for us, you'd be pleased we were hanging out together. But maybe you don't want that for me. Maybe you want to keep things just as they are?'

Sarah takes a step back, shocked by Liza's vitriol. Has she been harbouring these feelings towards her all along?

'Look at you when we moved in. Being all huffy with

him so I have to overcompensate. You think that's best? Or is there something else at play here? Is there? Some reason you won't even look him in the eye? You ask me to move in, which I'm grateful for, but then you act so weird that . . . Oh,' she throws her hands up in the air, 'fuck it. You tell me. What's really going on here, Sa?'

Sarah feels very frightened. *Something else at play? What's really going on?* Does Liza know more than she's letting on? All these conversations she and Ella have been having on WhatsApp? She freezes. She can't speak. That's a good thing, she thinks. If she says anything else, she might incriminate herself. Best be silent. But she wants to weep for the direction her and Liza's friendship seems to have taken – especially knowing that she only has herself to blame. She lets out a cry.

'I'm going then,' she falters, pausing just for a second to see if Liza will grab her hand, tell her not to be silly. But she doesn't, and Sarah's forced to flee.

She runs up the stairs back into the main house, great sobs coming out of her mouth, and switches on her computer. She's darned if she isn't going to find out what's going on. At least then, perhaps she'll be vindicated. Somehow. She types the address she's just found into the Google search bar. At first, a map loads up. Come on. Hurry up, she thinks. Where the fuck has her friend been? And could her suspicions be right about Gav?

An image loads up in the side toolbar on Google Maps. A very discreet corner building, attached to a large house that's painted black. Very strange. What the hell could it be? She zooms in, the argument with Liza sidelined for the moment. She sees a name on a dulled gold sign on the door. *Hilda Zettenberg Home*. Even stranger. For some reason her breath keeps catching, an impending sense of doom draped around her neck. She types *Hilda Zettenberg Home* into her search bar. The first search results make her laugh. She isn't sure why. Shock? Disbelief? *Nerves.* But she continues to scroll down and down. And then she bursts into tears. She's missed it. How could she have missed it? All this time? She thought she knew Liza back to front. She's known her breakfast habits for the past five years. She even calculated her own cycle by Liza's. But this? Nothing could have prepared her for this.

Gav. Everything becomes very clear to her now. *Everything.* It meant that she'd *never* tell the truth now about what happened about The Vale Club. It would all get too ugly, for Liza. If Gav for one minute thought that Liza had been neglectful in her maternal care, that she had chosen to take Sarah's word for it, things could get very dangerous for her friend indeed. A series of images scroll through her mind, each one making her gasp aloud. No – she could never, ever let Gav find out.

She's going to be decisive in her actions. Liza needs protecting. She needs love and support from her friends. Not snarky comments and bad behaviour. Sarah feels horrendous about the earlier harsh words spoken between them. But, thank God she hadn't replied to the journalist. Thank God she had moved Liza in, safe from harm. And thank God she hadn't yet spoken to the club. She'd had a constant low-level thought that she'd just come out with the truth at any given point, the facts bursting from her like an unchecked dam. But, now, if anything is going to set her decision about what she was going to tell them – it was this.

She wipes her face, tears all over her cheeks. Her absolute worst fears have been confirmed. The thoughts she'd stumbled upon and tried to dismiss – to bat away because they were too awful to contemplate. They are true and she needs to hurry and do something, before her friend is put in a very real and present danger.

LIZA

I hadn't initially thought about dressing up for Gav tonight. After all, he seems so disinterested in me I didn't think he'd even notice. But after I'd seen Sarah's expression before I'd got into the shower this morning – eyes wide and mouth dangling open before she'd quickly snapped it shut, no doubt gawping at the flab of my belly and my untamed body hair – I decided I need to make an effort. There was after all, I told myself, a difference between dressing for a man and a little bit of self-respect.

I think about mine and Sarah's earlier row. In five years of friendship, we've never raised voices at each other, yet her insistence that I stay away from Gav had made me completely lose it. Sarah – once again getting fixated on an idea, thinking she knows best, burying her way into people's lives, their relationships. Like with Ella Bradby. Why can't she just keep out of it and focus on the train wrecks in her own life, I think, with a stab of guilt. I resolve to try and focus on mine and Gav's supper tonight and put our argument to the back of my mind.

I'll see if she comes and apologises to me later – after all, it's her who's been acting so strangely.

'Hey Franny,' I shout to Jack's tutor, 'mind if I take Thea really quickly to the shops? You all right to stay here with Jack? Jack darling, is that OK?' He doesn't reply. I hope he hasn't been affected by mine and Sarah's argument; we didn't exactly keep our voices down.

'Course,' says Franny. 'I'm here for another two hours so take your time.'

I go and buy the finest fillet steak from the local butcher's. Then I get a nice bottle of red. By the time I get home, there's even enough time for me to do a full beauty routine.

I choose a jumpsuit from Whistles, which I've never worn. One of those that I've been saving for a special occasion, the likes of which had never really turned up – meaning it was still in its packaging in my drawer. I wax, moisturise, slip on the jumpsuit and put on some make-up. I even straighten my hair. I feel lighter, somehow. The guilt still simmers away; about the fall and that memory of Gav and Jack all those years ago, and the things said and done afterwards. But it is time to move on, despite what Sarah says. A small part of me wonders whether she is right, or if she can see something I can't. But tonight, we are going to be a family, and whatever his intentions are – to stay or go – I'm going to be an adult about this. Besides, Sarah knows nothing about the side of things that I've kept behind closed doors.

By the time Gav arrives, I've managed to put Thea down. I reapply my make-up, rolling on another layer of deodorant.

'Gav,' I open the door. He responds well to me. Smiles that great big grin of his and walks right on through, as though there'd never been anything wrong in our marriage in the first place. I think about when we'd first met. And our wedding day – under a tree with his mates' band playing in the corner of his aunt's Hampshire garden. Me in a flowing, vintage gown, him in a suit looking dapper, a top hat in his hand. Both my parents had been alive, Mum in her wheelchair waiting for me at the end of the aisle. Those were better days. I can't quite compute that this is where we are now. *But of course we are*, I tell myself. *Where else would we be after I'd done what I had?*

'Hello, you look nice.' He passes me a bunch of flowers. 'I thought you could do with these.'

'Thank you. I've made you steak. Jack is awake still but I'm going to put an audio story on for him in a bit. You go in and talk to him. I'll get dinner finished.'

'Wow. Thanks.'

'And I've got that wine you like too.' I feel my cheeks reddening. 'I mean, I know this is not, like . . . it's just that I thought you might like some. I'm not drinking tonight. Got awful insomnia.'

'Sure. A glass would be lovely.' He walks over to Jack. I hear them laughing together. I put some poivre sauce on the hob and take him a glass of red and some Twiglets, his favourite snack. It feels comforting to be like this. As a family, despite this limbo. I pour myself a ginger ale and sit, waiting for Jack to sleep.

By the time he's gently snoring, supper is on the table.

'You seem – stronger?' Gav says. 'Better than I've seen you for ages.'

I want to tell him everything – that I actually feel so fragile, and where I'd been yesterday. But I keep my mouth shut. I don't want the night to end in tears, in memories and recriminations. And, worst of all, Gav's panic.

'Thank you.' I pour him some more wine. 'You good?'

'I'm well. Thank you.' He tips his wine glass towards me. 'Cheers.'

'Cheers,' I say, holding up my drink.

'We haven't done this for a long time, have we?'

I want to tell him that that's not down to me. But again, I'm quiet. It seems that everything is loaded. 'I know. We should do it more often.' I nod my head towards Jack's direction. 'For the kids' sake if anything. Be grown-ups about it all.'

'I don't think it was me who wasn't being the grown-up,' he says. I snap my head up. Here we go. But I look up and see he's laughing. 'Just kidding. I know how I can be sometimes.'

'Do you?'

'I do. And I know that, well – I could have played things differently that time. After Jack was born.' I watch the bob of his Adam's apple. 'Perhaps we wouldn't be in this mess now. I think perhaps – maybe we should have spoken to someone. Together.' I want to interrupt here – tell him what I've done – but he is rarely this open, so I let him carry on. 'Not buried our heads in the sand. It sank us – what happened. Didn't it?'

'Yes it did. I'm learning too, Gav. I am.'

'Cheers again.' He lifts his glass into the air.

'Oh, that reminds me,' I say. 'About speaking to someone,' I falter. 'I thought we should get Jack some therapy. Of some sort. Talk to someone about the fall. I don't know what kind. But he's having trouble. He's really struggling. He's been OK with you but he hasn't seen you that much.' I try and keep the accusation out of my voice. 'I mean, I know how much you've been checking up on them,' I add quickly, 'I'm not saying . . .'

'I know you aren't. It's OK. Don't worry. Sure.' I know Gav's trying to level out his own emotions too. 'That's a good idea. I think that would be helpful. It had crossed my mind too actually.'

'I was worried you'd dismiss me.'

'Oh God. Liza. I'm sorry you thought that. For all your no-nonsense you're quite a softie at heart, aren't you.' He reaches over and takes my hand again. 'I know someone actually. Katy. She deals in post-traumatic stress disorder. And she's just starting to take kids on. She's great. She used to go out with Gordo. Remember him?'

'That funny guy who went to Zimbabwe for work and ran off with someone?'

'Yup. That's the one.'

'Well – what does she do? Can she help? I've asked Jan to look into it but if you think this is better, then I'm all for it.'

'I'm absolutely sure she can. She owes me a favour or two. She does something called scrambling. Helps people relive the moments before a trauma. Then she helps them replay the memory, whilst scrambling it.'

'Scrambling? Like . . . eggs?'

'They put the memory to funny music, or speed it up. Put some comic motion to it so the memory loses its poison. She helps the body release the trauma too. Something I'd have dismissed as crap in my twenties.' He bites his thumbnail. I think of Gav and the things he's been through too. The foster care and the generally shitty upbringing.

'Sounds amazing,' I say. 'Thank you.' We're still holding hands. There's no weirdness surrounding it. He squeezes my fingers. I can do this, I think. Whatever happens, I've got this. The room goes silent, both of us lost in thought. He looks like he wants to say something, but then we both hear a thud coming from upstairs.

'What the hell was that?' And then screams and shouts. It's Sarah. My first thought is that she's been burgled. But then I can hear Tom too.

'No,' he's shouting. 'I refuse to believe it.' I know that voice of Tom's. Irritation with a creep of panic. Then I can hear footsteps.

'He's here,' Sarah's shouting. 'He's here now. He's in the downstairs flat.'

They're coming closer to the door. My heart speeds up. I look at Gav. He's holding one finger up to his lips.

'What the hell?' I whisper but the words get stuck in my throat. And she's going on and on. I wonder if I should mention to Gav what happened earlier, the argument. Tom is telling her to be quiet but she's getting louder and louder, her screams are getting more and more shrill. And then it goes silent, except for small sobs that I can hear not far from where we are sitting. She must be sitting right at the top of the stairs that lead down to our basement. The swishing in my stomach is becoming almost unbearable. I reach for Gav's glass.

'What's going on?' he says. 'What the hell is going on?'

'I don't know,' I say, but I'm shaking. 'I haven't heard them before now, I didn't know you could hear anything upstairs.'

And then it goes totally silent. Nothing. Which in itself feels even more disconcerting. I get up and crane my neck towards where Jack is sleeping. No movement.

'What did she mean, *he's* here?' Gav says. 'Was she talking about . . . me? What's the big deal?'

'I don't know what her problem is, it's scaring me,' I tell him.

I've been hiding so much, from everyone and myself, it feels good to finally speak the truth. I say it again. 'I just don't know.'

West London Gazette editorial notes, October 2019
J Roper interview transcript: Angela Harrington, witness,
The Vale Club

I was there when it happened. The poor mother was
inside – watching her kid from the table that overlooks
the playground.

All I hear now is that everyone's talking about her,
saying what a bad parent she is. Well – all I can say that
it was totally different in my day. None of this new-
fangled helicopter-parenting and the likes. That poor
woman probably just needed a little break. She doesn't
deserve all of this nasty stuff.

It seems that everything now is based around this
strange parenting anxiety in these modern times. People
terrified that the world is going to end up in chaos – what
with political and climate change. Economic uncertainty.
So of course they do everything they can to protect their
kids from all of that. And then there's the internet. I'm
a member of this grandmas' site. Support for grand-
parents who do some of the childcare. I'm always aghast
at what's on it. And then on the mums' sites too: 'breast-
feeding only, no sugar, no playing in mud because of
parasites, play in mud because if you don't get germs

then you'll get leukaemia, sleep with your kids for a year, don't sleep with them or they'll get too attached . . .' It's never-ending.

No wonder the parents nowadays have so much pressure on them. It's awful. But then there's not the childcare support to go with it, is there? Unless you've got pots of money.

You see in my day none of this existed. We just played outside, entertaining ourselves in this blissful ignorance.

So really, I just thought to myself that this poor woman – she was probably just tired. She probably needed a break, and to sit down and have a cup of coffee. And well – bad stuff happens.

I told my daughter-in-law all of this when I dropped off Gracie but she got very cross with me. Said that if this mum couldn't look after her kid then maybe she should get childcare. I said maybe she couldn't afford it and then she went mad and said if she could afford The Vale Club, she could afford childcare. I don't think that's true. She just chose to spend her money on the health club. And she needed a rest. But I daren't say that at all. I once had a big row with them and I wasn't allowed to see my Gracie for a fortnight. So now, I just shut my mouth, you see.

Except really, it seems like I'm the only one. It's all anyone can talk about around here. Wherever I go – shops, tea parties, lunches – the rumours, the whispers about what really happened, about who is to blame, they're everywhere. It seems I'm best out of it. I don't really want to join that vipers' nest, even though I was actually there when it happened. But that's the decision I've made. To sit there quietly whilst the noise buzzes around me. I shut my mouth and get on with it.

SARAH

Her whole body aches. Her eyes sting, her muscles clenched tight. She's been sitting on the same step for twenty minutes now, stroking patterns into the carpet with her fingertips. Tom has stormed upstairs and Casper is watching *PAW Patrol*.

She had told Tom everything. The minute he'd walked through the door. He'd barely had a chance to take his coat off before she launched into the whole sorry lot.

'Here!' She had thrust her computer under his nose. 'Look what I found, Tom. Look – this is where Liza went yesterday. You know anything at all about this?'

He had put down his old, black briefcase and held up his hands. 'Hang on, Sa, I have no idea what you are talking about. Just give me a minute. I need the loo. And listen. I can't. Not right now . . . I've got a lot going on at work. Can this all just wait?'

She had waited for him right outside the bathroom door. 'No. I need to talk to you,' she had persisted, over the flush of water. 'Listen to this.' She explained the bits of the puzzle that she had pieced together from years ago.

300

She'd remembered other bits too, after she'd spent hours staring open-mouthed at the computer screen. Things Liza had said that now made sense. 'Did you know that this was happening?'

'Sarah – you are off your nut. What the hell is up with you at the moment? You're talking rubbish. Listen, I need to speak to you.' But before he can finish his sentence she starts to shake his elbow and jabs her finger on the keyboard. 'Look. Can't you see now what's been going on?'

'Sarah, they've been our friends now for over five years. I think we'd know if there was anything amiss. Or rather, anything as bad as this. Don't you? Listen please, just take a breath for a minute and stop being irrational.'

'Irrational? Are you going to tell me I've got PMT too?' She starts to shriek at this point, the tone of her voice wandering into alto territory. 'Tom, you need to fucking well listen to me. Think about it. Liza disappearing after Jack was born. Gav going AWOL. Liza not breathing a word of it to me – her best friend. It's really weird, Tom. Something is going on – has been for years. I never thought to question it that time Liza went off the map. Just thought she had postnatal depression after Jack. I mean, I was hardly in a position to help too much, was I? I did as much as I could. But now I see – it wasn't that. It wasn't that at all. And now Gav going off again and that weird controlling thing? And if you must know, he's seeing someone else.'

'What? Sarah, seriously. You're beginning to scare me. You're frantic, come and sit down . . .'

'Are you listening to anything that I'm saying?'

'I am. I hear you. But you've been behaving so oddly

lately that I'm not sure if anything you're saying is rooted in reality.'

She knows she shouldn't question her own mind. That everything surrounding the accident has made her feel stressed – but she also knows what she saw. She knows that Liza is not in a safe place. She *knows* that Gav is dangerous.

'You arsehole,' she hisses. 'Don't try and fuck with me. Listen to what I'm telling you.'

'Look, see? You can't talk to me rationally. You're letting this get out of control, Sarah. Gav's a good bloke. Sure, they've had rough patches, but you can't seriously think . . .'

It's at this point that she'd turned on her foot, stormed from the room and slammed the door. She is so enraged at Tom's reaction that she can't think straight. He'd looked at her like she'd totally lost her mind. Maybe she had? She doesn't know anything any more.

She doesn't care if Gav had heard her shouting. In a way, she hopes he had. But Tom – instead of reacting kindly, he'd just behaved as though she was making all this up, let alone said anything to support her, or Liza. After all she's been going through. It's like she barely knows her husband. Kind, supportive Tom who would normally by this point have scooped Liza up, brought her to the sofa, and offered her not only the clothes off his back, but his mattress for her to sleep on.

Sarah feels like shouting at him again but she doesn't have the energy. Today has taken absolutely everything out of her. She'll wait for him to come downstairs before she has another chat with him. Maybe she had cornered him too quickly. She tells herself not to spiral. That she must focus on Liza and stay calm for her. Focus and work out a plan. She'll ring for help. And there's absolutely no way now that Liza can move out of the flat. She'll lie down dead before that happens, before Liza is somewhere where she can't keep an eye on her. She also decides she'll march up to The Vale Club as soon as possible and give her statement. She'd had more missed calls from them earlier. She knows she's been putting it off, but now she doesn't need to any longer. She really has the bit between her teeth. The sooner she tells them that it was their fault – somehow they'd been negligent with the post – then Gav would leave Liza alone. Hell, he'd leave them *all* alone. It's the best thing she can do. Not just for herself, she thinks shamefully, but for Liza too.

Then she thinks of social services. The way she'd batted them off. Perhaps, perhaps she should tell Liza that they'd rung. Give her some hints that she had the help if she needed it. She would have to pretend she'd forgotten to mention it earlier. Oh hell – her brain feels like it's in overdrive.

She logs onto Airbnb and deletes the half-finished profile she'd started this morning. Then she texts Liza and tells her exactly what's happening. Two weeks? Hell to that. She can stay a full year if she likes. She's full of shame at what she's done to her friend. It's getting worse now she knows what Liza has been going through all this time – and now there's the added guilt at the argument they'd had earlier. She can feel it permeating right through to her bones.

She'll go and apologise to Tom, too, for how she's been handling things, but first she'll check on Casper. He's happily slumped on the sofa eating rice cakes. She

suddenly remembers a headline she read the other day –
something about rice cakes and arsenic. She whips them
away from him, bracing herself for his whining. She's
going to stand firm now. And not just with Casper.
Boundaries, boundaries, boundaries. It was all she'd been
told about at her and Tom's Relate sessions and now she
realises exactly what the lady had meant as she'd poured
them more tea and told them they needed to learn their
own positioning in life.

Sarah walks up the stairs breathing in and out slowly.
She feels her fingertips tingle. She opens the door, fully
prepared to tell Tom that she's sorry. To say that she
knows she shouldn't have accosted him like that and
that they'll have to let Liza stay for as long as she needs.
But when she opens the door, she realises something is
amiss. Tom is doing something she's never, ever seen him
do before. Not in nearly ten years of marriage and five
years of dating prior to that.

Tom is sitting straight-backed, arms folded on the bed,
tears running down his cheeks. Her Tom. Her lovely Tom
is sitting on their bed, weeping as though his life depended
on it.

WhatsApp group: Renegades
Members: Liza, Sarah

Sarah: Hi, just to say that I'm sorry about earlier. I really am. I shouldn't have acted that way. Especially when I think I know what's going on. With Gav. I hope you can forgive me. And don't worry. You're safe. I've got your back. You can stay as long as you like. Alright? Until things are sorted. We'll get through this. You and me. And the kids. But you have to get out of there. You have to get out. Ok? You can do it. With my help. With Tom's help. You'll be safe.

Liza: ??? Thanks! And no worries. Thanks for the apology. Me too. I'm sorry I snapped back. This isn't us, is it? And are u talking about Jack or what? The Vale Club? They're putting in massive safety procedures apparently. We'll hear updates soon after they've finished talking to people. And I think they said they'd put something in their newsletter about the changes they made and what happened. So they're dealing with it well, I think. Not trying to cover things up. Anyway – Gav here. We heard you shouting just now. All ok?

Sarah: All fine! More importantly – stay safe, my friend. Stay safe. I'm just upstairs if you need me. Ok?

Liza: er . . . you too? Thanks!

LIZA

Shit. Thea. Jack. I sit upright in my bed, paralysed with fear that if I get up and see the kids dead in the bed, my life will change forever. Fragments of last night's nightmare start replaying in my mind. Jack screaming for me, his body broken on the floor. I remember briefly coming to in the night, wondering if it was real – whether it was happening all over again. *Mummy. Mummy. Help me.* And every time I tried to reach him, his hand would pull further and further from my grasp.

I don't know what's better – the rampant insomnia, or the terrors that plague my mind when I do sleep. It's eight o'clock in the morning and I haven't tended to them once during the night. It feels like the moment I relax, something bad will happen. Better just stay here and not move. Then I realised that was stupid. They were fine. I was just having flashbacks from Jack's fall.

Until now I'd managed to stop thinking about it for a while. Managed to keep an even keel. I mentally run through the things that happened last night. Did anything go amiss? Did I do anything I wasn't supposed to?

Nice supper. Nice chat with Gav. Weird, weird shouting from Sarah and then those peculiar texts about me staying safe . . . Not to mention the row we'd had. I've begun to feel sorry for her. She looks like she's totally on the edge; pale skin, trembling hands and constantly watering eyes.

But last night had been a haven from all of that. The telly-watching after supper with Gav, laughing together like we used to. As I slowly recall everything, the strangled feeling loosens. All is OK. I had done nothing wrong.

Gav had stayed on the pull-out bed next to Jack. 'I think I'll just kip on the truckle,' he'd said, scraping our plates clean and loading the dishwasher before I'd gone to sleep. 'Is that OK?'

'Of course,' I'd said. 'Jack will be so happy.' Then I'd fallen asleep straight away – how alien that is to me these days.

I hear the sound of laughter. It's Jack. I walk into the other room.

'Gav, thanks for being here this morning. Wow. I haven't slept in this late since, well, I can't remember.'

'I know. I realised last night. I just want to say sorry to you that I haven't been here for you more in the nights. For the kids' sake, I should have at least helped you, rather than just sitting and watching that you're doing the right things.' He trails off.

'No worries. Not even a tiny bit for my sake too?' I laugh to try and keep the neediness out of my voice. And of course, I can't expect everything to be OK after one nice supper.

'I suppose. You're still my family, you know.'

I want to tell him sorry too. Sorry for the things I've done. Sorry for the awfulness of everything we've been through. That I've never allowed him to share his fear too. Instead, I've taken the brunt of it. Insomnia. Not being able to deal with it. Going underground in the way I've been doing for weeks on end.

'Coffee?' I take a breath, trying to hold onto the positives. 'I'm putting on the kettle.'

'Nah. Had two cups already. Thank you. Thea went straight back to sleep last night. I gave her some formula. Conks her right out, doesn't it?'

'It does.' I think of my own milk. How quickly it had dried up after Jack's fall.

'It's good for you,' he says. 'To have a break from feeding her.'

'Thank you. I was finding it difficult. With the both of them. Jack needing my attention. I couldn't do it.'

'I know.'

'Thanks.' I wonder where all this has come from. Gav's kindness. I'm pleased he's trying, but I also can't help feeling unsettled and unsure as to when his next 'temper' is going to arise. It's also strange, I reflect, that as Gav's behaviour has calmed, Sarah's totally gone off on one. Gav and I have bonded whilst mine and Sarah's friendship has started to fracture. I wonder whether the two are connected somehow. My mind is spinning with it all, a darkness descending on me with all the possibilities.

I think about Sarah's screams and shouts. *He's here now. He's in the downstairs flat.* As though Gav is some sort of monster. The more I think about her behaviour lately, the more I wonder whether she's having some sort of breakdown. I had waited for it, last year. After the week of horror as she referred to it. But it never came. She'd in fact carried on as normal. Even *more* sprightly than normal. The minute we left the hospital together, she'd pulled herself upright and told me there'd be no more tears.

'Yes. I feel *fine*,' she had said to everyone that had asked, a big grin stuck on her face a second or two longer than was natural.

I think about the way she's been unwilling to praise Ella for the things she's done since Jack had been unwell. I think about whether I'd missed some signs before Jack's fall. If we've both been so entrenched in our daily lives in these four small corners of the world that I've missed something monumental unfolding right in front of my very eyes.

'I'm just going to get ready,' I shout into the living room.

'No worries at all. Take your time. I'll get lunch sorted,' Gav shouts back.

I put on the same jumpsuit I wore last night. Gather my hair into a top-knot and put on a smudge of blusher and mascara. I don't know why. Gav's behaviour has triggered some sort of self-imposed expectations. I'm just about to walk back into the kitchen when I see him hunched over the sink. He's talking on his phone, using that soft voice he used to save only for me. I stand stock still. I don't know what to do. I stand there, listening to the low hum of conversation. When he puts down the phone he starts to sing.

'Gav?' My voice is shaky. 'Who was that? On the phone?'

'On the phone?' I will him not to lie. 'I was talking to Katy. She's the . . . I told you about her. The woman who specialises in PTSD?'

'But it's a Saturday?'

'I told you.' Thea starts whining. 'Shhhhh, it's OK,

little one,' he whispers before looking back up at me. 'She owes me a favour. She's all booked out for months. So she has to do it on the weekend.' His lips curl upwards, as though he's thinking of some shared joke, or secret. I'm trapped. I can't say anything. After everything I've put him through. And if I want my family intact, I need to stay calm.

'Right. Fine. OK. Well,' I push back strands of hair off my face.

'She's coming here. Today.'

Surely he wouldn't dangle a new love interest in front of me?

'Today? But . . . I'll go out. OK?'

'Out? Why would you do that?' He drums his fingers on the sideboard. A sign he wants to wrap up the conversation and move on. 'She's here to help you and Jack.'

'OK. Fine.' I try and keep the hurt out of my voice. 'What's her name?'

'Katy. Loftman.'

'Fine. And you say you know her from where?'

'I told you.' He frowns, unaware that isn't actually the question I'm asking. 'Didn't I? Or am I going mad? You know, through Gordo?'

'Yes. Yes you did. Just watch the kids for a minute, will you?'

I leave before he can answer. I sit on my bed. I knew it. I damn well knew it. The way things are going. Gav coming and helping. Telling me he's sorry? I always have a go at Sarah for thinking like this but, this time, I know exactly how she feels. I feel like he's manipulated this whole situation on purpose. That he's adopted a 'good guy' stance before turning around and saying, *Hey! Look at me, I've got a new girlfriend but you can't go blaming*

me because I'm an amazing ex-husband and father.
Maybe I'm paranoid. Maybe Sarah is right after all.
Maybe.

SARAH

Sarah had spent the previous night avoiding Tom. They'd gone to bed in silence and she *still* hasn't said anything to him this morning about the crying episode. What she wants to be is a good wife. A good *person*. She wants to take Tom into her arms and tell him that, whatever is the matter, they will sort it out together. But, her mind is elsewhere. She's just had a text from Liza, who thinks Gav is seeing someone. And she also dropped the bombshell that Jack is going to see a therapist. Scrambling, or whatever it is she'd called it. Liza must be trying to get their friendship back onto an even keel. Sarah's glad, but she's also shaking from head to toe, struggling to put one foot in front of the other. It's one thing telling a lie to The Vale Club. It's quite another to think that it might come to Jack's word against hers.

'Tom?' She decides to focus on her husband.

'I . . .' He says nothing else from beside her on the bed.

'What is it? You can talk to me?' But he doesn't reply.

'I'm feeling . . .' he says eventually. He shrugs his shoulders and looks down. 'Like I can't breathe.' She wants to tell him she feels like that too. 'By the way, I know,' he says. 'I know you were going to do the IVF thing without me. I found out just yesterday. On my way home. I bumped into Camilla and George. George let it slip. That Camilla was going to go with you for your first appointment. She nearly murdered him. Told him it was under the radar and that I didn't know. Why? Why didn't you tell me? Why were you going without me?' He's looking over at his top drawer. And then he puts his head in his hands. 'Oh God.'

She walks over to the drawer and takes out a small silver box.

'Here,' she says. He takes it and holds it tight. 'Have a look.'

He shakes his head but she goes right ahead anyway, pulling out photographs and the small cast of a footprint. She squeezes it tight, in an effort to try and do something with the all-consuming pain inside her chest.

'I didn't tell you because I'm scared. I am desperate for another child. But I'm also scared. Of having to go through this again. I mean, we've been wanting another child since Rosie and nothing's happened and it just felt like less pressure if you weren't there. Like I couldn't take on your sadness and stress too.' She knows she's missing out the part about the stress of Liza, but she feels too sad, too weak, to say anything else.

He takes her hand. 'Then, do you think we're ready for this?' He covers his mouth in a bid to stifle his own emotion. 'Maybe we need to speak to someone again. Maybe we need some support. We went to Relate but you never got any help for yourself and for your own feelings about . . .' He can't bring himself to say her name.

'I don't want to wait around much longer, Tom. It's time.'

He steeples his hands and takes a deep breath. 'OK, OK. Let's work it out. God. That was hard. Camilla and George. I had to talk to them as though I didn't mind you going to the IVF. Like I didn't care you hadn't told me. I couldn't let on that I was totally broken inside.'

He picks up one of the photographs. 'But all that time I wanted to rush back here, and I was just thinking about the minute I came back from the plane last year – that journey was the worst, not even knowing if you were OK – and then I found you on our bed.' His voice breaks. 'The way you were just curled up whilst Liza was downstairs.' She jolts at the mention of Liza. 'I'm sorry. I wish she was here now. Our daughter. She should be here now. And I never even got to meet her.'

Sarah looks down and gives his hand a squeeze. And then she feels her phone buzzing again in her pocket. That fucking Christmas fair, she thinks. It has to be. Who else would be so insistently trying to get hold of her at such a bad time? She reaches into her back pocket and presses the mute button, whilst trying to silence the sound of her own sobs.

'But thank God you had Liza. She was so good to you.' He puts the photograph back. 'Wasn't she. You – you wouldn't have got through it without her.'

Sarah's crying even more now – grief, overlaid with guilt. She wants him to stop. She'd always asked him to discuss Rosie in isolation. She never wanted the memory of her child tarnished by anyone, or anything else. But how was he to know that this also included Liza – the very person who had helped her the most? The person who had run straight to the hospital and galvanised the doctors and nurses into more action, who had called the necessary people and held her hand through the torturous eighteen-hour labour that Sarah had wanted to be even more painful to distract her from her sadness. How was he to know that she was also the person who was causing her the most horrifying guilt?

WhatsApp group: Private chats
Members: Ella, Charlotte G

Ella: Charlotte, can I pick your brains?

Charlotte G: Go for it.

Ella: What do you make of this text from Sarah? She sent it during the Christmas fair meeting. I just wondered if you thought she was all right? I'll forward it to your email. Read it and get back to me.

Charlotte G: Oh. My. God.

Ella: Don't tell anyone though.

Charlotte G: Of course I wouldn't tell a soul! You can trust me with your life, Ella.

WhatsApp group: Mums on the wine
Members: Charlotte G, Shereen, Minnie

Charlotte G: Guys look at this! Don't tell anyone but look at this – Sarah! She's lost the plot! Look at the text she sent Ella by mistake. Ella screenshotted it before Sarah deleted it.

And look what she says about all of us! Ps don't tell anyone. I told Ella I'd keep schtum.

Shereen: OMG!

Minnie: OMG – what is she on?

Actually I saw her today looking tearful at drop off. Maybe there's something wrong?

WhatsApp group: Year Four mums
Members: Saffy, Johanna, Claire, Mils T, Katie, Amina, Della, Mehreen

Saffy: Look at this! Sarah in Reception sent it to Ella Bradby by mistake! You know Ella?

Johanna: The tall model one? OMG!!!!!!!!!!!!!!!!!!!!!!!!!!

Mils T: This would be bloody hilarious if it wasn't just so heinously awful. AWFUL.

Amina: Sarah, she's got Casper, right? Reception? The little boy with the wonky fringe?

Saffy: That's the one. I can't believe it. I'll bet she won't be showing her face around here again!!!!

LIZA

I don't really know what to make of Katy when she walks through the door. My first thought is that she isn't Gav's usual type. Or rather, she doesn't look like me. And then I wonder if I ever was Gav's type in the first place. She's got black hair, a neat centre-parting tied back into a low ponytail (the sensible type, I can tell) and a long, pale face. She's wearing red lipstick. Odd, I think, for a Saturday therapy session with a five-year-old boy. I pace the room, opening and closing cupboards, checking we've got milk for the fourth time that hour.

'Liza, sit down,' Gav orders. 'You're making me nervous. It's OK. Jack will be OK.'

'It's . . . ha. That's normally your game. Making me nervous.' I sit down and then get up again. I don't even care how Gav is going to react. He wouldn't dare say anything in front of the therapist anyway. 'How long is she going to be in there with my son?'

'She's helping. Remember? It's what you wanted?'

'She said five minutes. That she'd spend five minutes alone with him. It's been—'

318

'Seven?'

'Still. That's longer than she said.' All sorts of thoughts are running through my mind. Might she one day be Jack's stepmother? What's she asking him? My palms are slick with sweat.

'Just chill. She's amazing. She'll sort him out.'

'Amazing?' I know I have no ownership on Gav, but it hurts me to hear him say this. 'She didn't look that amazing.'

'I didn't say she looked amazing, I said she *was* amazing.' Before we can get further into the discussion, Katy walks back in.

'Hi, both of you. Well, what a clever little boy.'

'He is, isn't he.' My chest expands. 'He's just been so off since this happened. I never expected him to be tip-top, of course. But I just don't want things to fester, you know.'

'I do know. And I just wanted to spend some time alone with him so he slowly gets used to me and trusts me. I'm going to go back in now and do some play therapy for another hour or so. If you don't mind?'

'Of course not. But it's a Saturday?' I look at my watch. Two p.m. 'You should be off surely?'

'That's OK.' She looks over at Gav and smiles, her teeth practically zinging in the sunlight. 'I owe this one here.'

'You do?' I try not to sound too accusatory.

'I do.' She doesn't explain further. I want to ask but I have to remind myself this is about Jack. No one else.

'And costing?' I ask, just in case she thinks I'm taking the complete piss.

'I'll do my initial assessment – and then a session tomorrow so you can see how it all works. Then I'll write to you with a proposal, how many sessions I think he'll need. That sort of thing. But just to let you know that certainly I'll be doing at least three of those with no charge.'

Again, she looks at Gav. 'Sound all right? You're under no obligation either. You can ask me any questions at all about how it all works. Speak to my clients. Anything you need. I'm here to help, not to do a massive sales push on you.'

'Great. Tomorrow's a Sunday though?' I wonder if this is all a sales technique in itself, then I tell myself not to be so cynical. 'Thank you, by the way.'

'Sunday's fine. In fact it's better for me, so I've got a clear run with no other patients. That OK?'

I nod, unsure of where to look next. I can't bring myself to face Gav, to see what sort of expression has crossed his face. I like her. Damn. I like her a lot. Something about her feels right. Good. As though she's melting away all my own troubles. She's looking directly at me, occasionally glancing over at Gav, who keeps nodding his head. Why does he feel the need to reassure her, I wonder. To make her feel like she's doing a 'good job'?

'Listen.' I don't have a chance to process what I'm about to say. 'Maybe this isn't such a good idea after all. I don't know. Just that maybe it's best to have someone totally new. Someone who doesn't know any of us?'

'I totally understand.' Understand? There *is* something to understand then, I think. 'Look,' she tucks her papers into her shiny, black briefcase. 'How about you go and speak to Jack? See what he says.'

I'm torn between doing what she's suggested and leaving them together. Maybe I should just ask Gav?

Maybe I should come right out with it. Here. But then I remember – I have no rights to his life any more. Not after what I did.

'One minute.' I walk into the other room. Jack is doodling with his good arm. There are a small set of scribbles in different colours on a scrap of white paper with an address at the top and her name. Katy Loftman, and her address! Excellent. I snatch the paper away from him. Maybe I can snoop.

I pretend to peer at the picture. It's something that looks close to a rocket. 'A spacecraft?'

'Mum, no, it's a dog. Can't you tell?' He's laughing. That dimpled grin is back. The sparkle in his eyes. 'It's a sausage dog. Maybe that's why you thought it was a rocket.'

'It's a lovely sausage dog.'

'Why are you crying, Mummy? What is there to be sad about?'

'I'm not sad. I'm . . . you looked like your old self again just for a minute. From before.'

'I am myself,' he laughs. 'Jack Barnstaple.'

'You liked that woman?'

'Yes. She's nice. Can I have a biscuit?'

'Course you can.' I leave the room, wondering what magic Katy has. If she can transform my son in the space of seven minutes flat, I don't really have a chance with my husband. I have a decision to make now. Either I can give in to all of this. Let her have Gav. Or I can go in with a fight. I'm going to say yes. That way I can see what's unfolding in front of my eyes. And, most importantly, Jack likes her. Maybe, just maybe, Gav will get off my back a bit then. Maybe he will ease up. Just maybe. He's been better in the past few days but I still feel like I'm on eggshells – nothing, after all, can change the things I've done. I'm stuck with this weird sensation of wanting my freedom, but not wanting to let Gav go. Somehow, though, we have to find a middle ground. Maybe this Katy woman is my key. I feel an overwhelming sadness at how things have turned out.

I grab a biscuit and am walking back into the room to speak to Gav and Katy when my phone pings. I should leave it. But it might be something else important. Jan or Franny maybe, trying to schedule our next physio or tutoring appointment. I slide my phone out of my pocket. It's a screenshot, from Shereen.

> I thought you should see this. I know you've got a lot going on but I know how close you are to Sarah. This has gone round the entire school.

My first thought is not to look. I've got enough on my plate. But something draws my eyes to the screenshot. It's a WhatsApp from Sarah to Camilla, about Ella and the rest of the mums at the Christmas fair group. I read it once. Then I read it again. My first reaction is to cover my hand with my mouth. My next is to laugh. Lastly, I gasp. *Sarah*, I think. Then I realise that I'm implicated in all of this too, just by association.

Sarah, I tut. *You silly girl*. I can't quite believe it and read the message again.

Because if I've taught her one bloody thing, it's always, always to bloody well stay on the right side of the school mums and dads. But she hasn't listened, and now the shit really is about to hit the fan.

SARAH

She now knows why her phone had been pinging so relentlessly earlier on. She'd managed to make herself feel stronger after her time with Tom. But now, the strangled feeling is back. She hadn't got away with it after all. She can't breathe. There's too much going on. Jack's fall. The investigation. That sodding journalist scurrying around. Gav's behaviour. Ella. And now this.

This. Which she supposes is Ella again. She thinks back to the way Ella had ignored the whole WhatsApp incident after the Christmas fair meeting. The way she'd just given her that small smile as if to say, *I know what you've done but I'm far too above it all.* Above it all my arse, Sarah thinks, she was clearly just waiting for the right time to unleash hell. Why now? Why did she wait until now? She supposes she'll find out soon enough, which makes her impending sense of doom go stratospheric. She looks down to her phone again to Camilla's message. She can't quite bring herself to read through her own little missive, but she skims a few of the words: *Desperate. Ella. Secret. Gossip. Hideous mothers' meeting. Nosey Parkers. Nothing better to do.* And then the worst. *LOSERS.* She'd actually put it in capitals and tapped out three crying emojis afterwards and then a series of knives. She looks properly sociopathic. Her stomach shrinks. Oh God. What the *hell* has she done! She hadn't even meant any of it. At all. Everything had been getting on top of her at the Christmas fair meeting and Ella had been sitting there all smug. She'd been trying to make Camilla laugh. Trying to get her 'Ella rage' out.

Her phone pings. It's a calendar notification. Christmas fair meeting on Monday. She switches her phone off. It's like it knows. How is she going to get through the day knowing that everyone has read her message? Knowing she's going to have to face every single person she's mentioned in that bloody WhatsApp? Oh God. She needs to physically get out of here. The entire place is suffocating her, with constant reminders of everything bad that has happened. She thinks about fleeing to her mother's. Not saying a word to anyone. She'll scribble a note to Tom telling him she needs a break from it all, because she certainly can't tell him what she's done, plus he seems so beaten by life just now.

She takes four deep breaths. She can hear Tom in the bedroom. She thinks about Ella, about the ease of her life. How she never has to struggle for anything. Sarah's absolutely sure of that. Even Ella's little secret is something cool. Something glamorous. A secret love child with Rufus North. When Sarah was a child she'd always wished she had a more interesting background than the one she was born into – nice house, nice family, nice school. *Nice. Nice. Nice.* How she wished she had a dark secret about her that would have made her more interesting to her peers, instead of just Sarah Biddlecombe, who always just looked like *someone* – someone nondescript you couldn't ever quite put their finger on. *You do remind me of . . . hmmm. I can't quite think.*

All this time she'd been trying to look after Liza. To look after Jack, given this was all her fault anyway. And now she's managed to wrap herself up in the eye of the storm. She looks at Ella's words underneath the screen-shot.

> Wondered if Sarah was ok. It's not that I mind so much what she's said. It's more that I hope she's all right. Seems like she's going through a tough time. Maybe she has too much on with Liza? Do you think we can help her at all?

Bitch, she thinks. Liza had defended Ella to the hilt but she can read through Ella's text beautifully. And more fool Charlotte G, Ella's messenger, for falling for it. Sarah's going to have to apologise to each and every person she's offended. She starts with Camilla – apologising that their conversation had leaked.

By the time she's had a chance to calm slightly and think about everything, she decides she can't go to her mum's. Running away from things won't help in the long run. And what about Casper? Has she forgotten she's a mother in all of this? Instead she decides to just get out of the house for a little while, perhaps head into Chiswick to get some space. And tomorrow she'll make her statement at The Vale Club and pop round to Ella's. She'll be back from her little trip now and Sarah really does need to do something which involves moving her body, if only to distract her from the terror churning through her mind. She'll find out where Ella has been. Apologise face to face. It will be the hardest thing she's ever had to do, but she's going to go through with it. For the sake of Liza.

'Tom? I'm going out,' she shouts. 'Casper's down here. I'm bringing his Lego down. I'll be half an hour. I'll go and get some groceries.'

She's putting on her coat when she hears the front door to the downstairs flat slam. She hurries out of her own door and sees it's neither Liza, nor Gav. Who on earth *is* that? She rushes down and catches up with the small, dark-haired lady. Lord, she's very pretty, is the first thought that crosses her mind. She feels ungainly next to her. A result of all the stress-eating she's been doing lately.

'Hi.' She offers a hand and for some inexplicable reason pretends to start jogging. Why, she has no idea, given she's dressed in grey Ugg boots and jeans, but all the adrenaline coursing through her is doing something strange. 'I'm Sarah. Liza's friend. She's staying with me at the moment. Whilst Jack, y'know.'

'I'm Katy. Ah Jack, he's so lovely. I'm practising some therapy with him.' The woman smiles – one of those smiles that makes Sarah think of Agas and roaring country fires. 'Just like his dad. They have the same mannerisms.'

'Just like his dad?' Sarah wants to shake the woman. 'You know Gav well?' And then she jolts. Could this be the lady she saw coming out of the IVF clinic? Her mind flicks back to that fateful day, just before she'd bumped into Charlotte G. She conjures up the image of that other lady Gav had been with. She had blonde hair, she's sure of it. Maybe she'd dyed it? She peers into Katy's face.

'How do you know Gav?'

'We met recently actually. I can't really go into it. But – actually he ended up helping me with something.'

'He did? He's like that. Helpful. Sometimes overly so.' Sarah thinks about the way Gav behaves towards Liza and about the information she knows about him. 'So what did he end up helping you with?' She realises, as she's talking, how unlike her this is. To be so pushy. She's been spending too much time with Charlotte G.

Katy takes a step back. 'I can't really talk about that,' she says, still smiling.

'Of course you can't,' Sarah carries on. 'Jack OK?'

'He's doing really great. I'm going to get to the bottom of what happened just before that fall and we're going to get him all better and sorted so he never has to think about it again. So that his body doesn't carry it for ever. In fact, we're starting tomorrow lunchtime.'

'I saw him. Before the fall.' Sarah doesn't know why she's said those words. But they've entered the air before she can stop herself and she needs to take some form of control given the timeframe. 'He was . . . fine.'

'Really? Well, maybe I can have your number? Just in case I need to chat to you? I like to get the details straight so we don't muck things up.'

'Course. Shoot, I've got to run and I've left my phone. But give me yours. Have you got a card?'

'I do. Here.' The woman passes her a light blue card with a dolphin on it. 'Give me a ring anytime about anything you remember. It would be really helpful.'

'Cool. I will. And it's lucky, you know, Gav and Liza. They're working things out together.' Sarah flinches as she says it; she certainly doesn't want Gav anywhere near her friend, but then again she doesn't want him near this lady either.

'Have a lovely day,' Katy says and walks off, shiny ponytail swinging in the breeze.

Sarah should get her phone. Text Liza. So if she's not the woman Gav's been seeing, who is?

She opens up the front door, slides her hand around to the hallway table and grabs her handset. Tom's chatting on the phone. Shit, he's talking to Gav! Does that mean Gav's left the house? Or is he still downstairs?

'Gav mate,' he's saying. 'Sarah's being so weird about Liza. I mean, I know their friendship wasn't quite what it was, even before the fall. But – she's acting so strangely about it. I'm worried. She's eating badly. Her skin's grey. Her eyes are always puffy and she's started doing this weird trembling thing when she's still. I'm at my wits' end. Know anything?'

She can't lean her head in any further and she doesn't want him to know she's overheard. *Their friendship wasn't quite what it was, even before the fall*? Has everyone been talking about it behind her back? She closes the door quietly and looks down at her hands. They're still. Thank God. Just then her phone pings with a text from Liza. SOS!!! it says. It's underneath the chat they'd been having about Gav – where Sarah had told her that she wouldn't let anything happen to her. Sarah's heart quickens. Liza must be in trouble – well, she knows that already, but she must mean she's in trouble *right now*. Gav is on the phone to Tom so at least he's occupied right this minute. But later on? An idea comes to her.

Don't worry, she types back. I'm on it.

She's got to do something. Things haven't gone quite as planned so far, in trying to make things up to her friend. However much she tries to make things better, nothing seems to help. She's got to go one step further.

She walks to the car, which is parked opposite the house. It's covered in birdshit, she thinks. Just like her life. When she's settled in the driver's seat and has set up the Bluetooth for her mobile, she takes three deep breaths and searches for a phone number. When she finds it, she tries to copy and paste it three times but her fingers are shaking too much. She hopes she's not doing this to distract herself from the atrocities of what she's about to face at school. She's just got to trust her decisions, for once. Except she doesn't know what that means any more. She thinks of all the parents at the school gates and she starts to dry-heave. The WhatsApp. Everyone has seen it! Something private she'd written has actually gone viral.

Just as she's on the verge of a full-blown panic attack, the phone clicks.

'Hello?' A kind-sounding man picks up. 'Craig speaking. How can I help you?'

'Hello? Hi.' Sarah starts the ignition. She stops for a minute. Is this really the right thing? Should she talk to someone first? Ella? Tom? No. She's not going to. It's time she took proper control instead of overthinking everything. She'd made mistake after mistake, and the WhatsApp was the last straw. She needs to start correcting things.

'Hello?' says the voice. 'It's all right. Just take a deep breath. You can talk. It's OK.'

'I need to tell you something.' She hasn't thought this through. She has no idea what to say next. 'I need your help.'

'Slow down, Madam. We're right here. You need to breathe.'

'OK. I'm, um . . . I'm trying.' She gasps at the air; it

feels hot and syrupy in her mouth. 'I think it's urgent,' she says. 'It's about my friend. My best friend.' And then she starts talking and, to her surprise, finds she can't stop.

SCREENSHOT
Sent to: Year Four mums
WhatsApp group: CFC board
Members: Sarah, Ella

Sarah: God these women are hideous. Hideous, hideous people. Listening to them droning on is painful. Like I'm being repeatedly hit on the head. Makes me want to stab myself in the face. Ella c-bag Bradby! Who the HELL does she think she is? Nothing better to do in her sorry little life. Bossing everyone around to make herself feel important. What a TWAT. Desperate bitch. Just cos she's got money, she thinks she can control us all. Bet her kids turn out to be right little bullies. It's like some deathly mothers' meeting – all these awful women squawking away about their revolting little children. Nosey parkers with Charlotte G going on about Jack. What the hell does she know anyway? What is the collective noun for a group of women like this? Ah – I know:

LOSERS

Crying face *Knife emojis*

LIZA

'Who you texting?' I watch Gav's thumbs skate across his phone's keypad. 'Looks interesting.' Gav had gone home last night but had arrived early this morning to see me and the children. It almost feels like the old Sunday mornings – where we'd mooch around all day doing nothing.

'Just Tom. Had a chat with him yesterday. Said Sarah's been behaving strangely. You know anything? Don't mention it though.'

It's been ages since Gav's confided in me like this. Katy must make him happy where I haven't been able to. Her and my son. I pull out my phone and show him the message I received yesterday.

'Well – since we're sharing it might be something to do with this.' I watch his brown eyes glance over the message, and then widen.

'Oh my God.' He bursts into laughter. 'This is going to go down like a shit-storm. What she's said is awful. And about other people's kids too. Oh my God. Isn't she meant to be running the fair?'

'Well. She was. But then Ella took over. Got all the sponsorship. I've just sent her an SOS message – to see if she knows that it's gone round the school – but she hasn't replied. She's probably in the middle of a massive shame spiral.'

'I'm sure she must be. Hang on. The ten k? Ella got it, just like that?' He nods his head in approval. 'Wow. I'm impressed.'

'She did. Ella magic.'

'You know where she got it?' he asks. 'Seems an awful lot to get in one fell swoop when you were expecting it to take months and months.'

'No. I've asked them not to involve me in any of it. God. Poor Sarah. I mean, what the hell has she done? No one's ever going to talk to her again.'

'Maybe not such a bad thing. To distance herself from all that weird school politics.'

'Maybe. I'm a bit worried about her though. She's been so strange since the accident.' I throw my head in Jack's direction. 'I can't put my finger on it. There's a distance between us but at the same time she's trying her best to be supportive. I keep thinking back to before. Whether she wasn't being herself and I didn't notice it – I know she's been cut up over Rosie since last year, but this behaviour, it's really something else.'

'Well, no one is ever going to get over anything like that, are they? She must still be grieving. Heavily.'

'Maybe. I suppose. She never talks about it though. Seems funny it should hit her now.'

'Not that weird,' he says. Something odd crosses his expression. A dark look, except I can't quite make out what it means. 'Things can hit you way later. Shock and stuff. So I wouldn't discount it. You know? Sometimes associations trigger old PTSD. That kind of thing.' The mood changes.

'Anyway,' I try and lighten the atmosphere. 'Oh, look, Sarah's finally replied to my SOS message.'

'What's she said?'

'Not sure she's understood my joke. She's written back saying something about me not worrying. That she is *on it*.' I lift up my handset. On what? 'I don't know why she's sounding so calm about it. It's the kind of thing that would normally make her hyperventilate. The entire school reading an awful message meant for a mate. And what she's written! I mean, my God.'

'You couldn't make it up, could you?' Gav gives a laugh. 'I wonder how everyone is reacting. I'd be so fucked off if that were me reading that. You heard anything?'

'Well I don't think they'd be texting me, with Jack and everything. They'd try and keep me out of it. And Ella started a new Christmas fair group, so I'm not privy to what everyone's been saying. But I'm guessing everyone is going mad.'

'Ella especially, I should think.'

'That's another thing.' I pick up Thea and put her over my shoulder. 'Ella. Sarah keeps going on and on about her. Saying she's not the person she says she is. She's got some crazy secret. A love child or something. All this stuff. It's like Ella's got a hold over her. I mean, she's always been obsessed but, I don't know. I've been having to stop Sarah from talking about her.'

'Here, let me.' Gav takes Thea and I sit down, thinking how strange Sarah's behaviour actually is. With some distance I can see things much more clearly now.

'Maybe she's right though, Sarah?' Gav rubs Thea's

soft hair. 'Maybe Ella is up to something? I mean, she was totally absent before, wasn't she? It seems a little strange she's suddenly so involved in everything.'

This is one of the things I love about Gav. The fact he's always onside with people. That he always looks at the other person's point of view. I'd forgotten how thoughtful he is and what good advice he gives. His calmness rubs off on me.

'Yes, you're so right,' I tell him. 'Thanks. I'll text Sarah tomorrow. See how she is. It'll be good when Jack is back to his old self. We can work on getting our friendship back on track, and do all the things we used to do every day.' I start to feel lighter. Something about the thought of Gav seeing someone else has reduced the pressure on our relationship. I haven't spoken to someone like this for ages.

'And don't worry,' he says. 'We'll get to the bottom of Jack. What happened before the fall. And his PTSD. Because that's what it is.' He stands up and leans over me, his arms slung around my neck. I hold his forearm and squeeze tight.

'Thank you.' I feel like I'm about to start crying. 'Thank you for being so decent.' Because despite everything, despite him and me separating, it's still my fault. 'I'm really trying,' I tell him. 'Really I am.'

'I know. Maybe you should speak to Katy? She might help? I know you pooh-pooh that kind of thing but . . .'

I think of three days ago. The trip to Marylebone. I want to tell him what I was doing. But I don't because I can't let him know it's got to this state. He'll never trust me again.

I keep silent. Just as Gav is about to pull loose from me, the doorbell goes. I look at him, frowning.

'You expecting anyone?' he says. I shake my head.

'It's not Sarah or Tom, we have a code. Three fast knocks and two slow. Just so that we know it's them.'

'Maybe . . .' He looks around the room to see if there's anything that's not meant to be here.

I look over to the basement window. I can see a small, rotund man in a green jacket. He's got his hands in his pockets and his head is bent down so I can't see his face properly. Just the side profile. He looks a bit like a pale walnut, wrinkles crevassing his cheeks, and his brown hair is combed over, gelled into waves. He looks like he's wiping mud off his feet.

'Thank God you're here,' I tell Gav, as he walks over to the door.

'Don't worry, he's probably just trying to sell something.'

'Annoying. On a Sunday.'

'Let's see.' He opens the door. 'Hi mate. You OK?'

'Yes. Hi. My name's Craig. Any chance I could come in?'

'Come in?'

'Sorry. I should explain.' Gav looks over at me. For some inexplicable reason my tongue feels swollen in my mouth and I'm struggling to breathe. 'I'm here to speak to Liza Barnstaple. Is she in? It's important.'

'Yes. She's here. And you are?'

'Craig Travers. My colleague Beth actually spoke to you the other day? You said you'd ring her back.'

'Oh.' I laugh with relief, looking at Gav. 'Sorry, that's not me. I didn't speak to anyone. This must be the wrong address. Now if you don't mind, we're very busy.'

'Well, I'm here from . . .' I watch as he cranes his neck through the door to look right at me. He clocks Jack on the sofa and Gav's still holding Thea. He looks around the flat, his eyes scanning the room. It looks like he's checking for leaks, or something. 'I'm here from social.' Both Gav and I look at each other, and then at Jack.

'Social?' I hear myself give a light, tinkly laugh as I think of tea parties. Meetings. School fundraisers. But I know. Already, I know. Inside, I'm thinking, oh my God. *He* knows too. He knows what happened all those years ago. How could he, though? It was just me and Gav who knew. There's not one other solitary person who had found out. Unless Gav has told someone. I think about running at this point. Just grabbing the kids and running. What would I take? My wallet. Keys. The kids. And then I'd run. I look over at Jack. His thin body, prostrate. And then Thea, her cheeks resting on her little shoulders as she shudders in her sleep on Gav's huge frame. How could he know? What would they do? Take my children away from me? Gav has already told me he'll always do what's best for the kids. That he doesn't care what it comes down to. That their welfare would be number one, no matter how much I begged and pleaded.

I start to sob, huge gulps coming out of my mouth. They are going to take my children. Or give them to Gav. Oh my God. He must have told Katy. I knew it. I knew there wasn't something right. It must have been a set-up. All that time, he was setting me up so that he could snatch the kids. Jack's fall must have triggered something in him. And he must know where I'd been three days ago. Who could have told him that?

Now, Gav would watch me fall and be ruined. I think about last night. How kind he'd been. Had he been worried I'd cottoned on to his plan? That I'd run? He'd never said anything. Never once said the words out loud about what I'd done. Referred to it only: *our secret*.

Craig takes a step forward into the flat. He's wearing big, black bovver boots that make him look like he's about to go climbing. I notice they're as shiny as anything. 'Like I said, I'm from social services. We've had a call.' Gav and I exchange glances again. 'I'm here to follow up. I'd like to speak to you, Liza. I'd like to speak to you right this minute. *Alone.*'

SARAH

It's time to go to The Vale Club and make her statement. Keep Liza safe from any more trouble and upsets. She'd been so shaken up after she'd made the phone call yesterday, she'd gone straight home and passed out on the sofa. But today is a new day. Today is the day for fixing everything. She's set the wheels in motion and soon Liza and the kids will be safe from Gav. Tom had agreed to look after Casper, and she's determined to sort things out.

If she goes quickly, no dawdling, it'll be easier. No feeling sick when she reels off the words in her head again and again. She thinks about what Ella would do. She would just go right in, the words tripping off her tongue, and never think of it again. Sadly, Sarah's body is telling a different story. She pats her stomach to silence the perpetual gurgle that has sounded since she left the house.

Liza, Liza, Liza, she tells herself on repeat. The thought of saving her friend from a terrible fate gives her strength she never knew she had. She clears her throat, alerting the receptionist to her presence, but nothing happens. Is she really that invisible? Sarah stares at the top of the girl's aubergine-purple-coloured head. She remembers dyeing her own hair that colour when she'd been a teenager.

'Excuse me,' she barks. 'I'm here.'

'Oh I am sorry.' The receptionist looks up, sounding anything but. 'All our systems are down. Filling everything out by hand at the moment. It's a disaster. And I'm trying to run this place alone as the other two reception staff have called in sick.' Sarah wants to both tell her to shut up and apologise for being mean at the same time. She goes with neither.

'Listen. I need to speak to your manager. About the boy's fall. Jack Barnstaple.' She looks down the corridor. She can hear the screams of children, and just about make out the brightly coloured soft-play. She grips onto the counter.

'Sure.' The receptionist sounds flat. 'I'll go and get her.'

By the time the manager returns Sarah's confidence has begun to diminish. She looks at photographs of Liza on her phone to keep up her will.

'Hello,' says a tall, pale woman who looks like she's never seen a treadmill in her life. 'My name's Arlene. I understand you're here to speak to me about the incident the other day.'

'Do you mean the fall? The little boy's fall?' Sarah falters. 'Yes. Yes, I am.'

They go into a small side room that reminds her of a prison cell. She delivers her lines perfectly. She has no idea what she'd been worried about. All she'd had to do this entire time was think of what that despicable man Gav had been doing to her friend. How it would be dangerous for him to know the real chain of events; she couldn't give him any more ammunition against Liza. The lies slip off her tongue like fish thrown back into the water.

'I saw him. I waved. I think he saw me. But he was fine. At the bottom of the post.' And then she remembers the CCTV. Shit. What if she's caught out? 'I think he saw me anyway. But what about all your CCTV? Don't you have the footage?'

'It doesn't reach that part of the playground.' Arlene doesn't look up at her. 'Thank you,' she stands, signalling for her to go. 'For coming to see us. That's very helpful.'

'Is that it?' Sarah sidesteps from leg to leg. 'Can I go?'

'Yes.' Arlene extends a hand. 'You can.'

She's done it. Now to tell Ella and they can all move on.

Sarah gets in the car and swings back down to Ella's house, Chiswick way. She feels lighter all of a sudden. She sneaks a look at herself in the rear-view mirror. Maybe it has taken years off her. When she parks up by Ella's she can't see anyone in the house. She steps out, ready to tell Ella that she's done her part. That the manager had written down her short sentences. She hadn't spoken too much (she hadn't learnt nothing from all those real-life-crime series she'd watched on Netflix) and she hadn't even mentioned Ella's name. They would never speak of it again.

Her finger hovers over the bell, and she pushes down to ring. She has no idea what – or even if – she's going to tell Ella about the information she's holding about Gav. Please answer, she thinks. Please answer quickly. The previous high levels of adrenaline drop and she feels wobbly. She needs to sit down. She has no idea what's brought her here really. The source of all her troubles – and here she is asking her for help and a friendly ear.

'Hi.' Christian opens the door.

She peers behind him. 'Sorry. I need to speak to Ella.' She presses urgency into her voice. He looks like he's just been for a run, skin bright, in his exercise gear. His hair golden. She doesn't for one minute think about introducing herself, or jolting his memory that they've met before, but then he offers his hand.

'I remember you from somewhere,' he says. She brings a hand up to her chest and lets out a laugh that she wants to kick herself for. For God's sake, she thinks. Pull yourself together. But she can't help the exhilaration she feels.

'Ah yes, it was NCT,' she says. He frowns. 'Years ago?' she prompts.

'Oh, was it? That's not what I thought. I've seen your face more recently than that, I'm sure of it.' He gives a laid-back shrug. 'Anyway, come on in. I'll get Ella for you. She's upstairs in the yoga studio. Kids are out at the moment with my mum, so we've got some peace and quiet.'

'Thanks.' Sarah walks in. Everything feels calm and clean in here. Nothing is out of place. A few plastic kids' toys are out and the newspapers are spread out over the Jasper Conran sofa. There's a selection of all of the Sundays. Her eyes flicker towards them as she tries to work out which ones have been read. Is Ella more of a *Mail* reader or a Guardianista? Perhaps a bit of both.

'Els?' Christian shouts up the stairs. Sarah sits down as he runs up. She prays he won't sit with them. She tries to pick up *YOU* magazine but her hands are all sweaty and she doesn't want to get black ink smudges all over her face. A thousand thoughts are going through her head. How will she explain to Ella she needs to talk to her alone? She has nowhere else to turn. And then she hears a whistling sound. For God's sake, she's always happy too, she thinks, whistling a merry tune. Then it stops. Silence. She finds it unnerving. She hasn't heard Ella coming down the stairs. She starts to stand up but, as she does so, she hears the turnaround of footsteps. And then she sees a scruff of blond hair peering around the doorframe. Christian is back.

'You,' he says. 'It's you. I *knew* I knew you from somewhere.'

The earlier exhilaration dissipates. This can't be good. What can he know? Has she accidentally 'liked' one of his Facebook photos? Her mind jumps to and from every single move she's made since Jack's fall. And then she thinks of the accidental WhatsApp messages. She rubs her stomach.

'Listen,' she says.

'No, you listen. I know exactly who you are.'

Fuck it. She should have removed that ridiculous WhatsApp profile picture of her making that stupid face at the school social earlier in the term.

'That WhatsApp message,' his voice doesn't change. 'She's not one to be easily upset, you know.'

She does know. But she also knows that she's played straight into Ella's hands. That her majesty has used Sarah's mistake to her advantage and is now milking it for all it's worth. She thinks of the way all the other mothers and fathers (especially the fathers with all their tongues hanging out) would now be fawning all over Ella. Poor Ella. Slighted by Sarah Biddlecombe, *of all people*.

'But I'm sure you had your reasons,' Christian continues. He looks her up and down pityingly, which makes her feel a thousand, billion times worse. *I know I'm no Ella*, she wants to shout. 'Ella said so anyway. That she thought you might be going through something. But just to let you know, my kids are good kids. So keep them out of it.'

She nods, close to tears. Typical of Ella too, she thinks. Pretending to be nice even now. If only Sarah could tell Christian the *real* reasons. Lying about a child's fall. And the rest of the stuff that she knows Ella is up to.

She presses her hands on her cheeks and then her forehead. 'I just need to sit down,' she says. 'Is she here?'

'She is. Yes. I think she's just finishing her yoga. She'll be down when she's ready. Drink?'

'No. Thanks.' She thinks of Tom in this situation. How he'd react if someone had slighted her, the love of his life. His wife with whom he'd chosen to spend the best part of fifteen years. He'd go mad. Flaming, apoplectic mad. She starts to well up at the thought. *She's got a cheek coming round here*, he'd say, his voice getting all clipped, hand smoothing back his strawberry-blond hair. *She's not welcome in this house*. His loyalty wouldn't have wavered for one minute. Sarah looks around. All of Ella and Christian's expensive things. The sculptures. The beautifully embroidered cushions. The photos of Ella and someone who looks not unlike her – both absolutely beautiful, laughing into the camera with their shiny hair and white teeth.

'Just wait here, Sarah. I've just got a few bits to do. I'll be in my office but Ella should be down shortly,' he says. 'Read the papers, make yourself comfortable.'

'Thanks.' She flicks through the Sunday magazines

feeling blue. Various headlines catch her eye. *Couple Tries MDMA Therapy. Woman Leaves City job to Become a Shaman*. She feels totally pedestrian. But then she wonders how her own ridiculous life would be summed up in headlines. The four corners of her little West London world, which have actually turned into a festering, over-flowing mess. She guesses they'd go something like this:

Perimenopausal Woman Lies About Boy Falling off Post in Posh West London Members' Club.

Best Friends Torn Apart by Husband.

39-year-old Woman Eaten Alive by Parents at the School Gates.

She can't focus on the words on the page. She flicks through, trying to breathe through her nerves. What's happening to her? And then, as she's rearranging the papers, an envelope falls out of the pile of magazines.

It's addressed to Christian Bradby. She clocks the logo on the top left-hand corner of the envelope. She's seen that logo before – all green and white geometric shapes. Maybe it's one of those famous ones she's just never noticed. She can't quite make the link, even though it's at the forefront of her mind, but, with everything else going on, it's just out of her grasp. Other connections spring to mind too. But no – she can't get it. And before she can think any further, she slides the letter out, reads it and puts it back without anyone seeing. She can feel the thud of her heart. It's so strong lights flash in front of her eyes. She tries to digest it but she's suddenly panicked they've got some nanny cam in the house.

She takes a deep breath and diverts her thoughts, focuses on the fact that they get the papers delivered to the house. Wow. They don't even need to move a muscle on a Sunday morning. She pictures the scene. Ella wafting down in her short, silk dressing gown, her long bare legs gazelle-like around the house. Carrying up a wholewheat croissant, or some almond butter, spirulina, hodge-podge creation, on a lovely vintage tray. Papers underneath freshly squeezed orange juice.

Then Sarah thinks of her own Sunday morning ritual. The way she preps herself the night before to get up, put on her gym kit and do some exercise. The way she opens her eyes and the first thing she does is inwardly beg for some illness to ravage her body so that she can lie underneath her duvet for hours, away from the world. She'd want something that would disappear quickly – of course. Nothing too bad that Casper would think his mummy was dying. Nothing too mild that she'd have to get up and go about her business regardless (because of course that's what she normally has to do, whereas Tom lies in bed whimpering at any sniffle). But no – this morning, for her sins, she'd felt as well as anything and still hadn't got to the gym. Just as she's thinking about other types of illness that she could have, the door swings open.

'Hi, Sarah.' Ella leans against the doorframe, her head nearly reaching the top. 'I see you've made yourself at home. I'm glad. Can I get you a drink?'

With a glimmer of satisfaction, Sarah notices Ella looks tired. Distracted. She's twisting the huge diamond around her finger. She certainly doesn't look as though she's been doing yoga.

'Hi. Ella – I just wanted to say sorry.' Sarah speaks fast, before she loses her nerve. 'For that WhatsApp. I was just trying to be funny. Make Camilla laugh. It wasn't meant to be personal.' She's half standing. She doesn't want to be sitting down, giving her apology. But halfway up, she's paralysed.

'It didn't come across that way, you know, Sarah.'

She nearly laughs. You can say that again, she thinks, but she keeps her mouth shut.

'I'd worked really hard to get those funds together for the school. For our children. I want my kids to have the best opportunity, whilst experiencing,' Sarah holds her breath, '*real life*. And just so you know, they're amazing little people. I very much doubt they'll grow up to be *bullies*, as you so kindly put it.'

Sarah feels like a bully herself, caught somewhere between shame and indignation. 'Real *life*? You think that by sending your kids to the local primary you're . . .'

She throws her hands in the air. Jesus wept, she thinks. Why on earth has Ella Bradby sent her kids to the local primary *anyway*? If Sarah had all the money in the world, a private education would be the first thing they'd spend it on.

'Forget it. Listen. I need to talk to you. Firstly, I've given my statement. To The Vale Club, I mean. I didn't mention your name. Just told them what we'd discussed.'

'You didn't mention my name? But we were together?' Ella puts a hand on her hip. 'Why did you do that? It looks weird.'

'I don't know. I just did. I thought I was doing a good job. Keeping you out of it.' Bloody hell. Can she do nothing right? 'But anyway, there's something else I need to speak to you about. I'm sorry. I don't know where else to turn.'

Sarah explains about everything that has happened in the past week. The woman she'd seen Gav with. The therapist. The SOS text message from Liza. She thinks about the phone call she'd made only yesterday.

'Good God,' says Ella. 'Are you sure?' And then she

slumps onto the sofa. 'Oh my God,' she says. 'You think he's been hurting the kids too?' Sarah watches tears film over those grey eyes. 'It all makes sense now.' What makes sense, she thinks. 'We have to do something. Oh, Sarah.'

'I already have,' she says. 'I called them. Social services.'

'Without . . . wait, you didn't talk to Liza?' Ella leans forward. 'She's never going to forgive you for that, you know.'

Sarah opens her mouth but quickly shuts it again – for all Ella's confidence, it looks like she's momentarily broken. She wants to ask her how she knows this. Is she playing games again?

'I don't mean to hurt you. But she won't. Forgive you, I mean. Or at least, it will take years.' Ella's speaking more fluently now, her eyes flickering over her nails. 'So, be prepared. Or just make sure you never, ever tell her it was you that put that phone call in.'

'They won't tell her who called them, will they? Social services? I mean, it's all anonymous, isn't it? So it's fine. She'll never know.' Sarah starts to panic. 'I was doing what I thought best.'

'Perhaps. But, well, I think she'll feel very angry. Want to lash out. She'll feel distressed that she couldn't sort this out alone. All sorts of feelings.' Sarah watches Ella clamp her mouth shut. 'Not that I'd know,' she snaps. 'It's just that.' She shakes her head.

'Really?' Sarah starts to cry. 'You think? I mean, she's my best friend.' Ella's at it again. She's playing her. Pitting her and Liza against each other. That's exactly what she's doing. Freaking her out that Liza will never speak to her again. Then Ella will be free to swoop in. Peck at Liza's carcass, what's left of her after all this, and fly off without any squawking from Sarah.

348

'No.' Sarah slaps her hands on her thighs. 'Look. That's not why I came. But it's one of the reasons. Liza and I will be fine, our friendship will survive *anything.*'

Ella raises her eyebrows.

'Listen. I need your help about something else too. The therapist, Katy.'

'Liza told me. What about her?'

'She's going to do this thing with Jack. Scrambling, it's called. For PTSD. You play back the events of your trauma and then replay them in your mind. Set to funny music or something. The body lets go of the trauma and it all begins to lose its potency. Apparently. So they're going to do it with Jack. Apparently he's been acting really bad. Unsurprisingly. But, well, you know.'

'You know?' Ella leans forward, seemingly scanning her face for clues. 'What do you mean, you know?' Sarah wonders now if she is being deliberately obtuse. 'It's a great idea. I mean, whatever helps Jack, right?'

'Right. It would be a great idea. If it wouldn't come out that I hadn't actually been anywhere near him. Have you forgotten your role in all of this since, what, three minutes ago?'

She mimics the way Ella had been standing when she'd been reading The Vale Club menu back in the soft-play. Not looking anyone in the eye. She tries to stretch her legs so they'll vaguely approximate Ella's but she feels like some sort of baby elephant.

'*Yes. She checked on him. He's fine.*' Her imitation of Ella's voice sounds disastrous. Flat and monotone like a kid learning to read. She hears Ella make a noise. She's laughing. The bitch is laughing! It's certainly not what Sarah expected.

'You know, that has nothing to do with anything.' Ella

looks down at her fingernails. 'I don't know why you're here. I really don't. I think you've forgotten that the most important person in all of this is Jack. Then Liza. And all this time you're just thinking of . . .' Sarah hears herself gasp. Don't you dare, she thinks. Don't you *dare*.

'I *am* thinking of Liza.' She should have stopped. Let Ella finish her sentence, but she couldn't quite bring herself to. 'I'm thinking of Liza *and* Jack. And how best to move on from this awful thing. And you aren't helping me. You were there. You told Liza that I'd seen Jack. I hadn't. You knew that. You were trying to distract me from your bloody *secret*.'

She wipes her mouth. 'Speaking of which, you think I said a lot on that WhatsApp? I've got a lot more in that arsenal, my friend.' She feels like she's about to start rocking back and forth in hysterical, witchy laughter. *Get a grip*, she tells herself. Why can't she own what she's saying, instead of all this nonsense coming out of her mouth?

'Look. Just calm down. Let's just focus here.'

'Focus? You were the one who said Liza would never check the security cameras. All of that. Remember? You were complicit too, or have you already forgotten? Only trying to hide the fact that you . . .'

'You what?' Ella's eyes take on a fiery look that Sarah hasn't seen before. 'Go on. If you know so much about me. What is it?'

'Oh please.' There's a triumphant tone in her voice, but only for a second until she feels the tremble of her chin and she thinks she's about to cry. She knows full well that Ella has her over a barrel. Ella knows that the likelihood Sarah will ever own up to the fall is slim. And that even if she does, Ella can easily deny everything. 'Don't pretend you have no idea what I'm talking about.

350

Your little disappearing act, about . . . what was it, nine years ago now? Rufus? I've worked it all out.'

Ella looks up at the ceiling as though trying to recall exactly what it was that had happened nine years ago.

'Oh stop it. I've got this on you, Ella. And you may think you are in the stronger position here – that you could tell Liza you really did think I had seen Jack. Or that I'd told you I had. But you aren't this all-perfect, all-singing, all-dancing being. And then you disappeared again after Felix was born. I wonder what you were up to then too?'

Ella's face takes on a different look suddenly – one that Sarah's never seen before. Sadness. Anger? She doesn't know what.

Come on, she thinks. Come on. Find her Achilles' heel. She looks around the room again. The artwork. The magazines fanned out on the coffee table. The letter addressed to Christian that she still can't get a grasp on. Even that looks expensive, the white paper thick and lustrous. Ella catches Sarah's gaze and, without a moment's hesitation, she snatches it away from her eyeline. As though she's some sort of Peeping Tom going through their private things.

'You're mad and I have absolutely no idea what you are on about. But by the way,' Ella says after a festering silence, 'how do you know? That Gav's been . . . did Liza say something? Or you saw something?'

'She's never said anything to me.' Sarah shrugs, feeling stung even as she says it out loud. 'Not even hinted at it. I mean, sure – she tells me about Gav's controlling behaviour. But not this.'

'So how do you know then?' Ella sounds slightly impatient. 'I mean, it's such a big thing.'

'She asked me to watch Jack the other day. She was being so secretive and weird when I asked her where she was going. I knew something was up. Normally she'd have told me every planned second of her journey.'

'And?'

'And . . .' Sarah feels a bit shifty – that she'd been poking around in Liza's phone. But things have got so bad lately that she knows it's the least of her worries. 'Well, I looked at her phone. Saw where she'd been in her Uber.'

'Do you mean you opened up her Uber app?' Ella looks taken aback.

'Yes. I mean, I just wanted to know she was OK.' Sarah tries not to sound so defensive. 'But anyway, it's bloody lucky I did. Isn't it? So I found out her route and looked up where she'd been on Google Maps. It was the Hilda Zettenberg Home.'

'Off Marylebone High Street?' Ella nods. 'The film production offices I do some consulting for are right past that building. It's a beautiful old street. Lovely houses.' Sarah wants to ask Ella why she's frowning and pulling at her bottom lip. 'But what makes you jump to that conclusion? That Gav's beating her? I mean – it's pretty odd?'

'Odd? Really? Considering what the place is for?'

'Well, it isn't really in use any more. They do some therapy sessions there. For post-partum mums who are struggling with some issues – or who have had birth traumas. In fact, I know that because there were leaflets about it in my office. I remember the name. Hilda Zettenberg building. And I remember thinking what a good idea it was. So, what made you jump to the conclusion that, because she went there, she's now married to a wife-beater? I mean, have you ever even seen any bruises on her?'

'It's a house for domestic abuse.' Sarah's cross now. Ella always has to take the other side. But come to think of it, she's never seen anything untoward on Liza's body. 'The Hilda Zettenberg Home. For *women*.'

'Er, yes.' Ella pulls out her phone. 'Like, over a hundred years ago. Back then it was a sanctuary for abused women. But look.' She passes the phone to Sarah. 'Now it's for therapy.'

'But Liza's not . . .'

'Struggling?'

'Yes, she's so pulled together. Even with Gav on at her. And Thea's birth was easy. Why would she . . .'

'Need to go and talk to someone? Get some support? It's not that weird. I know Liza's had some issues.'

'Like what?' Sarah looks up. 'Like, what?' she softens. But Ella shakes her head as though remembering something she doesn't wish to discuss.

'I know more about Liza than you think,' she carries on. Sarah opens her mouth and shuts it again. 'She never said anything to you at all?' Ella asks. 'About the time with Jack?'

'Said anything about what?'

'Oh. Never mind. If she didn't tell you.' Ella stretches out an arm as though looking for blemishes. Sarah feels black in her stomach. No. Liza had never told her. What the hell does Ella know that she doesn't? And now she's only gone and accused her husband of beating her best friend up. Has in fact called social services.

Social services.

Oh, God. What if Jack gets taken away? And Thea? And Sarah had put them off when they'd rung the other day. They must have thought that was suspicious too.

She'll go around there now. Despite Ella's opinions on it all, she'll admit everything. Warn them that social services will be paying a visit. She'll go and sort it all out. Say it was a massive mistake. That she had been drunk when she called. The therapist is going over too today – her brain is scrambled but Liza had definitely mentioned she was coming on Sunday. *Lunchtime*. Sarah doesn't have long. Gav was going to be there too for the initial PTSD scrambling session for Jack. She'll send the therapist away and tell Gav and Liza she has an extremely important announcement to make.

'Ella, my God. I think I've made an awful mistake. I've got to go.' She straightens her back. 'They're going to take the kids. Oh my God. Jack. They'll think . . .' She can now barely get her words out she's crying so much. 'They'll think that the fall was their fault. They'll think, oh my God. Ella, you promise you'll be here with me?' she presses, one more time. 'Promise?' She cannot do this alone.

She's fully expecting Ella to tell her where to go. To give her that annoying once-over she does, eyes sweeping the full length of her body, lips in a barely there pout. But Ella doesn't. She stands up off the sofa, and then reaches an arm out. This is the very moment that Sarah realises how bad things have got.

And then her phone pings. It's Liza.

Social services are here. What the hell?

'Oh my God,' she gasps. 'Ella. They're there. They are there already. Social services. I thought I had time. I . . . I . . . I only rang early yesterday evening.'

'Well, I suppose if they thought kids were in danger,' Ella says helplessly. 'They'd move pretty fast. Wouldn't they? Even on a weekend.'

Sarah's legs have frozen. She tries to pick one up but cannot, like she's stuck in quicksand. 'What have I done?' But then she feels Ella's fingers digging into her skin.

'Sarah, listen to me.' Her shoulders are being shaken now. 'You need to move. You need to get there quick. Do you understand me?' Sarah tries to speak but nothing comes out. 'You need to go now. Are you listening? Do you want to fix this?'

'I do,' the words come out in great gulps, as though she's surfacing from being held down underwater. 'Yes. Of course.'

'Then go,' Ella says quietly. 'You need to run.'

West London Gazette editorial notes, October 2019
J Roper interview transcript: Freelance mums' group,
The Vale Club

*Ade: We started this club – a freelance working mums'
club for those of us who have just had babies and are
slowly getting back into work.*

*Jane: It's to save our sanity. After we became mums
we lost our senses of selves really. So we needed the
company. We all met here.*

*Frankie: And we can do our exercises and then meet
up and work together on our various projects whilst the
kids are with the nannies. There's a few of us now. We
help each other out. Because it can be really lonely
otherwise. New mums trying to identify with an old self
that's nearly disappeared.*

*Georgina: Yeah – straddling these two different worlds
– we want to be our old selves but we don't know quite
how to follow the rules of our 'new' post-baby selves.
It's quite a learning curve so it's amazing to have other
people going through the same thing.*

Jane: Yeah – at least we've got each other now.

*Ade: It's true. I struggled the most with my first holiday
with bub. I went with loads of mates who weren't parents.*

*Some of them don't want kids. Some of them aren't ready.
Christa was only six months. I tried to be my old self
with them all – putting Christa to bed and then getting
absolutely smashed like I used to. I'd then have to get
up at six a.m. whilst the rest of them would lie in bed
all day and I'd be alone with the baby waiting for
everyone to wake up. I know better now – but it's that
weird in-between stage that's the toughest. Look – I'm
not moaning. We all know how lucky we are. I mean,
some of us have been through gruelling rounds of IVF
to get here.*

Georgina: *Yeah, it's this weird thing where people
think we're ungrateful if we say it's tough.*

Jane: *We're getting there, though, aren't we? But –
anyway – we were all there the day of the fall and
actually we didn't see what happened. It's just that we
wanted to show that mum some solidarity. We've all seen
the hate and rumours and online vitriol towards her. But
it wasn't her fault. I mean, I'm sure when our kids are
old enough we'll be doing the same thing.*

Ade: *It's so true. I'm so glad we spoke out. If we can
make her feel a tiny bit better after what happened, we
will.*

LIZA

'If you could just . . .' Craig from social services motions towards Gav. 'I need time with Liza. Alone. Thank you.' Gav is too shocked to say or do anything but stand there with his mouth open.

'What is this all about?' Gav shushes Thea and picks up her bottle. 'Can you at least tell me? This is my wife and my kids we're talking about. This is my . . .' He shuts his mouth before he realises it's not his home. 'You think I'm leaving you alone with them?'

I watch Gav's jaw set – his temper starting to rise. He's been better in the past few days – but maybe now he's going to completely lose it. *Please, Gav.* I breathe great gulps of air, hoping it will signal my internal danger radar to switch off. If I'm calm, maybe Gav will be too.

'I showed Liza this before but please,' Craig pulls a laminated identification from his pocket, 'take a look.'

Gav peers over and makes a big show of looking at the photo on the card, and then up to Craig's face. 'You have to tell me what you are doing here.'

'I need to discuss things with your wife.'

'Gav.' I pat him on the shoulder. 'Just let me find out what he has to say.' I want Gav just to do as he's told, so I can get this over and done with and find out what the hell is going on. I feel bad for my earlier suspicion that Gav has orchestrated everything – that he was being nice so that he could get social services involved. He quite clearly has absolutely no idea what is going on.

'Gav.' I speak quite firmly now. 'You need to go. Just out for a walk. Around the block. Take Thea and I'll put an audio book in Jack's headphones. He won't be able to hear us in the kitchen. Just, please.'

Gav gives Craig one final look and moves towards the door, hoisting Thea's pram up the basement stairs, before turning around and pointing a finger at him.

'Just so you know, if you . . .' But he pulls up and doesn't finish what he's going to say. 'Make it quick.' And then he gives me a look – one of reassurance.

'Tea?' When Gav's gone, I go to the kitchen cupboard but I'm struggling to send messages from my brain to my hands and I keep nearly dropping things.

'Water. Please.'

'Right.' I fill up a glass and bring it over to where Craig has pulled up an old wooden chair, well away from Jack right under the window. 'Now, are you going to tell me what's going on, please?' I want to shake him to hurry up. I think that my heart might actually explode in my mouth if he doesn't just come out with it.

'I'm an emergency social services worker. And you are a priority call today. Because we've had a warning that you're being hurt, Liza.'

'Hurt?' I almost let out a snort. 'Do you mean . . .'

'Hurt. Physically. By your husband. A Mr Gavin Barnstaple.' I can't quite process his words but I take in just enough that I need to check that Jack can't hear me.

'Jack darling?' I shout, but there's no response. I turn back to Craig. 'Sorry? Hurt me? Why, yes he hurt me because he left me but . . .'

'He has?'

'I mean, we're not together any more.' I twist my fingers. 'We . . .'

'Could you explain further please?'

'Well, we're separated. Me and Gav. He split up with me quite recently. A month or so ago. We're not together. So yes, he hurt me in that sense.'

'Ms Barnstaple.' I wonder what's warranted me being downgraded – or upgraded – to the use of my surname. 'I'm asking you if your husband is putting you in physical danger. You, or the children.' He looks over at Jack. 'We'll be needing to discuss the fall with you. Jack's fall, too. It's quite procedural. Once a child has been in hospital. But we also got a phone call alerting us to what might be going on in your household, and of course,' Craig picks up the glass of water and glugs it back in one, 'my colleague tried to get hold of you and it seems you've been avoiding us. We know you must feel too frightened to talk to us.'

This situation is all too peculiar. I'm wondering if I've heard him right.

'You think Gav's been, what, physically hurting me? Is that what someone told you?' I can't believe it. Someone's actually rung up social services and told them Gav's been abusing me. Who would do such a thing? Does someone have it in for Gav? Does someone believe it's true? Oh my God. 'I need to sit down. Sorry.' It's so confusing I can't gather my thoughts.

'It's OK. Take your time.' He slides his thumbnail down the ridge of his water glass. 'We're in absolutely no rush.'

'No. He has never, ever laid a finger on me.'

'You sure? You can trust us, Liza. We won't be doing anything unless you ask for our help.'

'I'm quite, quite sure.'

'And,' he clears his throat. 'Emotional abuse. There's been some concern that your husband has been, well, using methods of coercive control. With you.'

I stop. I think about the tactics Gav has used to keep me, well, under control. I can't deny that some of them, in isolated cases, have been – well – what could be classed as abusive.

'Well.' I feel like I'm under oath. 'No.' I want to talk but I find myself absolutely silenced. Muted. Like those mime artists, I start to move my hands around. I almost burst into laughter. I look like Peter Crouch doing the robot dance.

'Liza? Are you OK? Do you need some time?'

'No. No – I don't. Everything's fine. I just don't know why you are here.' I panic that I'm going to get in trouble for lying. I know that's not the point of social services. That they're not cross-examining me. But I feel that way. 'Please. I think you should leave now. Thank you ever so much for coming. Whoever called you made a massive mistake.' I give a false laugh. 'You must get that all the time. Revenge? People looking to prank other people? Weird pranks if you ask me but, you know, it takes all sorts.'

'So Gav never controls you? Bullying, gaslighting? And what about the kids? Does he control the way you bring them up too? Isolate you all from your friends and family? Because these days, we class that behaviour as emotional abuse, Liza, and if it's happening with both you and the kids – we can get you some help.'

With the kids. That's when I know I need him out. If he starts looking more closely – looking into our past, questioning Gav – things might come out that might destroy everything. Destroy *me.*

'No.' I stand up and start walking to the door. 'Never. He's a good husband and a good father.' I don't falter on the words. Gav's behaviour has been far from perfect in the past few years, but he's had his reasons, I suppose. And I don't need to look very far to know what those reasons are.

'OK. Thank you. Well, just to let you know that we're here if you need anything. Our number one priority is looking out for you and your children, Liza. So, I'll be around again to check everything's OK and to speak to your kids. Speaking of which,' he throws his head towards Jack, 'how is he doing? I heard he fractured his neck in the fall. It's so awful.'

'I know, poor thing. Been a bit traumatised.' I keep my tone light and breezy. I want him out of here as soon as possible. 'But me and his father have done a really good job of keeping him sane and happy.'

'Well, we're going to be sending round a health visitor to see you and your son next week. Just for a check-up and to discuss things. As I said, my colleague said she spoke to you.'

'Spoke to me?' I'm totally baffled now but I don't want to labour the point. I just want him out of the house. 'Yes. Yes she did,' I mutter.

'Fine. I'll get her to ring again first thing tomorrow. And this isn't your normal home, is that right?'

'That's right. We're on one floor here. My friend Sarah offered as the flat was going free. It's easier.'

'So I took a quick look at your notes. The hospital visits you've made. You've had your usual admissions for the past few years,' he says, looking down at his hands. 'There's been the croup, and the influenza. The usual. And there was something else.'

The lights above me start flickering. Or maybe it's my eyes. I can't quite tell. But I know what's coming. Everything around me starts to lurch. He's been waiting for this moment. To trap me. What if they take them, I think. What if they take my children? Gav and I had made a promise to each other. I hear Craig's voice start up again and all of a sudden I'm absolutely desperate for Gav to come back.

'In December 2014 your husband brought you into the hospital at two in the morning, with Jack. He was two months old. There was also a phone call, logged to the police, saying you'd gone missing, which was then retracted. Can I ask you about this?'

'Sure.' I will the words to start flowing. 'Of course you can.' I have them ready in my head, just in case this day ever came. It's all so hazy, what happened around then, and, out of nowhere, I think of Ella and her face. *I'm just walking the dog*, she'd said that night. I shut my eyes. 'One second.'

Just as I'm about to start talking, we hear a strange panting sound outside the door. Like a dehydrated animal. And then a groaning. We look through the window of the basement to see a figure hunched over double outside, hair in a messy top-knot. Sarah. She's wearing that huge coat she got from Zara that she bought because she thought it made her look smaller. She's knocking on the window now and then she starts pummelling on the door.

'It's me,' she's shouting. I get up. 'Open. Quick.' She catches sight of Craig. Is something wrong, I wonder. I start to jog towards her. Casper? Tom? Maybe something awful has happened.

'Ella,' she gasps. 'She was meant to be staying at home but she's coming. I just got a text from her. She's coming too.' She sucks at the air. 'I've come,' she says again.

'What have you come for?' I turn to Craig and back to Sarah. 'What's going on?'

'That's what I'm here for,' she says again. 'I'm here to make everything right. I'm here to sort it all out.' She takes another deep breath, and pushes herself, her coat shushing against the walls. Just as I'm about to slam the door, I see a shadow, darkening the entire wall outside. I examine it. A long, low ponytail. Sleek, flat hair. I recognise her straight away. It's Katy here too, early for the assessment with Jack.

'I'm here. It was me. I'm sorry. I called you,' Sarah cries, sticking out her hand to Craig. 'It was a mistake. I'm sorry. I was,' she looks around the room, 'I was drunk. I'd had a row with Liza. I was angry.'

Craig is looking flummoxed. 'We still have to look into each and every case. So I'll still be investigating.' Now he looks at her with sorrowful eyes.

'Katy,' I call, as she steps into the room. 'Can you please go and check on Jack? Is that OK? We can start his session soon.' My voice sounds all stretched. And then just as I'm about to turn to Sarah and ask her what the hell she's been playing at, I see Gav's face at the window. I'm trying desperately to tell him, through some kind of weird telepathy, that Craig knows about my hospital visit all those years ago, but he's just looking at me blankly, throwing his hands up in the air. Then he sees Sarah and looks even more confused.

Gav, I think. Please, please. Stick to the game plan. Don't think I've told Craig the truth. Please. I'm almost in tears, silently talking to Gav through the airwaves. If you do this one thing, Gav, I'll be yours forever more. Whatever you want from me, I'll give it to you.

Mumsandmore forum, new thread: #boyfallatTheValeClub

Mumofdd2: Guys – What do you make of that boy falling? I mean, I don't want to be judgy or anything – but, where was the mum? Just wondering . . .

Unicornlover: You don't want to be judgy?????

Mumofdd2: No. I just want to know where she was. Apparently she was nowhere near where the accident happened. Just wondered what you all make of it? I mean . . . I'm not saying I'm perfect . . . .

Unicornlover: No. You're certainly not that.

Mumofdd2: No need to get narky @unicornlover. I'm just trying to have a real discussion here about things to do with our DDs.

Unicornlover: The mother probably went to get a coffee or something. Have you never done that? And if not, then you're a better person than 99.999999% of the rest of us parents. I suggest now you get a life.

Mumofdd2: I have a life. Thank you very much. And a very fulfilled one too. I suggest you stop being so rude. I thought this was a safe space, where we could discuss things together.

The Fallout

Unicornlover: Well, I thought you'd have gathered from the title of your thread that there are no safe spaces in this world, Mumofdd2. #accidentshappen.

GAV

So you want me to start from the beginning, do you? I can certainly do that, Mr . . . Craig? Sorry, I've forgotten what it says on your badge. Travers. Mr Travers.

It was a tricky time, you see. Me and Liza. We'd just had Jack. So we were new parents. Anxious. Always making sure he was OK. But you know what it's like when they're first here. It's all new. Lovely, lovely little boy he was. Still is. But you should have seen him when he was born. Here. Let me show you a pic. This is him. Beautiful little chappie.

But in those first few months, he suffered from the most dreadful colic. Awful. Poor lad. Screamed day in, day out. Liza had terrible insomnia anyway. That started when she was pregnant. But it just got worse and worse. Are you a dad yourself? Then you'll totally remember, I'm sure, what those first days are like. So we went to the hospital because – well – Liza wasn't coping with Jack's colic. I'd been out one night – I'd gone straight from work so I hadn't seen them all day. I came back. Poor Jack was in a dreadful state. We were worried about him then. Really worried. Actually, I think Liza thought something was really badly wrong with him. You see, we had no reference point. They don't tell you about things like that, do they? So she got the proper fear in her. We drove to the hospital in the middle of the night. Just to get him checked over. But they told us he was absolutely fine. That it was colic. They gave us some medicine.

But you know, if your baby is screaming like that and won't stop, you might think you were missing something. You read all those stories, don't you. Twisted intestines, the beginnings of sepsis. All the rest. And of course your rational brain is telling you: *You'd know if something was wrong.* And then there's that other constant little tic: *What if you're wrong? What if your child is* dying *and you did nothing? Then what?* And it's hard to keep a check on it. Isn't it? When they're new. You're learning on the job.

Anyway, at the hospital they got totally the wrong end of the stick. Thought that Liza had walked out on Jack. Silly really. I'd rung the police earlier, you see, as I couldn't find her. Funny how your mind goes into all sorts of strange places. Especially when you've had no sleep. I couldn't get hold of her so assumed the worst. I don't know what I assumed in fact. That something bad had happened anyway. It sounds so utterly ridiculous now I say it out loud. But anyway the police went out looking for her around the area and all that time she was out smoking in the garden. Right as rain she was and we'd never even thought to look there. The back door was shut. She hadn't wanted any smoke to get into the house. We'd even looked out of the window, but she'd gone right behind the garden shed, terrified I'd catch her out. And later she was flabbergasted and horrified that the police had been looking for her all that time. I mean, we can laugh about it now. Sort of.

If I'm honest I'm really glad that social services checked up on us after that. That they worked with the police, even though it was a closed case. It made me trust in the system. That if people needed help, I mean really needed it, there would be someone there for them.

You want to observe the kids? Go right ahead. You'll see them for what they are. Happy, well-adjusted children. Well – obviously we're in unusual circumstances at the moment, poor Jack, it was a terrible accident, but he's doing so well. Thea's obviously only just over two months. But you'll absolutely see that we're brilliant parents. Liza's on the PTA. I used to be a school governor before Thea came along. My kids are wonderful human beings. So I think, Mr Travers, that it's time for you to leave. Thank you, thank you for your concern. We appreciate it. I'll show you out, shall I? I'll just show you to the door.

You have a good day now, won't you?

SARAH

Sarah knows she's intruding. But she can't help but stare at Liza, who has draped herself around Gav's neck. 'Oh my God, Gav,' she's saying.

'It's all right.' He's patting her on the back. 'You can breathe. It's OK. It's over now. I promise.'

Even Gav looks like he's close to tears. She had no idea that it had been that bad for them both. None at all. Liza, who is so emotionally sturdy, in the hospital at two in the morning for the sake of Jack's colic? She'd never said a word despite their constant flow of WhatsApp chats. And all that funny stuff about the police?

'You promise?' Liza's shut her eyes now. 'You promise it's over?' Sarah wonders if they are aware that both she and Katy are watching but before she can open her mouth and explain more, she feels someone tugging at her arm.

'Come with me now.' It's Katy, leading her to Jack. 'Let's leave them. Give them both a moment, shall we? I'm so glad you're here. I meant to ring you. I wanted you here. Whilst I go through the scrambling. I mean – not right here. But I thought it would be useful if you

371

could wait outside the room. Just so I can come and get you if I need to jog his memory about what happened. Would that be OK?'

'Sure,' Sarah says, knowing it's absolutely not OK. Nothing about this is OK.

'Ready?' Katy asks. By this point, Liza and Gav have gone silent and are watching her too.

'Sarah?' Liza walks over, blowing her nose. 'You're going to help?'

'Oh,' Katy exclaims, as though she's just popped some chewing gum. 'I'm so sorry you didn't know the sequence of events, Liza. I spoke to Gav about this last night. Did he not tell you?'

'No. But it's OK. It's fine. No worries at all. Sarah, you can do that?'

Sarah nods her head and says OK, but she can't actually hear any noise come out of her mouth. She's going to lie, about what happened to a five-year-old, in front of him, his therapist, and his parents. She can't. She can't do it. She'd done it at The Vale Club. But this is different. A five-year-old child. And if it comes down to it, it will be his word against hers. She swallows back a sour taste in her mouth. But then again she can't slow down her thoughts enough to work out what else she should do. She's completely stuck in her tracks. Ella would know. Ella would know *exactly* what to do.

'Wait,' she says. 'Of course I can. But Ella's on her way. And we need to wait. I need Ella with me because . . .' She fumbles around for something to say. 'Because Ella is helping me with some breathing techniques.'

'Breathing techniques?' Liza snorts. 'What the hell are you talking about, Sarah? You've never gone in for that sort of stuff.'

'I've just been feeling, well, panicky lately. That's why. Ella said she'd help.'

'Oh Sarah.' Liza moves over from Gav to her. 'Why didn't you say? You've been acting so bloody odd, for goodness' sake. I thought, well, I don't know what I thought. I wish you'd told me.'

'It's fine. And anyway – I'm so sorry about what happened back there. That was me. I called them. I'm so, so sorry.'

'It was *you*?' Gav shouts. Sarah takes a step back; he looks like he's about to pounce on her. 'You called them?'

'Calm, calm,' Liza holds her hands out. 'Why did you actually? I was so shocked I haven't managed to break that bit down. Wait Gav. Please. Let's just hear what Sarah has to say first, shall we?'

'I don't know.' Sarah can't admit to Liza she's been snooping on her. That she had opened up her Uber app and found out where she's been going. She takes a deep breath. She knows what she's about to say might break a relationship irrevocably. But what choice does she have? 'I'm so sorry, Gav. I thought you were . . . I'm not sure why. I must have been mistaken. I *know* I was mistaken, rather. I think I misinterpreted something Liza said.'

'What did she say?' Gav roars. 'What the hell has Liza been saying?'

'Nothing, it's—'

'Then I expect you to do better than that.' She can feel Gav's breath on her arm now. Liza fending him off. 'Better than,' he adopts a trembling voice, '*I think I misinterpreted something Liza said.*'

'Look.' Katy claps her hands like she's a school teacher. 'Jack can hear absolutely everything you are saying. So shall we just start his session? Sarah, why don't you go into the other room and wait there until I need you.'

Sarah nods. She scurries into Liza's bedroom and sits down, head in hands. She can hear Gav hissing at Liza in the kitchen.

'She's a fucking . . .' he's saying. 'You should never have . . . trusted . . .' She places an ear to the door but can't make everything out. Although she can certainly hear a few choice words. *Fucking* and *imbecile* being just two of them.

She texts Ella. She cannot do this alone. She thinks she might throw up all over the bedspread. Any minute now, Katy's going to come bursting in and ask her about the moments before the fall. And it's make or break. She either tells the truth, that she lied to Liza, or comes clean – and if she does that, she'll have to move out of London. She can't face Liza's hatred towards her. She can't face the other mothers and fathers – they hate her enough already after the WhatsApp she'd mistakenly sent to Ella. Shereen has been texting her updates to say that no one is talking to her. She'll be vilified at the school gates. Perhaps she'll ask Ella to walk in with her tomorrow. That would give everyone something to gossip about. She could do a massive distraction stunt. Then she hears Liza whispering.

'She's been through enough, Gav. Last year. Really brutal. I mean, really. You weren't there to see her. At the hospital.'

Sarah can't hear any more but she knows her friend is sticking up for her and, after everything she's done, with Jack and the fall, this reduces her to tears.

Stop it, she tells herself, sadness beating her down like a tonne of bricks. This interminable, deep, deep sadness that's plagued her since Rosie had been born, that has burrowed right into her subconscious and stuck there.

No time to feel sorry for herself now, though. She has Jack to think about. Ella texts her back. I'm on my way. Thank God. She will follow Ella's lead. She no longer trusts herself. To either say, or do, the right thing. She thinks of little Casper at home, and this again reduces her to tears, his jaggedy fringe and his small hand over her stomach as she'd come home last year from the hospital telling him she'd had a small 'thing' done to her. It wasn't that she hadn't wanted to tell him the truth. She had, but somehow the words simply wouldn't come out.

There's silence in the other room now. She's filled with an absolute terror. She can feel it all over her body. It's closing in on her. Maybe she *should* voice everything that had happened the day Jack fell. Maybe then the fear would go away. But now she knows she can't just think about herself. That she can't just be selfish and try and rid herself of the poison that's seeped into her body. Because of course, it's Liza, and Jack too. They have to move on from this with as few traumatic effects as possible. She starts to shiver.

Just as she's prepping herself on what to say (*Yes he waved. At least I think he did. He was just at the back of the sandpit. Near the bottom of the post. He saw me. I saw him. I was with Ella*), she hears the doorbell go. It's her. Ella. Thank God. Her nemesis has come to save her. She leaps up and goes to open the door, but Liza gets there first.

She sees Ella at the door, looking impossibly glamorous, despite the casual clothes she's wearing. Leggings and a baggy white T-shirt with a pattern on the front, which she's artfully tucked into her waistband. Sarah recognises that pattern. Her gaze rests on the T-shirt and her mind flickers from memory to memory. She doesn't have to think long to understand where she's seen it before. The logo on the letter she'd seen at Ella's house. The one that said that the sum of money had been withdrawn and donated straight to their chosen field. WLPA. Oh my God. The *school* – how could she have been so bloody stupid. The school fund. West London Primary Academy. She's seen it written down enough times, after all. And then her mind tracks back to the launch party photographs she'd seen on Ella's Facebook profile. The party to launch . . . hang on – she remembers googling this – Ella's company. She remembers searching for the company name: Echo Limited. And then her mind shifts into gear. A flash of the Christmas fair meeting. A paper with the sponsorship money details on it. The sponsorship money for the Christmas fair. With Ella and Christian's company logo on it. Except, she'd never declared that it was their company. She remembers distinctly, Ella waving her arms dismissively. '*It was hard work,*' she had said. Good heavens. Ella had sponsored the Christmas fair with her own money. What on earth is she playing at?

Is she trying to dodge tax by giving to charitable causes? Ten thousand pounds! Imagine having that kind of money. Sarah thinks about how easy it would have been for Christian and Ella, all they had to do was dip into their pockets. Yet Liza had had to sweat blood and tears to get sponsorship sorted. It's all getting stranger and stranger.

There's a knock at the door. 'Sarah? It's Katy. Your friend Ella is here too. She says she was with you during the fall. That she can help you with this.'

376

Sarah opens the door and shuffles closer to Ella, whilst staring directly at her T-shirt. It's not the time or place, but she can't hold it in any longer.

'The sponsorship money.' She lowers her voice and points a finger at Ella's chest. 'Your company. I know now.' She's pleased with herself for having joined the dots. 'What on earth are you doing? Why the big secret?'

Ella has the decency to go a shade of red. Even that looks fetching on her.

'I can explain,' she hisses. 'But now is not the time. What are *you* playing at, bringing this up now? Digging around trying to find things out about me. Talking about all this nonsense from nine years ago. If you want to know about that text message at The Vale Club, I'll bloody well tell you. But not now. Totally inappropriate. This is your best friend's son. Now focus.'

Of course, Ella is right. Sarah presses her hands against her cheeks. What on earth is she thinking? They both look over at Jack. His tiny body underneath his duvet. He's almost lost inside it. His face looks sunken and some of his limbs are jerking around the bed.

'Don't worry,' says Katy. 'That's good. He's releasing the trauma from his body. This is working. He's done so, so well, haven't you darling.'

Jack breaks out into the biggest grin.

'Is it over now?' he says. 'I want it to be over now.'

'It's over soon. Just one last scramble. But we have to now focus on the bit you've forgotten. The moments before the fall.' She leaves a silence to let him digest what has been said. 'Then we'll work on replaying the whole memory at once and that will be the last bit of our session today.'

He's nodding his head but he looks confused. Like

he's trying desperately, desperately to remember but he can't. It's OK, Sarah thinks. He won't remember. She's safe. They're safe. But then will the scrambling work? Will the trauma be released from him? She couldn't bear to do that to a five-year-old. Potentially ruin the rest of his life. She thinks back to last year. Rosie. Her subsequent battle to get pregnant again. She knows full well what trauma does to your body.

'I can't remember at all what happened.' His little face scrunches up. 'I'm trying. I'm really trying.'

'Sarah?' Katy calls. She feels Ella squeezing her arm. The heat of her flesh. 'The floor's yours. Perhaps if you tell Jack what you remember, he'll recall and then we can work on the release. Jack, this is very important for you to know that this isn't your memory, it's Sarah's. All right darling? Imagine Sarah is watching you. Imagine from her eyes. You're looking at yourself.'

Come on, Sarah thinks. How's a five-year-old meant to get that?

But sure enough, Jack nods. 'Sort of like I'm watching myself on the television?'

'Exactly like that. What a clever little man. Right. Sarah. You ready?'

She nods her head. And then she notices Liza staring at her and Ella. And just as she's watching her friend's expression, she sees it darken. Liza looks frozen, shocked, her mouth wide open. As though she's just remembered she's forgotten to turn her hair straighteners off when she's four hundred miles away. Weird. She wonders what Liza saw just now to make her react like that? But she can't carry on the thought because she's focusing on getting air into her lungs.

She clears her throat. She looks right back at Liza,

then at Ella and finally at Jack. *Tell the truth, lose a friend, tell a lie, keep her close.* Which one? Come on Sarah. Think. She's waiting for Ella to do, or say, something but she too is stock still.

'Sarah?' Katy tilts her head. 'I know this must be really difficult for you too. But please know that whatever you say now is going to help Jack enormously with his recovery. There's no right or wrong answer. If bits of the memory aren't quite clear, that's fine. Just start with maybe something else – who you were talking to, if anyone. The weather. Anything at all that you can fix on. Usually if you start talking about the surrounding memories, your mind will do the rest.'

'OK,' Sarah says. She's made her decision now. One that will no doubt stay with her for the rest of her life. And, like it or not, she's going to have to go with it. She's screwed up enough lately. 'It was grey that day. That's what I remember the most. Waking up. Everything was grey, grey, grey. Liza and I had been having coffee,' she pauses. Is this relevant? She doesn't know. But the words keep coming out of her mouth. 'And I said I'd check on him. I said I'd check on Jack.'

She shuts her eyes. She doesn't think she can go on, but her mouth is still moving in different shapes. Words, carrying across the air.

'And so I went. I walked through the café and I got us some drinks. I then went to the balcony to look for Jack. On the way I bumped into Ella. We had a chat and—'

'And?' Sarah's unaware of who has asked the question.

She tries to carry on. But she keeps getting flashes in her mind. Jack lying on the ground. His eyes, searching, searching. The look on Liza's face as Ella had told her that yes, yes she had checked on him. She hadn't really dwelled too much on that before now. But right this second, it's as clear as anything. A look of gratitude, and relief. Thanks, my friend, it said. Thanks for having my back. And then she can no longer hold it in. She lets out a great sob.

'I'm sorry,' she cries. 'I'm sorry.' It's all she can say. Nothing else. Nothing more. 'I'm really, so very sorry.'

West London Gazette editorial notes, October 2019
J Roper interview transcript (phone): Sally Hargreaves,
main witness, The Vale Club

*I'm currently in South Africa on holiday and didn't see
your emails or calls until this morning. I saw him fall,
yes. I just happened to look up at that moment. He didn't
see me, though. But I looked up just as he was trying
to get someone's attention. He was waving his arms and
then he was mouthing the words: 'Look! Look at me.'
At least that's what I think he was saying. But I shouldn't
imagine that anyone saw him because he started waving
harder at that point.*

*And then just as I was about to stop, to shout for him
to get down, he did it again. He had both hands off the
post. Then I knew – right at that point, I knew he was
going to fall.*

*I haven't forgotten that look on his face. The moment
he realised he was going down. Awful. Truly awful. I
couldn't shut my eyes for a couple of nights after that.*

*His legs seemed to lose their grip and that was it. I
screamed and then I heard the most awful thump on the
ground. It was loud. Much louder than I would have
expected because – well – he seemed so tiny. For a second*

I thought there's no way he can get out of this alive, but at that point he was the other side of the fence so I couldn't see him. The rest is a blur. But I know someone opened up the gate to the cricket pitch and we all gathered around. His eyes were open at that point and then his mother came.

I was going to get in touch with her – the mother of the little boy, I mean. I still might do. But in truth, I've been reading some of the Facebook pages surrounding it all – and all the forums on those mum sites. She really needs a break. That poor woman being vilified by all these people who have no idea of the surrounding circumstances. But that's how it goes, isn't it? Especially around there. Everyone has something to say about everything. It's exhausting, frankly. I think it's fear. Fear that as a parent, you're doing something wrong, so you end up judging everyone else for their behaviour. So that – you know – you can justify to yourself that your way is the right way. Fear that if you make a mistake – say the wrong thing, do the wrong thing, be yourself even – your kid might get ostracised. Everyone's just always on edge, all the time. And so when something like this happens – everyone just well, explodes.

Anyway, I'm not a mother myself. I was just out the back of the playground having a look at the new tennis courts – so I don't truly know what it's like. But anyhow, I feel sorry for her. And I don't really want to say too much more. I have made my statement to the club and, as far as I'm concerned, the incident is being dealt with. But – whatever happens – I hope something good comes out of this. I hope that people stop sniping, gossiping. Everyone's in this together – parents or no parents. I hope that people can take a long, hard look at them-selves.

Anyway, I do thank you for your call.

Interviewee hangs up.

LIZA

'Time out.' Katy looks over at Sarah, who's stuffed the sleeve of her jumper into her mouth to stifle her own sobs. 'Look, this is no good for Jack. It's meant to be a peaceful time for him – there are already too many people in here, and now – Sarah, are you OK?'

Sarah's sobs continue. What on earth is going on? She barely seems to register that Katy's spoken to her.

'She'll be fine.' I glance over at Sarah. 'Won't you, Sarah? You'll be OK. In five minutes?' I'm keen for this all to be over and I'm still gobsmacked that she's rung social services. *Furious* in fact, and I have no idea why *she's* the one crying. 'Come on now, Sarah. You need to pull yourself together. For Jack.' My voice sharpens. 'All right?'

'Shhhh,' Gav walks through the front door. 'I've seen our friend Mr Travers out.' He throws me a look. 'And been for a quick breather. So now you just need to let Katy take charge and do her job. She knows what she's doing.'

For some reason, this sends me wild – the implication

that Katy knows what's best for me. For my son. For any of us.

'I don't even know where you two met,' I shout, 'and I'm trusting you coming into my home. Doing this with my son. You're bloody seeing each other for all I know.'

Katy coughs.

'Seeing each other?' She combs her perfect fingernails through her ponytail. 'Me and Gav?'

'Don't you dare,' I shout. 'Don't pretend. Enough pretending.'

'Gav, maybe you should tell her the truth? If you don't mind? Clearly I've been a source of *something*. I'm not sure what. But I think it would be best.'

I look around the room. Ella and Sarah – both of their eyes shut for just a millisecond and they're both exhaling.

'Do you want me to ask everyone to leave?' Gav asks.

'No,' I say. 'Just tell me what the heck is going on.' I don't want to lose any momentum or derail the conversation.

'Fine.' Gav stands, smoothing his hands over his trousers. 'I've been seeing Katy. I mean, she's been helping me.'

For a minute, I don't understand. Gav? Seeing a therapist? Of course not. He would always laugh at people who paid for help. It was part of the reason I'd never told him *I'd* seen someone.

'She's been helping me with various repetitive memories,' he continues. 'Trying to make them have less of a hold over me.' He stares at Jack, then at me. And finally, I understand. I understand everything. He's been scrambling his own trauma over what had happened just after Jack had been born. My God.

'She's been helping you? That's good. That's great. You seemed better in the past few days. Less . . .'

'Anxious? Yes. We had a breakthrough. I've been seeing her for a bit. But I had to accelerate our sessions after Jack's fall. It brought stuff back. But she's helping. It's taken a while. But with the double time in the past week I feel that something's shifted. That I don't need to be in as much . . .' He looks up, searching for the right word. 'Control. And that's why I was so adamant that she help Jack.'

But something still doesn't make sense.

'But she said she owed you one? Surely it's the other way around.'

'Oh, I took Sally, her sister—' He looks over at Katy and she nods. 'It's OK,' she mouths. 'I don't mind.' 'I took her to an emergency scan. The morning after Jack's fall. I was with Katy. Having an emergency PTSD session because I really thought I was losing it. Anyway, halfway through, Sally banged on Katy's office door. Desperate. She was bleeding. Pregnant. She had no car and she's a single parent. So I left the session. Got Sally an Uber to the nearest place we could find for a scan. I sat and waited with her. It all turned out to be absolutely fine. Sally and baby are in fine health.'

The old Gav. I feel something lift. This is what the old Gav would have done.

'And he followed it up after that,' Katy says, looking at Gav. 'He sat with her for two hours whilst they went through everything with her.'

'So that's where you were. When you were meant to be at the hospital with Jack.' I try and keep the accusation out of my voice. I don't even mean to sound like that. I am pleased that he'd been with her. I think of Sarah and how relieved I'd felt that I could be there for her last year.

'I know. I didn't know what to do but when you told me Jack was asleep, that he was OK, I thought it would be fine for me to do this. I actually rang the hospital. I spoke to Dr Qureshi just to be sure. She told me I'd be fine not to be there for a couple of hours and that it was you who needed the support. I thought – well, I can give that to you, but right at that moment, when it was all happening, I just couldn't tell you all this.'

'Oh,' I cry. 'I wish you had.'

'Anyway,' Katy says. 'I'm totally indebted to him for helping us out. As luck would have it I had to go and take our mum to the hospital just after our session, so I couldn't go with them.'

'He's a good dad,' Jack pipes up.

All of us had forgotten he was there, listening, but he looks like a different little boy even from five minutes ago. He must have sensed my relief that Katy and Gav aren't seeing each other. Like *that* anyway. I feel bad he's been privy to this part of the conversation – but when I look at him, his limbs are relaxed, his dimples out in force. I feel like weeping. I've got my boy back. I want to clap and shout and jump. He's back. I've got my boy back. And then I look over and I see Gav is crying. I've never seen Gav cry in my life. I lead him into the bedroom, leaving everyone watching, open-mouthed. We sit quietly. Waiting for him to catch his breath.

'I'm sorry,' he says. 'I'm so, so sorry. My wife, and my son. And now I've got a little girl. And you needed help all that time. And I didn't give it to you. I had a reali-sation, after that social services guy came – and how I had to lie to him – about how much my behaviour must have affected you. I remembered the look on your face as you came back that night, after the hospital visit with

Jack. You were broken. I should have helped you. I tried to make it all OK but then I guess my anxiety took over to the point that I forgot what I was meant to be doing. My fear. My constant need for control in case you left him again. But of course, you weren't well. And I suppose after that, nor was I.'

He wipes his eyes. 'Jesus. Liza. I'm so sorry. I don't know how to apologise. How to make it up to you. The way I spoke to you after Jack's fall.' He doesn't look at me. His huge frame shuddering up and down as he tries to stop crying.

But then something doesn't add up. 'You got so much worse,' I say. 'After Thea was born? Why was that?'

'It was something Sarah said. Jack had been playing up. Thea had a bit of a cold. Sarah was joking around and said you'd probably throw in the towel if things didn't get better. That you were pulling your hair out and that you'd probably just walk out one day. She was laughing as she said it. But it brought all the trauma with Jack back and I hated you for it. I absolutely hated you. I couldn't even look at you. Or talk about it. It was like that moment you wake up from a dream where your partner's been cheating on you and, all day, you can't separate fiction from reality. I knew Sarah didn't mean it and I knew you wouldn't. But I suppose I was ill myself. Postnatal depression. But for fathers. If that's a thing. I hated you for being ill when Jack was a baby – when all that time I should have helped you. And myself. But neither you or I had anywhere to turn, did we? I mean, if they'd found out . . .' I squeeze his arm. 'So anyway, that's when I decided I had to leave. But of course, I couldn't. I was too fucked up. Too frightened that if I ceded control for one second, something would go wrong. I became hyper vigilant. Over everything. It's been awful. I'm so sorry.'

'Shhhh,' I put my hand over his. 'It's over now. It's over. OK? It's finished.' I remember now how Sarah had made a joke about me wanting to up sticks and get trashed just after Thea was born. I remember that exact moment; how Gav's face had turned and he had told me he was leaving me that night.

We sit in silence, holding hands. My Gav. Deep down I've always wondered if I can ever forgive him for the way he's been behaving.

'Katy,' he continues, sniffing. 'She does couples' counselling too. For traumatic things that have happened.' He looks over at me. 'Will you?'

Both of us are crying now. 'We can't let things slide without trying. Can we?'

He shakes his head. 'It's going to be a long, long road,' he says. 'And this conversation has only scratched the surface. Come on then. Let's go back out.' He follows me, hand on my back, ready to face the rest of the day.

'Oh hi, both,' Katy says. 'Thank you. For being here. Jack is ready. So shall we carry on then? We've just got this tiny bit left. Sarah? Are you feeling all right now? Have a few more moments.'

I feel much clearer about things after having spoken to Gav. 'We can go on now, Sarah.' But she's still looking at Ella, frozen. And then out of nowhere, my entire body tenses. That bloody look. *Again.* The one I'd seen just minutes ago when Sarah had been looking at Ella. Where have I seen that look? It feels like déjà vu. Where? Where? Wh— and then my entire world shrinks. I know *exactly* where I've seen it before. *I waved at him. He's absolutely fine*. And I think, right now, I'm about to throw up absolutely everywhere.

I replay the memory in my head. It appears, fragmented and distorted, as though it's been stretched and spliced with other unwanted memories.

Everything shifts into sharp focus. And then I remember the fall. The grey day. Thea, restless. Jack in the sandpit. Ella and Sarah walking towards me. My heart sinking. And then, the screaming. The sound of my parka jacket as it fell to the floor. And then, *the look*. I'd told myself that I would dissect it later. I had read it, in that heart-stopping moment, as a look that said: *Oh my God. Look at her. Look at the crazy bitch overreacting*. But now, in the cold light of day, I see it for what it is.

Guilt.

I have a nasty sinking feeling and everything feels blacker than black. And then suddenly, everything crystallises into sharp focus. Sarah's reluctance to answer Katy. Her look of total fear whenever I spoke about Jack reliving the memory for his therapy sessions. Her look of fear right this minute, skin soaking up her tears. Like she's turned into glass and could shatter at any given moment. Her strange behaviour. Us, living in her flat. Oh God, I realise, this is why. *This is why*.

I could do one of two things at this very minute. I could step in. Let her off the hook. Or I could confront her, and see what she says. I look over at Ella, who looks totally in control and calm. And then I think about Ella. Why had she answered for Sarah? Why had she covered up for her? Or was she just thinking that I was being an overprotective parent? *Silly Liza*. Of course my son was fine and no one needed to check on him at all. Or had it been *me* she's been trying to protect?

I start to shake, thinking of Jack. Could it have been prevented? If Sarah had told me she hadn't checked on him, would my little boy be here, in a neck brace, lying on the bed?

Or worse – *had* she checked him and he'd already been up the post? I dismiss that thought as quickly as it enters my head.

'Liza?' It's Katy, but I can't answer. 'Are you OK? You look . . .'

'I'm fine,' I say. I'm frozen. Because of course, whatever I choose, it's all tied up with my own parenting mistakes. I look over at Sarah whose hands are clamped right over her mouth. She'd been doing that exact pose last time we went on a PTA night out. 'I'm going to vomit, let me out!' she had shrieked in the back of the Uber. How we'd laughed.

I think about Jack. And ultimately I have to do what is best for him. I've failed him once already, and I'm not willing to do it again.

'I'm fine,' I say. 'But I need to speak to Sarah.' I catch her looking at Ella again, who gives her the tiniest nod. One that says, *Don't worry, I'm here.*

'Alone.' My voice comes out as barely a whisper. 'I need to speak to Sarah alone.'

SARAH

Montages of American real-life-crime series keep flooding her brain: the executioner's chair; dead man walking. Liza wants to speak to her. Alone. No hiding behind Ella now.

She has a mind to lie down on the floor and wish for some horrendous catastrophe to consume her, right then and there. But then Casper would be without a mother. And Tom would probably marry that accountant from his old work who she's always secretly thought more suited to him than her – his pathetic excuse for a wife and a human being.

My God, she's failed spectacularly at everything.

'Fine.' She sounds surlier than she means to. If she's going to have to tell the truth now, she's going to have to own it. 'Fine,' she says again, softening her voice. 'Ready when you are.' But she can't hide the shakiness in her words. It's too late now, she no longer looks at Ella. She blinkers herself from Katy. 'Where would you like to go?'

'Outside.'

Liza's arms are crossed. Her arms are never crossed.

'OK.' Sarah starts to grab her coat and bag but then decides to leave it all. This is her house, after all. She can come back. She starts to shiver. She holds an arm out signalling for Liza to go first. And then she thinks about their friendship – the fact that there was always a good balance of power between them, and that was what had made it so comfortable, so easy. She starts to cry.

'One minute.' Liza turns to her son. 'Jack? Mummy loves you so much. I'm just going to talk to Sarah. But before I go, I want to let you know that you deserve only good things in life. OK?'

Sarah's stung as she feels Liza's glare on her. She knows she can't expect anything else, but even when Liza's stressed, or upset, it's always *Aunty Sarah*. She now knows that things will never be the same again.

She isn't aware of herself, climbing the metal steps on the stairwell. She is aware, though, that her body feels like someone's trying to erase her insides. She steps over a small stick on the middle step. She's not sure why. She thinks it's because she doesn't want to hurt anything else – even an already broken piece of wood. When they reach the top, she grips tightly onto the metal railing. It's OK, she tells herself; maybe Liza wants to speak to her about something else? But she knows, deep in her gut, that's not the case. She wonders how she found out. It can't have been Ella. Sarah knows, though, it was in those few moments just passed that Liza had worked it out. The look of dawning on her face, crossed with pure rage. They stand there for a minute. She's still shivering.

'You lied, didn't you? You lied when you said you saw Jack, that you'd checked on him.' Liza's chin juts forward. 'Why? Why did you do it?'

Sarah rocks back slightly, half expecting a slap around the face. Some shouting. Some aggression. But there's nothing. A flat, resigned voice, which makes her feel even worse.

'I hate you for it,' says Liza, almost matter-of-factly, as if the realisation of it is so final that to convey it with emotion would be pointless. 'In the past few minutes I've gone from loving you like a sister, to hating you. You lied to me. About my *son*. He broke his neck, Sarah. And I've only just realised the truth of it. The look you and Ella gave each other – I realised you've been lying to me, all this time. How could you?' Liza sounds so disappointed, so deeply let down. Sarah feels hollowed out with anguish.

'I don't know.' She picks at a flake of metal, digging it off with her fingernail. 'It's so small and so stupid but it's the truth. I don't know why I did it.' There had been so much behind her decision that day she doesn't know how to untangle it all. Ella, her anxiety, life dragging her down. 'It was . . .'

'It was what?' Liza peers into her face. 'I need you to explain. It's the least I deserve. We trusted each other. Always. You told me, you *told* me he was OK.' Her voice starts to crack.

Sarah takes a breath. She can't hide from it, or herself, any longer. 'OK, I'll tell you. I'll tell you everything.' She does. She starts right at the beginning. The edgy feeling she'd been wrestling with in the pit of her stomach during the months before. Rosie. The way she'd felt when she'd seen Ella – invisible and useless.

'I swear to you, I'm not trying to excuse it, or use my,' she chokes up, 'my grief. I'm just trying to be honest about the chain of events that led to this. That it wasn't quite so simple as me not bothering and then Jack falling from the post. What followed was me trying to protect you. Gav, too, if you can believe it. It was all tied up in that shitty decision which I'll carry with me for the rest of my life.' They both go quiet, watching a bird track the sky above them.

Sarah talks some more. She tells Liza how she'd gone outside to check on Jack. That she'd seen him up the post, then bumped into Ella on the outside balcony. That she'd been distracted with Ella – with that message on her phone – and hadn't called for Jack to get down. And that it is a moment that she'll regret for the rest of her life. She doesn't leave out anything. Every word slips from her mouth, pushing her further and further away from her friend, but she can't help that now.

'So, you see, when Ella replied for me, the wheels had already been set in motion. It had started.'

'So why did Ella cover up for you?' Liza pushes her hand on the top of the railing.

'I don't know.' Because that's the truth. She doesn't know. But then Sarah thinks back to Ella – *I know more about Liza than you think* – and feels a shiver run right down her spine. 'I just don't. I'm sorry, Liza. I'm so, so sorry. I love you and I love Jack. I don't know what,' she gulps back air, 'I don't know how I let all this happen. I was trying so hard to . . . to . . .' But what can she say? How can she possibly say she'd been trying to help when this, *this*, is the result?

'And you didn't feel you could, or should speak up? I never would have thought you could have actually seen him up the post and not called him to get down. The lack of care over another human being. My son. How dare you. You have had SO many chances.' Liza is screaming now, shaking with rage so her whole body is vibrating.

'It just seemed better for everyone if I didn't. I thought about it. I thought about it constantly. Not for one second has it not been on my mind. *Should I? Shouldn't I?* And at that point I wasn't really thinking of myself, Liza. I was thinking about you. And the kids. Have you never done something like that? Something that would eat you up for the rest of your life?'

Sarah watches Liza open her mouth, about to say something. But she snaps it shut, remains silent and shakes her head.

'No,' she says. 'No I haven't.'

LIZA

I want to tell her. By God I do. I want to tell Sarah what happened with Jack when he was born, but I also want her to carry the weight of what she's done. If I tell her, it'll let her off the hook – and if there's one thing I won't do right now, it's that.

A siren echoes past, the only sound other than the birds chirping, and my own breath. It feels like absolutely everything is about to erupt – including the pavement beneath my feet, like some treacherous volcano. Has it been long enough for her to feel the force of her actions? Should I punish her more? And should I ever tell her what happened five years ago?

I think back to Gav, what he'd said to the man earlier from social services. And how it was only a half-baked version of the truth. Our chat – how things had started to resolve, despite us never actually voicing what had happened out loud. I had watched, then, something fall from his face.

And then I remember Ella – who *had* actually found out, despite not knowing the full story at the time. Or maybe she had known and she'd never let on. The way she'd initially walked past me with her tiny terrier, snouting around in the dark. I'd been lost, wandering around and then I'd stopped, unable to take one more step. I'd been standing in the same place for God knows how long, electric with fear. All the streets looked the same; despite having lived in the area for years, I had no idea where I was. The houses had taken on sinister shapes, barbed with evil intentions. And then I'd seen her. I hadn't been aware of who it was at the time. I think I'd passed others who'd been out late, loose-limbed from drink, or tired from a late night at the office. But they had given me a wide berth. Until Ella had turned on her heel, heading back towards me.

'Gosh, I didn't recognise you for a minute. Liza – what are you doing out so late?' She'd pulled at her dog's lead. 'Come on, Bramble.'

'Getting some fresh air,' I'd managed. I hadn't realised it at the time but my body had given me away, limbs shaking, hair dripping with sweat.

'Come on. Let me walk you home,' she'd soothed. Except when I looked closely into her face, I thought she'd been crying – her eyes were red and she looked like she'd been blowing her nose. I was too tired and ill, though, to think about anything other than what I'd done.

'You're OK, Liza. You're OK. Where's Gav?'

I'd shrugged, allowing myself to be led by her.

'Thank you,' I'd said as we arrived at my house. I'd stopped her from coming inside. For a minute, I'd forgotten that I'd left Jack in there. Although I didn't know it at the time, it was around about half an hour earlier that Gav had been dialling 999. The police were out searching for me. Him, staying at home in case I should make an appearance. It had been a surprise that they hadn't found me, wandering around the streets in my nightie, like I'd been drugged.

'Thank you, Ella,' I'd monotoned. And she'd left without another word. When I walked back into the house, still shaking, I'd told Gav what had really happened. How the piercing noise of Jack's screaming had done something to my psyche, already shredded with fatigue – imprinting terror onto it before any rational thought could take hold.

'You're scaring me,' he'd said. 'Why are you speaking in that weird voice? Just tell me what happened. Quick. Before the police come back.'

'I wanted to hurt him,' I'd replied. 'I wanted to hurt my own child. I wanted to shake him. To shut him up. And so I left him. I've been gone since lunch. I left him nearly all day. I've been walking around. I don't know what I've been doing. I don't even really know how I got back here.'

'Jesus fucking Christ,' he'd whispered. I hadn't dared look at him then. And then I'd hung my head as he'd gone through the motions of what we were going to tell the police.

'But afterwards, take Jack to the hospital,' I'd said, after we'd rehearsed our alibi. 'I think there's something wrong with him. And then take me.'

We'd told the police, doctors and nurses it was a mistake.

'I know,' I'd held up my hands. 'I shouldn't smoke. Please, spare me the lectures this minute. I just want you to check that my son is OK. That it's colic and nothing worse.'

And Gav, poor Gav, who had been terrified ever since,

had had the responsibility of nursing me back to health alone, petrified of being caught out. Petrified I'd do it again. Petrified they'd take the kids away from us. Petrified but sad and also, though he tried to never say it, angry. They'd sent us health visitors anyway, after that. I'd found a place in Marylebone which dealt in that kind of thing.

And so if I tell Sarah any of this now, it'll make her feel in some way vindicated. It's OK, she'll think. His own *mother* left him alone for nearly a day. He could have had dehydration. If she'd left him longer, who knows what could have happened, she'd have been thinking, judgement creeping over her features.

'Liza? Are you OK?' she says. 'You look faint.'

'I'm OK. I need to go back inside.' I think back to the way things had changed since I'd left Jack alone. Gav's behaviour. Me disappearing from the world for two weeks trying to come to terms with what I'd done. And then Ella.

'Look, if you need anything,' she'd said after she'd found me wandering around that night, 'just contact me. You've got my number.'

I'd thought about coming clean. Or at least, in part, explaining. But she'd deleted herself soon after from the WhatsApp group, only for us never to hear from her again. Until now.

And just as Sarah and I stand in silence, we see her walking past, her long legs striding purposefully away from us.

'Wait,' I tell Sarah. 'I need to talk to Ella. Alone.' She nods and looks down at her fingernails.

I run after Ella. She stops, turns and looks at me, her grey eyes softening.

'Sarah?' Ella says. 'She told you?'

'I guessed. It was the way she looked at you. It brought it back. The moments after the fall. And you?'

'I'm sorry.' She continues her gaze, right into my soul. 'I really am.'

'Is that all you have to say to me?' I feel the anger rising again. 'Is that all I get? No explanation?'

'I know what people think of me,' she says. 'I know people think I'm aloof. That I don't give much away. I've had to become like that.'

I think of what Sarah had been itching to tell me. Something about Ella's secret love child with Rufus North. If that is as bad as it gets for Ella Bradby, God help us all. She'll never, ever understand a thing. I'm not going to allow her this.

'But that moment I saw you again at The Vale Club, it all came rushing back to me. The time I found you outside after you'd had Jack. Looking ill. Very ill. I was going through my own stuff too, so I couldn't give you all of myself, but when you asked if Sarah had checked on Jack, my answer was a reflex action. I was trying to protect you.'

'From what?'

'Yourself.'

My stomach starts to hurt. I have flashes of her, squeezing my arm. Bramble her dog, at our feet. But I cannot remember much else.

'I know that you'd left Jack alone all those years ago. You said something about not being with him. Gav, being out. I don't even know if you were aware you were talking, though, you were in such a state. When I got you back into the house, Gav was already there, feeding Jack, so I knew he was OK. Being looked after.'

I shake my head. I have no recollection of any of this.

'And then I had to leave. I had important stuff going on at home.' What, like your fling with Rufus North to attend to, I think nastily. 'And then that day, in The Vale Club, I could see something in your eyes again. Yes, I told you Sarah had checked on Jack. That he was fine. I wanted you to know, somehow, telepathically – although I realise how stupid that is now – that I remembered. That I had your back. That he was fine. You were fine. Except he wasn't. And then Sarah . . . *Sarah*.' She shakes her head.

'My God, the two of you.' I'm too exhausted and upset to say any more. 'Please leave now.'

She nods. 'I understand,' she whispers. And it seems she does, because she doesn't try to say anything else. I watch as she walks off, the leaves whipping up around her.

She was here and now she's gone and I wonder what might be different if the mysterious Ella Bradby had never walked so carelessly back into our lives. Life spinning so routinely, until she had come and tilted it right off its axis. I walk back towards the house where Sarah is still standing, watching, her body hunched in on itself.

'Liza, will you . . .' She looks like she's about to follow me inside, but then stops. 'Will you . . .' Her voice is carried away by the wind.

'No,' I tell her. I don't even know what she'd been about to ask. But I'd given her my answer. And now it's time. I leave her, outside, wiping the tears from her face.

It's time to go and collect my family. It's time now for us – the four of us – to go back home.

West London Gazette Online
Author: G Paphides

The Vale Club have issued a statement about an incident that occurred mid-October and they have asked us to publish it in full on our website:

We would like to unreservedly apologise to our members for any distress caused as a result of an incident in which a five-year-old boy fell from a post in our West London branch.

The club has had all health and safety checks done and we were found not to be at fault. However, we are aware that this accident has raised issues amongst our members.

We have since put up more signage that no child should be left unattended and we have hired an extra site manager, who will be available at all times to answer any questions our members might have – or to look into any concerns about the safety of our equipment and surroundings.

We would like to extend our thoughts to the family involved.

Please call us if you have any questions or comments, but due to some harmful and unsavoury comments and

trolling, we have frozen our Facebook pages until further notice.
  Arlene Richards
  The Vale Club Manager

COMMENTS:

Gravytrain456: No doubt our Vale Club membership prices will be pushed up now. Paying for an extra site manager because that woman wasn't watching her son!!!!!! Too busy moaning about her life and slurping on her skinny cap. How much is that going to be from our pockets into the PC coffers!!!

WestLondonLover: I KNOW. It's disgusting. We can't be expected to pay for someone else's fuck-ups. As if it isn't enough that they hiked up the prices on the menu last month. I noticed the salmon dishes have gone up by fifty pence. No doubt blaming Brexit instead of their management.

PhillyMumofMaxandSophia: Please go to the PC FB page that I've set up (since they couldn't handle the complaints on the official one) to air any grievances, which I'll then collate as I've got a meeting with Arlene next week. We've got nearly 4000 members!

Bunny: For fuck's sake guys – have you got nothing better to talk about? And what about that poor kid? Get a grip.

Comments have now been moderated.

To: J.Roper@westlondongazette.com
From: G.Paphides@westlondongazette.com

J

It's come to my attention that despite our earlier correspondence, you've been talking to people at The Vale Club and to a lot of people who witnessed the boy's fall. I don't know what you want to do with the information – whether you have intentions of publishing it anonymously, or trying to sell it to a broadsheet. Whatever the case, we really admire your reporting skills and your tenacity in trying to carry on with the story. Obviously you can't publish this whilst you are still working for me – so instead of doing anything with it, I'd like to offer you the position of features editor with a view to doing one investigative piece a week for the paper.

Best,
G

Ella: Forgive the WhatsApp attachment – but I had to type this up in a Word document as it felt more appropriate. It seems that a few things need to be cleared up after what just happened at yours, with Liza and Jack. I hope you are ok and you and Liza managed to sort things out.

Firstly – the adoption. I'm telling you this to stop any false rumours. I now see what you thought you'd gleaned when you read my message on the balcony at The Vale Club, and then put two and two together and got five.

The adopted son – 9 years – in said text, did not refer to my ex-boyfriend Rufus North, from nine years ago. It didn't refer to some love child him and I had, that I subsequently hid. It referred to my sister's son – her 9-year-old boy, Xavier, whom I am currently in the process of adopting. The reason I didn't tell you this is because Xav himself didn't know that procedures were being put in place. My beloved sister Daisy died around five years ago now. Me and Christian and my parents nursed her in our house around about the time that Felix was born. We were all holding her hands when she took her last breath when Felix was only a couple of months old. Xav then flew out with his estranged father to Trinidad after she died. But sadly, he has decided that single parenting is not for him. I've flown out a few times recently to try and persuade him otherwise – but he won't change his mind. I didn't particularly want to share this sensitive information with you – effectively a total stranger. But I did tell you I would explain. We are all still absolutely reeling from our loss.

This leads me onto the sponsorship money for the Christmas fair. Daisy's dying wish was that I bring Xavier up in the way she would have brought him up, if she'd had the chance. That means a state education – the type we both had. She didn't agree with fee-paying schools. It means giving him a life full of love, laughter and experiences. It means me living and breathing Daisy's wishes so I can be a mother to her little boy. Whatever that means. I'm still working it out, and will be until the day I die.

Christian and I would probably have done things differently. But I love my sister so much, and I'll always stay true to what she wanted for her son, whilst also trying to do the very best for my own children. We enrolled Felix into West London Primary with Xav in mind, and the truth is that he's very happy there and he's so, so excited to be sharing his school with his new big brother. Christian and I chose to sponsor the fair through our new company for this reason – we would have spent a large chunk of this money on Felix and Wolf's school fees. We have a lot of cash. I can't help that. But I can help the kids have access to good activities and equipment and, by heading up the PTA, I can try and control where best that money is spent.

The reason I'm telling you all this is because I would now like you to please, please, just leave me alone. The minute you walked back into my life, I've had nothing but trouble.

I know how people view me. How everyone thinks I have it so easy. My so-called 'perfect life'. I recognised that look in your eyes too. The casual dismissal of me and my feelings. Because – well – why would I have anything difficult to face? Why would I have any challenges? Look at me! I've got everything. And I see now that you wished for my downfall, because then in part you'd be vindicated, wouldn't you? You would have been right all along. No one can be *that* perfect. Well, now you know. And I lied to you too. I knew about the Hilda Zettenberg Home not because I used to work around there. But because I'd been going there for years, after my pregnancy and Daisy's death triggered a relapse of an eating disorder I've suffered badly with since I was a teenager, and for which I've been hospitalised on many an occasion. So little Miss Perfect Ella Bradby turns out to be not quite so perfect after all. I hope you feel better about that and can now console yourself that you were right, after all. Lord knows why I feel the need to defend myself to you.

But now, my advice to you is to get some help.

Move away from here if need be but just get some perspective. Anything. Forget about all the shit – the unnecessary noise. Forget about the other judgy mothers (and some fathers!). Forget about everything that you can forget about. And just focus on what I know you are really good at. Which is loving Casper, your sweet and kind little boy.

Sarah: Typing . . .

Ella has left the group.

ONE YEAR LATER

'Everybody's damaged. It's just a question of how badly, and whether you're healing or still bleeding.'

— Angela N. Blount, *Once Upon a Road Trip*

To: LizaBarnstaple@btinternet.com
From: Sarah_Biddy@hotmail.com

Dear Liza,

I hope you don't mind me writing out of the blue like this. I also hope you got my letter. I know that you said we could never speak to each other again. I've always wanted to respect that, which is why I haven't tried to contact you before now.

I'm not sure how much you know – if anything – of our lives now. After that autumn half-term, I couldn't face the school gates any more – the whispers and the rumours. I should have braved up to things and just got on with it. I know that's what you would have done if you had been in my position. But I couldn't. And I'm trying to come to terms with that too. But I constantly felt like I was under the microscope – even though I know that in reality, everyone's got better things to think about than my mistakes.

Soon after everything that happened, Tom got asked by his company to set up an office in Cheltenham. And in truth, I think he was so relieved that the decision had been made for us. That he didn't have to carry on pretending that everything was ok. With me. With him. He suffered a lot more than I thought he did, after Rosie. Another thing I got wrong. But I've been trying so hard to repair that.

So we packed up and left – renting a small cottage in a tiny village near Mum. Never thought I'd say those words! But she's happy we're here and she's spent so much time with Casper that it's been totally worth it for that alone. Things worked out on that front, at least.

And I got a job as – would you believe it – school admissions admin assistant at the local primary here. It's just a part-time thing. But it brings in a bit of extra cash and it keeps me busy. And Casper's little face lights up when he sees me in the office.

The change has been good for us and for our marriage. Ella told me I needed to get away. She was right, as usual. Again. Never thought I'd say those words!

Which brings me to the real reason I'm writing. I wanted to let you know that Tom and I had a baby girl last week. Isla Elizabeth (9lb 11 – my pelvic floors are screwed forever). Anyway, I don't know why I felt so strongly that you should hear it from me. And I don't want you to feel emotionally obliged to reply, especially after we agreed not to be in touch – so please, don't feel that you have to write back.

But I did also want to tell you that since Isla's birth, I've been thinking so much about Rosie. About what happened, with you. I'll never, ever forget what you did for me the day that my first daughter was born. The way you quietly, fero-ciously, gripped my hand when the doctors took her away from me was something that only a true friend could have done. I never really thanked you for it. I suppose I'd buried it so deeply that I never got to tell you what your friendship – particularly at that time – meant to me. You did not deserve what I did to you. To Jack. And I'm so sorry. I'm trying not to make this about me – so I'm not going to go on about how much of a bad person I feel. But for what it is worth, everything that happened with you and Jack, it changed me. I have changed.

To that end, I think that's why I wanted to tell you about Isla – she reminds me of you. A fighter with a strong spirit.

I know that we'll never be in each other's lives again – but I also know that I'll never regret our friendship. You taught me so much about myself. About how to live. And about how not to live. I think of you all the time – you, Gav, Jack and Thea. Not a day goes past that my heart doesn't feel heavy without you all in my life. I wish you every happiness, joy and luck with everything. And if our paths ever should cross again – I hope we can remember the good times that we shared.

Yours,
Sarah

To: Sarah_Biddy@hotmail.com
From: LizaBarnstaple@btinternet.com

Dear Sarah,

I'm so pleased to hear about Isla. And I'm pleased you told me, too. Thank you for sharing your good news and letting me know how you are all getting on. I know that Gav is sad that he lost his friendship with Tom, so I'll make sure I pass on everything you've told me.

Gav, Jack, Thea and I are all really well. Jack has grown up so much and is now loving judo. Thea is now walking and saying her first words. (Bread – she takes after me.) I'm with the kids during the day – thinking about what to do in the future – and Gav has set up a business with Katy Loftman. He's training in PTSD and trauma psychology.

He is much happier now. And to that end, we will be renewing our vows next year in Somerset. (I know!) But last year felt like, in some ways, a chance to start afresh. We went to counselling together and tried to come to terms with the idea that we can't control everything. Since then, we've learnt to take each day as it comes. Sometimes it works. Sometimes it doesn't. But that's ok too. We had some family sessions as well (minus Thea!). We are all much closer because of it and we've learnt to accept others, and most of all – ourselves.

You don't need to say thank you to me about being there when Rosie was born. I wouldn't have had it any other way. It was an absolute honour to have met her, to have held her hand – and yours.

And I think of her often. She was absolutely beautiful and she looked so like you. I know that Isla will never be a replacement, but I know that she will bring you as much joy as Rosie would have done – and her memory will always live on.

I wish, somehow, I'd managed to 'access' you more after her burial. Looking back, I can see how much you and Tom were struggling, despite never really talking about what happened. Perhaps that was my fault. Perhaps I was so consumed with everything that was going on with Gav that I hadn't realised the depths of what you were feeling. Perhaps I should have insisted you went to counselling, or got some sort of help. Perhaps that's where I went wrong in all of this – because – well, as I get older, I realise things aren't always that one-sided.

I also realise we all felt totally lost after Jack's fall. But of course, we were lost before then too. We had blamed ourselves for things that weren't necessarily in our control. I hope you know that there was nothing in this world you could have done to prevent Rosie's death. You mentioned this at the hospital – that you blamed yourself. That you thought you could – or should (that wonderful word!) – have protected her. You were a wonderful mother to her and there was nothing you could have done differently. You were so harsh on yourself afterwards. You tried, so hard, to carry on and do what was best for everyone, and to live up to an invisible standard. To do what was expected of you from everyone else – swallowing your own pain to satisfy other people's opinions

*of you (why do we all do this?!). And then you
berated yourself for doing that too. All the time.
I did it too, with certain events of my life. We told
each other it was ok – so why didn't we tell
ourselves the same thing?*

*And then came Ella – perfect Ella – who took
on the mantle of all that we thought we should
be, but that we could never quite achieve. And
who highlighted the disconnect between our own
public and private personas – especially for you,
who was so fragile at the time. But for the record,
to me, you were always perfect just as you were.
And as it turns out, Ella wasn't so great after all,
was she?*

*I'm aware she had her own pain to deal with.
But despite that, I guess she never felt the need to
make her apologies for who she was. She already
felt seen. She already felt she was enough. And Sarah,
you are too.*

*I am still sad about what happened – and angry
– and all the other emotions that I went through
after Jack's fall and all the bits afterwards, and
although I know I can't go back to how we were,
I do still miss having you all in my life too. I miss
you all very, very much. Jack still asks for Casper
often. I tell him this: that friendships come into
our lives and do incredible things but just because
they leave us sometimes, it doesn't negate the
impact they made. Or that the impact they made
doesn't mean it isn't right, when it is time, for us
to let them go. That the love doesn't fade, even if
the people leave, because he is worth loving. Just
as he is.*

The Fallout

And so the days pass, don't they? I wish you happiness, Sarah, I truly do – in all the rest of yours.

Liza

WhatsApp group: Christmas fair '20!!!
Members: Charlotte G, Ems, Bella, Mehreen, Millie, Amina, Charlotte T, Charlotte M, Amelia, Shereen, Fizz, Becky D, Becky G, Isa, Marion, Mimi, Nabila

Charlotte G: Hello All! You lovely PTA lot! It's that time of year! Now as we all know – last year's fair didn't quite work out as we'd hoped. We put Ella Bradby's sponsorship money towards a playground extension, but we missed out on many of our children's enrichment funds, due to everything that went on after that. I'm here to take charge now – and will ensure we do the VERY best for the future of our children.

Aren't we lucky! And best of all – you have me – your very own Charlotte G, running the show!

Isa: Thanks Charlotte. Happy to help in any way I can. I've spoken to the local deli and they're happy to donate some cakes.

Marion: Great stuff! I'm in too to help in any way that I can. @Amelia – I also just wanted to tell you that my son Adam tells me Ellen has been rifling through his school bag during the day. We've had some things go missing lately. An expensive pen I bought him.

Amelia: I hope you are not suggesting Ellen has taken Adam's things. On a public forum.

Marion: I am just repeating what Adam told me.

Charlotte G: This is not a place to be discussing your children – if you want a forum to discuss those issues, please do so in your own specific WhatsApp group, or in private! Thank you so much!

WhatsApp group: Is she for real?
Members: Amelia, Fizz

Amelia: Oh my god the absolute bitch. Is she actually accusing Ellen of stealing?

Fizz: I think so! Ha! She's got it in for you. She's such a cow. Time for revenge!!!!!!!! *rubs hands together*

WhatsApp group: Guess what?
Members: Amelia, Lena, Bella

Amelia: You'll never believe it – some kid has been pushing all the children in class and in the playground. Ellen came back yesterday in tears. She didn't name any names but she *did* say that Marion's child, Adam, was standing *right* behind her before she got pushed . . .

Lena: Oh my god! Of course we won't tell anyone. But bloody hell! What have the teachers done? Marion's kid – Adam? It's got to be him. He's a little thug.

Amelia: I know! I'll find out what the teachers are doing about it. I hope something – it's awful. Poor Ellen was so upset about it all. The little poppet.

WhatsApp group: Mums updates (dads welcome too!!)
Members: Isa, Kristen, Ava, Jo, Arianna, Lena, Liza

Lena: Guys – just a little warning – Marion's kid Adam has been going round pushing the other kids. Really hard. I think someone should have a chat with Marion – or the teachers. Apparently it's getting dangerous.

Kristen: OMG – Amelia's just told me. Crazy! He could really hurt someone. Pushing kids like that.

Arianna: Do you think we should complain about it? I mean – you know – it's in situations like these where really bad accidents happen . . .

Liza has left the group.

Acknowledgements

Nelle Andrew, I am forever grateful for your unwavering belief in me. I am so lucky to be on your team and I have learnt so much from you, agent extraordinaire, who knows when and how to say the right thing – on top of everything else you do for your authors. Thank you. Thank you. Thank you.

Charlotte Brabbin, as soon as we spoke I knew that you got me and the book – and that I'd love working with you. And I have. It's been an absolute dream for me. Thank you so much for everything.

And to Kim Young, Fleur Clarke, Ellie Wood, Jennifer Harlow, Claire Ward, Cliff Webb, Isabel Coburn and Alice Gomer and the entire team at HarperFiction. I'm so grateful for all the work and energy that's gone into this book.

To Rhian McKay – what an amazing job you did. Thank you.

Ben Oliveira and Angela Blount for your fabulous quotes which add so much to the book.

To all the authors, bloggers and past readers who've shown so much support.

Elizabeth Day, Tim Logan and Susan Lewis.

Asia Mackay – my writing and everything else (EAC) partner in crime. Sometimes I forget to tell my husband things because I've already told you. Thanks for always being there, for getting it all and for making me laugh so much. You are the best.

Lynn West – who unwittingly gave me the idea for this novel. Thank you for that – and absolutely everything else. I am so glad we bonded all those years ago on a school outing. Lucky me to have a best mate who happens to be across the road.

Alanna Clear – for being an amazing friend and helping me with details of the accident itself and the aftermath. All mistakes are my own.

In no particular order and for being there all the way: Caroline Jones (as well as your constant support and friendship, I have to mention your amazing proof-reading skills!), Elizabeth Thornton, Isabel Cooper, Elizabeth Day, Gemma Deighton, Mahim Qureshi (I will never forget that laughing fit), Charlotte Wilkins, Sarah Wheeler, Maria Guven, Daniel Cavanagh, Emilie Bennetts, Edwina Gieve, Alison Hitchcock, Neil Alexander, Ayisha Malik, Josh West and Vikki Sloboda. I'm so lucky this list hasn't changed since my first novel and I'm grateful for you all on a daily basis. Thank you guys for allowing me to be myself – neuroses and all.

And to all my other friends who have supported me in this chapter. I can't thank you enough. You know who you are.

To Ching, who is greatly missed. Much love to Val, Sebastian and Francesca.

Louisa Barnett and Jamie and Carly Spero.

To my in-laws, Karen and Ellis. My parents, and to

Emily, Jasper, Matt, Alia and Chester. I wanted to say a huge thank you for helping me so much last year. I couldn't have done it without you all. I am eternally thankful.

And to Olly – for everything you do for us.

Finally, this book is for Walter and Dom, with all of my love.